BENEATH

a

SHOOTING

STAR

BENEATH

a

SHOOTING

STAR

a novel

SUSAN HARRISON RASHID

Mill City Press ✳ Maitland

Mill City Press, Inc.
2301 Lucien Way #415
Maitland, FL 32751
407.339.4217
www.millcitypublishing.com

ISBN-13: 978-1-63505-218-3

Edited by Laura Goodman
Cover Design by C. Tramell
Typeset by M.K. Ross

Printed in the United States of America

For my husband Zafar
And my Pakistani family who have
enriched my life beyond measure

Beneath a shooting star,
The Earth is torn asunder
By unrepentant mankind.

Susan Harrison Rashid

There is in every woman's heart, a spark of heavenly fire, which lies dormant in the broad daylight of prosperity, but which kindles up and beams and blazes in the dark hour of adversity.

Washington Irving

PROLOGUE

Fear bound her tighter than the rope encircling her wrists and ankles; like a python's coils it constricted her chest, and made each breath difficult. Her body was a constant reminder she was not trapped in some horrible dream, her cheeks pinched by the tape across her mouth, the inside of her throat dry and sore. Beads of sweat rolled down her forehead and left a maddening itch behind as they dripped off the tip of her nose onto the front of her kameez, darkening the fabric like blood from a wound. And if that was not reminder enough, there was the gunman right in front of her, all too real. Every time his eyes swept over her, she felt naked under his scrutiny. If only she could tunnel into her mind and hide in a snug burrow of her creation. But her discomfort fixed her in reality.

At first, she kept her head up, eyes staring straight ahead, the only show of defiance possible, but it forced her to look into the dark tunnel of an automatic weapon barrel which frightened her even more. She redirected her gaze downward, her view limited to her legs and feet, the roped extremities of her family who sat on either side of her and the floor. She noticed a worn spot near the edge of the antique, Bokhara rug and a gap in its white fringed border where several pieces of cotton warp had broken off just below the knot. Crumbs had escaped from someone's plate during their afternoon tea and sullied the carpet's surface, a reminder normality had existed just a short while ago. Time inched along at a sloth's pace. In the absence of conversation, sounds amplified, the whir of the fan above her head, the distant clap, clap of leather sandals against stone, the squeal of wooden furniture being dragged across the floor, cupboard doors opening and closing, and the occasional bark of an order to the men scavenging in the other rooms of the house.

She considered their situation. Escape was impossible and the likelihood of rescue seemed remote. The walls that surrounded the house for protection and privacy provided the same advantages to the criminals who had breached them. In her helplessness, the only thing she could do was pray to Allah to keep them safe, each silent prayer slipping between her lips like prayer beads through her fingers. But, her petitions failed to push away the thought that fate had caught up with her and this was how her life would end.

As this sense of doom held her in its grasp and all hope fled, she struggled to conjure up pleasant memories to provide some comfort and instead was ambushed by her regrets. If only she could go back to the beginning, back to when anything was possible, back before her missteps had sacrificed the life she'd dreamed of and distanced people she loved.

PART ONE

*

Chapter 1

On the 26th day of March, 1971, the night of Nadira's birth, Allah set off celestial fireworks in her honor; at least that's what her father always told her. By his account, the Lahore night was particularly beautiful; the air washed clean by a late afternoon rain storm carried the scent of jasmine. A breeze blew away the leftover clouds and lifted strands of her mother's hair off her forehead as she stepped outside. Walking toward the car, her father stopped for a moment so her mother could wait out the pain of a contraction. She leaned on him and raising her head up to the heavens, whispered a prayer to Allah for herself and her unborn child. As she gazed at the sky, a thin, brilliant waterfall of light poured from the dark bowl of the stratosphere.

"Look, a shooting star," her mother said. "It must be a sign our child will be blessed."

"Of course, signs are superstitious nonsense," her

always rational, physicist father had instructed her. "But just this once, I prayed she was right."

She remembered how his words voiced in serious, hushed tones became part of her bedtime routine, a final tale after the closing of a book, as comforting as a lullaby before going to sleep. When she was very young she had believed her father's prayer had been answered, and the shooting star had carried a blessing. This blessing was a personal charm which protected her from the evil jinn and the monsters that crept into her room once the light was switched off and the door closed. The story comforted her, and it wasn't until she was old enough to put herself to bed that it was relegated to her childhood like a discarded toy left to gather dust in a storage cupboard.

Her birthday story was one of many ways her father tried to make Nadira feel special. But as far back as she could remember, she came second in the family. Her older brother Asim was first in the order of things, both as the oldest child and as the all-important son. He was also the one with the sunny disposition and compliant nature who set the standard for behavior.

"Why can't you follow your older brother's example," her mother admonished her whenever Nadira did something wrong.

It wasn't until she was surprised by a scolding, Nadira realized she was bad. She never chose wrong-doing: trouble just somehow seemed to find her. There were so many rules to follow, many of them puzzling. What was the difference between her mother tasting the contents of a pot on the stove, and her sticking a finger in the bowl of rice pudding cooling on the table? What harm had she done when she followed the cook out the gate to the road where his children were pushing small cars through the dust? She'd been so tired of being in the house without a playmate, and the dirt on her shalwar kameez would wash out without much trouble. What was even more puzzling to her, then and for years to come, was why her mother couldn't be more like her father? Even as a busy professor at Punjab University, he found time to join her for a tea party with her dolls, or play games with her. And when they talked, he paid her the same close attention as he did to adults. His playfulness belied his age, and he was the funniest person she knew, often making her laugh until she got the hiccups. When she went to him with her small accomplishments, he enlarged them into major triumphs. And he bookended her days, getting her up in the morning and putting her to bed at night, providing her with a constancy and sense of safety which allowed her to launch herself out into the world without hesitation.

By the time she was four, Nadira finally thought she had figured out how to navigate through her world. Then a new baby arrived and nothing was as it had been. His name was Kareem but she called him "baby," because if she used his name it would make him somebody and he was nobody to her. She waited for him to be left alone so she could hide him until he was forgotten, and life could go back to the way it was before. But, it was as if her thoughts were written on her face because whenever she got near him, an adult watched her, not even allowing her time to take his unmarked skin between her fingers and pinch, hard.

Just a few days after his birth, her older brother, Asim, departed with the driver and didn't return all morning. Nadira didn't know what to think. Uneasiness crept inside her and once it made itself at home, it opened the door for fear to walk in. Nadira became silent and stayed close to her mother's side, until finally she caught hold of her tunic-like kameez, and attached herself like a burr.

"Nadira, don't hang on me," her mother said. "Go get a toy and play."

Nadira shook her head, her braid whipping through the air like a lash while her hand retained its grip on her mother's kameez.

Her mother started to uncurled her fingers from the cloth and though she clamped her teeth together and tried as hard as she could, she wasn't strong enough to hold on. When her arm hung free and her mother was a step away, she felt all by herself, uncared for, and she let out a whimper.

"Nadira, what's the matter with you?"

"Please don't send me away. I promise I'll be good," Nadira said, raising her tear stained face to her mother.

Her mother sat down and pulled Nadira into her lap. "What are you talking about? Why would I send you away?"

"You got a new baby and sent Asim away. Maybe tomorrow it will be me." This thought made her weep again. She didn't feel big enough or brave enough to be on her own.

Her mother wiped her tears away with a corner of her dupatta. For a second, Nadira thought she saw a smile begin to emerge, but then her mother's face turned serious. She waited to be punished for her bad thoughts about the baby and her desire to have what once was hers returned.

"Is that what's worrying you? I didn't send your brother away. He's at school and will be back in a few hours."

School? Questions sprang from Nadira like runners sprinting to the finish line, leaving her breathless when she came to the end.

Nadira's mother laughed and then explained how school was a place where children went to learn how to read, write and use numbers, everything necessary for a good future. Nadira looked at her, eager for more information, the small details which would allow her to picture a day at school. But her baby brother started to cry and her mother lifted Nadira off her lap and picked him up, walking back and forth and crooning in the high, cheerful voice she reserved for him. It ended any further disclosures about school. But the idea of this special place for children took hold of Nadira and for the moment, she forgot all her grievances. She decided there was nothing she wanted more than to go to school. Tugging on her mother's kameez, she asked if she could start school the next day. Her mother told her "No, you're too young for school," in a tone of voice that ruled out any further debate. But Nadira wasn't willing to give up after this one refusal. She decided to wait until her father came home and ask for his permission. As soon as he stepped through the door, Nadira confronted him with her request. Usually, her father found it impossible to say no to her, but this time he agreed with her mother. When Nadira sobbed with disappointment and refused to be comforted, her father offered her the compromise of taking lessons from him at home. Should she accept? She wouldn't have the company of other children, and she would still be at home with a crying baby, but she guessed it was better than nothing, and so agreed.

Little by little her father taught her the alphabet. She was astonished when letters arranged in the correct order formed words; when strung together, words became sentences, and groups of sentences created stories. On her father's lap with a book propped up in front of them, reading held her restless body still. She'd listen with unwavering attention as he spoke each word and underlined it with his finger. From the beginning, her books were very special and she took care of them, unlike her clothes, left in a pile on the floor when she undressed, or her misplaced, broken or abandoned toys scattered throughout the house. She would rub her grimy hands clean on the front of her kameez before she opened a cover or turned a page, and when she was finished with the book, it was put away without delay in its appointed place on her bedroom shelf.

Her father also taught her to count to twenty, and simple addition and subtraction using pieces of fruit or crayons or whatever else was at hand. Nadira could see that in some ways, numbers were like letters, unchangeable when singular but becoming something else when combined with other numbers. But unlike letters, numbers appeared to be ordered and disciplined, obedient to underlying rules, a constant she could rely on in her otherwise messy world. If asked which she preferred - letters or numbers - she couldn't say. They were both important to her for different reasons.

But, as much as she enjoyed the lessons with her father, she never gave up on her desire for a real classroom, and every few months, she asked the same question, if she were old enough yet for school. In her sixth year, she finally got the answer she'd been waiting for and went to find Asim. When she announced she'd be going to school with him, he told her, no, she would not; his school was just for boys; she'd be going to a girls' school. This dampened her excitement a little. Might his school be better in some way?

Not daunted for long, Nadira counted the days to the beginning of classes. She'd open her cupboard every morning and look at the new uniforms her mother's tailor had stitched for her to confirm she was really about to start school. Then, on the first day, she'd woken up early, very early, her body feeling jumpy and her mind jumbled with worries – about the other girls, what her teacher would be like, if asked questions would she know the answers? Grey, dusky light began to fill the room. She lay in bed and stared at the ceiling for what seemed like hours until she wondered if she somehow had slept through the call for prayer and it was late. She got up, washed her hands and face and pulled on clean underwear before stepping into the starched blue shalwar, taking care to point her toes so her feet could pass through the narrow bottom cuffs of the wide pant legs. Then she thrust her arms into the sleeves of the blue and white, window pane print kameez and pulled the tunic over her head. Finally she put her head and arm through the one-piece blue sash so it rested on her right shoulder and hung in a neat diagonal line, across her chest. She was ready.

She went to her parents' room and was surprised to see they were still sleeping. Back in her own room, she smoothed out her kameez before sitting down to wait. Now that she was still, weariness leaned her head back and tugged her eyelids down and soon she was asleep. Her bedroom was bright with daylight when her father's voice woke her.

Panicked, Nadira jumped up. "Abu, have I missed school?" she asked.

"No, no," he told her, a smile creasing his face. "I came to wake you but it looks like you've been up for a while," he said as he continued smiling at her. "Maybe it's your school uniform, but you appear very grown up this morning."

Nadira studied her image in the mirror so she could see what he was seeing. Almost all her features mimicked family traits. Her once chubby face had become oval like her mother's and she had her mother's short, straight nose and upturned mouth with its slightly fuller upper lip. Her almond shaped eyes framed by long eyelashes came from her father's family, but the wave in her long, thick, black hair was all her own.

An hour later, Nadira and her mother entered a class-room filled with women and girls. Her head swiveled as she took in her surroundings, and she shifted from one foot to the other as her mother talked with the teacher. She only suspended her inspection when her mother pulled her forward for introductions. As her mother continued talking to her teacher, Nadira studied the classroom some more. So this was it. She had expected something different, a special place made for people her age. The classroom of her imagination had lemon yellow walls, a blue ceiling with painted stars, floor cushions around low tables, and maybe a floppy eared rabbit in a cage. Everything here was so drab and ordinary.

In front of the teacher's desk, the student's seats were lined up in precise rows on either side of a center aisle. Side aisles separated the rows from a wall on the right with three tall windows and a solid wall on the left, once white but now the color of aged parchment. There was a blackboard on the front wall with the letters of the Urdu alphabet arranged above it. The back wall had a large framed photo of a man with a thin face, a long, narrow nose and deep set, intense eyes that looked right through her. Later, the teacher informed the class he was Muhammad Ali Jinnah, the founder of Pakistan. On either side of Mr. Jinnah's photograph, there was a world map and a map of Pakistan. Totally engrossed, Nadira jumped when her mother's hand landed on her shoulder. Bending down, her mother took hold of her arms, gazed straight into her eyes and told her to listen to the teacher and do everything that was asked of her.

"Remember, your behavior reflects on your family," she said.

Nadira saw the distrust in her mother's steady gaze and heard the sharpness in her voice which promised consequences if she failed to obey. Why did her mother assume she needed reminding? Nadira had every intention of being respectful and doing as she was told.

Nadira arranged a serious expression on her face and nodded her head. Her mother gave her arm an affectionate squeeze before rising to leave. She felt only a momentary pang of loss as she watched her mother go, her excitement and the activity around her drawing her attention into the room.

The day could have gone better.

Nadira felt lucky her assigned desk was in the last row at the end near the windows. From there she could watch what everyone in the classroom was doing and also see outside.

The teacher clapped her hands for the class's attention and Nadira tried hard to concentrate as she began going over the alphabet. But this was just baby stuff, and she wondered why the teacher was giving instruction on something she already knew? The lesson was going on far too long, and the outside enticed her. They'd been told to remain in their seats unless given permission to get up, so she raised her hand.

"What is it – she looked down for a moment, consulting her seating chart – Nadira?"

"May I be excused please," Nadira asked.

"Do you have to go to the toilet?"

"No, I'd like to go outside."

The teacher's eye's widened, forehead furrowed and the corners of her pursed mouth slid downhill, reminding Nadira of her mother's expression of disapproval.

"You'll remain in your seat until I dismiss the class," she said. Her voice, as sharp as a needle, punctured Nadira's sense of well-being.

Some of the girls giggled. Nadira wasn't sure what she'd done wrong but flushed with embarrassment. When the teacher resumed the lesson, she amused herself with what was at hand. First she tested the wooden surface of her chair by sliding back and forth, and then ran her pencil through the trenched scratches on her desk top, her imagination constructing pictures from the random tracks. Out the window, she saw a guard standing in the shade of a tree smoking a cigarette. A gardener trimmed the branches of the bushes bordering the walkway while a bird pecked for bugs in the dirt nearby, making Nadira wonder what a bug tasted like. Was it salty, sweet or bitter? Was it chewy or crunchy? Maybe if she asked the teacher, she would have the answer. Then cutting through her reverie, she heard the teacher call her name, and was told to pay attention, her scolding tone not encouraging any questions. She tried to listen for a while, but her eyes strayed back to the window or to the girl two seats in front of her who was biting her pencil.

By the end of the first week, her seat was changed to the middle of the first row right under her teacher's watchful eyes.

When she complained to her father about her dislike of school and her teacher, he was not sympathetic. He ran his hand over the back of his head, sighed and said the trouble might be his fault for starting her education so early. "But you must pay attention in class," he told her. "Some things you already know, but there will also be new things, and you'll miss out if you don't listen. You should give your teacher the same respect I demand of my students. Promise me you'll do that."

Nadira visualized her father standing in front of a class full of students, and it made a difference in how she felt about her teacher. She promised him she would, and from then on, Nadira did pay attention in class. Most of the time, anyway. At times her resolve weakened, but she found if she kept her gaze on her teacher, her mind could wander where it pleased with no one the wiser. Once the class had caught up with her and new subjects were introduced, school became interesting. She especially enjoyed learning the intricacies of English, a language of different letters and sounds, presenting a new challenge for her. Sitting still was always difficult, but her attentiveness was rewarded by schoolwork unmarked by her teacher's red pen, and praise from her parents when at the end of each year she always stood first in her class.

The change in Nadira's seat assignment had one beneficial effect. She now occupied a desk next to a girl she had noticed earlier and had wondered how to approach. The girl's name was Hameeda and Nadira was fascinated by her uncommon appearance. She had the look of a Pathan from the far northern regions of Pakistan, with fair skin, dark brown hair, a round face, gray-green eyes, a slender elegant nose and an upturned mouth that always seemed to be smiling. She stood out among girls with dark eyes, black hair and skin tones ranging from golden to shades of brown. If it weren't for her appearance, Nadira might have overlooked her. Hameeda had a way of disappearing into the background, her body still, her words kept to herself unless questioned. When called upon, she spoke in a whispery voice that sent a pleasant, shivery feeling down Nadira's spine she longed to have repeated. Without even knowing her, she craved her friendship and spent the whole morning deciding how she would introduce herself, unaware this first, social interaction would change the direction of her life.

Chapter 2

Before Hameeda was even conceived, she was shaped by another birth, that of the nation of Pakistan. Her grandfather Majid's experience in the cataclysm of Partition left an invisible scar which cut deeper than the one that marked his forehead, and influenced the legacy he passed down to the next two generations.

*   *   *

Majid never forgot the old days, the days when he identified himself not as Pakistani but as Indian and lived in Dehli, a city generations of his family had called home. When he was growing up, his family was among the few Muslims in a predominantly Hindu neighborhood. In those days, Hindus, Muslims and Sikhs were, for the most part, at peace and mingled in their homes, the streets and shops. Religious differences were overlooked most of the time in their common desire to win their freedom from British rule, and any conflicts were minor and over cultural and social matters.

As the oldest son, Majid had always known he would work in the family business once he reached an age when he could be of help. His father owned a small shop, housed in a squat, mud brick building with a rusted tin roof, one barred front window and a wooden door fitted with a hasp so it could be padlocked at night. Inside, a bare bulb hung down from the center of the ceiling, and left the corners of the room shrouded in shadow. Floor to ceiling plank shelves lined the shop's walls and a narrow table ran down the center of the room. Every available surface was crowded with aluminum pots and pans, flat iron tavas for making chapattis, wok-like karahis, long handled spoons, tongs, grinding stones, graters, sieves, mortars and pestles, knives and other kitchen implements. At a young age, he would go to the shop as soon as school let out to sweep the concrete floor, restock the shelves, and help carry large purchases out to waiting rickshaws. He could hear the shouts of his friends playing in the neighboring streets as he worked, but even the knowledge that he was missing out on their games did not decrease the enjoyment he received from helping his father in the store. In his spot near the door, he would observe the women as they navigated the narrow aisles in their bright saris, or patterned shalwar kameezes, their black hair, shiny with oil, snaking down their backs or coiled at the nape of their necks. When the customers called him by name, joked with him, or asked his opinion of an item they were thinking of purchasing, he swelled with importance. He soon learned the art of wooing the ladies with his thickly lashed, dark eyes and the clever use of his tongue, talking them into buying things they hadn't intended to get when they entered the shop.

By 1946, Majid had inherited the shop from his

father and had enlarged it by taking over the building adjacent to it. He thought it was his welcoming personality and apolitical nature that had garnered him a large clientele. But he had no control over the political rhetoric of the Hindu Congress Party and the Muslim League which awakened dormant animosities between religious groups. Over time, many of his Hindu customers had taken their business to more distant shops owned by their co-religionists, and he had to rely almost entirely on non-Hindus for his livelihood. Every day the newspapers printed stories of rioting in other cities, and word of mouth delivered reports of disputes between Hindus and Muslims in Delhi. Majid hoped these clashes were the result of anxiety over an uncertain future after independence. The British, and India's own contentious populous had left the question of a united India up in the air. There was the possibility a separate Muslim nation would be created, but even if that came about, how the boundary line would be determined and where it would be located was still in question. Everyone, including Majid, wondered how their lives would change, and if it would be for better or worse.

A year later on a fine April evening, Majid walked home from his shop. He smiled and nodded at a group of men talking by the neighborhood water taps. Until a couple of years ago, there had been one tap, now there were two. Above each tap was a black-lettered, wooden placard, one labeled Hindu water, and the other Muslim water; each group afraid of being contaminated by the other. It was just one more sign of the growing divisiveness within the community.

That night, Majid was not the only one enjoying the good weather. On either side of the street he saw people sitting outside on their doorsteps or balconies, the men relaxing with a smoke, the women chatting with their neighbors or tending to their children. He watched as a young girl leaned over the balustrade above him and waved to a friend on the street below. Her dupatta started to slip off her head and as she reached up for it with her free arm, the bowl she was holding in the other arm tilted and an onion rolled out. Falling through the air, it landed on the shoulder of a Hindu man in the street below and then rolled into the gutter. The Hindu let out a howl and looked up as the girl pulled back from the edge, her hand held over her mouth in dismay.

"That Muslim girl threw a stone at me," he cried out.

Majid watched in alarm as other Hindus gathered around the outraged man, making angry statements and shaking their fists at the now empty balcony. The man who had been hit hammered on the front door of the house while other men jammed together behind him like metal filings clinging to a magnet. Majid hesitated for a moment. Could he defuse the situation without them turning on him? Seeing a familiar face on the outskirts of the crowd, he became hopeful he could avert a tragedy. He yelled out to the men.

"Wait, you've made a mistake; it was an accident." When the group of men turned and faced him, he pointed to the onion and explained what had happened. The men stared at him, their faces twisted with malice.

"He's a Muslim; of course he'll defend one of his own," a voice shouted.

Fear took hold of Majid as the group came toward him. Then his friend moved to the front of the crowd and halted them with his upraised arms.

"Stop; you know this man. It's our friend Majid, the shopkeeper. What he says is true. Look around. There's no rock in the street, only the onion."

The crowd halted. Grumbling still rose from the men's throats, but the group began to pull apart as individuals drifted back to whatever they were doing before the commotion began. Majid hurried over to his friend and thanked him.

"What are we coming to when a dropped onion can cause a riot," he said to Majid as he shook his head in disbelief. "But you must be more careful my friend; these days doing what you did was foolish – more than foolish - dangerous. Next time there may be nobody to come to your aid."

For Majid, not only was a beautiful evening destroyed, but also his belief in a united India where all faiths co-existed in peace.

He wasn't alone in his assessment of the situation. The first week in June, the British announced the Indian subcontinent would be partitioned into two countries, the predominantly Hindu India, and the Muslim majority Pakistan. A few days later, three Hindus whom Majid recognized from the neighborhood came into his shop. He extended a courteous greeting and offered them refreshments. They refused his offer with barely a smile, and walked up and down the aisles of well-ordered merchandise. As they browsed, they picked up objects and turned them over this way and that before setting them down. They showed an interest in everything in the shop but left without purchasing anything. If he'd had any doubts before, Majid knew then that as a Muslim, Delhi no longer offered safety or financial security, and his only option was to move to the new country of Pakistan. The very next day, he left to visit his cousins in Karachi, soon to be part of Pakistan. While there, he deposited whatever liquid assets he had in a bank account. On his return to Delhi, he visited a Hindu who had been a close friend since childhood and had done very well for himself. He told his friend once the country of Pakistan was established, he was leaving and would be willing to sell him his shop for fifty percent of its value. There was one condition. He needed a bank draft for the full amount of the sale on the day he left. His friend told him he understood his position since he had family in Multan who were making arrangements to cross over the new border into territory controlled by India. They consoled each other, cursed the British and their own politicians, and shook hands on the deal. Majid planned to leave on August twelfth, two days before Pakistan's Independence Day, which left him with a very tight schedule to move his household and wind up remaining business matters. But during June, the violence between Hindus,

Muslims and Sikhs increased and spread throughout the country. In early July, Majid decided to put his wife and children on a train to Karachi with his brother, who was also departing with his family. His wife begged him to come with them, but he told her he would need at least three more weeks to get everything done so he could hand over his business. Once that was taken care of, he would get on the first train out.

Two days before Pakistan became a nation, Majid met his friend at the shop. His friend handed him a bank draft for the agreed upon amount, and Majid placed it in his money belt and secured it underneath his kurta. He looked around at the shop which held so many good memories for him. With great sadness, he gave his friend the deed to the building, keys to the shop, a list of his suppliers - although who knew how many would still remain - the financial books and a quick embrace. Then, he picked up his one small bag and headed to the railroad station.

When he got to the station, he pushed his way through crowds of people trying to get on a train to any destination over the border in Pakistan. It took him thirty minutes just to get from the terminal building to the platform. By the time he got to his train, his body was bruised from being elbowed and shoved, and his bag had almost been wrested from his grip by the crush of the crowd. At the train, complete bedlam prevailed. Controlling the crowd was impossible with the limited station personnel and soldiers on hand, and people without tickets fought their way onto the train. He showed his ticket to a conductor who got him into one of the open flatbed cars which had been added behind the last carriage. The cars had once hauled logs, and offered crude accommodations - wood plank floors and foot high side walls with spaced metal rings which had once anchored the chains securing the logs. He was quick to find a spot against a wall as men, women and children crammed into the car. Once all the cars were full, desperate people, who saw the train as their last means of escaping a horror that earlier riots had only hinted at, climbed up on the coach roofs. At last, the train blew its whistle and pulled out of the station. As it accelerated, dust and cinders blew back at him from the coal fired engine and the wheels of the cars in front of them. He was forced to pull a shirt out of his bag and use it as a shield to protect his face. After an hour, people began reaching into bags and sacks to unpack food and water so they could eat before it got dark. With all his careful planning, he had forgotten to bring food for the journey. The family next to him, seeing he had nothing, offered him a share of their meal, and he accepted with many thanks. They hadn't been traveling long, but his cramped position made his body stiffen and his muscles ache. Soon, the sun set and he watched as the moon appeared and stars pricked the dark curtain of the night sky. His discomfort prevented him from sleeping, and as he rode through the night he listened to the wheels on the rails and watched unidentifiable shapes in the landscape flash by, each mile taking him farther and farther from a home he might never see again. Some of his fellow passengers slept, but the eyes of those still awake shone in the dark like animals just beyond the reach of a campfire's light.

The next morning the sun rose in a cloudless summer sky. In the blazing heat, time became elastic and stretched out far beyond its real limits. When they were a few miles from the border, he got an excruciating leg cramp. Risking a fall off the car, he slid up onto the side ledge so he could straighten his leg and massage out the cramp. Just as he repositioned himself, the train squealed to an abrupt stop and he was thrown over the side and down the embankment. He tumbled over and over through the undergrowth until a tree halted his trajectory and rendered him unconscious.

When he came to, he heard horrible screams coming from the train. He worked his way up through the tall grass to the top of the slope and careful to stay concealed, peered out. A horde of Sikh guerillas with long knives and guns were butchering the passengers. Easing his way back down the embankment, he retreated into a small grove of trees. He found a thicket which was hollowed out in the middle, crawled in, pulled some branches over the opening and waited. Something trickled down his cheek. When he touched a finger to his face, it came away covered in blood. Exploring further, he discovered a large, deep gash on his forehead. He tore off a piece of cloth from the bottom of his kurta and tied it around his head.

The screaming went on for a long time, penetrating the hands he'd placed over his ears like a steel blade. Once, he thought he saw a movement on the slope above him and feared the guerillas were conducting a search of the area. He'd been a marginally observant Muslim, bookmarking his place in the vast volume of Islamic observance by going to Friday and Eid prayers at the mosque. Afraid for his life, he began to pray.

"Most merciful Allah, please help your humble servant. If you bring me safely through this massacre, I promise I'll live fully in the ways of the Qur'an and the hadith."

Finally the screams stopped. He heard someone shouting instructions and after a little while, there was a roaring noise and acrid smoke contaminated the air. Now there were a few scattered screams, even more horrible than before, and the smell of burning flesh. Whatever was in his stomach came up and he heaved until his throat was raw. The faces of the men, women and children he had traveled with on the train appeared in front of him, and he began sobbing, his hand held over his mouth to muffle the noise of his despair. From above, the crackling, roaring fire overrode any other sound.

He stayed in his hiding spot through the night to make sure the attackers were long gone. When he climbed back up the bank, he saw a cloud of vultures circling overhead. The train was a long line of blackened coaches with their windows blown out. A framework with wheels attached was all that was left of the flatbed car he'd traveled in only hours before. Underneath it, between the heat twisted rails, was a pile of charred, misshapen forms. Off in the distance, there were mounds on the ground moving up and down. As he got closer, he realized vultures were feeding on the bodies that had escaped the fire. He felt as if he would be sick again and fell to his knees. The screeching of vultures fighting over scraps and the smell drove him back up to his feet. He moved some distance from the tracks but stayed close enough that he could keep sight of them, and started off in the direction the train had been traveling before the attack. Concentrating on his balance, he put each foot down in the dust like a toddler taking his first steps. Weakened from some loss of blood and lack of food and water, he had to stop often to rest and it was late in the day when he finally reached the border. Police and soldiers listened to a story which was becoming all too common. A doctor cleaned and stitched up his forehead and helped him arrange transportation to his family in Karachi.

For the first leg of the journey, he was crammed into an old bus whose entire outside surface was covered in hand-painted, multi-colored geometric designs. It gave the vehicle a festive air that belied the state of mind of its passengers. The bus was so crowded with refugees, three people had to share slatted wooden seats meant for two. He was squeezed between two men, their bodies touching at the shoulder, arm, hip, thigh, knee, calf and ankle. As the bus jounced and swayed, they rubbed against each other with the intimacy of lovers. Each passenger kept a tight grip on a bundle of possessions in their lap as if it was the only thing keeping them anchored to life. Majid shut his eyes tight to avoid the pain on the faces around him; his stitched head throbbed, marking time like a ticking clock. Finally, days later, he arrived in Karachi. As Majid made his way to his cousin's house, he saw other less fortunate refugees bedded down next to the road. When he rang the bell at the gate, his wife opened the door and cried out when she saw him. His clothes were dirty and torn, and a large blood stained bandage covered his forehead. Sobbing, he fell into her arms like a young child coming home to his mother after a bully's beating, and when his tears were exhausted, he let his wife lead him to their room. Closeting himself in the bathroom, he scrubbed his body with strong soap and bucket upon bucket of water until the tank was drained. He changed his bloody bandage, put on fresh clothes, and after making the ritual ablution, he faced Mecca and stumbled through his prayers. Emerging from the bedroom, he followed the sound of conversation to the sitting room where he found the rest of the family gathered. Having heard the train had been attacked, they asked him what had taken place, but he couldn't say a word. He sat there shivering as if he had a fever, and his face must have mirrored his inner torment because they did not press him on the matter.

During the night, he woke up screaming from the horrific visions in his dreams, and his wife pleaded with him to tell her what had happened. But he'd already started to construct a wall around what he'd seen and had no words for her. Over the remaining years of their marriage, he would never speak about this experience which changed him in an irrevocable way. After the train journey from India, Majid pulled his religion as close around him as a winding sheet. He grew a beard, and became a very devout

Muslim, and as head of the family, made sure the rest of the household followed his example. He also changed in one other respect which he could tell puzzled his wife. He no longer ate nor did he let her prepare any grilled meat, and when she asked him why, he told her the smell sickened him.

Majid never stopped missing Delhi. Despite many years in Karachi, he couldn't develop an emotional attachment to his adopted city nor did he feel secure there. Although his business acumen brought him financial success and afforded him a beautiful house and comfortable life style, Karachi was never a place he was able to call home. There was animosity between the original inhabitants and the muhajirun who had sought refuge after Partition. To make matters worse, Majid was a Shia Muslim, one of a very small minority among Pakistan's Sunni Muslim population. The city had a volatile temperament, and when it exploded, Majid and his family's status as outsiders placed them in a dangerous position. Living there was like performing in a high wire act; one misstep could have dire consequences. So when his son was accepted at the University of the Punjab, the first of them to go to college, he didn't hesitate to move his business and his entire family to Lahore in the belief this would finally put them out of harm's way. As much as he admired his new home, it wasn't until his grandchildren arrived, the first generation to claim Lahore as their place of birth, that he felt tied to the city.

Of all his grandchildren, Hameeda was his favorite. Fate placed his son in another city the day she was born, and gave Majid an early role in her life. Normally intimidated by the fragile, vulnerable appearance of newborns, he had held back until his other grandchildren developed a toddler's sturdier constitution. But in his son's absence, he had kept a vigil at the hospital while his daughter-in-law was in labor with Hameeda. When he first saw his granddaughter with her distinctive pale skin and wide-set hazel eyes, he was drawn to her. Without hesitation, he asked to hold her, marveling at the perfection of Allah's creation. She became Allah's blessing to him. Her gentle innocence pushed aside his reserve, drew him out from under the dark veil of his past, and pulled him back into life.

Chapter 3

It wasn't until Hameeda was pregnant with her first child that she began to think about her own infancy and childhood. Before she felt the baby kick, she hadn't any inclination to ponder her birth or earliest memories. But now she looked back to find lessons for herself as a mother.

Who had she been in the instant she emerged from the womb before being placed in her mother's arms? Had Allah assigned her certain traits, or was she created to be malleable? What if her start in life had been different? Would her fate have changed if she hadn't arrived two weeks earlier than expected while her father was away on business, her dada, Majid, stepping into his shoes? For as her mother told her, it was not her father, but her grandfather, who first entered the hospital room and received her from her mother's arms. Holding her against his chest, he leaned his head down, and with his mouth close to her right ear and then her left, whispered the Azaan -"God is great," and the Kalimah - "There is no god but God, Muhammad is God's messenger," introducing her to Islam, and finding a special place for her in his heart.

When she asked her dada what he had thought the first time he saw her, he put his arm around her, drew her to his side, kissed the top of her head, and said she'd been a gift from Allah, and made their lives joyful during difficult times.

"You were like a sunbeam, brightening the dark corners of 1971 when the war between East and West Pakistan brought hardship and sadness to so many families. And right from the beginning, you were such a good girl, a blessed presence in the house. When you were seven days old, and the nails of your hands and feet were trimmed and your head was shaved, your only form of protest was to wrinkle your brow and screw your eyes shut. Your parents had not yet decided on a name but upon seeing your behavior, your father chose to call you Hameeda, praiseworthy. And from the beginning, you've lived up to your name."

Hameeda recalled the family's expectations, solidified by their reflexive smiles of approval and pats on the head, their preconceptions as real as the blanket she dragged around, or the thumb she sucked. She had always tried not to do anything to correct them, wanting to be the perfect child their minds had created.

She puzzled over who she would have been if instead of frowning, she had started screaming when the cold razor touched her scalp. Then what name would they have given her? If her parents hadn't depended on her to inform their decision, and had named her Aafreen, hoping for bravery, or Nabiha, hoping for intelligence, would she have lived up to those names instead? Had she disappointed them by being who she had been from the beginning – only

31

someone in need of approval? Would her life have been easier if she'd been different? What traits would she have wished for if she'd been able to choose? No, she wouldn't change anything, maybe because she couldn't visualize herself as anyone else, or imagine substituting another past for the happy memories she had of her childhood.

Every picture of her early years Hameeda's mind conjured up included her mother, holding her hand, washing her face, brushing out the tangles in her hair, listening to her concerns, expressing her love in so many ways. When she was small, her favorite place was perched in her mother's lap, snuggled in her embrace. Most of the time she'd had her lap to herself since her much more independent brothers, Omar, eight years older, and Rafiq, six years older, never claimed her mother's attention unless they were hurt or sick. She'd spent a large portion of every day with her mother and felt bound to her in a way that was unique in the constellation of her relationships. It was such a close connection, as if her umbilical cord had been replaced by an invisible line which her mother had cast between them.

Hameeda's mother was first in her heart, but she also adored her brothers. She liked their earthy, salty smell when they came in from playing outdoors, the way her hand fit into theirs without getting lost, and being able to find their faces without stretching her neck too far back. She admired them for the abilities she hadn't yet acquired and the confidence they brought to everything they did. When her brothers were in the same room she'd made sure she was near them, standing in front of them and leaning on their knees if they were seated, or following on their heels if they were on the move.

"Take me with you," she would plead.

But they granted her the pleasure of their company only on rare occasions. Often she'd found herself crying with disappointment on the other side of a closed door, wondering why they didn't like her. But every once in a while, they surprised her and pampered her with sweets, galloped her through the house on their backs, or drew pictures with her. When they paid attention to her, the memories of teasing, being left behind, or ignored were erased, giving them a clean slate until the next time they deserted her.

Some people didn't believe her when she said her memories extended back to age three. But she had one very distinct memory from that year, and she was sure it was hers alone, not a story told by someone else. She was sitting with her mother in the lounge when her brother Rafiq tore through the room, in his usual rush, breaking the rule against running in the house. His carelessness caused him to bump into a small, nearby table. A vase filled with flowers fell and shattered on the terrazzo floor, scattering broken glass, water and flowers everywhere. A small, glass shard embedded itself in the leather strap of her sandal and another one grazed her mother's ankle, drawing a thin red line down its length as Hameeda watched. Her mother had cried out and grabbed a startled Rafiq by his arm. She could still visualize her mother, her once soft features hard, the light gone from her eyes, her mouth twisted out of shape and her voice loud and high pitched. In an instant, she became a stranger, and Hameeda had been as frightened as her brother who leaned away from her, his free arm curled over his head and his eyes wide. The happiness she'd felt just seconds before vanished and was replaced by a tightness in her chest. She had started to whimper, then cry, louder and louder, each wail feeding on the previous one until she couldn't stop. Her mother left off berating Rafiq, picked her up, and tried to comfort her with gentle words. But Hameeda hadn't been able to calm herself, her crying already out of control. It had taken quite a while of her mother's shushing, and the sight of Rafiq making funny faces before a smile had twitched at the corners of her lips, and her weeping had wound down, replaced by hiccups. When she recalled this vivid memory, she realized this episode had shifted something deep inside her and changed her in some fundamental way.

Growing up, Hameeda was aware there were some things people feared which didn't bother her, for the most part quite small things crawling about the house. It had surprised her when the sight of a spider made her mother cringe on the other side of the room until a servant came with a broom and disposed of the poor creature. Hameeda hadn't understood the panic caused by an insect which only a short time before had entertained her by spinning an astonishing web. Yet, she'd never thought of herself as courageous because there were other things which made her just as fearful, the most distressing of all being angry voices or cold silences. In their presence, she was subject to stomach cramps, had trouble swallowing and was overcome with the urge to flee to the safety of her room. When she was young, her brothers had used this to their advantage. When they got into trouble and were called in by their parents for punishment, they asked Hameeda to plead their case. Hameeda had always agreed. She had felt helping her brothers was also helping herself because how could she be happy if they were miserable. So, Hameeda would beg her father not to punish them, her innocent face and little girl voice lending truthfulness to her statements. She would describe how sorry her brothers' were and how they had promised never to get into mischief again, convinced it was true. More often than not, her parents would dismiss her brothers or give them a lighter punishment. When not in their parents' presence, her brothers called Hameeda their "little defense barrister."

During childhood, as now, Hameeda's waking hours were governed by a distinct, immutable pattern. She had always treasured the unvarying daily divisions which gave her something to rely on in the unexpectedness of each day. She couldn't remember a time when she wasn't aware of the dividing lines of the five prayers - dawn, noon, afternoon, sunset and evening - separating the hours into segments. Before Hameeda knew what prayer was or could pray herself, she was drawn to witness it. She had found it both mysterious and comforting for reasons she hadn't under-stood. The ritual of prayer was an intricate ballet which captured her total attention: the bowing of her mother's covered head, the silent movement of her lips mouthing the words of the Qur'an, the cupping of hands, the standing, kneeling and prostrating of the body; everything else had receded into the background while she'd watched her mother pray. Daily prayers were the familiar, if incomprehensible, poetry of her existence.

At age five, her dada had expressed pleasure at her interest in the prayers. To encourage her, he began a weekly routine of reading her portions of the Qur'an, and explaining in simple terms what they meant. Hameeda had looked forward to her time with her dada. The other children had been a little wary of him, seeing only his bushy eyebrows, long beard and the pearl white railroad track of scar tissue that ran across the dark terrain of his forehead. But Hameeda had seen his kind eyes, had heard his soft, caressing voice, and had sensed the depth of his interest in her. Over the years, she often went to him with her questions when something confused her, and she had considered him her personal imam who helped her understand what Allah wished of her.

In a household where she was by far the youngest, Hameeda often wished for someone her own age she could talk to and play with. When she finally confided her feelings to her mother, she told Hameeda that in a few months she would be starting school where she would meet lots of girls her age and would soon have many friends just as her brothers did.

But Hameeda hadn't realized to have friends she would sacrifice her mother's companionship during school hours.

In the beginning, the separation left her with a physical ache. All day long she worked hard to hold in the tears that threatened to spill down her cheeks. She prayed the teacher wouldn't call on her because she was afraid if she opened her mouth, a wail would escape. She kept looking at the clock on the wall, and imagined what her mother was doing at that particular time of the day, counting the minutes until she could go home. But after a few days, she was too busy navigating her new relationships with her teacher and classmates to think about much else. She found these strangers were very much like the people she already knew.

Over the course of her short life, she had watched people, becoming an unconscious expert at observing the stiffness or relaxation of a body, the placement of arms and hands, the narrowing or widening of eyes, the wrinkling of noses, the position of a mouth and the tone of a person's voice, and was adept at adjusting her response so she could get the positive reaction she desired. She began to make the friends she'd wished for, and found this new environment, like daily prayers, had a definite, reliable structure, and held its own, unique satisfactions.

The second week of school the girl sitting next to her was moved to a back row and a girl named Nadira was given her seat. At first, Nadira's bold stares had made her uncomfortable. But every time she caught her at it, instead of turning her head in embarrassment, Nadira would smile at her. Hameeda couldn't place this girl in a familiar category, making her feel off-balance. She admired the fact that from the first day, Nadira wasn't fazed by the new subjects and had all the correct answers. Hameeda, feeling lost and struggling to keep up, longed for this girl's cleverness and air of confidence. However, she saw right away Nadira was having other problems, as she failed to comprehend some of the rules and displeased the teacher. This flaw made her more approachable in Hameeda's eyes. Still, it was Nadira who made the first overture, taking the lead as would often be her habit in the years to come.

Chapter 4

Hameeda felt a tap on her shoulder. It was Nadira, trying to get her attention.

"Sit with me at lunch," she said.

"All right."

The beginning of their complicated friendship was as simple as that.

While they collected their lunches and sat down, Nadira talked non-stop, continuing through most of their meal, hampered only by bites of food. As her words tumbled out, her hands went back and forth, up and down, as if she were writing on an invisible blackboard. She described her relatives like characters from a book, having traits which made them funny, odd, endearing, or irritating, all of them entertaining in some way, leaving Hameeda with a desire to hear more.

"My parents were born in Lahore. Anywhere we go they bump into someone they know, or someone who knows someone they know. It's amazing and maddening," Nadira said, her eyes widening, leaning in toward Hameeda as if she were going to confide a secret. "Can you imagine how often I have to stand there listening to boring conversations about people I've never met and don't care to meet?" she said, straightening up again before continuing. "Are your parents from Lahore? Maybe my parents know them."

Hameeda was hypnotized by Nadira's performance, lost in the continuous flow of words so that she had to be prompted a second time before she answered.

"My Amma is from Karachi, and my Abu moved there from Dehli when he was eight years old," Hameeda said, as she struggled and failed to think of even the smallest fact to add. She was fortunate this didn't hamper Nadira.

"Oh," she said, pausing only for a moment before bombarding Hameeda with new questions, smiling when something Hameeda said pleased her, and sometimes interrupting with comments. Hameeda had never met another child who was so unrestrained and curious. The more she directed her attention at Nadira and the more she laughed at her attempts to amuse her, the more animated Nadira became. Hameeda didn't mind her doing most of the talking, relieved not to have to find something to say. Given the opportunity, she wasn't sure what she would talk about. But finally, Nadira appeared to reach the end of her supply of stories; her comments and questions ceased, and she looked at Hameeda and waited.

Hameeda knew she was expected to say something and would have to be quick about it. She wanted Nadira to like her, and to capture her attention as hers had been captured, this wish so strong it was almost a physical sensation. But she didn't have much skill carrying on conversations, especially with people she didn't know well. Talk at home was dominated by adults. Hameeda and her brothers had been taught to answer only when questioned, and to otherwise remain silent. She wondered how you found the right words, and what, if anything, she knew that Nadira might find interesting. There was one thing. For some reason she didn't understand, she was privy to private stories her classmates had brought with them to school. They were tales older children would have known to leave at home, embarrassing incidents presented for her admiration like curios from a foreign country. But even if she was able to mine these stories for interesting tidbits, she knew passing them on was wrong. Often enough, she'd heard her dada tell her tittle tattling aunts that Islam prohibited the spreading of gossip. Yet in her eagerness for Nadira's friendship, she was tempted, and at that moment, she realized Satan didn't have a voice of his own, an utterance so sweet and seductive you forgot who was whispering in your ear, but instead spoke in the inner voice of your overwhelming desire.

Seconds ticked by as her eyes scanned the room for inspiration, and a feeling of panic gripped her. Finally, she asked Nadira what she thought of their teacher, both listening to her answer and trying to plan a response. Failing to come up with anything, she had to endure the silence before Nadira took up the slack.

At home that night, Hameeda went over and over their conversation in her mind, coming up with things she might have said and memorizing them for the future. She felt she'd failed some kind of test, and feared Nadira wouldn't approach her a second time. But Nadira continued to seek her out at lunch, and on the odd day Hameeda was already seated with other girls, she inserted herself into the group, once even going so far as to ask the girl sitting next to Hameeda if she'd change seats with her. When it happened, excitement lifted her up and left her suspended in the happy realization that a friendship with Nadira was taking shape and was something she could manage. As they spent more time together, she found it easier and easier to talk to her friend, sharing their common experiences at school and information about their lives outside the classroom.

After a few weeks, Nadira invited Hameeda to come to her house on the following Saturday.

"My uncle just got back from London and brought me a new game of Chinese checkers I want to try out."

"I'll ask my parents and let you know tomorrow," Hameeda said.

Hameeda decided to ask her mother's permission and let her mother take the request to her father. She wasn't sure if they would let her go, having seen how strict they were with her brothers, careful to monitor their friends and where they went.

When Hameeda had asked her mother, she questioned her about where Nadira lived and if she knew anything about her family. It was fortunate Nadira's talkativeness had provided her with the answers. Her mother said she would have to discuss it with her father before giving her a decision. Hameeda went to bed without having heard anything, and hoped for their approval before she left for school in the morning.

Later that night, she woke from a bad dream and

crossed the hall to her parents' bedroom. The door was open a crack and she heard her mother's voice.

"They're only children," her mother said.

"I still don't like it," her father replied.

"Please, this is so important to her."

"She's going to get hurt."

"How can you know that?"

"All right, I'll give my permission, but I'm going to keep a close eye on things."

Hameeda had tiptoed away, not understanding the conversation but knowing it was about her, and she was not supposed to hear it.

Before leaving for school the next day, she was told she could accept Nadira's invitation, and her mother requested she find out when they should drop her off. Excited, Hameeda counted the days until the weekend. But Saturday on her way to Nadira's house, nervousness overcame her the way it always did before a new experience. Her head whirled, making her feel dizzy, as if she were standing on the edge of a steep precipice with a view of the ground far below her, courting a fall.

When Hameeda's parents accompanied her to the front entrance, they were met by Nadira and her parents. After greetings and introductions, her parents were invited to stay for tea while Hameeda and Nadira entertained themselves in her friend's room. The visit had gone well, and afterward, as often happened in such cases, she wondered why she had been so worried. Her mother even made a point of telling her she had enjoyed herself.

"Even though they're Sunnis, they seem like very nice people," her mother had said.

Hearing her mother's statement, Hameeda was confused. "Did that mean Nadira was not a Muslim?" she asked.

Her mother smiled at her and said that Sunnis were also Muslims, having in common their belief in the five pillars of Islam. "Can you recite them for me?" she asked.

Hameeda frowned in concentration, looked upward as if for Allah's assistance, and recited, "One God and Muhammad is his messenger, five daily prayers, fasting during Ramadan, purifying almsgiving, and pilgrimage to Mecca."

"Very good," her mother said giving her a congratulatory hug.

The beliefs Hameeda had recited were all she knew of Islam, and she was surprised there were other parts of her religion she hadn't learned yet.

"What else is there to know?" she asked.

"These five pillars are the most important thing. The main differences between Shias and Sunnis are small in comparison, and arose long, long ago over who should take Muhammad's place as leader of the Muslim nation after he died. Our ancestors believed the leadership must stay in the family of Muhammad, peace be upon him, while Sunnis believed the leadership should go to one of his close companions."

Hameeda was having trouble understanding what this had to do with the commandments Allah had given Muhammad.

"Also, in our tradition, the imam is the unquestionable head of the Muslim community and his authority comes direct from Allah. Sunni's believe an imam is a pious, learned man whose leadership is earned and may be taken away by the people. Other differences grew out of these two things, but it is nothing you need to be concerned about," her mother continued.

Hameeda thought of the imam from their mosque, a stern man with a long, white beard, looking as old as the world itself. But the image of the imam did not help clear up her confusion over what her mother had said.

Her mother finished by saying, "The most important thing to remember is that Sunnis are our sisters and brothers in Islam."

Hameeda was relieved and thrilled by her mother's final revelation. Forgetting everything which had come before, she grabbed hold of this last piece of information. How wonderful to have shared beliefs which made Nadira not only her friend, but also her sister.

*   *   *

Nadira was surprised at how fast Hameeda was accepted by her family. From the very first moment, everyone was smitten with her. Her brothers were polite and attentive, so unlike them, and Nadira caught her parents exchanging delighted smiles, as if they'd found an unexpected treasure. Nadira paid attention to what Hameeda did and said, but whatever skill she used to charm them was hidden from view. Two conflicting emotions tugged at her. She was proud of Hameeda for winning over her family, almost as if she'd had a part in her accomplishment, and was also jealous, thinking of her as a prize she'd won and wished she didn't have to share.

The weekend following Hameeda's visit, the invitation was reciprocated. Nadira was only allowed to go after enduring a lecture from her mother on proper behavior. When she arrived, a servant answered the door and ushered her into the foyer, asking her to wait a moment. Nadira didn't even have time to glance around before Hameeda and her mother appeared. After the usual greetings, she was led up a staircase to a door which opened into a spacious sitting area.

"Hameeda, why don't you play with Nadira in your room where you can have some privacy." her mother suggested.

Hameeda led the way down a short hallway on the far side of the room. Nadira was silent as she followed her friend, a sudden shyness robbing her of any words. In this strange house, she felt like she was meeting Hameeda for the first time.

Entering the bedroom, her friend announced, "This is my room."

"It's very nice," Nadira said as she looked around. She found, in some ways, it was not much different from her own room. The bed was covered with a colorful quilt, a copy of the holy Qur'an, a string of prayer beads and an alarm clock lay on top of a nightstand, and an upholstered chair squatted under the window next to a desk and a crowded bookcase. The similarities ended with the wall decorations. Here there were items with religious themes, a picture of the Kaa'ba in Mecca, scenes depicting events from the life of the Prophet Muhammad, and above the bed, the name of Allah was written in brass calligraphy, mounted on black velvet and surrounded by an ornate gold frame. To Nadira, it seemed like the room of someone much older. She wondered if Hameeda's mother had chosen her decorations, but she didn't want to ask. Nadira had made her own choices for her bedroom walls which were covered with cut-outs of Mickey Mouse and Goofy, and two large, felted namda rugs, one appliqued with elephants, camels and tigers, and the other with oversized flowers in primary colors.

That afternoon proved to be a blueprint for all the visits which followed, regardless of whose house they played in. They spent their time talking about the big and small events that made up their world, put puzzles together, drew on paper with crayons, or made up stories using their dolls. Hameeda favored happy, domestic tales with a mother and father taking care of their children, while Nadira preferred fighting dragons or scaling castle walls to rescue damsels in distress.

From the beginning though, Nadira felt out of place in Hameeda's house. At home she was used to lots of activity and the noise of a boisterous family. At her friend's house, they were always left to their own devices and spent their time together in her room. Hameeda's parents and the other adults in the household spent quiet weekends studying the Qur'an, or entertaining relatives and friends. Hameeda's brothers were busy with their own friends and took any noisy activities outside. When she was there, Nadira felt like she was too big for her surroundings, her gestures too broad, and her voice too loud in a place where people were subdued and soft spoken, and whispering and tiptoeing seemed more appropriate. Nadira wished she felt welcome at Hameeda's, but the smiles and greetings had a mechanical air. She thought she must be doing something wrong, but couldn't figure out what it was. She saw in Hameeda an inherent ability to say and do just the right things, a way of always floating on life's waves like a seagull on the ocean; while she often felt she was thrashing about as if fighting an undertow. Nadira wondered if by associating with her friend, she could acquire whatever it was that enabled her to fit in so well.

If her friend's family found her lacking, it didn't seem to affect Hameeda's opinion of her. She confided to Nadira she felt lucky to have her as a friend. Nadira thought it was the other way around; she was the lucky one. At school, Hameeda was the more popular of the two of them, and Nadira understood the attraction. She also felt the warmth her friend gave without asking for anything in return, and saw how she passed out generous smiles, and viewed everyone in their best light. Nadira knew she was nothing like that. Instead, she tended to judge her classmates like a farmer choosing livestock, each person's behavior examined to determine whether or not they had traits she found agreeable. When there were hard feelings between individuals, Hameeda took on the role of peacemaker to smooth things over, and when someone was upset, she was the first one to offer comfort. Her friend also had a generous nature. If someone admired something she possessed, she wouldn't hesitate to share it with them.

With the whole class to choose from, Nadira was never quite certain why Hameeda had singled her out. Although she and Hameeda had some similar interests, they were otherwise very different, and she gave her friend the credit for them getting along so well. Somehow, she always knew how to respond to whatever Nadira was feeling, heightening her good moods and finding ways to banish her bad ones. She was very grateful Hameeda was her friend, and after her initial bafflement, she stopped thinking about the why of their friendship and was just happy to settle into the fact of it.

*   *   *

After Hameeda and Nadira had visited back and forth for a while, they fell into the habit of always meeting at Nadira's house. Hameeda was happy to accept this arrangement. Her father was rather stiff around Nadira and although her mother tried to make up for it, Hameeda always worried her friend felt the lack of warmth. At Nadira's house, she was treated as a fourth child and included in any planned activities, all more exciting than anything her family did. Sometimes, Nadira's mother provided a hamper filled with their favorite foods, and her father took them to a cricket match for the day. Once or twice, they went to the zoo. While Nadira's brothers ran from one exhibit to the next, her father took the two of them by the hand and talked about each animal as they strolled from cage to cage. Other days, Nadira's mother allowed them to go shopping with her, and together they explored the stalls lining the narrow streets of the Anarkali Bazaar, stopping for some sweets or a glass of sugar cane juice from a vendor. Hameeda loved getting sugar cane juice just so she could watch a cane being fed through the press. At the front of the hand cranked machine, the juice ran down a spout into a glass while the cane came out the back side as flat as a chapatti. It was simple pleasures like these, pleasures whch required no skill other than to be present in the moment, Hameeda liked the most. Matching her natural inclinations, these activities allowed her to be comfortable and a part of the group, unlike competitive pursuits at which she was terrible, the striving and rivalry of it making her feel stressed and isolated.

When it was a windy day, Nadira's father took all the children up to their flat roof for kite flying. He would get a kite aloft for both of them before handing over the spool. Once the kite was hers to command, Hameeda was never quite prepared for the force of the pull on her hand as she battled the wind for control. When an updraft caught the kite, it would rush skyward like a prisoner making a break for freedom only to find itself handcuffed to the earth by its string. But the most skill was required when the wind abated and withdrew its support, resulting in the kite nose diving toward the ground. When this happened, she would yell for Nadira's father. In a second, he would be at her side. He'd grasp the string above her hand, running forward, tugging in quick, short downward strokes, teasing the kite back up before releasing his hold so she could take over again. Nadira was more expert with her kite and only in rare instances would she accept help, wanting to do everything for herself. Once during Basant, Lahore's spring kite festival, Nadira's father took all of them to a friend's house in the old part of the city to watch boys and men fly the fighting kites with their crushed glass coated strings. Like bright colored birds of prey, the kites dipped and soared until one kite cut the string of another and mortally wounded, it plummeted to earth.

Nadira, her two brothers and Hameeda all had their favorite activities and were often at odds if given a choice. But there was one activity they all agreed on – going to the cinema. Before becoming friends with Nadira, she had never been to the cinema since her dada objected to movies, in particular American westerns or war movies.

"Movies with fighting and killing shouldn't be allowed. They make such behavior seem easy and acceptable and cheapen the value of human life," he had proclaimed as he rubbed his finger across the scar on his forehead.

Hameeda thought violent films had turned her dada against movies in general. As head of the family, her dada's advice was heeded by her parents, who also didn't go to the cinema. And while they never forbid Hameeda or her brothers from seeing movies, the opportunity was never provided, and she knew, as with everything else, she was expected to follow their example.

Hameeda never forgot her first movie. When Nadira's father offered to take them, she had not known what to do. She could already picture her friend's disappointment if she said she couldn't go and the awkwardness of having to return home after she'd just arrived. Maybe she would go just this once. The other girls at school had described the movie experience to her, and she thought the dark interior of the theatre would keep anyone from noticing if she closed her eyes and plugged her ears during objectionable parts.

Even the first sight of the cinema excited Hameeda's imagination. The lintel of the front door was painted a deep purple and the columns on either side were a bright orange. Cables attached to the top of the building supported a large, white sign board with red letters, spelling out the name of the current film and its actors. Dramatic posters depicting movie scenes hung on either side of the front door.

Hameeda looked over at Nadira and her brothers whose smiles and restless bodies spoke of their anticipation. Why did movies cause such excitement? When they entered the theatre, Nadira's father went up to a booth and purchased their tickets from a man who joked with him as if they were old friends. Then they walked through double doors into a room with rows of chairs bolted to the floor and an enormous white rectangle on the front wall. They found seats near the middle and sat down, waiting while the theatre filled with people. Without warning, the lights dimmed and then went out, and, in an instant, the room was flooded with color and sound. Larger than life people seemed ready to jump off the screen, and Hameeda felt as if she was a bystander in each scene. The story held her in its grasp and she grew attached to the characters, feeling as if they were people she had known for a long time. As if a wonderful tale and beautiful costumes weren't enough, there was also singing and dancing. She wanted it to last forever. When it ended and the lights came up, she sat there, still lost in the artificial world of the film until she felt the hard tip of Nadira's finger poking her.

"Get up, we're leaving. My father always takes us for a fancy tea at the Gymkhana Club afterward."

When they reached the car, Nadira's father turned to Hameeda with a smile and asked how she liked the movie.

"I loved it," Hameeda said, the corners of her mouth reaching for her ears.

"You're welcome to come with us anytime," Nadira's father said as he opened the car door for her.

Hameeda knew she was somehow crossing a line she hadn't crossed before, but she couldn't bear the thought of never seeing another movie. How could something so beautiful be bad?

"Thank you, that would be wonderful," she said, pushing aside her guilty feelings. All the way to the Club, she hummed the movie's songs under her breath, hoping they would go again soon.

Going to the cinema became her one secret act of

disobedience, and she continued to enjoy this activity until one day in the early eighties. They had arrived only a few minutes before show time and as they walked up, they saw a chain had been threaded through the handles of the double doors and secured with a large padlock. The owner sat to one side of the entrance with his chair tipped back against the wall, smoking a cigarette. Nadira's father asked him what was going on. The owner pointed to an official looking document pasted over one of the movie posters. Clustering around it, they saw it was an order from the government of General Zia-ul-Haq announcing the closure of all cinemas in Lahore.

"So my friend, what does Zia have against films?" Nadira's father asked.

"They've suddenly become un-Islamic, too many men and women gazing at each other with longing, with love. I tell you, it's no surprise. Zia looks like a cold fish with his military bearing, plastered down hair, clipped mustache and opaque eyes. I bet his wife has booted him out of their bed, and you can tell just by his tight-lipped expression that he's constipated all the time."

Nadira's father laughed and told the man he was probably right. Then he spoke with him for a while asking after his wife and numerous children and inquiring about what he would do now that his livelihood had been taken away.

The man took a long drag on his cigarette and blew out a stream of smoke. "Something will come along, insha Allah."

Her friend's father told him he might be able to find

some work for him and to come see him the following week. Hameeda always remembered his kind offer, and it increased her fondness for him.

For several years Hameeda and Nadira were unable to go to the cinema and satisfied their appetite for films by viewing video cassettes at Nadira's house. She often felt guilty when she arrived home, her mind still lost in the world some movie had created, her parents there to greet her with undeserved smiles.

Life had been so different before Nadira became her friend. When Hameeda was with Nadira she got caught up in her enthusiasms and felt as if she was plugged into an energy source. In her company, she put aside her timidity and enjoyed the outside world in a way she couldn't on her own.

Chapter 5

Beyond the boundaries of school and the comfort and connection of being with Hameeda and other girls her own age, Nadira was learning where she fit within the framework of two large extended families. You could never forget your identity was shaped by your family, its history and place in society. At family gatherings, the old stories so often told by her parents and grandparents spoke of their pride in being native Lahoris for many generations. Both her grandfathers had served in the British civil service and looked to Great Britain for their higher education. Her father often spoke of his college days in England, where he had gone to the same school as his father before him. But despite their connection to their British rulers and England, members of her family had also been in favor of independence and the push for the creation of the country of Pakistan. One great uncle had even been arrested and spent a month in prison after participating in an anti-British demonstration. Her family considered themselves up-to-date and modern, a sentiment which often prefaced the expression of a particular viewpoint. After all, they had traveled outside the boundaries of their own country and seen something of the outside world. But their modern views co-existed with a strong attachment to Punjab and their cultural and religious traditions. They considered themselves observant Muslims, but by the time Nadira was an adult, she would find others in their society disagreed.

As the only girl, she had to withstand the teasing and rough and tumble of her brothers and cousins and was often left out of their games.

"You can't play cricket with us; it's a boys sport," they told her when she tried to join in. Refusing to be put off, she'd stand in their way thinking it would force her inclusion, but the boys would grab her by the arms and pull her off to the side, leaving her fuming at the unfairness of her world.

Soon though, she realized being the only girl also came with certain advantages. Her father's oldest sister, Saabira Auntie, spoiled her with special outings and her favorite sweets. She also got the undivided attention of her maternal grandmother, her adored nani, under the guise of cooking and sewing instruction. But when she lorded those activities over her brothers, they just laughed.

The summer she was seven, soaring temperatures and three squabbling children became too much, and her mother sent Nadira to her grandparents' house for a few days. Their house was located in the older neighborhood of Gulberg on a street bordered on both sides by mature trees whose branches trespassed over the eight foot high boundary walls surrounding the houses. Her grandparents' house was reached either by driving into the walled compound through a wide, heavy timbered gate or walking through a small door adjacent to the gate. An intercom next to the exterior door operated a buzzer to announce a visitor. The house, similar to its neighbors, was a two story, flat roofed, concrete structure with large windows protected by vertical metal bars. Flowering vines climbed up the exterior walls, adding a splash of color and softening its hard lines. In front, there was a wide expanse of lawn, and shaped bushes marched single file across the house's foundation. Behind the house, the yard was crowded with well tended flower beds that erupted with color; orange zinnias, white blossomed cupid's dart, yellow coreopsis, the purple cone flowers of echinacea, the red and green felted leaves of coleus, and draping the rear boundary wall, curtains of lavender passion flower vines. The veranda was shaded by an old, enormous Banyan tree. Looking at the tree, it was difficult to imagine it had started out as fig seedlings that wrapped themselves around the host tree's trunk and root system until it was strangled to death. The trunk of the host tree rotted away over time, so not even a ghost of its identity remained under the immense tubular lattice of lignified roots that served as the Banyan tree's trunk. Outside the reach of the Banyan tree's shade were mango, orange and lemon trees.

Once through the gate, Nadira most often entered through the unlocked kitchen door on the side of the house. She was a favorite of their cook and by going through the kitchen she often got a taste of whatever was simmering on the stove, or a sweet. But on this particular day, she decided to pretend she was a guest and went up to the front door. Grabbing hold of the elephant head doorknocker by its trunk, she rapped it twice against its brass base. Almost at once, her nana, her mother's father, opened the door.

"My goodness, your nani didn't tell me we were entertaining a VIP today," her nana said, bending his taller than average frame so he was at her eye level.

Once Nadira entered the foyer, her nana took her small suitcase from her, kissed her forehead and gave her a one-armed hug which lifted her off her feet. Their footsteps echoed on the grey and white speckled terrazzo floor as he led her into the spacious lounge where her nani was waiting for them. In here, the floor was covered by two large, burgundy Bokhara rugs patterned with cream and black geometric designs, perfect for sprawling on when a chair wouldn't do. An oil painting of an English landscape in an ornate gilt frame hung on the wall facing her as she entered the room, and it always made her feel as if she was peering out a magic window into a place far removed from her familiar surroundings. Under the painting was a rosewood sideboard with carved leaves and bunches of grapes popping up from the center panel of each door, begging to be fingered, and a top crowded with framed photos of ancestors and current family members. Heavy velvet drapes faded to a soft rose color were drawn across the windows sealing them off from the outside. Lamps positioned throughout the room shed a soft yellow glow, and the blades of the ceiling fan high above Nadira's head pushed the still air, its motor buzzing like a swarm of flies. On a side wall was an overstuffed sofa whose cushions were covered with a moss green, paisley throw, hiding the frayed and balding spots of the original beige brocade. Her nani sat at one end of the sofa, a trolley in front of her which held a teapot, cups and saucers, and plates of food. Nadira said her salaams and then waited while her nana was served his tea and took a seat in one of the straight backed chairs flanking the sofa. The sight of food awakened Nadira's appetite, and she filled a plate with boiled egg sandwiches and biscuits, and was handed a cup of tea mixed with lots of milk and sugar. Mindful of her full cup and plate, she took small, slow steps across the room and placed her tea things on an end table where she could reach them from her favorite perch. Then she climbed onto the cushion of the jhula, a large, teakwood swing, its surface carved with elaborate designs and inlaid with ivory, hanging from a similarly embellished framework consisting of a pole suspended between angled supports. The jhula had been purchased in Gujarat as part of her great grandmother's dowry and then passed down to her nani who counted it as one of her prize possessions. In between bites from her plate, she leaned against the pillows piled on the back and traced the jhula's intricate designs with her finger. She liked imagining her nani when she was her age sitting in this very spot, daydreaming about her future.

After tea, her nana read the newspaper, and she and her nani went into the sewing room. This was Nadira's favorite room in the house. Although it was small, its large windows shaded by the deep roof of the back veranda provided a beautiful view of the garden's greenery. Protected from the sun, the drapes were allowed to remain open and the room filled with natural light. Her nani's sewing machine was set up against the outside window wall. On one side of the room were two large cupboards, their wooden shelves piled with plain and patterned fabric, boxes crammed with a rainbow of threaded spools, chipped and cracked tea cups filled with colored sequins, buttons, and beads, lengths of lace, and stacked rolls of ribbon whose curled ends trailed off the edge of the boards like dyed monkeys' tails. Nadira plopped into an overstuffed chair. Her descent formed a comfortable hollow in the down seat cushion, a temporary substitute for her nani's unavailable lap, while the chair's large rolled arms encompassed her like the walls of a fort. She watched from this seat as her nani cut out a new outfit, using an old, disassembled shalwar kameez as a pattern.

"See how I'm making a line a couple of inches outside the edge of the pattern to enlarge the size?" her nani said. "This is what happens when you eat too many sweets." She winked at Nadira, who laughed at her reference to their mutual fondness for desserts and chocolate bars.

While her nani sewed, she had Nadira help pin the pieces of the garment together before she stitched it. When Nadira grew bored with this task, she marked out a pattern on the top of a pillow cover and let her sew on beads or try some embroidery stitches. But the best part of the day, of many she spent with her nani, was the stories she told while she worked. She was a wonderful story teller, as expert at stitching words together as she was at sewing a new garment. Her stories weren't fantasies fabricated by her imagination, but about real events and people.

One story her nani told more often than any of the others, and it always reminded Nadira of a fairy tale without the usual happy ending.

"When I was growing up, I had a beautiful aunt," her nani started. "She married a handsome man and they had a beautiful young daughter. Everyone said she had been twice blessed. One morning during the monsoon season, her husband left for his office, his leave taking no different than it had been on any other work day. He climbed into a horse drawn tonga, took the tiffin box with his lunch that my aunt passed up to him, and waved goodbye as he disappeared around a bend in the road. A few hours later, a neighbor came to her door with a policeman. She was told the horse had lost its footing in shallow water and fallen, tipping over the cart and trapping her husband under one of its wheels, a broken spoke piercing his chest. The horse had been pulled from between the shafts, the tonga righted and her husband loaded into another vehicle and rushed to the hospital. But he bled to death before a doctor had a chance to examine him. Within a week my aunt acquired the face of an old woman. She had a young daughter to care for and no idea what to do. While she wept at home, her family held a meeting and decisions were made for her future." At this point in the story, her nani always paused, and looking at Nadira would say, "Remember Nadira, your first duty is to your family. They will be there for you when nobody else will." Then she picked up the dropped thread of the story and followed it to the end.

"The family decided living alone was improper for a young widow with a child. All the property my aunt's husband left to her was sold and the proceeds were put into an account for her expenses. My aunt was informed she would live with each of her three brothers and her sister in turn. All her choices were taken away and her life narrowed as she was forced to fit herself into the place allotted to her in the lives of her siblings. People looked at her and saw not her, but her circumstances. My aunt once told me she felt like a cloak of invisibility had been thrown over her."

That day, the first time her nani told her the story, Nadira interrupted with a question. "Did a prince come and rescue her?"

"No, there was no prince, not even a match with a widower," her nani said with a slow shake of her head. "Her nomadic existence only ended when her daughter married and she went to live with the couple."

"And did she live happily ever after?" Nadira asked, her eyes wide and her body leaning forward in anticipation.

"By then, life had worn her down like a river smoothing a stone, and she fell ill and died a few months later."

"I don't like stories with unhappy endings," Nadira told her, feeling sad and disappointed.

"I'm telling you this story because it illustrates a very important point. You never know where life's path will take you, and you need to prepare yourself for whatever Allah, in his wisdom, has in store for you. Study hard in school and complete college so you can make an independent life for yourself whether or not you're married. Times are changing. When you're grown, you'll have choices women don't have now. Learn from this story and remember its lesson."

Nadira never forgot this tragic tale. It remained imprinted on her brain, every detail as readily accessible in later life as those of "The Ugly Duckling" or "Red Riding Hood."

*   *   *

As an adult, Nadira realized that one event dramatically changed both her childhood and her country. Though the crisis took place outside of Pakistan, it couldn't be contained by national borders, and set in motion an unpredictable chain reaction which refashioned the bright future she might have had into something dark and twisted.

On a December day in 1979, eight year old Nadira sat on a floor cushion in the corner of the drawing room, feigning invisibility. She disliked missing out on anything important, and she discovered if she was very quiet and out of the center of things, adults often forgot she was in the room. Her father was talking to Saabira Auntie about the Soviet invasion of Afghanistan, mocking the Soviets for thinking they could conquer the country when Alexander the Great, tribes from India, Arabs, Mongols, Persians and the British had failed.

"The terrain and the people will defeat them. It may take longer because of their modern equipment, but still they will leave in defeat." he said.

Over the following months, Nadira heard stories of the Afghanis fierce resistance and how the Soviets bombed villages in an effort to eliminate local support for the mujahedeen fighters. One day at school, her teacher explained how the war had sent millions of refugees over the border into Pakistan, and described their desperate plight in overcrowded camps in the same instructive tone as when she taught a history lesson.

Nadira heard a sound, so soft she wondered if she had imagined it. When she turned she saw Hameeda, shoulders hunched, her hand over her mouth and her eyes on the verge of brimming over. As she looked at her friend's face, the words she'd just heard were transformed into images of fathers, mothers and children, their hardships etched on their faces.

"We can all do something," she heard her teacher say. And then she asked for three volunteers to help her organize a class collection drive for supplies.

For the first time Nadira could remember, Hameeda's hand shot up. Her friend was in the habit of not doing anything to draw attention to herself, and this unexpected behavior startled Nadira. She wished her hand had gone up first, but she had to settle for second.

Over the next couple of weeks, Nadira and all the other girls in the class worked hard collecting clothing and blankets from family and friends. When a representative from a charity came with a truck to pick everything up for transport, he shook the hand of each girl in the class, thanking them for their contributions. When Nadira felt the pressure of his hand, she remembered the emotion on Hameeda's face the day the teacher had told them about the refugees. She concluded that of all the girls, it was her friend who had come to this task in the most natural manner. She considered how goodness was as instinctive as breathing to some people, like Hameeda. She wished she was made that way instead of often having to be pointed in the right direction. Her deficiency pressed down on her and pushed out a sigh. And then, Hameeda's hand slipped into hers. Maybe her friend recognized something in her she couldn't see, and this thought made her feel lighter.

After her class's involvement with helping the refugees, Nadira forgot about the war. Although the neighboring conflict was a continuing subject of conversation in Lahore, it seemed very distant from daily life which went on as always. But once in a while, she saw or heard something which seemed connected to the war.

One morning, Nadira went out to the front gate to wait for one of her cousins. The door next to the gate was pushed halfway open. When she went to close it, she saw the neighborhood guard and their driver leaning on the wall a few yards away, smoking and talking. The man who had patrolled the neighborhood for years had fallen ill a few months earlier and had been replaced with a young man who had served in the army for a brief period. Nadira had been friends with the previous guard, but the new one put her off for reasons she couldn't explain. He had the face of a fighter with narrow eyes beneath tufted eyebrows, one of which was bisected by a thin, white scar. His nose took up much of the territory on his face and a thick, drooping mustache formed parentheses around the corners of his mouth. He treated the children of the neighborhood with scowls unless they were with their parents, and she had overheard their cook telling their maid to stay away from him. Today, a brand new gun was slung over his shoulder, replacing his old hunting rifle. Curious, Nadira moved down the wall on the inside until she could hear their words, and then slid down into a squat and listened in on their conversation.

"You want a handgun or a Chinese assault rifle with ammunition?" the guard asked. "I have a brother who can get it for you very cheap."

"Why would I want such a thing? I don't even hunt," she heard the driver reply.

"I'm just saying he can get them. This rifle, he got it for me, a gift of course. He can even get grenades or a stinger anti-aircraft missile."

"That sounds dangerous," the driver said. "What kind of business is your brother mixed up in?"

"He's helping the jihadists by bringing opium in from Afghanistan and then purchasing weapons for them with the drug money," the guard replied. "Think of him as a pipeline between interested parties."

"What has that got to do with selling guns in Pakistan?"

"Moving drugs and guns for the jihadists - that's for Allah; making money out of it on the side - that's business."

"Is this something we should be talking about? What if someone should hear us?"

"Who's going to hear us? Besides, fighting the infidel

Russians is our religious duty, and as a friend, I trust you to keep this to yourself," the guard said. "We wouldn't want anyone to get the wrong idea."

"Of course, of course."

The driver got the words out so fast he stuttered, not sounding at all like his usual cocky self. After a brief pause, he told the guard he'd better get back to work before he was missed. Nadira already thinking it had not been such a good idea to listen, jumped up, lost her footing and fell against a bush, breaking a branch with a crack.

"Who's there," the guard shouted out.

Nadira struggled to right herself and started running toward the house just as the guard came through the open door. He caught up with her and grabbed her by the arm. When she looked into his face, his eyes pinned her down like a butterfly on a collection board.

"What did you hear girl? Quick, tell me," he said, squeezing her forearm.

Nadira wrenched her arm out of his grasp.

"I don't know what you're talking about. I was chasing a cat, hoping she would lead me to her kittens, and now you've made me lose her." Nadira feigned indignation so well, she almost forgot how scared she was.

"You better not be lying to me."

"It's true; a stray cat had a litter of kittens behind the servants' quarters last week and has since moved them," the driver said.

The guard glared at Nadira, and she stared back at him without flinching.

"Well then, go find your cat," the guard said, waving his arm in the direction of the house.

Nadira left, wanting to run but holding herself to a walk. Once inside, her heart pounded as she peeked out the window. She watched as the guard went back out to the road, and the driver closed the door behind him and returned to his chore of washing the car. She sighed with relief. The guard frightened her, and the conversation she'd overheard made her anxious. She wanted to ask her father what it meant, but the lectures she had received in the past for eavesdropping were fresh in her memory. The only person she told was Hameeda who thought she shouldn't concern herself with a servant's personal business, which had nothing to do with her. Nadira told Hameeda it wasn't just what the guard said but how angry he'd gotten when he'd thought she'd been listening that made her nervous. But her friend said servants were always up to something they didn't want you to know about. Just the other day, her mother's maid had lied about having to take her pregnant sister to the doctor so she could interview for another job. Nadira didn't see how it was the same, but dropped the subject, filing the guard's conversation away with the hope she would discover other information to help her interpret its meaning. A week later, the guard was gone, saying he was going into his family's business. He was replaced by a nice, middle-aged man. Nadira was relieved, mistaken in the belief she had seen the last of the disagreeable guard. Many years later when their paths crossed again, she would recall this first encounter.

A couple of months afterward, Nadira and her family were in Karachi visiting her aunt and uncle. When they were out in the streets, she heard an undercurrent of Dari or Pashto in the river of Urdu that flowed around her. That evening at dinner, her uncle talked about the change with her father.

"The influx of Pathans from Afghanistan is straining our resources, not just near the border in Peshawar and Quetta, but also here in Karachi. And the worst of it is they've brought the emotions and tools of war with them. You're lucky Lahore hasn't been affected."

"Not directly maybe, but we're all affected," her father had replied.

Nadira remembered the words of the guard she'd overheard, and somehow knew it was proof he was right. Lahore was changing too.

The months came and went, winter passing into spring and then into summer with a heat that burned through to the bone. Nadira was out shopping with her mother for material which would be sewn into winter clothing. She couldn't understand the necessity of venturing out into an inferno when winter was so very far away and wished she was home with her brothers.

Sweat soaked the thin, cotton cloth of Nadira's shalwar kameez taping it to her body. She peeled her kameez away from her chest and shook it to get some air moving against her skin. Every once in a while, her mother pulled a bolt of fabric toward her and asked Nadira if she liked the color or pattern. Why did her mother ask her opinion when she always made the final decision?

The duration of their time in the shop was evidenced by the pile of unfurled bolts lying on the table. The ceiling fans caused the loose cloth to rise and fall as if it was inhaling and exhaling.

"Amma, can we go home now?"

"It will just be a little while longer."

Her mother fingered a piece of fabric and asked the shopkeeper how much. The shopkeeper gave her a price which was much too high and the bargaining began. Nadira knew it would not be the promised "little while longer" before her mother reached an agreement. With that in mind, she wandered outside. The shop fronted a narrow alleyway where similar two-story buildings were lined up cheek to cheek on both sides. Canvas awnings stretched across the alley, bathing the scene in half light. She leaned against the concrete wall of the shop, its surface giving off the last remnants of night air, cooling her back. Laziness took hold of her as she watched the steady stream of people passing by. A man sat on the ground in front of the next shop. His once fine clothes were wrinkled, spattered with the residue of at least one meal, and smudged with dirt from the roadway. The shoes at the end of his outstretched legs were scuffed and scratched, and he shivered as if it were the coldest of winter days. He was fingering a coin when a spasm shook his hand and the coin fell from his grasp and rolled across the ground, stopping near Nadira's toe. She picked up the coin and started toward him. As she got closer, he turned and looked up at her. His face was gaunt and pale, the down-turned corners of his mouth disappeared into an unkempt beard, and he stared at her with eyes whose pupils were obsidian pools, flooding his irises until only a thin border of brown remained. They were the dead eyes of someone whose soul has left his body. He reached out and grabbed her by the ankle. Startled and repulsed, Nadira pulled back trying to loosen his bony grip. Without warning, a foot kicked his wrist, and he released her with a howl. Her mother's hand grasped her upper arm, and she was dragged away from the man and pulled back into the shop.

"Nadira, don't ever leave without me again," her mother said, her voice breathless, the fingers gripping her arm trembling. Her mother pointed to the back of the shop. "Go stand over there and *don't* move."

Nadira watched a few feet away as her mother had a hurried conversation with the shopkeeper who picked up the phone and made a call. The stranger's eyes focused on her as he stood by the doorway, his body swaying a little. At first she didn't know why he was staring at her and then realized she still held the coin in her hand, but didn't dare do anything about it. Everything had happened so fast she hadn't had time to feel scared. Now safe, her former curiosity was replaced by an uneasy feeling that skittered down her spine like a light footed bug and then lodged in her belly.

In a little while, two policemen arrived and took charge of the haunted looking man. She could hear his screams of protest as they dragged him over to their vehicle and drove away.

In the days that followed, Nadira would be at the dinner table or in the lounge reading, and feel her mother's eyes on her. But when she looked up, her mother's attention was somewhere else. A week later, she was leaving the house to walk down the street to a neighbor's, and her mother happened to see her at the front door.

"Where are you going beti?"

"Just down the street to play with Seema."

"You'll have to wait a few minutes until I can walk you over there," her mother said, adjusting the bundle of laundry in her arms.

"Why? I always go by myself," Nadira said, already pulling the door open.

"The city is not the same as it was. Go sit in the lounge until I'm ready," her mother said, watching as Nadira closed the door and stepped away. "I don't want you leaving the house unless an adult is with you."

"Amma please, it's only a few houses down." Nadira rested her hand on her mother's arm and looked up at her.

"You heard what I said, Nadira."

As she waited, Nadira thought about this new, inconvenient rule. Since their shopping trip, her mother had been nervous, yelling at the driver if he left the gate open for even a minute and reminding everyone to relock the door when they came inside. Had her mother's mood infected her? Maybe it was the cause of the recurring dream that woke her up at night. In the dream, the stranger was shadowing her as she walked through the marketplace. When she turned around, his imploring face with its impenetrable stare confronted her, a bony hand reaching out to grab her. She'd wake up, clutching her blanket, her breathing uneven, relieved to find herself in the familiar territory of her bedroom.

As she sat in the sunlit room, the dream seemed silly and insubstantial, and the stranger more pitiable than threatening, easy to forget. What she felt most was frustration over this new restriction and a sense her life was being compressed, pushing her into a smaller and smaller space.

Chapter 6

Later, Hameeda would think of school as a test Allah had designed for her, a struggle that never got easier. Although she did well in Urdu, English and Islamic studies, the rest of the subjects, especially math, were difficult for her. In a strange way, her good results in some subjects made her poor performance in others seem much worse, as if it was due to some unacknowledged willfulness on her part. She was reasonably sure it was not for lack of studying. For days before an exam, she sat hunched over her books, reading and rereading material and struggling through problem after problem, in an effort to clear a path through the fog that veiled her brain. She always felt pretty confident on the day of the exam, certain she had done everything possible to prepare and knew the material. But once in the classroom, the questions in front of her swam in and out of focus, and with the clock ticking away, answers would elude her. Eventually, she would manage to pluck some out while others tormented her by staying out of reach. If only she had more time, she was sure the information she needed would come to her.

When she was eleven, her teacher sent her home with a note for her parents. She was certain it was because of a recent poor showing on three of her exams. Later, her mother came into her room to talk to her. She stroked Hameeda's back as she had when she was a child and was having difficulty falling asleep, and told her they were engaging a tutor for her. She emphasized that they knew she was doing her best, but said she would have to try harder. Years ago, high marks on exams were not so important for girls, she told her. But these days when it came time to marry, it was very important to have at least some university training. Only with this qualification could you hope to attract the most eligible young men.

"I know you're too young to really understand this, but for a woman, a good marriage is the most important goal."

Hameeda could feel the tears forming in her eyes and couldn't remember the last time she'd felt so miserable.

"I'm sorry I've disappointed you Amma, I'll do better," Hameeda said, feeling the hot flush of embarrassment on her face, and dismayed her mother had to have this conversation with her.

"Beti, you're a good girl, and you've never disappointed me," her mother said giving her a hug. "We'll help you as much as we can, and I'm sure you'll do fine."

Hameeda had never thought much about her future and had no particular ambitions of her own. She'd always looked to her parents to give her direction. If she did her best, she assumed everything would work out according to Allah's plan for her. The fact she'd fallen short was frightening, and her future, never a concern, now worried her. It had been nice to let life carry her along, always existing in the here and now, never pondering where she was headed. But from now on she'd have to pay attention.

The next day at lunch, Hameeda was still thinking about the conversation she'd had with her mother and didn't respond to one of Nadira's questions. Her friend frowned and asked if anything was wrong. Hameeda looked around, and then cupping her hand next to Nadira's ear, she whispered her shameful secret. Nadira told her that she would be glad to help her with her homework assignments.

"Thanks, but I don't want you to give up your free time to help me with my studies," Hameeda said, burying her head in her arms.

"I don't mind. I have to do the work anyway, and doing it together will be more fun," she heard Nadira say, but she couldn't bear to look up and see the pity in her friend's eyes. She felt a tug on her braid, and when she lifted her head, only a smile graced her friend's face. "Don't worry, I guarantee you, everything will be fine." And for some reason, Hameeda believed her.

Their parents agreed to let them stay for an hour after classes let out so they could do their homework together in the school library. In Hameeda's opinion, it wasn't the tutor but Nadira's help that made the difference. With her friend, she wasn't afraid to admit to a lack of comprehension or reveal memory lapses which required additional drilling on the facts. And, Nadira was so inventive in finding ways for them to learn the subject matter. On weekends before exams, they would closet themselves in Nadira's room, and she would have them marching around, singing, chanting, and rhyming the material into submission. Once Nadira's mother had knocked on the door to discover the source of the commotion and to make sure they were studying. They assured her mother they were preparing for the exam, and after she left, closing the door behind her, they both collapsed on the floor in a fit of laughter. Now when she took a test and was searching for an answer, Hameeda would hear Nadira's voice, encouraging her like a coach from the sidelines, providing her with the information she needed.

After a few months, Hameeda managed to get her grades up where they needed to be. She knew she would never be one of those people who acquired knowledge with ease, and maintaining good grades would always require long hours of study. So, even after her grades were acceptable, she and Nadira kept up their routine of doing their homework together. She believed it was one more thing that deepened their friendship.

In addition to her regular schooling, the imam from their mosque came once a week to teach Hameeda the Qur'an and her daily prayers. She loved these sessions, and felt each sura she mastered drew her closer to Allah. Her dada also continued studying the Qur'an with her like he had when she was much younger. Once Hameeda knew her prayers, her dada gave her a beautiful prayer rug. It was woven out of royal blue silk with an image of the Kaa'ba in the center and a pale gold border with a motif of arabesques in green and light blue. Hameeda thought it was the most beautiful gift she had ever received. From then on, she spread her rug on the floor next to her mother, and pulling her dupatta over her head, she joined her in reciting the prayers.

Her religiosity was one area of her life she felt uncomfortable sharing with Nadira. It was something they never talked about. From what she'd seen, her friend's religious observance was something she tried to fit into her schedule, rather than fitting her schedule around the dictates of Islam. Nadira was more than happy to say her prayers with Hameeda if they were together when the call to prayer sounded. But if she was absorbed in something at the time, she would often let Hameeda go off by herself to pray, saying she would just add her afternoon prayers to her evening prayers. This caused Hameeda to worry about her. She wanted to tell Nadira she should be more careful about obeying Allah's commandments, but she felt it wasn't a discussion her friend would welcome. Hameeda just hoped Allah would take into account all the good things Nadira did, like volunteering to help her with her studies.

Hameeda got used to her new routine; her teachers were pleased with her progress, and finally life seemed to be going along the way it should. She stopped worrying about the future and let the days pull her along. Then one morning, near the end of the following school year, Nadira met her by the school gate and told her she would be leaving Lahore for a while. At first Hameeda thought she hadn't heard correctly.

"What?" she said, thinking she'd misunderstood because Nadira didn't appear very upset. When her friend repeated her statement, this indigestible nugget of information made her tongue tied, unable to respond. "When? How long?" she finally managed.

Nadira put her arm around her shoulder. "It won't be forever, only two years."

Two years! Hameeda felt sick. She asked her friend how she could take it so well, and Nadira got mad. She said she had no choice and was trying to make the best of things.

Feeling the sting of her friend's rebuke, Hameeda tried to find something comforting to say. "I'll write you every day," she said, which garnered a smile from Nadira and an assurance she would do the same.

Later alone in her room, Hameeda tried to remember who she had been, and the shape of her days before Nadira had entered them. But she couldn't find her way back to that time in her life. She tried to convince herself two years wasn't very long compared to the countless years they would have together. But in her mind, the number refused to stay small, expanding first to twenty-four months, then 104 weeks and ending up at 720 days. Their separation stretched so far out in front of her, she couldn't visualize the end of it. The thought of her imminent loss weighed on her and bent her into a sad huddle whenever she was alone. And, there was another component to their separation she wouldn't be aware of until much later - the timing of it couldn't have been worse. Poised on the brink of adolescence, they were most vulnerable to change, each subject to a transformation which would have a lasting effect on their friendship.

Chapter 7

When Nadira was twelve, her father made a decision which changed the way she viewed the world forever. For weeks she heard her parents' voices behind the closed door of their bedroom, rising and falling like the waves of a stormy sea. It was out of the ordinary, and soon she became worried. She tried to figure out what might be wrong, but her parents seemed much the same when the family was together, and their daily lives went on as usual. Then one night when they had almost finished dinner, her father stood up and said, "I have an important announcement."

Nadira and her brothers looked at him while her mother studied her hands, folded on the table in front of her.

"I've received a Fulbright scholarship to Stanford University's physics PhD program, and I'm taking all of you with me," he said, opening his arms wide as if to embrace everyone at the table.

Asim was first with a question. "Where's Stanford?"

"Stanford is in the state of California on the west coast of the United States," her father said, as he drew an imaginary map in the air and pointed to a space to the left of the kitchen door. "I'll get a proper map tomorrow so you can really see it."

"Will we be there all summer?" Nadira asked, thinking how much she would miss their usual vacation in the mountains of Murree, and how the horse wallah would let someone else ride her favorite mount.

"Is it near the ocean so we can go to the beach?" Kareem chimed in.

"We're not going just for the summer," her father said. "We'll leave at the end of June for a two-year stay."

Her father's words were greeted with complete silence. An almost visible space opened up in the conversation for what seemed like minutes. Nadira was so surprised, she felt like a machine short circuited by a sudden surge of electricity. She pulled her braid over her shoulder and soothed herself by running her fingers over it while she waited for something to restart her thought process.

Finally, she heard her older brother's voice, sounding louder than normal as it cut through the quiet.

"Abu, what about school?" he asked, his forehead creased by a frown.

"You'll go to an American school near the University. It will be a wonderful experience for you," her father said, with a big smile, nodding his head as if in agreement with the soundness of his opinion.

Nadira tried to catch hold of her father's enthusiasm, but a similar note didn't sound inside her. Instead, the news flattened her. Two years seemed like a very long time away from everything she knew. She tried picturing America, but found her only reference was the cowboys and Indians from an American movie she had once seen. She looked across the table at her brothers. Asim sat there, head in his hands, with a glum look on his face. Like her mother, he disliked change. Eight year old Kareem appeared the least affected, busy plowing a furrow across the tablecloth with his fork.

"Well, doesn't anyone have a question or comment?" her father asked.

At that moment, Nadira's mind was still in a muddle and she couldn't come up with anything. Flinging her braid back behind her, she looked across the table at Asim, who remained silent, his features composing themselves into a sulky expression. For whatever reason, her mother must have decided she wasn't going to help her father out, her expression hidden by her bent head, and her only sound a slight clearing of her throat. It was Kareem who finally broke the silence.

"Abu, can we have dessert now?"

Her mother gave a short, off-key laugh as she got up, and shook her head at her father before disappearing into the kitchen. There was no more discussion of the move that night, but during the coming week her father had a one on one conversation with each of them and with the family as a group until the subject was worn as thin as a threadbare shirt.

Nadira still had a month of school left and she spent the time as a minor celebrity. Everyone in her class was envious of her upcoming stay in California, and one of the girls asked if she would go to Disneyland every week. She talked to her father, and inquired about plans to see Disneyland. He said it was a long way from where they'd be living, and he couldn't say whether or not they'd be able to go. Nadira decided there was no reason to share this piece of information with her friends. Their envy made her see what a great adventure her move was, and soon she was looking forward to their departure. Her excitement crowded out her concerns about leaving her home, family and Hameeda. Whenever she glimpsed Hameeda's downcast face she felt bad, but her time away would only be a short interruption, and afterwards, they would have the rest of their lives together.

Her last day in Lahore, Nadira was allowed to spend the afternoon at Hameeda's house. She lay next to Hameeda on her bed, their bodies touching and hands clasped, her eyes averted to avoid the sadness in her friend's face while she tried to keep up her side of a halting conversation. Was her friend also trying to find an avenue of thought which led anywhere but to the goodbye that was coming, and was she failing in the same way Nadira was?

Whenever words were put aside, Nadira could feel a matching pulse in Hameeda's wrist and hear their breathing synchronizing little by little, as if their bodies were merging together, their hearts and minds touching and connecting in some effortless, inevitable way. Nadira realized she had let the novelty of the trip seduce her. Why hadn't she given a thought to Hameeda's irreplaceability, or how with anyone else she would have to present an edited version of herself? She tightened her grip on Hameeda's hand, not wanting to let go. But too soon, they had to say goodbye. An hour later, when she stood at the door, she saw her own tears mirrored on Hameeda's face. And in her head, as if she had finished the last page of a book, the words "the end" kept repeating themselves.

The day they left, all the family members in Lahore saw them off at the airport. Her dada held a Qur'an in one hand and placed his other hand on each of their heads in turn, saying a prayer for their safe journey. Then, the rest of the family crowded in, voicing their goodbyes. As she was being passed from relative to relative for one final hug, the excitement which had bubbled inside her for the last few weeks disappeared, and she felt as flat as a bottle of soda left uncapped too long. When her nani came up to her, she started to cry, put her arms around her and wouldn't let go. Faced with boarding the plane, she couldn't remember why going had seemed so appealing. Her father came over and with a gentle tug, pulled her away.

"The time will go by fast, and you'll be home before you know it," he said. Then he clasped her hand in his and walked her through the gate to the waiting bus that took them across the familiar, potholed, dusty tarmac to the plane.

Her father let her have the window seat so she could see Lahore from the air. She watched miniaturized buildings and streets recede until only light and dark shapes intersected by lines remained. The only home she'd ever known reduced to a complicated plane geometry problem. Then the plane nosed its way through the clouds and the city disappeared.

*　　*　　*

After a thirteen hour flight, Nadira's introduction to the United States was not promising. Required to disembark in New York for immigration and customs before proceeding on to San Francisco, the only view she had was of a narrow, windowless corridor that led to a vast subterranean hall. This enormous area was filled with multiple queues of men, women and children, who shuffled forward in serpentine lines which ended at raised booths occupied by uniformed men and women. The wails of babies, voices in languages both strange and familiar, and yells of "next," bounced off the concrete walls. She inched forward in the line, her small carry-on bag banging against her ankle, her muscles aching, and her eyes irritated from the dry, conditioned air. The line for foreigners crept along at a much slower pace than the line for returning Americans. These privileged citizens exuded none of the weary endurance of outsiders, and instead exhibited a combination of confidence, anticipation, and impatience. Nadira wished she was not the stranger here but the one returning home.

After their passports were stamped, they were ushered into a transit lounge where they sat in hard, molded plastic chairs, waiting to board the plane for the last leg of their journey. Nadira thought of how far from Lahore they had come, and soon they would put even more miles between her and her country. The full weight of her displacement settled on her, a burden she would need to lift every morning on waking, and carry around with her the rest of the day.

Things got better when they reached the San Francisco airport. Once freed from the baggage area, they entered a space where walls of windows filled every corner with light, and everything looked fresh and new. It was nothing like the old, shabby, stripped down barrenness of the Lahore airport. There was also a smiling face holding a sign with their name on it - a new colleague of her father's who would drive them to their apartment. Nadira was amazed that he looked just like the Americans in the Western she'd seen at the cinema, a ten gallon hat perched on his head, his belt decorated with a silver steer head buckle and his feet encased in fancy cowboy boots. He introduced himself in heavily accented English as Professor Jim Calhoun. He told them he was a foreigner too – originally from Texas. And then, he gave a big laugh as he looked at the puzzled expressions on their faces.

As they walked through the terminal, Nadira saw shops, snack food vendors and restaurants. She wished she could stop and take a closer look. She felt excitement edging its way back in, energizing her tired body. She slowed down and paused whenever something piqued her interest until her mother's sharp voice hurried her along. "Nadira, let's go, let's go."

Outside, her father and Professor Calhoun loaded their belongings into his station wagon and they left for their new home. Nadira was exhausted from the flight and even her first glimpse of the country's scenery couldn't keep her eyes open. Very soon, the motion of the car and the thrumming of the tires on the pavement lulled her to sleep. When she woke up, they were parked in front of the tallest building she had ever seen. She counted fourteen rows of windows tiered one above the other. As she stood there, she watched people entering and exiting the building, their faces representing a similar diversity to what she'd seen at the airport. Later, her father told them graduate students came to Stanford from all over the world.

Getting to their apartment, she had her first elevator ride. She was fascinated when the doors glided shut with the push of a button, and they were lifted upward almost without a sound, the motion as smooth as a spoon drawn through cream, going up and up, until with a slight jerk, they stopped at their floor. Once off the elevator, they walked down a long hallway with numbered doors on either side, halting at number 603. They all crowded inside, eager to see their new, temporary home. Exploring this dollhouse of a space took them only a few minutes. They entered into an L shaped room. The long arm was a furnished lounge with the bare minimum of furniture and a small alcove off to the right on the far end. The alcove looked like it had been designed for a desk, or as a storage area, but now a narrow bed occupied the space with a swing-arm lamp on the wall above the head of the bed and a brass nailed trunk at its foot. A pole hung with curtains bridged the opening, providing a means to close it off from the lounge. The short arm contained a dining table and chairs, and in the middle of the two arms was a tiny galley kitchen.

A hallway off the living room led to two bedrooms and a bathroom. One bedroom had a large bed, a dresser and a built-in closet. The other smaller bedroom had two narrow beds stacked on top of each other with a ladder at the end, called a bunk bed by Professor Calhoun. It also had a small chest of drawers and a closet.

As soon as her father's colleague left, Nadira's mother complained about how tiny the apartment was and asked her father if he could find other accommodations. Her father explained that student housing was included in his living allowance, and if they moved elsewhere, he'd have to pay the difference himself, which would be too expensive. He said, in time, her mother would get used to it, and a small place had the advantage of being much easier to keep clean.

When her father stopped speaking, he glanced at her mother with a hopeful look. Nadira turned toward her mother and found an unhappy expression still in place.

Asim and Kareem were given the room with the bunk bed, leaving the alcove for Nadira. At night, with the curtain closed, hidden from the rest of the household, she would imagine she was in the berth of a train or ship, traveling to exotic locations. In her miniature but private space, she was able to read her books, write letters to Hameeda, or let her imagination rescript her life without being disturbed. Her private hide-away was the first of many happy memories she had of those two years.

The first week, they took a taxi to the shopping mall to get clothes for the upcoming months. Nadira found the vastness of the mall's interior overwhelming. It was like an indoor city with boulevards lined with small shops, a main courtyard with an enormous fountain, and a huge square bordered by food kiosks and populated with dozens of tables and chairs so you could sit down and eat.

Her mother found all the separate shops confusing, so they went into a department store at the far end of the mall where they could shop for everything in one place. Nadira was thrilled with her mother's choices for her - one red and one navy short sleeve t-shirt, a pair of khaki pants, a white cardigan with pink flower buttons, and a couple of patterned skirts with matching solid colored blouses. Only one thing almost spoiled the day. As they were walking out of the children's department, she saw a stack of blue jeans.

She dragged her mother over to the table. "Amma look, can I have a pair of blue jeans, *please?*"

Her mother shook her head. "No, they aren't appropriate for a young girl."

"But I see girls in our building wearing them," Nadira said, her hand stroking the denim.

"I'm not concerned with what other girls wear, only with what *you* wear," her mother said, turning away from the table.

Nadira knew once her mother made up her mind, there was no use arguing with her. She didn't understand what the point was of going abroad if you brought all your old attitudes with you. She could see her mother intended to set up their household here along the same lines as it had been in Lahore. But it was early days and maybe, just maybe, things would change after a while. With a lot of reluctance, she followed the rest of the family out of the store.

At lunch, her disappointment spoiled her appetite, and she ate only half of her burger and turned down her father's offer of dessert. When they went into the pharmacy on their way out, her father told her mother he would return in a few minutes. When he came back, he had a department store bag.

"What did you get, Abu?" Kareem asked, making a grab for the bag.

"It's a surprise," he said with a wink, holding the bag up out of her brother's reach. "You'll see when we get home."

Her mother frowned. "Nadeem, what have you done?"

Her father just gave her mother a pat on the shoulder, and led them outside to the taxi stand. When they got back to the apartment, her father put his hand into the bag and pulled out three pairs of blue jeans.

"Nadeem, you're impossible!"

"To paraphrase an old expression; when in America wear what the Americans wear."

"Abu, can we put them on now?" Kareem asked.

"Ask your mother."

"Now I'm consulted?" her mother said in an exasperated tone. "Fine, go change."

Nadira whooped with joy and ran to claim the bathroom first. She wriggled out of her old clothes and slipped one of her new t-shirts over her head. Then, she stepped into the stiff, indigo jeans, pulled up the zipper, pushed the bronze metal button through the buttonhole, and dug her hands deep into the front pockets to test them out. The full-length mirror mounted on the door reflected back someone new, a girl who appeared tougher and ready for anything. Hooking her thumbs in the belt loops she struck a pose she had seen in a Western and smiled. The jeans were more than clothes, she thought, they were the key to her American experience.

Her father started his assistantship and his classes the week after their arrival, but for Nadira, summer vacation stretched out ahead of her in the same pleasurable expanse it had back home.

Nadira had been worried about making friends, but living in an apartment complex made it much easier. Her building and those adjacent to it were filled with children who grouped themselves by age and interests into informal tribes that roamed the complex and its environs. One quick smile at a girl in the elevator who looked about her age had started a conversation and earned Nadira her first friend, and it only took a few more days to acquire two more. There was a Chinese girl from Taiwan, a girl whose family was from India but who had been born in New York City, and an American girl from a place called Chicago. They spent their time playing games which required the simplest supplies. Grids were chalked on the sidewalk for hopscotch, and one of the girls had a jump rope she shared. They found string and learned the intricacies of cats' cradle, made clover chains and sat in the shade of the trees talking and giggling. Whatever barriers there might have been were transcended by the fact they were all in a new place, far from home.

Nadira found Stanford to be quite different from Lahore. When you went outside you weren't accosted by beggars every few feet with their pleading voices and thrusting hands; the roadways weren't bordered by improvised canvas shelters, where the poorest of the poor publicly conducted every aspect of their meager existence; there were no skinny, feral dogs nosing through the garbage; and the air was not heavy with dust, gasoline fumes and charcoal smoke.

The large Stanford campus, with its cream colored stucco buildings, red tile roofs and towering palm trees, was as fresh and clean as a shirt just removed from its factory wrapping of cellophane. It was populated with smiling, helpful people who greeted strangers with a polite "Hi, how are you." Nadira felt as safe on campus as she did within the walls of their apartment, and her parents must have felt the same way because their rules changed.

Her father purchased secondhand bikes for Nadira and her brothers so they could get around the campus in a reasonable amount of time. At first, he borrowed a bike and rode with them. But within a couple of weeks, he relaxed his usual close supervision. Although her mother needed some persuading, Nadira was finally accorded the same privileges as her brothers, and rode her bike all over Stanford with her friends. If she was meeting her father on campus, she could even go on her own as long as she went directly there. Of course, she first had to endure her mother's admonitions – "stay on the main road, obey the crossing signs, and no talking to strangers." Sometimes she would leave earlier than necessary so she could have some time by herself. Once out of sight of her building, she did as she pleased, taking routes she had not yet explored. At first, she was afraid someone would see her and report her misbehavior to her parents. Once a friend of her father's recognized her when she was at the far end of campus, and she waited for a scolding. But when nothing happened, she realized, here, everyone thought her behavior was normal. Over time, she explored every inch of the campus and soon knew the fastest route to any destination within its borders. She often stopped and watched the students playing Frisbee on the lawn, sitting in groups and talking intently, or walking with books under their arms to classes or activities she couldn't begin to imagine. Observing them, she felt a stab of envy. They were so lucky to have such perfect lives, making their own decisions about what to do and where to go, and how they would shape their futures. She vowed someday she would be just like them.

That first summer, Nadira and her father established a routine which continued for the two years they lived there. At the end of each day, she took her bike and rode across campus to meet her father at the physics building. It was their special time together, and she enjoyed having his undivided attention without her brothers' constant interruptions. Usually, she walked her bike on the way back to the apartment so they could talk. She told her father about her day, and he explained what he'd been working on or commented on something he'd read in the morning paper. Sometimes they scrutinized the people they passed and tried guessing where each person was from and what he or she did. Other times, they took turns on the bike, shouting out sentences as they rode circles around each other. Her father looked so funny on her bike, his knees almost hitting his chin as his long legs worked the pedals. Nadira wondered if her friends' fathers had the same talent for transforming into younger versions of themselves.

One day Nadira exited the apartment building to meet her friends. She was early, and stood there with just her thoughts keeping her company. Scenes from her first weeks in California flashed through her mind, and she contemplated the months stretching out into the future with all their possibilities. Her body began feeling lighter and lighter, as if she were a balloon filling up with helium. Lifting her face up to the sky, closing her eyes against the bright summer sun, and raising her arms over her head, she spun around and around until dizziness landed her on her back in the grass, her body stationary, her head still spinning. She stayed there, stretched out on the ground, waiting for the whirling to stop. She felt buoyant with happiness. It astonished her that in this country where everything was so foreign, it all felt so natural, so right, as if her presence here had been preordained.

Vacation flew by as it always had, and one morning she woke up to the first day of school. Unlike in Lahore, she and her brothers would be attending the same school. She felt every bit the foreigner when she walked into the unfamiliar atmosphere of the classroom, and the relaxed ease she'd acquired over the summer disappeared in an instant. But when the teacher introduced her to the other students, they smiled and chorused a greeting that dispelled some of her anxiety. In those first weeks, her classmates were very welcoming, which helped her adjust to the strange environment.

This was the first time she'd been in a co-ed school, and the presence of boys changed the atmosphere in the classroom. Nadira recognized many of her brothers' traits in her male classmates. In terms of physicality, boys seemed akin to girls raised to the fourth power. Among themselves they participated in a masculine dance composed of playful shoving, punches and high fives. They pushed against the rules in the same way they pushed against each other, sitting sideways in their chairs, flinging paper clips behind the teacher's back and running in the halls. When they spoke, their voices were often at full volume. Nadira enjoyed the extra energy and excitement these masculine attributes contributed to her classes.

Her teachers had a very different way of conducting lessons compared to what she'd been used to at home. They acted more like an older friend than the stern disciplinarians back in Lahore. Even the classroom setting was new. Everything was more relaxed. Their desks were arranged in a circle facing each other rather than in straight rows, and instead of just reciting back the information they were taught, something called "class participation" was encouraged. It took Nadira a while before she was comfortable asking questions or offering her opinion. Although she spoke fluent English, it was British English and some American words and slang made her feel like her classmates were speaking another language. But after a while, she felt she was "catching on."

Outside of class, Nadira played sports like football, which her American friends called soccer, and she was introduced to softball. She'd always had a problem sitting still, and playing sports kept her in motion. There was also satisfaction in mastering new skills, a sense of accomplishment each time the side of her foot made solid contact with the soccer ball or the softball landed with a satisfying smack in the pocket of her glove. Her father sometimes kicked a ball around with Nadira and her brothers on weekends and kept track of how their teams were doing. But her mother, observing a purpling bruise on her leg, or a skinned elbow, trophies from hard fought games, shook her head in silence, her lips pressed together in a thin line.

In addition to the friends she'd made in their building during the summer, Nadira also formed friendships with girls in her class. Sometimes they invited her to their homes, and she saw how Americans lived. Their houses were much smaller, ranked close together with no boundary wall or fence distinguishing one property from another. Although her friends lived in close proximity to their neighbors, they seemed more removed from their lives than was common at home. She was astounded that they were usually mere acquaintances of the people living next door to them. Following the teachings of the Qur'an, all the families she knew maintained cordial relationships with the people who lived on their street and adjoining streets. The men and boys met at the neighborhood mosque for Friday prayers, and the families often got together at each other's homes to share in celebrations, support each other during difficult times, and help out when needed. The vast interconnected network of family and friends held you in its net, by turns saving you or keeping you captive, and even among the millions of people in Lahore, there was no escaping it.

It seemed to Nadira, the lives of her American friends were quieter and less crowded than her own, contending only with their parents and siblings on a daily basis. Nadira wondered if these living arrangements were because of the size of the accommodations or something else. Why wasn't their extended family with them, taking up space, filling the air with contented or quarrelsome voices, creating discord and delight? Back home she and her friends lived with at least grandparents and sometimes aunts, uncles and cousins as well. There was a constant flow of family through their house at all hours of the day. Even the vocabulary of family was different. In English there was only one term for grandmother, grandfather, aunt, uncle and cousin. In Urdu, there were two separate terms for each, depending on whether they were paternal or maternal. You were also often reminded of your role when addressed by a family member. You would be referred to as daughter, son, sister, brother and so on. When Nadira thought of her relatives, their separate titles provided her with the reference points of family connections, each one occupying a precise place in the map of her universe. She wondered what it would be like living in a home where a prolonged period of solitude was possible. Nadira often felt pulled in two directions, her new life in Stanford tugging her one way and the ties of home and family pulling her another way.

Sometimes her classmates asked her to their houses on weekends, but most of the time she couldn't accept because her mother liked having the family together on Saturdays and Sundays. While they were at Stanford, they made numerous trips to places which remained fixed in Nadira's memory, the passing years filing off the sharpness of the details and leaving behind recollections with a dream-like quality.

Outings started early in the morning, her father getting them out of bed by whisking the covers off their sleeping forms, shaking their shoulders and in a loud voice demanding "up, up." While Nadira and her brothers ate breakfast, her mother packed a picnic lunch of kabobs wrapped in homemade chapattis or egg salad sandwiches cut into crustless triangles which they would eat with the cold sodas they bought at their destination. They often went into San Francisco, hiking up and down the hills until their legs gave out and they caught a ride on a cable car. There were trips to the tiny town of Sausalito where houses were stacked like colorful children's blocks on steep hillsides overlooking the bay. One October afternoon they walked through the giant redwoods of Muir Woods. The quiet was as deep as the shadows beneath the enormous trees. Among these arboreal dinosaurs, Nadira felt as if she had drunk from one of Alice in Wonderland's bottles and dwindled down to a fraction of her size. And in the laser beams of sunshine that worked their way between the redwoods' needled caps, she felt the presence of Allah in a way she never had at home.

In the beginning, Nadira wrote to Hameeda one or more times a week with details of every aspect of her new life. She also received frequent letters from Hameeda, keeping her up-to-date with all the latest news from home. But as Nadira became entangled in a web of new experiences and daily activities, the time span between her letters to her old friend got longer and longer. Aside from being busy, she was becoming more and more assimilated to life in the States. There were times when being a Muslim in a Christian country meant nothing and other instances when it meant everything, causing Islamic requirements to go unobserved. In her effort to fit in, she made choices that would have been difficult to explain to Hameeda in a way she would understand. It was as if her life had become a foreign language which required translation. She found herself censoring her letters, nervous about how Hameeda would judge her. Sometimes, she wrote Hameeda "remember when" letters, dwelling in the past in an effort to recapture feelings of similarity and closeness that were slipping away.

Life at Stanford, even with its compromises, seemed perfect to Nadira. She fought less with her brothers, spent more time with her father, and even got along somewhat better with her mother. She was happy at school and with her new friends. But their time there was short, and just when she felt most comfortable, they were going home.

Returning to Lahore was not what Nadira wanted. Although she sometimes missed her grandparents, aunts, uncles and cousins, she dreaded returning to the restrictions she remembered. Her friend Rajasi's family lived in the States and spent their summers in India. She thought making California their home and visiting Lahore on vacations and during the summer would also be the perfect solution for her family. When she came to this conclusion, the thought of her friend Hameeda didn't alter her opinion. Instead, she planned how she would fit Hameeda into this new life, imagining summers together in Lahore, and Hameeda visiting her in Stanford during her mid-term break. It would be fun showing Hameeda around, and teaching her about the States, in the same way she had tutored her in math. With this in mind, she spent their last month at Stanford, begging her parents to stay.

"Nadira, enough; this is an adult decision, not one for a child. There are things you can't possibly understand," her mother said to her in exasperation. "Besides, once you're back home for a while it will be like you never left, and you'll forget about this place."

But her mother was wrong. Back in Lahore, her new freedoms were taken away, and she was once more imprisoned by musts and must nots. At school, she was like a singer who becomes tone deaf overnight and is often caught singing off-key. The girls teased her about the way she spoke, saying she had a strange accent. When the other girls made jokes, she didn't understand them. She was told she was too forward and boyish, and the teachers scolded her for asking too many questions instead of concentrating on drilling for her exams. She had once excelled in all her subjects but had fallen so far behind in Urdu and Islamic studies that her parents hired a tutor for her. She found it difficult sitting still in her seat all day and missed playing sports. She was laughed at for her fastidious habits when she wouldn't eat from the filthy street carts opposite the school. Where she had been welcomed into her new class in Stanford, here most of her former classmates were cool toward her. She would have felt very much alone if it wasn't for Hameeda.

Chapter 8

In the first few weeks after Nadira's departure, Hameeda found it difficult to believe she wasn't in the mountains of Murree with her family for their usual six week summer vacation. But as the weeks stretched out into months, Hameeda felt the void opened up by Nadira's absence getting bigger and bigger. She realized how much her friend had filled up the empty corners of her life and enlivened the bland routine of her days. Nadira's departure even appeared to set in motion disturbing changes in Hameeda's universe, as if her friend's move from Lahore to Palo Alto had thrown the world off balance, causing Pakistan to follow a new direction.

Hameeda had never paid attention to politics, but now it invaded the conversations at the dinner table, and was impossible to avoid. She learned the country was feeling the weight of General Zia-ul-Haq's rule, and his Islamization program had motivated the Shia community to become politically active. Both her dada and father agreed that Zia's concept of Islamization was really Sunnification since the laws and regulations were based on Sunni interpretations of sharia law and thus in opposition to Shia religious principles. However, the two of them disagreed on what to do about it. Her dada spent his time praying to Allah regarding these injustices, while her father joined the TNFJ, the new Shia political party, which was proactive and demonstrated to allow Shias to regulate their own religious life. Loving both of them, their disagreement pained Hameeda and destroyed the sanctuary family life had always been for her. The atmosphere around her house became as tense as a stretched rubber band. Sometimes, there were arguments at the once peaceful dinner table.

"If you put your hand into a wasp's nest, you're going to get stung," her dada said to her father, jabbing his finger into the air for emphasis.

"If we do nothing, Zia will take away our religious rights," her father said, crossing his arms over his chest and frowning.

"I'm your father and I've lived many more years; you should respect my judgment."

As Hameeda's father started to answer, she saw her mother place her hand on his sleeve, and his mouth snapped shut.

She could tell they were both trying to control their anger by the tight, low timbre of her father's voice, and the way her dada rubbed his scar. The conflict caused Hameeda to lose her appetite, and she spent the meal picking at her food and trying to ignore the arguments and silences which were often served as unpalatable side dishes at the dinner table.

Home was not the only place where Zia's policies had an impact. One day at school Hameeda overheard one classmate tell another that according to her father, the TNFJ was trying to force the Shia interpretation of sharia law on the country.

"My father says if Shias can't learn their place, they should be exiled," the girl proclaimed.

Hameeda couldn't believe what she was hearing. For the first time, she felt different from her classmates. It began to overshadow everything she had in common with them, and she dreaded going to school. Every morning, as soon as she opened her eyes, her body tensed in anticipation of having to struggle through another school day which seemed to get longer and longer as the weeks passed.

The shunning started with only a couple of the girls, then another and another were persuaded by their strong, sure opinion. Others who seemed to disagree still tried to avoid being included in her snubbing by keeping their distance. She could tell they were uncomfortable with the way she was being ignored because they would shrug their shoulders and tuck their chins in apology when they rejected her overtures. The number of invitations for parties and outings diminished, and often the only thing she had to occupy her time was the drudgery of her studies. She missed Nadira's company more and more, and as each day passed she mentally checked it off, thinking she was one day closer to her return. If only Nadira were with her, she was sure the world would right itself again.

With her reduced social schedule, Hameeda had more than enough time to write lengthy letters to Nadira once or twice a week. Correspondence from the States took at least a week and sometimes two to arrive. Still, every day she looked through the mail on the foyer table, hoping to see the blue paper of an aerogram among the pile of white envelopes. She kept Nadira's letters in a special box. Daily, she took them out, unfolded them and read them until the creases in the paper became as thin as a dragonfly's wing, and prone to tears, which she repaired with cellophane tape. At first Nadira matched her letter for letter. But after a few months, she began writing less often. Hameeda wondered if some of her letters had been lost in the mail. But when at last a letter showed up like a tardy child without an excuse, she found indications among its contents that Nadira was responding to several of her missives. What was keeping her so busy that she'd waited such a long time to answer? She pictured Nadira laughing with new friends, too occupied to give her a thought. An unfamiliar feeling clung to her. Tightness settled in her chest like a winter cold along with a lethargy that persisted for days. Was this what abandonment felt like?

One day, her mother suggested Hameeda go with her when she went to visit a friend.

"Her daughter will be at home, and she's just a year older than you. I think you might find you have similar interests."

Hameeda thought her mother was trying to find her a replacement for Nadira – impossible. Still, she appreciated her concern and agreed to go. To her surprise, she enjoyed her time with the daughter. Farideh had a quiet personality and was as immersed in their Shia religious traditions as Hameeda. She still missed Nadira's high spirits and the excitement of never knowing what will happen next. But being with her friend had often been exhausting while Farideh's many similarities made her company as comfortable as putting on a pair of well-worn slippers. At first she felt disloyal to Nadira but reasoned she wasn't replacing her, only adding a new friend. Farideh also introduced her to a few girls from the Shia community, and within a short period of time Hameeda was also too busy to write as often. On weekends, she and her new group of Shia friends met to study the Qur'an and have a meal together. They often cooked the dishes themselves to practice their culinary skills. Her father would come in to greet them and ask after their parents, sometimes sitting and talking with them for a short while. It was something he'd never done when Nadira was visiting, making Hameeda both pleased and perturbed. The world seemed to be dividing and sub-dividing, pushing people into tighter and tighter groups where fewer people belonged and more were outsiders.

Nadira was still absent when Hameeda decided to cover her head. The idea of it came to her after her friend Farideh adopted the practice. When she had asked her new friend what encouraged her to take this step, she told her that physical changes had prompted her to do it. Hameeda had blushed, thinking how in the last couple of months the flat plain of her chest had developed curves that still felt like they belonged to someone else. After this conversation with Farideh, Hameeda thought about her own situation. Was her body confirming a turning point she had, until now, refused to acknowledge? It seemed like such a big step to leave childhood behind and take on the burden of adult responsibilities, and she was reluctant to let go of her familiar role. But, she was thirteen now, she thought, too old to be considered a child any longer. In her need for affirmation, she went to her mother and asked her when she had started covering her head.

"I was about your age when I lifted my dupatta off my shoulders and on to my head, just as my mother did before me. This last year, I've watched you mature in so many ways, amazed at how fast time has passed since you were my baby girl," her mother said, her voice sounding sad. "I've been waiting for you to decide it was time to adopt an outward sign of womanhood."

Hameeda wondered what changes her mother had seen in her. She felt no different, still held back by the same uncertainties and insecurities. Maybe taking on the trappings of a woman would somehow imbue her with a new confidence.

The first day she wore her dupatta on her head, her dadi and aunts came over at tea time and made a fuss over her, turning it into a special occasion. Hameeda couldn't remember when she'd felt so happy. Throughout the day, she kept stealing glances in the mirror, admiring how well she looked with her face framed by fabric. Finally, her mother took her aside and said with a laugh, she'd never seen a change designed to enhance modesty encourage so much vanity.

That night as she uncovered her head, she started planning how she would describe the experience in her next letter to Nadira. She wondered what her friend would think. Maybe she'd wait until she came home; it was only a few more months. It was possible by then Nadira would also be covering her head. Yes, maybe she would wait.

Chapter 9

Her first night back in Lahore, Nadira felt like a guest in someone else's house. She had gotten so used to her sleeping alcove, her old room felt cavernous. Exhausted, yet unable to sleep, she rolled herself up in her sheet and tucked it under her chin to create a cocoon for herself. The cooler hummed and clanked as it pulled the late August, hot air through its water moistened pad, lowering the temperature, and perfuming the air with the smell of a sun heated sidewalk after a rainstorm. She finally fell asleep, only to be jerked awake by the 5:00 a.m. call to prayer. The chant was taken up one at a time by the nearby mosques, their calls overlapping and at last trailing off as the last muezzin finished. It was at once foreign and familiar, tugging her back into the Lahore she remembered.

Nadira turned over and went back to sleep, only waking when the sound of voices and household activity invaded her room. Still feeling disoriented, she untangled herself and went to take a shower and dress. When she opened her closet, a row of shalwar kameezes greeted her. She went hunting for her Western clothes and found them in a small suitcase pushed to the back of the bottom shelf. After pulling on a pair of jeans and a wrinkled Stanford t-shirt, she appeared in the dining room for breakfast, and her mother sent her back to her room to change. Nadira sat on her bed in her underwear and wished she could transform back into her old self as easily as she changed clothes, and knowing it would be much more difficult.

Later, Nadira received a phone call from Hameeda, eager to meet. It was agreed she would come over to Nadira's house after lunch and spend the afternoon.

When Nadira met Hameeda at the door, she was startled to see her head enveloped in her dupatta. Was this a sign she was different from the person who had said goodbye to her two years ago? She had a difficult time keeping her eyes off her friend's head covering, but when she focused on her friend's face, she saw the identical kind eyes and warm smile she remembered from the day she left, and this reassured her.

Hameeda grabbed her in a hug and said she looked just the same, only taller. Nadira laughed and told her she also looked just the same, only taller, and in that moment, it was true. After Hameeda greeted her parents and spoke to them for a short while, they escaped to her room. Nadira pulled out the presents she'd brought for her, a box of Ghirardelli chocolates, and a bracelet made out of silver links and blue sea glass beads she'd gotten at the San Francisco Aquarium gift shop.

Nadira received another hug with Hameeda's thanks, and she realized just how much she'd missed her. When she asked her friend to catch her up on all the latest news, she found that Hameeda had also held back information in her letters. As Hameeda described her study group and her new friends, Nadira tried to look interested, but the subject annoyed her. She wondered if she had been displaced by these Shia girls, and if Hameeda's decision to cover her head was due to their influence. Would differences in religious practice become a barrier between them?

In the past, had she ever thought of Hameeda as a Shia? She couldn't remember ever defining her that way. If someone had asked her to describe her friend, she would have focused on her personality and physical appearance. A religious label was not part of how she'd thought of her. But now, Nadira couldn't ignore that it was an aspect of their lives that separated them. Because of their religious differences, there were some experiences they couldn't share, a gap in their understanding of each other she had never thought about before. Nadira felt sure there were things Hameeda discussed with her new friends she would never discuss with her, just as there were experiences she'd had in the States she wouldn't attempt to explain to Hameeda. Before, their shared activities, thoughts and emotions had drawn them as close as conjoined twins. But she began to doubt her assumption that they would slip back into their previous relationship without any problem. She impulsively grabbed Hameeda's hand as if the physical connection would retrieve the closeness they once had. Hameeda started with surprise, then smiled and squeezed her fingers. Her untroubled expression allowed Nadira to attribute her concerns to a lack of sleep and a feeling of dislocation.

The following week, Nadira returned to the same school she had attended before going to the States. But in only two years, a lot had changed. Although Hameeda still had her admirers, Nadira noticed many of the girls had withdrawn their friendship. This puzzled her. When she asked Hameeda what was going on, her friend explained that while she was gone, some people had turned against Shias, making life more difficult for them. A feeling of shame overcame Nadira when she recalled that, no matter how benignly, she also had considered their religious differences. Then, her sting of conscience turned into anger at the girls' narrow-minded cruelty. She wished they would whisper a negative comment about Hameeda to her so she could chastise them. But she soon found that confidences from her classmates were very unlikely.

Some of the girls acted as if they had never known Nadira, treating her like an interloper. The same girls that had clamored for her attention in the days before her departure had an air of resentment about them. Whatever they had once liked about her was forgotten in her absence. One girl came up to her before class and told Nadira she was wrong if she thought living abroad made her better than the rest of them. Nadira couldn't remember doing or saying anything to deserve such a comment, but by the time she thought of a response, the girl had walked away.

Nadira longed to lash out at someone on Hameeda's and her own behalf. But without an overt action or hurled epithet to react to, it was like fighting phantoms. Over time, defensive because of real or perceived slights, she chose to withdraw from her classmates and turned only to Hameeda for company.

It wasn't just her classmates giving her difficulties. Despite her best efforts, Nadira couldn't find her footing. She went to her father for advice, but the vocabulary to describe what she was feeling eluded her, and she stayed silent. She found the quite different social formalities and conversational requirements of Pakistani culture, once as automatic as breathing, had been subsumed by her Americanized self. The only constant was her friendship with Hameeda. In those first months they became even closer, returning to their old routines, and spending most of their free time with each other.

Despite yearning for the greater independence she'd had in the States, as the months passed, overall, life got better, and Lahore began to feel like home again, but never in the same way as before her time away.

Chapter 10

At fifteen, Nadira's life had sunk into a boring routine. It seemed like nothing interesting had happened to her since her time at Stanford. She felt hemmed in, stagnant, as if she was waiting for something. So when Hameeda mentioned the upcoming Moharram holiday, Nadira became alert. She had forgotten about the Shia observance since it didn't concern her in a direct way. She had always wanted to see the Ashura public procession which commemorated the death of Hussein bin Ali, whom the Shias had supported over a Sunni candidate for Caliph in the 7th Century. In those days, the Caliph was a leader who wielded both political and religious power over the Muslim community. Her father frequently said the quest for power was the root cause of much of the world's problems, and once acquired, often destroyed even the best of motives and the most righteous intentions.

She had heard the Ashura participants worked themselves into an emotional frenzy. It mystified her how people could still become distraught over the death of a man who had died in battle centuries ago. No matter how tragic, she thought, it was past history, something to be studied dispassionately, even if its impact was tremendously important.

But that was not the case. Each year, Shias renewed their grief, taking it out and examining it like a treasured family heirloom passed down from one generation to the next. How was this emotion sustained over the years? Was it taught like math or science, a lesson drummed into you from the time you reached the age of understanding? Or, was there something in the annual mourning ritual that recreated this emotion? Nadira wanted to see for herself.

Afterward, Nadira would regret asking Hameeda to take her to the procession. It was an event that would forever divide her life into a before and after. Whether it was true or not, she came to believe if she hadn't been present, she wouldn't have been associated with the day's tragedy and would have avoided the personal repercussions which followed. But she couldn't go back and change the fact that once she'd latched on to the idea of going, she refused to let go of it, insistent in the face of Hameeda's reluctance. Maybe it was curiosity or a longing for the held breath of anticipation and the rush of excitement that had made her so adamant. Her arguments were bolstered when she found out Hameeda's father and grandfather were marching in the procession, and her uncle, aunt and a female cousin were going as spectators. She cajoled and pressured Hameeda until she relented. Nadira's father gave his permission without hesitation, telling her it would be good for her to learn about Hameeda's Shia traditions first hand.

The morning of the procession was a typical October day, sunny with pleasant morning temperatures, which

Nadira took as a good omen. Her mother had advised her to wear a simple dark grey outfit to match the somberness of the occasion. When Hameeda and her relatives picked her up, they were dressed in black, making Nadira grateful for her mother's good sense.

Hameeda's Uncle was hoping to be at the site of the procession early enough to get a place near the middle of the route with a good view of the proceedings. The procession was to be held on streets just outside the old city. Despite the hour, many people were there ahead of them, and they had to park the car a short walk away. Four policemen with holstered pistols, holding wooden lathis, lounged at the end of the street where the crowd was gathering. The policemen were busy talking and didn't even glance at them when they walked past. As they made their way down the street, Hameeda and her relatives stopped again and again to greet family friends. Although, she was introduced as Hameeda's friend and an effort was made to include her in their talk, Nadira felt awkward, unused to being the only stranger in an unfamiliar situation. Just as she was tiring of introductions and polite conversation, they found an unpopulated spot that Hameeda's uncle thought would be a good vantage point.

They had just settled in when the street was flooded by a tide of men streaming out of the mosque where they had gone for special prayers. Pressed into a compact mass by the gathered crowd of watchers, the men jostled each other as they danced with upraised arms, chanting "Allahu Akbar," and "Ya Hussain." On either side of the street, women and girls hung over balcony railings, or leaned against the buildings, draping the red bricks in a black curtain while men, three or four deep, filled the road. Nadira and Hameeda stood on their tiptoes, trying to see above the people in front of them. Hameeda's uncle commandeered some empty wooden crates for them to stand on. The extra height allowed Nadira a clear view of the street. She saw a group of bare chested, silent men wearing white shalwars lined up, waiting for an imam to place a handful of ash on the top of their heads. The sun glinted off the thin lengths of chain some of the men held in their hands. At least one of the men had attached razor blades to the end of his chains, and looking at them made Nadira shudder. She wondered if she would be able to watch the whipping without getting sick.

She recalled her first experience with bloodletting at the age of six, observing the Eid al-Adha sacrifice of a goat she and her brothers had made a pet of the previous day. Her father and the butcher had dragged their bleating goat to a bare expanse of ground behind the house. Even knowing what would happen next, she had remained where she was. She remembered the butcher trapping the goat between his knees as if he were riding it, grabbing it by its chin, and pulling its head back. Unable to turn away, she watched as he severed the goat's jugular with one sweep of his long, razor-sharp knife, so quick it seemed as if nothing had happened. It wasn't until she saw a necklace of blood decorate the goat's white coat and widen into a stream that pooled beneath its limp body, that she knew their goat was dead. She didn't remember being disturbed. Maybe she'd been inoculated against sentimentality by watching the cook cut the necks of chickens and pluck them naked. Or maybe she'd been too focused on the delicious holiday delicacies that would be made from the goat meat. But, these were men not goats, and the flaying would be painful, the blood, human blood.

"Look, there's my abu and dada," Hameeda said, pointing down toward the end of the line of marchers.

As Hameeda pointed out her father and grandfather, the sound of beating drums came toward them and two men led a riderless, white horse with a much decorated bridle and saddle to the head of the procession. The men clung to the reins hanging from the bridle's bit as the horse pranced and half reared up, throwing its head from side to side, trying to shake itself loose from its handlers and the noisy crowd.

Once the procession got under way, the drumming and chanting of the men and women grew louder and louder and drowned out every other sound and all thought. It enveloped Nadira until her body seemed to vibrate in time with the shouted words. "Ya, Hussain, Ya Hussain, Ya Hussain." She was infected by the fevered chanting, and she too took up the repetitive recitation. She watched as the marchers beat their chests with their fists. The men carrying chains flayed the bare skin on their backs until it tore apart. Blood bubbled to the surface like water from an underground spring, thin rivulets running down until it pooled in the waist bands of their shalwars, dyeing the white material scarlet. Every time a man raised a chain, Nadira's shoulders hunched and her muscles tensed as if the blow was about to land on her back. As she turned her head away from the sight, she glanced over at Hameeda. She was also chanting but had climbed off her box. Nadira got down and asked her if she was all right. Hameeda nodded but her face had paled, and her forehead was beaded with perspiration.

The marchers passed by and were a few feet ahead of them when another sound interrupted the cadence of the chanting. Nadira got back on her box to see what was happening. Knots of men had appeared on either side of the marchers, their faces twisted into ugly expressions, mouths open, shouting language as foul as sewage at the mourners. Nadira noticed policemen scattered along the street and waited for them to move the intruders away from the procession. But they didn't interfere, looking on as if it had nothing to do with them. She saw a pebble fly through the air and bounce off the bare arm of a man already bloody from self-mutilation. She looked again at the policemen. Still they did nothing. More pebbles were thrown, then a rock. The Shia men went after the assailants only to have other attackers materialize out of the crowd. Women started to scream. The street roiled with fighting. Nadira was pressed between the crowd and the wall, trapped and panicky. A hand grabbed her arm and she pulled back in alarm. It was Hameeda's uncle.

"Come, we must get out of here," he said.

"What about Abu and Dada?" Hameeda asked him.

"Once I get you to safety, I'll come back and look for them."

He told them to hold each other's hands and not to let go no matter what. Taking his wife's hand, he pushed and shoved his way through, the surging, heaving crowd while the rest of them were quick to slip through the holes he'd punched out, trailing behind him like a tail on a kite. Finally, he turned into a narrow, still unpopulated side street. People called down from windows asking what was happening, but he continued on without answering. Taking a circuitous route, they worked their way back to the car. Her uncle made sure they locked themselves inside the vehicle before he started back. By this time others had joined their flight. A steady flow of people passed by their windows, escaping the chaos behind them. Hameeda's Aunt studied each face, looking for her husband while dabbing her eyes with a corner of her dupatta. Next to her, Hameeda's cousin shivered despite the heat, while Nadira held Hameeda's hand, mute with shock. The stream of people became a trickle and still Hameeda's uncle did not appear. An ambulance went by, its siren blaring.

"I shouldn't have let him go back," Hameeda's aunt said, her hands wringing the tail end of her dupatta.

Every time Nadira looked at her friend's face, her fearful expression accentuated her own worries and brought to the surface an uneasiness she would have preferred to leave undisturbed. She had the same shaky feeling she got at the end of a day of fasting, and it made her incapable of offering Hameeda more than the hand she still clutched.

She tried to distract herself by turning her attention to the scene outside the car window. At first she saw only the fronts of unfamiliar buildings in a neighborhood that felt hundreds of miles away from home. Then as time went on, she began to focus on familiar objects within her view and catalogue them as if they were pieces in a museum collection; a bit of white string snagged on the rough corner of a protruding brick, the water stained window casing below a broken gutter, curtains with a sun faded pattern of leaves and vines, a clay pot filled with yellow flowers, towels hung to dry on a balcony railing, a young child's pull toy, a dirty rag flung over the rim of a green plastic bucket and a bike with taped handle bars and a dented rear fender. She found studying these ordinary things made her hopeful in a strange way and wished she had the words to transfer this comfort to her friend.

She didn't know how long they sat there before Hameeda's uncle reappeared. Trickles of sweat ran down his face into his beard and soaked the fabric of his collar and the area under his arms. As soon as he opened the car door, Hameeda's aunt asked him what had happened and leaned over the seat, looking him up and down as if to make sure he was undamaged.

He told them the attackers had been driven away but a number of the marchers had been hurt, Hameeda's dada among them. The injured had been transported to the hospital. He would take them home and then join Hameeda's father there. Hameeda, her aunt and cousin began to cry. Horrified, Nadira put her arm around Hameeda in an effort to console her friend. Dry eyed, she felt conspicuous and uncomfortable amidst the sobbing women, an outsider without any claim to emotion. She reasoned the attackers were Sunni extremists, and despite the fact they in no way represented her or the majority of Sunnis, she was ashamed.

They dropped off Nadira first. As she got out of the car, she told Hameeda to let her know as soon as she heard anything about her dada. Walking into her house, she felt the release of an internal tension she hadn't realized was there, and she began to tremble.

"Nadira what's wrong? You look ill," her mother said, walking over to her and placing a hand on her forehead.

"Something terrible has happened," she said, and choked out a brief description of the riot.

Her mother pulled Nadira to her chest, holding her close. And in the warmth and safety of her mother's embrace, she finally cried.

Chapter 11

After the riot, Hameeda wanted to submerge herself in the solace of a normal routine, something that would help her push aside the fear that still clung to her. But her dada's hospitalization disrupted the household and forced her to endure the unfamiliar. She dreaded the daily trips to the hospital when even the walk from the car park to the building had her jumping at the slightest noise, and every shadowy corner held the possibility of men lying in wait to attack them. She found herself returning to the childhood habit of catching hold of her mother's hand as they walked along.

Even in the safety of her home, she couldn't evade the sense of foreboding let loose by her experience. Every evening a nightmare lay in wait, emerging once sleep disarmed her attempts to turn her thoughts to some safe subject. Her dream was always the same; she was in a crowd of people, their bodies pressing against her from all sides, squeezing her tighter, and tighter, until it seemed as if the last bit of air would be expelled from her lungs. Then she would wake up, gasping for breath, her heart thumping with an uneven beat.

Daylight just substituted one nightmare for another.

Long hours were spent at the hospital with her mother, brothers, aunts, uncles, and cousins. They took turns sitting by her dada's bed, spelling her father who spent the nights there so her dada would never be left alone or without a family member at his side.

The rock had struck her dada on the side of his head just above the temple. The doctor said a little further down and he wouldn't have survived. She thought she would feel better once she saw him, but his appearance only made her more worried. His shaved head was encased in layers of white gauze and tubes sprouted from his motionless body. The only indication he was alive was the intermittent cloud of an exhalation inside his oxygen mask. The family huddled around him, speaking to him as if any moment he would enter the conversation. They prayed without ceasing; when one person tired, another took over, the murmur of their voices interrupted only by the beeping of a monitor. For five days they talked and prayed beside his unresponsive form. On the sixth day he died.

The night of her dada's death, Hameeda found it difficult to believe he was gone. She and her mother went downstairs to sit with her dadi, while her father and his brother washed her dada's body in preparation for burial. As she entered the lounge, her eyes went to his favorite chair, half expecting him to be sitting there, gesturing to her to sit by him. But his chair was empty. Her dadi was giving her mother instructions on what needed to be done the next day when all at once she was overcome by a fit of weeping. After a while she stopped and wiped her eyes with a handkerchief. She told them if her dada was there, he would say they shouldn't weep over Allah's will. Recalling his survival of the journey from India during Partition, she said her dada had considered it a miracle, and often said Allah had taken pity on him, granting him another chance to make a better life, all the years since a special gift.

From the time she was a young child, her dada had instructed Hameeda the will of Allah ruled them all. Even now, when he was no longer with her, his words reminded her to acquiesce to what Allah had ordained. A feeling of acceptance settled inside her, bandaging the raw wound of her grief.

The day of the funeral as she recited the prayers, tears filmed her eyes and clung to her lashes like dew on a spider's web. She had to keep blinking them away so she could see the words on the pages of her Qur'an. In the midst of her own sorrow, Hameeda observed how differently family members reacted to her dada's death. The women of the family were subdued and quiet, putting aside any differences to comfort each other, grief softening them. But the men's grief appeared to have a hard core of bitterness and anger. There was much talk of how her dada would still be alive if it weren't for the Sunnis and the lack of action by the police.

Their friends from the Shia community made the three day mourning period as easy as possible for them. Meals were brought in to feed both the family and the visitors who arrived daily for condolence calls. All of Hameeda's friends from her study group came to sit with them. She had only spoken to Nadira once since the Ashura procession, her days at the hospital preventing them from talking again. But even the one conversation had helped Hameeda feel better. The constraint she felt with everyone else did not extend to Nadira who had experienced that horrible day with her. She was able to open up with her friend who also expressed a need to talk about what had happened. She knew Nadira truly understood what she was feeling, and she had never felt closer to her, or valued their friendship more.

The second day after the funeral Nadira called and let her know she and her family were coming over in the afternoon to offer their condolences. Hameeda was grateful for their support and sure her parents would appreciate their thoughtfulness. She was talking to a neighbor when she heard the gate buzzer. Her father went to answer it. She heard Nadira's father's voice and then was dismayed when her father told him they were not receiving visitors. She pictured the line of cars on the road outside their house, an obvious sign her father was lying. Why was he refusing to see them? What would Nadira and her family think? Hameeda started to get up, but her mother shook her head. The rest of the afternoon she couldn't keep her mind off what her father had done and often lost the thread of the conversation and had to have a question repeated.

After everyone had left, Hameeda went over to her father. It was the worst possible time to question him, but she had to know why he had turned Nadira and her family away.

"Abu, why did you tell Nadira's father we weren't

receiving visitors when they came to call today?" Hameeda looked up into his face, strained with grief.

"Sunnis are not welcome in our home, and you're not to associate with Nadira or her family any longer."

"But why?" In her need to resolve her confusion, she ignored the visible stiffening of her father's body.

"Your dada is dead at the hands of Sunnis, and you ask me why?"

Hameeda could see the anger in her father's face, and hear it in his voice, and knew any further resistance on her part would only exacerbate his fury. But, she needed to make him see that Nadira and her family were different from the people who had attacked the procession and pressed on.

"They are not like the others. Nadira's my closest friend and her family has always treated me well."

"Your friend only went to the Ashura procession to gawk at it like a circus spectacle. Why do you trouble yourself over this Sunni girl who can never be a true friend to you? You must learn not to trust anyone outside the Shia community. If it comes to a conflict between Shia and Sunni, they will side with their own people just as we will side with ours."

His words hit her like stones. "No Abu, please…"

"What has happened to my obedient daughter? I can see this Sunni girl has been a bad influence on you. You will not question my decision and will show proper respect to me. Now go to your room." His outstretched arm pointed the way.

Used to being favored by her father, Hameeda felt his displeasure like a slap in the face. As she lay crying in her room, her mother came to her. Hameeda told her she didn't know how she would face Nadira at school or explain the reason she could no longer spend time with her. Her mother wiped away her tears with a gentle touch before delivering the final blow. She told Hameeda they had already made arrangements for her to transfer to another school which had a higher percentage of Shia students. A couple of the girls from her study group went to the school so she would already have some friends there.

It was obvious her parents had made their decision even before her dada's death, and their deception wounded Hameeda and robbed her of speech for a moment.

"Can I call Nadira to say goodbye?" she said, searching her mother's face for a sign she would relent.

"Your father has already said you can't contact her again."

Her mother reached out and drew Hameeda to her side, and hoping it was a sign her mother was softening, she pleaded with her.

"Can't you ask him to let me talk to her just one more time?"

"I know you think your father is being very hard on you and your friend, but your dada's killing has brought up many bad memories. When he was growing up in Karachi, there was a lot of dissention between Shias and Sunnis. Now this sectarianism is spreading to Lahore. He's only trying to protect us. Most important, your father is head of this family, and we must abide by his decisions. Speaking to Nadira is an act of disloyalty."

How could her father be so cruel? Anger, alarming her with its vehemence, flooded her body and swept away her tender feelings for her father, leaving behind something cold and unyielding. Hameeda began to cry again, this new loss more than she thought she could bear.

Her mother stroked her hair and said in a soft voice, "I'm sorry Hameeda, but try and understand. I can't oppose your father in this matter."

Hameeda knew it was as close as her mother would ever come to telling her she disagreed with her father's mandate.

For days afterward, Hameeda was not allowed near the phone. It seemed to her, it rang more often. Once she heard her father say she didn't want to talk to the caller. She imagined Nadira on the other end of the line hearing those words, and worse still, believing them. She thought about sneaking away and calling her, or writing her a letter, but the ingrained habit of obedience and her mother's words about family loyalty stopped her. For the first time in her life, she disagreed with her parents, but challenging her father had taken all her courage and left her feeling power-less. In addition, the once friendly outside world now filled her with trepidation, making her family even more important. Defying her parents would take away whatever safety remained and separate her from all she held most dear. No, she couldn't go against them, and would have to forget about Nadira.

Unfortunately, her compliance didn't end her anger, which grew inside her like a malignant tumor, making her silent in her father's presence and hampering her ability to eat and sleep. A few days later, her mother sat down with her, and said she had to find a way to forgive him. She reminded her that no one is without fault, and quoted the portion of the Qur'an which instructed them that Allah forgives those who forgive others for their shortcomings. Her father also attempted to draw her close again, making an effort to talk to her, and once bringing her a box of her favorite sweets. Gradually, her anger dissipated until, with relief, she let it go, resigning herself to her change in circumstances.

Two weeks after her dada's death, she started at her new school. The two girls she knew watched over her and included her, and she was grateful, but she had no desire to make new friends. Nadira was a ghostly companion keeping her company. She couldn't stop thinking about the hurt and anger her friend must feel. An aching sadness engulfed her, and she observed her surroundings and the daily goings on, as if from a great distance, navigating the hours of her days with all the effort of slogging through heavy mud. She forgot how to smile and open her heart to others, and knew she was a quiet, almost unnoticed presence in the classroom. It was only when she was lost in prayer that she could escape the misery of her separation from her friend. Nadira's disappearance from her life was so sudden and complete, it was as if she had died along with her dada. The pain caused by the absence of these two important people would dull over time but never entirely go away.

*　　*　　*

Nadira couldn't believe they had been turned away when they went to Hameeda's house. She'd heard Hameeda's father's voice over the intercom and believed he alone didn't want them there. Thinking she might hear from Hameeda later that day, she stayed near the phone, but her friend didn't call.

She went to her father with her anger, and he rejected it like an unwanted gift.

"You must learn to use your head before diving into your emotions," he said, putting the book he'd been reading aside.

"How can you be so calm in the face of such an insult?" Nadira asked, pacing the floor in front of him.

"Look at me."

Nadira stopped and turned to face him.

Her father shook his head. "You disappoint me, beti. Hameeda's grandfather has just been killed by a Sunni mob. Now, when their sorrow is so fresh, is not when you should judge them. You have to give them time to think more clearly. I'm sure once their emotions cool, their attitude will change."

Nadira crossed her arms over her chest, annoyed and frustrated by his response.

"You're assuming they'll react like you would," she said. "Her family isn't like ours."

Her father raised his eyebrows. "What? They're not thinking, feeling human beings? This riot happened because people focused on what separates us instead of what unites us. Besides, only good, kind people could raise a daughter like Hameeda."

Sometimes her father was so naïve. Nadira was sure Hameeda's father had already made up his mind, and if he only listened to like-minded people, how would he reconsider his position? She hoped her father was right, but thought she was better off trying to somehow get around Hameeda's father and talk to her friend. The next day she tried calling and was told Hameeda didn't want to speak to her. She didn't believe it.

The first thing she did when she entered the classroom the following day was to look for her friend, but her seat remained empty for that day and the rest of the week. When she asked the teacher when Hameeda would be coming back, she was stunned to find out she had transferred to another school. What would she do now?

Over the next few days, she called Hameeda three more times, varying the hour of the day, hoping she would pick up the phone. But everyone who answered told her Hameeda didn't want to talk to her. The last time she called, Hameeda's mother answered the phone and said it would be better for both of them if she stopped trying to reach Hameeda. Nadira began to have doubts, and wonder if it was Hameeda's decision not to talk to her. If their places had been reversed, she would have found a way to get in touch. After all the years of their friendship, didn't she deserve some sort of explanation?

At school, her classmates didn't comment on Hameeda's absence. For nine years she had been a constant, solid presence among them and then poof; she disappeared with the suddenness of an audience volunteer in a magician's trick. Every time Nadira entered the classroom her eyes went to the empty desk, expecting to see her friend despite what she'd been told - this possibility seemed no crazier to her than the events of the last few weeks. But the only place Hameeda appeared was in her mind's imaginings. There, Hameeda was a silent onlooker to Nadira's debate over her friend's role in the decision to dissolve the bond that had held them together. Was it solely her father's doing or had she played a part in her banishment? In trying to figure out the situation, what she'd known of Hameeda pulled her one way and Hameeda's silence pulled her the other.

As the months and years passed, Nadira's memories faded or were reshaped and colored by current emotions. She forgot as they escaped the riot; Hameeda, in front of her, had held onto her so tightly there were finger bruises on the back of her hand for days afterward. She forgot the sound of her friend's voice, her quiet laugh, her wide smile, and how she had always put Nadira's wishes before her own. The time they had spent together was changed, distorted, and recapturing a picture of the friendship they'd had was as difficult as trying to grab a minnow at the bottom of a pool of water. She was left with a scabbed over wound which never fully healed, and an emptiness that new friendships never filled.

Chapter 12

Nadira spent the beginning of her sixteenth year in opposition to everything and everyone around her. She refused well-meant attempts by her family and classmates to compensate for the loss of her friend, pushing people away, both needing and regretting her isolation. There were arguments with her parents and brothers during long periods of irritability, and hours behind the closed door of her room, her well of tears stoppered by a tightening in her throat. Some nights, unable to sleep, she sat in the yellow circle of her desk lamp, penciling math problems, trying to solve her way out of insomnia. Every morning Nadira resolved to retrace her steps back to her old self, but some inconsequential word or action would throw her back into her self-destructive pattern. Then her nana became seriously ill, and his rapid decline tore away the carapace of her self-involvement. The once unfamiliar specter of death seemed to hang over everything, inserting itself into her daily thoughts and darkening even the sunniest days.

Her visits with her grandparents became a trial, a test of her ability to do what she least wanted to do. After being sick for a few months, her nana resembled someone who required an introduction. Once endowed with the upright posture of a man proud of his height, a stocky build, and meticulous about his appearance, now he was bent and bony, his clothes wrinkled and his hair uncombed. When she was with him, their once easy conversations were stiff and uncomfortable. Her nani also changed as her husband shrank; her bulk increased, opening up tears in the seams of her kameez that matched her torn composure. The cheerful energy that had characterized her nani's personality was depleted until only the occasional pallid smile remained. Unexpressed feelings and concerns filled the rooms of her grandparents' home with disquiet. It often seemed as if the house itself was holding its breath, waiting. These abrupt changes left Nadira feeling unsettled and suffering from a host of mysterious aches and pains. It was as if her body, rather than her emotions, was under attack. So, when her father entered her room one afternoon, his shoulders bent under the weight of the news of her nana's death, Nadira felt a guilty relief.

In the following weeks, her nana was never far from her thoughts. Something would come up she wanted to tell him, or a sight or sound would trigger a memory of him, and she would find herself in tears. His death also brought Hameeda to mind. Now, she could truly relate to her sorrow over her dada's death and commiserate with her. But, her knowledge came too late.

After the funeral, her parents asked her nani to move in with them. But her nani chose to remain where she was, sharing her large home with two old servants and her memories. It was her nani's solitary existence that finally released Nadira from her self-imposed isolation. At her nani's request, she went to her house after school on Tuesdays and Thursdays to keep her company as she took care of her errands for the week.

"When I undertake a task, my mind is always too optimistic, forgetful of the much older body that must do its bidding," her nani said with a shake of her head. "And that often gets me into trouble. But, you must promise never to reveal how much you assist me. Otherwise, the family will keep after me until I move out, and I'll spend the rest of my life as an ornament in someone else's home."

For Nadira, these afternoon visits lessened the ache of loneliness, and no longer taking her nani's continued presence for granted, she wanted to spend as much time as possible with her. As always, their time together was memorable and never boring.

While helping her, Nadira went to neighborhoods of Lahore she had never had the chance to explore, neighborhoods that revealed Pakistan's historic past and provided a physical record of its slow disintegration. Instead of shopping in the convenient stores of Gulberg's neighborhood marketplace, her nani preferred the shops in the convoluted streets of Lahore's old city. Here, she frequented family establishments she had been going to since the early days of her marriage.

The protective walls that once surrounded this part of the city had been destroyed by the British, and only five of the original thirteen massive stone gates remained. Nadira and her nani always entered through one of two gates. Sometimes they passed through the Kashmiri Gate, and just beyond its threshold, were welcomed by a bazaar of the same name. Other times they went through the Roshnai Gate which was located between two architectural marvels. On one side was the Alamgiri Gate, its massive arched opening flanked by fluted bastions, giving access to the trapezoidal citadel of the Lahore Fort. Within the Fort's walled enclosure, ancient mansions, pavilions, towers and open fields were spread out over fifty acres. On the other side of the gate was the Badshahi Mosque with its red sandstone walls, four soaring minarets and three white marble domes inlaid with arabesque floral patterns. The Roshnai Gate's proximity to these important sites may have been why it was in close to original condition, its stone walls gleaming as white as bleached bone in the sunshine.

Nadira often imagined ancient, elephant caravans passing through the Gate's arched opening, the tasseled howdahs straddling the animals' massive backs, swaying with their heavy footed gait. It was a pretty picture compared to the reality inside the old city. The once grand havelis had been divided up into small apartments for its poor residents. Once beautiful carved and decorated Mughal facades with cantilevered, ornate wooden balconies had been ravaged by time and lack of attention, and only sporadic, surviving surfaces provided a tiny glimpse of their past magnificence.

Trips to the old city were like passing over an invisible border and entering another country where Nadira often felt as awkward as a foreigner. A very different kind of existence from the one she inhabited confronted her as they navigated around the broken pavement of the narrow streets. Large bouquets of refuse were strewn by the roadside and their malodorous perfume permeated even the closed windows of the car. Men and women with the lethargic gait of the undernourished, wearing the dirty, old clothes of the underpaid, crowded the shoulder of the road. Girls, some no more than seven or eight, hefted babies or pulled younger siblings along by their hands, the harried look of an adult already imprinted on their faces. Young boys, their backs bent under heavy loads, moved in and out of the small shops and beggars propped themselves up against the walls of sagging brick buildings. Nadira had seen poverty before, but it had always been at a distance, surrounded by all the familiar places and people of her class, easily dismissed with a turn of her head. Everywhere she looked in the narrow streets, she saw deterioration and the faces of people who spent their days just managing to put one foot in front of the other, and she longed for her old self-absorbed ignorance. Her image of Lahore was tarnished; it was no longer the entertaining, perfect city she'd thought it was.

When the car stopped to allow a man with his goats to cross the road, a beggar woman came up, tapped on the glass with the boney fingers of an outstretched hand and beseeched them for a few rupees. Her nani rolled down the window and handed the woman some coins. The woman bowed and smiled revealing a mouth with only two, discolored teeth. Nadira turned her head away and slid down in the seat, the woman forcing her to confront everything she took for granted without a second thought: the new clothes each season, the abundant meals, and the summer vacations in the mountains. She cringed remembering her petty complaints to her parents.

Her nani patted her hand. "There's nothing wrong with being well off, for whatever wealth we have is due to the blessings of Allah. But we are obligated to help those less fortunate through fulfilling the duty of zakat. And we should not only give this proscribed percentage of our assets to those who are in need, but also give of ourselves in other ways. It's only if we don't do these things, we should feel ashamed," her nani said as if picking up a thread in the fabric of Nadira's thoughts.

Nadira slipped her fingers over the soft, wrinkled skin of her nani's hand, enfolded it and gathered its warmth into the cup of her palm, as she imagined a day when her nani wouldn't be there to provide her with the answers to unasked questions. Her nana's death had changed Nadira's view of the future. Life had once seemed like it would go on in the same way forever. Now she felt uncertain, as if she was traveling on a twisting mountain road, never knowing what was around the next curve.

Though mundane, it was food shopping with her nani Nadira enjoyed the most. Whereas her mother delegated such shopping to their cook, her nani preferred doing it herself. In this way, Nadira was introduced to the sprawling produce market, a maze of small stalls set up on beaten earth. Some stalls were under a canvas cover, while other sellers sat on the ground, unprotected from the sun, with their wares in front of them. As soon as they entered the market, the dusty air was filled with the scent of spices piled in shallow woven baskets or round tin trays. Mounds of yellow turmeric, red chilies, green cardamom pods, gnarled roots of ginger, papery skinned bulbs of garlic, and bunches of freshly picked cilantro nestled next to each other like the colors on an artist's palette. Pyramids of fruits and vegetables, the riches of the Punjab's valleys, filled several long rows. Sides of beef and lamb, speckled with black flies, hung from hooks, while cages of squawking chickens and pens of bleating goats competed with the yells of venders hawking their wares. Tables held bolts of patterned, cotton fabric and piles of cheap, aluminum pots and pans, while multi-colored budgies and bright yellow canaries chirped in bamboo cages. Leaning on Nadira's arm, her nani bargained with the vendors, handing her granddaughter the plastic bag containing each purchase until Nadira's hands were full and her shoulders ached. Her reward came when they finished their shopping. She and her nani always made their way to one corner of the market where a man made fresh jelebis. Her mouth watered in anticipation as she watched the jelebi wallah drizzle the saffron flavored batter in concentric circles into a vat of boiling oil until, fried to a crisp, the sweet treat was dipped into orange colored sugar syrup. Her nani would purchase two jelebis for each of them, and they would sit in the shade to eat them while they were still warm, licking the last sugary taste from their fingers before leaving for home. Years later when sterile,

Western style grocery stores had taken over for most of Lahore's old food markets, Nadira would remember with fondness her shopping trips with her nani. These companionable afternoons never seemed long enough, the hours disappearing as quickly as a box of chocolates in the hands of an unsupervised child.

One afternoon, while her nani was napping, Nadira decided to finish cleaning out her nana's desk. Her mother had already started the project, and the desk top was covered with neat piles of household account ledgers organized by year, check book stubs, blank pads of paper, balled elastic bands, rolls of adding machine tape, assorted pens and pencils, envelopes of various sizes, an address book, a half full bottle of rubber cement and a stack of old black and white photos. The drawers on the right hand side of the knee hole were already empty. She removed the remaining contents from the top two drawers on the left side, placing them in the appropriate stacks. When she tried to open the bottom drawer, it was stuck. She wiggled and pulled on it, but it resisted her efforts. Giving one final, hard yank, something seemed to shift and the drawer popped open. At first she thought it was empty, but looking closer, she saw an envelope addressed to her nana curled up against the back. Both the envelope and the pages she removed had brownish stains on them that looked like dried blood. The top of the first page showed a date of March 27, 1971 - the second day of the war between East and West Pakistan, and most important, the first full day of her life. She thought the coincidence was an invitation to read it. The three sheets of paper were filled with small, crabbed hand-writing in faded ink that took quite a while to decipher.

Uncle, you have always been more than my father's closest friend. For as long as I can remember you have been like a second father to me. With my father gone, you are the only one I can trust with my disclosures. I apologize for placing this heavy burden on you, but I need someone to know what I witnessed in case anything happens to me. I have always admired your strength and wisdom, and I know you will see this information is communicated to the right people.

I'm writing this letter in an empty house in Dhaka where I have taken temporary shelter with a young servant boy. I've given him a few rupees, and he has promised to mail it for me. I will wait for him to leave before I try and find someone to help me, although who that would be, I can't imagine. The local Bengalis have, understand-ably, taken against us, and if my affiliation is recognized, I will receive no mercy. I shall have to put myself in Allah's hands and hope for the best.

The story I will relate is a true account of what I observed from my post at Dhaka University. The facts are so horrific, I hesitate to tell you, concerned they will be permanently seared into your memory as they are in mine. If I survive, I'm afraid they will inhabit my nightmares for the rest of my life.

Last night, when we entered the University campus, I was one of two soldiers stationed on the roof of build-

ings on either side of the quadrangle, assigned to keep a look-out for rebels approaching from outside the walls, or anyone slipping through the net of soldiers on the ground. From my perch, I had a clear view of everything happening down below.

I tried to focus on my job but couldn't keep my eyes off the unfolding calamity. Pleading voices winged upward, and filled the air around me like a flock of frightened birds. I couldn't tell whether the entreaties of the captured men were directed to my fellow Pakistani soldiers or to Allah. In either case they had no effect. There were bursts of noise as bullets exploded from muzzles, followed by screams as they tore into tender flesh. Soldiers strode over to the sprawled men, and it is my belief, they got close enough to see the individual characteristics of their victims, the greying hair and lined faces of the older men, the bearded faces of the religious, and the smooth faces of boys whose time on earth had been too short.

One of the soldiers came forward with a pistol in his hand and methodically shot each person in the head, ensuring there were no survivors. Another contingent of armed men went into the student hostel across the yard from my vantage point. Through the open windows, I heard their boots echoing in the hallway, the crashing of rifle butts against wooden doors, and the screams of the students as they were pulled from their rooms and hauled outside where the executions continued. The air was thick with the smell of gunpowder and blood, and the fallen bodies took on the appearance of piles of dirty clothes *waiting to be laundered. I could sense the presence of the angel of death, doing Allah's bidding, collecting the souls of the murdered men.*

Then as quickly as it started, the killing stopped. My fellow soldiers huddled together just beyond the reach of the buildings' lights, well away from the heaps of tangled corpses. Army vehicles approached, the sound faint at first, then louder and louder. Soon truck after truck rolled up and parked with engines idling, their headlights illu-minating the staging area. A soldier waved his arms, pantomiming instructions over the mechanical din. At his direction, bodies were carried over to the trucks and stacked inside. Once the grisly cargo was hidden behind closed tailgates under strapped down canvas; the caravan left.

As the whine of engines and the rumble of wheels faded away, an unnatural quiet descended on the campus, only broken by a muffled voice, or the clinking of metal against metal when the buckle of a rifle sling hit against a gun barrel. A few minutes later, I heard someone climbing the steps to the roof. With one swift motion, I picked up my rifle, raised it into firing position and stared at the doorway. A soldier from my regiment appeared in the opening, halting, wide-eyed when he saw the rifle trained on him. I lowered my gun. The soldier relayed orders from the Company Commander to report to the front gate at 0100 hours.

I told him to proceed to the gate, and I'd be there directly. After he left, I stared at the rifle in my hand, once

*a mere tool of my trade, like a tailor's needle or a garden-
er's spade; now it was a symbol of senseless death and
destruction, and abhorrent to me. I placed it against the
parapet and consulted my watch; I had forty-five minutes
to make a decision.*

*The night's events pressed down on me, and I looked
back to see how I had arrived at this point. Before dawn,
I had been pulled from my bed by a Captain from West
Pakistan. I was shown a document stating that East Pakistani rebels were attempting to secede from Pakistan and
set up an independent country. Intelligence information
indicated there were traitors within the military ranks.
Orders were given to disarm all East Pakistani officers and
soldiers residing in the Dhaka barracks. I had complied
without question. It hadn't been easy. These were men who
had trained with me, fought next to me, played cards with
me, and entertained me in their homes. But at least it
had made tactical sense. The slaughter of professors and
students at the University was incomprehensible insanity.
If they could kill hundreds of innocent people at the
University, what would they do to the soldiers imprisoned
in the barracks? Despite the fact I hadn't yet fired a shot,
I considered myself a participant in what had happened,
as culpable as if my own hands were stained with blood.
I thought about mother and my wife. Giti and I grew
up next door to each other and have been very close since
childhood. Since before we were married, we shared everything – our possessions, our experiences, our laughter, our
tears, even our inner most thoughts and feelings. What*

could I tell her about today? For the first time, I have nothing to share with her, only secrets to keep.

Taking nothing with me, I crept down the stairs, taking care to skirt any soldiers heading toward the front gate. I made my way to a back corner of the boundary wall, deep in the shadows and laced with well-established, thick bougainvillea vines. I hesitated for a second, and took a quick look around before testing the strength of a toe hold and reaching up for a branch above my head. I wondered if I would ever see my family again. I had almost reached the top of the wall and made my escape, when a bullet stabbed me in the shoulder. Somehow, I made it over the wall and found shelter in this house whose inhabitants had fled the fighting spreading throughout the city, leaving the boy behind to guard their possessions.

I exchanged my bloody uniform for a shalwar kurta the boy got me from the servants' quarters, hoping to pass as a civilian. If I see you again, I will reclaim this letter and relieve you of this burden. If I don't return home please...

Here the words reached the end of the page. The letter must have continued on a fourth page that had somehow gone missing.

By the time she finished reading, Nadira's cheeks were wet with tears. She knew the military would have considered this soldier a deserter, and if he'd been caught he would have been executed. But there was no doubt in her mind he had followed the right course of action and instead should have been rewarded for his bravery. While she was thinking how unfair life could be, she remembered something Hameeda often said when, despite Nadira's good intentions, she had gotten into trouble. It was not humans but Allah who was the ultimate judge. This thought eased the pain she felt on behalf of the writer of the letter, but she was still sorry her curiosity had gotten the better of her. Now she was privy to another of her country's self-inflicted wounds, and this unknown man's nightmare would be added to her own disturbing night visions. She shivered as she realized during her birth, young people at the University had been dying The darkness of the event eclipsed the shooting star that had appeared in Lahore's night sky and stripped away her last subconscious sense of protection from the world's evils.

It was clear the letter was meant to be read only by her nana. She considered putting a match to it but couldn't bring herself to do it. Instead, she placed the letter back in the envelope and tucked it into the waistband of her shalwar. Knowing what it felt like to be forgotten, she didn't want her nana's death to erase the soldier as if he'd only been a series of random marks on a piece of paper. She would take the letter home with her, safeguard the soldier's last words, and honor his memory.

*　　*　　*

Over the course of the next few years, Nadira observed her nani with a deliberateness born of wanting to learn as much as possible from her while she could. She saw how her mind was never unoccupied and her hands never still. A smile reappeared on her nani's face, and if she was sad, she kept it to herself, maintaining a cheerful demeanor when Nadira was with her. During their time together, her nani continued teaching her life lessons, some of which she would only fully understand years later. Her nani taught her what it is to be a woman alone, a woman in charge, a woman who has found her place in the world, and a woman who knows how to live with grace in the midst of grief. Thinking of her lesser sorrows, Nadira was ashamed of holding on to them, and worked on emulating her nani. As the months went by, sadness loosened its hold on her as she reacquainted herself with happiness.

Chapter 13

The summer after Hameeda's second year in college, she felt at loose ends. Her few friends were all away on vacation with their families while she was left on her own in Lahore. A year of required reading for college courses extinguished any desire to pick up a book, and the excessive heat left her no energy for any other activity and made her summer holiday stretch in front of her like a penance.

A few days later, a conversation with her mother banished her lethargy.

"Hameeda, remember when I told you we've been receiving a lot more interest in you from the parents of marriageable young men?" her mother asked.

"Yes, I remember." Hameeda looked at her mother's serious expression and could tell she was about to say something important.

"Well, one young man sounds perfect for you. His name is Zubair Khan and he's a doctor. He's just returned to Lahore after completing his medical residency in England, so providing for you and your future children will not be a problem. He comes from a good family who share our values. Amina Auntie has a friend who is acquainted with his mother, and Hamid Uncle is a close friend of his father.

They both agree that it's a good match. We've talked to the parents and have arranged a meeting of the families for tea two weeks from this Sunday.

Hameeda wasn't surprised about the proposed match. Her parents had been talking to families with marriage-able sons for the last two years, but nothing had happened. Sometimes the family was not from a similar background, their religious views were too liberal, the members of the two families were not compatible, or in her parents' judg-ment the young man's personality didn't seem like a good fit for her. She had met one young man last year whom she'd rejected after the first meeting. She'd found him arro-gant, his dress ostentatious, and his bragging about the large amount of money he made distasteful.

"I know you'll impress the Khans just by being your-self, but it won't hurt if you make something for tea which will show off your cooking skills," her mother said. "How about making sewayian for the sweet dish? You do that so well." Her mother smiled at her.

"Whatever you think is best, Amma," Hameeda said, already worried how her dessert would measure up and anxious about making a good impression on this young man whom her parents already thought was so promising.

Hameeda was happy to let her mother take charge of all the arrangements. The prospect of a potential match gave her something new to focus on. Having been fed on a steady diet of Bollywood romances since childhood, she spent the next two weeks daydreaming about a handsome doctor who would sweep her off her feet just like in the movies.

The day of the tea Hameeda was more nervous than she had ever been. Part of her was afraid Zubair wouldn't measure up to her daydreams, and the other part was afraid he would be her Prince Charming, but she wouldn't be the princess he had in mind.

Before the Khans arrived, her mother had her sit in the chair facing the door where they would enter. Hameeda knew she looked as pretty as she ever would. The pale green shalwar kameez and matching dupatta brought out the green in her hazel eyes, and heightened the paleness of her skin.

"Remember, you should be modest and keep your eyes down until I introduce our guests," she said, her hand giving Hameeda's shoulder a comforting squeeze. "Speak only when you're spoken to, and don't stare at Zubair."

With a nod of her head, Hameeda indicated she understood, and prayed she would not do anything to embarrass herself or her parents.

A few minutes later, she heard the ringing of the gate bell and then the sound of a car driving up to the front terrace. Her parents went to the door to greet their guests. Hameeda knew this would be one of only two or three opportunities for judging this potential husband before making a decision. Staring down at her hands clasped in her lap, she listened to everyone exchange greetings and make introductions. In the seconds before they arrived in the room, she pushed extraneous thoughts away and drew her mind up to attention.

Their footsteps echoed on the marble floors as they

entered the drawing room and walked toward her. When the group stopped in front of her, and her mother spoke her name, Hameeda looked up. She saw a slim older man with a bald head and eyes magnified by black framed glasses sitting askew on a nose that dipped down to a close cropped goatee. Next to him was a stocky woman wearing a shalwar kameez with a red floral pattern that would have looked better on someone younger. Her thick, black hair was pulled back in a bun away from a square face with skin the shade of wet earth. She had wide-set, narrow eyes, a broad nose and a receding chin. The bodies of the couple blocked her view of the young man behind them.

"As salaam aleikum," Hameeda said.

"Wa aleikum salaam," two quiet male voices and one loud female voice responded.

"Hameeda, this is Salima Auntie, Daud Uncle and their son Zubair."

"I'm happy to meet you," Hameeda said just as Zubair stepped out from behind his parents.

Zubair was as thin as a noodle in the dish of sewayian she'd made. He wore an immaculate, white button down shirt, dark grey pants with a sharp crease, a tie with blue and grey diagonal stripes and shoes buffed to a mirror shine. His angular face was softened by the sweep of hair that fell across a high forehead and rested just above his chocolate brown eyes. Completing the picture, a long nose descended to full lips and a narrow chin.

During the tea, he rarely spoke unless asked a question. No matter how trivial the query, he would pause half a beat, appearing to give it serious consideration before answering. His voice was soft and had a musical quality to it. Hameeda felt an immediate attraction to him and questioned herself in an effort to figure out why. Was it the meticulous way he presented himself to the world that gave her the impression he was careful with everything that concerned him? Was it the deliberateness with which he spoke, or the attentiveness with which he looked into the eyes of the person questioning him? Was it the fact that despite his obvious accomplishments, he didn't push himself forward but let others take center stage? Was it his confident posture, a hand gesture, the way his features composed themselves into a portrait of absolute calm, or the words he used that drew her to him? By the time their guests left, Zubair's seduction of her was complete, and she was certain that if he would have her, she would marry him.

Later alone in her room, Hameeda's body felt as if an electric current was passing through it, every cell hummed with energy. She paced up and down. The need to talk to someone was overwhelming, and without thinking she reached for the phone to call Nadira. Realizing her mistake, she sank down on her bed. After five long years, Nadira was still the person who came to mind during important moments. She wondered when she would finally escape the grasp of the past.

That night, Hameeda prayed to Allah for guidance and for Zubair to like her. Hameeda and Zubair's families got together two more times, and the day after the last visit, Hameeda's mother came and talked to her.

"You've made a favorable impression on Zubair and his

parents," her mother said taking both of Hameeda's hands in hers. "They've called and said they will be bringing a marriage proposal to us. Will you accept a proposal from Zubair?" Her mother's eyes never left Hameeda's face.

"Yes," she exclaimed, finding her good fortune almost unbelievable.

Her mother smiled with pleasure and embraced her.

"Then I'll tell your father he can accept on your behalf, and we'll proceed with the arrangements for the engagement. Insha Allah, Zubair will be a good husband to you and bring you much happiness," her mother said kissing her cheeks with tears in her eyes.

That night, her mind untroubled, Hameeda dreamt of a beautiful house with many doors. Behind each door was an image of her heart's desires, a wonderful husband, children, and all of Allah's blessings shared with family and friends.

After the engagement ceremony, Hameeda spoke to her mother about whether she should complete her last two years of college. Her mother said she could finish her degree requirements if she wanted, but her current situation made it unnecessary. Hameeda was relieved. With the exception of a couple of courses, she had struggled with her studies, and she had never expected to do anything other than get married once she graduated. As she looked forward to a release from school, Nadira's horrified voice echoed in her brain, telling her she was making a big mistake. With a shake of her head, Hameeda tried dismissing Nadira from her thoughts. But there was her voice again, telling her not to leave college. Hameeda pushed it away once more.

Nadira's opinion should no longer be of any consequence, so why did she feel guilty all of a sudden?

The months prior to her marriage were crowded with the tasks associated with her status as a bride-to-be; there was the exercise of going to the shops, the standing for fittings until her back ached, the list making that seemed like a school assignment, and the effort of responding to requests for instant decisions, sometimes beyond her ability. As each day slipped into the past, Hameeda found herself clinging to the familiar - the rhythm of her daily routines and the faces of family members. When people asked her if she was happy, she could answer yes with honesty's ease, but thought, her looming departure had made her fully conscious of her childhood and the happiness it had held, soon to be relinquished in favor of an unknown future.

In the week before the marriage ceremony, out-of-town relatives filled their house to overflowing, leaving Hameeda with not one second to herself. At the end of each day, she fell into her bed exhausted. But in the few minutes before sleep claimed her, an incomprehensible feeling of melancholy swept over her. It wasn't until her wedding reception she realized the origin of this feeling. Intermittently during the evening, her girlfriends had come to sit and talk to her and tease her new husband. She was thinking how often she had day-dreamed about this day and how it had been almost how she had envisioned it, almost perfect in every respect – almost. She couldn't forget there was one important person missing; one familiar voice and beloved visage, absent.

Chapter 14

When it came time for Nadira to apply to college, her mother insisted she choose among the colleges in Lahore and live at home. Her father agreed. He told her, soon enough she'd be gone. She compiled a list of every classmate who was going away to school and gave it to her parents. She argued they were old-fashioned and overprotective. But they didn't budge. Their only concession was to give her the use of one of their cars so she could drive herself back and forth to campus and have it for outings with her friends. She considered it inadequate compensation.

Nadira had envisioned college as a way of breaking with her past, a place where she would be unknown and empowered to reinvent herself. She wanted to go abroad to study or at least venture to Islamabad or Karachi where she could live on her own in a student hostel. Every night for the last year, she had counted the weeks until graduation, trying to hurry the passage of time and reach the day when she could free herself from the confining framework of her youth. She saw her parents' decision as deterring her progress, leaving her where she had always been instead of moving forward. But there was nothing she could do but wait for time to pass, yet again.

A few weeks into her first semester, Nadira was walking toward the parking lot to get her car and go home. She heard loud voices and saw a boy and a girl yelling at each other. As she approached, the boy turned and walked away. The girl went after him and grabbed his arm, but he shook her off and ran.

"How am I supposed to get home?" the girl called after him, an arm stretched out toward his retreating form as if reaching to pull him back.

Nadira realized she had seen the girl in two of her classes. She walked over to her.

"Are you all right?"

"I could be better. I just had an argument with my cousin, and he's left me without a ride home. I'm sure he'll be back once he cools off, but who knows when that will be." She sighed and shifted the pile of books in her arms.

"I was just leaving. Can I drop you somewhere?"

The girl cocked her head to one side and looked at her. "Thanks, that's really nice of you. I've seen you in class, haven't I?"

"Probably, I'm Nadira," she said, extending her hand.

"Sharnaz," she replied, shifting her books to one side so they could shake.

Sharnaz told her where she lived and asked her if it was out of her way. Fortunately, Sharnaz's neighborhood was not far from Nadira's house. During the drive, Nadira was relieved that Sharnaz did most of the talking, leaving room for only a sentence or two from her. After their brief encounter, Nadira thought the only consequence of their meeting would be an acknowledgement of each other whenever they crossed paths. But, Sharnaz made it a point to search Nadira out, and claimed her as a friend. Nadira wasn't sure she wanted a friend. She had grown used to acquaintances, girls who were pleasant companions at parties, on shopping trips, and huddled around small tea shop tables, demanding nothing more than cheerful company. But Sharnaz wasn't interested in a superficial friendship. She wanted to know everything about her - likes, dislikes, politics and feelings on every subject that came within their orbit. Nadira had forgotten how to open herself up to someone, but Sharnaz persisted. She was either oblivious to Nadira's hesitation and the way she avoided saying anything meaningful, or decided to ignore it, inserting herself into Nadira's life as if she had been holding a space vacant, waiting for her.

She didn't know how to chase Sharnaz away without being rude. She started paying closer attention to what her new friend was saying, finding her smart with very definite views and an easy laugh. She was also quite convincing, and talked Nadira into joining the college paper and enlisted her help with various causes. Sharnaz was an irresistible force, her personality so compelling and appealing, Nadira allowed a friendship to develop, surprised by the pleasure of it, and found a closeness she hadn't had since Hameeda disappeared from her life.

*   *   *

As she entered her last year of college, Nadira felt both excited and sad. She was looking forward to graduation and starting a career but sorry about leaving the academic environment and the friends she'd made. In college, Nadira had taken on the daunting task of completing a double major in math and accounting. She chose to major in math because the universe of numbers captivated her. She enjoyed testing herself against the abstract complexities of the subject, absorbed by its challenges, and reveling in her successes as she conquered each of its principles. But, she also heeded her nani's advice and picked accounting as a second major because it led to a distinct career path. She had already survived her most difficult courses and expected to complete her final year without much effort, except for the dreaded senior project requirement. All accounting majors were paired up, and each pair created a business plan for a fictitious company and then produced the book-keeping and financials for a one year period. Fortunately, Nadira and Sharnaz were partnered. They had both done well in their accounting courses and had a similar way of approaching tasks. That and their friendship made working on the project together enjoyable.

One afternoon, Nadira was at Sharnaz's house. They were sitting at the dining room table going over some figures, and she took no notice when Sharnaz's older brother, with a friend in tow, walked past the table on their way to the kitchen. In their wake, quiet returned to the room, but she sensed another presence which had not been there a few minutes earlier. She looked up to see a young man standing in the doorway staring at her. He was taller than average with an athletic build. His hair was clipped short above a square jawed face with even features and heavy lidded eyes as round as paisa coins. He was, without a doubt, handsome. Nadira brushed her finger across her lips, making sure there were no crumbs from the biscuits she'd been eating and tucked a stray hair behind her ear. She needn't have worried. Sohail later told her he was struck by her beauty, in particular, her captivating, oriental eyes, and impressed by the bold way she stared back at him.

This good looking stranger lifted one eyebrow at her before asking what they were doing.

"We're working on a school project," Sharnaz replied without raising her head from her ledger. "Go away, Sohail."

When Sohail retreated back into the kitchen, Nadira felt like a little girl who has been offered a treat and then had it taken away. For the next few months, almost every time she was at Sharnaz's house, Sohail showed up. He would pull up a chair and talk with them for a while before joining Sharnaz's brother. Sohail was smart and funny and had an easy going way about him, and Nadira began to look forward to seeing him. Once when he was sitting next to her, he reached across to take a piece of fruit from the bowl in the center of the table and his arm brushed against her hand. Sensations rippled out from where she'd been touched and lapped all over her body as if she were a pool of water into which he had cast a stone. The heat of a blush filled her cheeks.

Confused about her feelings, she wished there was

someone who she could consult. It was at times like this she felt Hameeda's absence. In her mind, a conversation with her old friend played out. She could hear Hameeda's soft but firm voice as clearly as if she were in the room with her.

"Nadira, I'm surprised at you. Your meetings with Sohail are unseemly. How could you let it go on so long?"

"There's nothing unseemly about it. Sharnaz is always in the room. I'm never alone with him."

"Then it's not just you who's doing something wrong, but also Sharnaz. You're putting yourself in the way of temptation, and she's helping you. What you're doing is haram, forbidden, and you must stop."

"Hameeda, you're so old fashioned; you act like we're still in the dark ages. I can't see anything wrong with what I'm doing."

"If you already know the answer, why bother asking me the question?"

That was her problem; she had trouble listening to advice, preferring to follow her own counsel, which sometimes resulted in preventable mistakes. But not feeling comfortable talking to anyone else about her situation, she stopped going to Sharnaz's house and instead suggested they meet at school or at her own house. If this puzzled Sharnaz, she didn't say anything.

Nadira pushed away her confusion over her feelings for Sohail, and instead focused on her studies and finding an accounting position. She interviewed with campus recruiters and with companies where her father had a connection. Standing at the top of her class, she went into her first interviews with confidence. But as the weeks passed, the positions were filled by less qualified young men. She'd been naïve to think the excellent record she'd worked so hard to achieve would get her the job she wanted. It wasn't until an interviewer suggested she give up on a job, get married and have family as Allah intended, that she realized the type of mind set she was up against. Frustrated and angry, Nadira discussed her problem with her father.

"I wish I could say this is unexpected, but it was something I thought might happen. Now, we educate our girls like we do our boys, but the business world hasn't taken the next step of applying the same criteria when hiring," her father said.

"What am I to do?" Nadira asked.

"The teaching field is very accepting of women. Would you be interested in teaching math or accounting?"

Teaching had never held any interest for Nadira. It was something she would have to think about. But before she could come to a decision, an unexpected event changed her fate.

Later, Nadira found out that during her absence, Sohail had taken matters into his own hands. He told his parents he'd met a young woman at his friend's home and asked if they would contact her parents about a possible match. After using a network of family and friends the CIA would envy, Sohail's parents were satisfied that Nadira's family met their criteria, and she was acceptable as a possible bride for their son.

Three months after she'd last seen Sohail, Nadira was sitting at the breakfast table with her parents and younger brother when the phone rang. Her mother went into the lounge to answer it. She heard a muffled conversation, and then her mother called to her father and asked him to come into the room. She didn't think anything of it and was talking to her brother when her parents returned to the table.

"Kareem, please go to your room," her mother said.

"What've I done?" he said, looking puzzled.

"Nothing yet; we want to have a private word with Nadira."

She became uneasy when she saw her mother's stern expression.

"Nadira, you must have really done something wrong this time," Kareem said with a smirk. "I want to stay and hear this."

"Kareem, do as you're told; we'll tell you whatever we think you need to know later," her mother said, raising her voice. And, I don't want to look up in a few minutes and see you standing outside this door." Her mother wagged a finger in front of his face. "Stay in your room until we come get you."

While her mother was giving instructions to her brother, Nadira pondered what she could have done, but nothing came to mind.

"Nadira I just got a phone call from a Mrs. Malik," her mother said. "She has a son, Sohail, who says he knows you. It seems Sohail has told his parents he's interested in marrying you."

Nadira opened her mouth, but no words emerged. It was as if all signals from her brain had ceased. She felt dizzy and disoriented.

"How long have you known this boy?" her mother asked, her arms folded across her chest and her voice sharp with displeasure.

She didn't respond, still catching up to the trajectory of events put in motion without her knowledge or consent.

"Nadira, answer me."

"A few months," she said, forced to look up at her mother from her seated position, and feeling at a distinct disadvantage.

"You've been seeing him a few months? What else have you been hiding from us? What's been going on between you?" Her mother motioned to her father who had kept his distance, to come closer.

Nadira was offended by the unfair implications of her mother's questions. "Nothing Amma." She shook her head. "He just talks to me and Sharnaz."

"Sharnaz, what does Sharnaz have to do with it?" her mother said, looking puzzled.

She explained the circumstances leading up to her being in Sohail's company.

"So, it's not just you but also Sharnaz this boy has been spending time with?"

"Yes." Nadira was so annoyed with her mother's interrogation she made up her mind not to volunteer any more information.

"And you've never been alone in the room with him?"

"Certainly not," she replied, unable to keep the irritation out of her voice.

"Still, you're forbidden from having any contact with him, even with a proper chaperone, until we've met with his parents. I don't know what you were thinking, seeing this boy without talking to me," her mother said, in a tone that vacillated between anger and relief. "Your father has allowed you too much freedom, and I blame myself for not stepping in years ago."

Her father tried looking contrite while at the same time giving Nadira a wink.

"I saw that," her mother said. "It's this kind of attitude from you that got us where we are today."

Later that night, Nadira explored all her past interactions with Sohail and her feelings for him. Defining those pleasurable experiences was still impossible. Was Sohail the right one for her? She tried imagining what her life would be like with someone else, but Sohail's face kept superimposing itself on any future scenario she created. In the days that followed, she felt as if she had waded into a river and midstream was caught by a strong current. Instead of fighting it, she allowed her emotions to pull her along.

After an unconventional beginning, everything had worked out. The families got along well, and Nadira and Sohail were formally engaged. The next few months, her days were so filled with wedding preparations she barely had time to think. Through it all, she felt a constant undercurrent of excitement and anticipation, as if she were an adventurer planning her first solo expedition, with no parental hand-holding to spoil it. This, she thought, must be how explorers felt as they looked forward to taking their first step onto the soil of unmapped territory.

It was not until her wedding day, as the finality of the commitment she was about to make struck her, that she lost her certainty and became jittery. And only after she had given her assent and signed the marriage contract, her fate sealed, did she begin to relax.

She had reached a divide in her life, leaving her childhood behind and beginning anew, her old life and old identity gone. From this day on, she'd take her husband's name, and move from the house where she'd spent her first twenty-two years to the small apartment she and Sohail would share. She was hopeful her marriage would be a turning point, a perfect opportunity to transform into the person she had always hoped to be.

At the bride's reception, Nadira sat at Sohail's side looking out over the wedding hall filled with over 500 family members and friends. Every person who had touched her life in some important way was there. Even her father's closest friend from Stanford, Professor Calhoun, was present. In a twist of fate, he was a guest lecturer at Punjab University for the semester. She could see him off to the side, amused by something her uncle had said, head flung back, his big Texas laugh audible above the other conversations. With his black string tie and cowboy boots peeking out below the cuffs of his suit trousers, he was recognizable as an American even before you heard his accent. Earlier in the evening, he and his bleached blond wife were telling her about their experiences since they'd arrived. The professor mentioned how impressed he was with his students, and his wife commented on how welcoming and hospitable Pakistanis had been to them, both in Lahore and on their travels elsewhere in the country. On a trip to Islamabad, they had gotten lost coming back from dinner. A stranger had seen them looking around and had come to their assistance, walking them back to their hotel and then inviting them to his home the next afternoon for tea with his family. Listening to them, Nadira had felt a surge of pride in Pakistan and its people.

All at once, a few yards away, she saw a woman from the back, her head covered, and her walk familiar. Nadira's heart started racing and she half rose from her seat. She was sure it was Hameeda. Somehow she'd found out about her marriage and had come to her Shaadi to give her the gift of renewed friendship. But when the woman turned around, her face was the face of a stranger. She sat back down. How foolish she'd been to even think such a thing was possible. Still, she was overcome with emotion, turning away from Sohail, and bowing her head to hide the tears stinging her eyes.

"What is it?" Sohail asked.

"Nothing, I thought I lost a bangle but I was mistaken," Nadira said managing to turn back toward him with a smile.

"So you haven't lost anything?" Sohail asked.

She lied and told him "no." But, she had suffered the loss of something much more precious than jewelry, something priceless and irreplaceable.

PART TWO

*

Chapter 1

Fifteen years into her marriage, Nadira looked forward to spending time with a friend who allowed her to be someone other than Sohail's wife. As she sat in a restaurant stirring her milky tea, waiting for the arrival of Sharnaz, she traded her worries for idle thoughts. Outside the window, she saw an old car drive past and then return a few minutes later. The car looked like a derelict; the hood was a different color from the rest of the body, its surface tattooed with dents and pitted with rusted out craters above the wheel wells. As the car slowed down, she heard the engine emit an asthmatic cough and saw its muffler was held up by baling wire. The driver stopped the car in front of the restaurant and parked. Through the car's dusty window, she observed him as he leaned forward and reached for something below her line of vision before he straightened up, stepped out of the car, and leaving the door open started running down the street.

Oh no, please no! She thought. An instant later the noise of an explosion assaulted her ears and the car disintegrated into a ball of fire and metal projectiles. Her mind told her she should dive for cover, but her body wouldn't respond. Frozen in place, she watched as the window across the room bulged inward and then collapsed like a breached dam to send a torrent of glass shards flying toward her. The debris had almost engulfed her when she jerked awake.

The high pitched squeal of a loudspeaker preceded the muezzin's voice blasting the call to prayer from the mosque down the street. Her body, still residing inside her dream, trembled and her breath came in short gasps. Searching for a way to calm down, she focused on the muezzin's chanting and let the familiar words and cadences even out her ragged breathing.

"Allahu Akbar, Allahu Akbar, God is great, God is great." As a child she loved waking to the sound of the muezzin's unassisted voice softened by the distance between the mosque's minaret and their house. She always felt his insistent chant was directed solely at her ears, saying: Arise; begin your morning prayers and your day. Now the loudspeaker gave his call a mechanical edge, and she heard it off and on due to the static of yet another aging, faulty system. Nadira sighed and pulled herself from bed, careful not to disturb her sleeping husband. She padded in her bare feet over to the cupboard to retrieve her prayer rug, but her dream was still too real, and she didn't think she could clear enough of it from her mind to make room for her prayers. Instead, she changed out of her night clothes into an old shalwar kameez, wrapped her duputta around her shoulders and went down the hall into the lounge. She pulled apart the drapes, opened the window and sat where she could see and hear the day begin. As the sun rose in the sky, the garden view changed from an abstract pencil sketch in shades of gray to a detailed, brightly colored oil painting. Two doves settled on a tree branch and cooed to each other, the noise of a car traveling down the street came to her from beyond the garden wall, voices rose and fell in conversation somewhere in the distance, and the neighbor's gate creaked open and then clanged shut. The everyday sights and sounds soothed away her night terrors. She heard a bedroom door open and turned, catching sight of her son, Arif, still rumpled with sleep, walking across the lounge toward her.

"Amma, what are you doing out here?" he asked with a yawn.

"Just thinking beta; what got you out of bed so early?"

"I have homework that needs finishing."

"What, I thought you'd finished it last night?" Nadira shook her head. "Why must you leave everything to the last minute?"

Arif gave her a disarming smile as he leaned forward and kissed her cheek. "Because that's the way I am Amma. If it was done early, you'd think I'd come down with some strange disease. Isn't that so?"

Nadira tried withholding her laughter, but it escaped despite her best efforts. "You're impossible Arif; go then; go do your homework." She shooed him away with her hands.

Arif made a deep bow and said, "Your wish is my command," and then disappeared back into his room.

Nadira touched her face where Arif's upper lip had brushed it, his skin no longer baby smooth but tickly with the first downy hairs of an incipient mustache, a reminder that his childhood was quickly slipping away. When she was very young, she remembered experiencing time second by second, her days passing in slow motion, but lately time seemed to travel as fast as a fleeting thought.

Nadira mentally shook herself. In the distant past, Arif would have received a severe reprimand from her for his procrastination, but these days she found it very difficult disciplining the children. Every morning she dropped them off at school and watched as armed guards checked their IDs before they were allowed past the barricade and through the entrance gate and was reminded of how vulnerable they were. When the gate opened to admit them, she glimpsed the green lawn and beautiful shade trees that had once been visible from the street but were now hidden by high brick walls topped with barb wire. While she waited until they were out of sight, she thought about her list of activities for the day. An unoccupied mind was dangerous since her imagination often populated any empty space with dire scenarios, which if allowed to take up residency in her brain, would prevent her from going on as usual. And, it was crucial for the boys for her to act as if everything was normal. Still, no matter how they misbehaved in the morning, she didn't scold, so really, how successful was she at hiding her feelings?

"What's all the noise about?" Now it was her husband. Sohail stood in the doorway rubbing the top of his head.

Nadira smiled at his hair standing up in spikey tufts. At a distance, except for the slight thickening at his waist and the shadow of a beard on his face, he resembled a sleepy adolescent.

"I was just talking to Arif. Sorry we woke you."

"That's all right; I was getting up anyway," Sohail said, sinking down on the sofa next to her. "Do you need your car today? I was thinking of having the driver take it for servicing."

She reached up and smoothed down his hair. "I'll need it. I'm doing some errands for your cousin Nighat this morning. She's been so busy taking care of her husband she hasn't been able to get out of the house."

"What's wrong with him?" Sohail asked, a look of concern crossing his face.

"I'm sure I told you. He was beaten up and robbed in the middle of the afternoon, right in front of their gate. To make matters worse, he filed a report with the police, but nothing has been done about it." Nadira thought how once this story would have been unbelievable, but now it was only remarkable because it had happened to someone they knew.

Sohail got up and began to pace. When he spoke his voice was low but shook with emotion.

"I often wonder why I continue on as if we have viable government institutions. I pay our taxes when the vast majority do not, think it's normal when I place rupees in the outstretched hand of an official so he will do the job he's already getting paid for, and watch crimes go unpunished because the police, who are supposed to protect us, are either incompetent or corrupt. And most of us just shrug our shoulders and say there is nothing we can do because the forces arrayed against us are too many and too powerful. Our country is falling apart, while we watch, accepting the role of a captive audience."

When he stopped pacing and faced Nadira, his jaw was clenched and his hands were balled into fists. Nadira was surprised at the vehemence of his reaction. Usually, he was the calm one in the family. The last time she'd seen him so upset was two years ago when Arif flunked a history exam. This was the perfect opportunity, she decided, to bring up something she'd been thinking about in recent months as the increasing violence filled her with dread.

"Maybe it's time to go." Finally, she'd said it. "Would you be willing to leave Pakistan if we could get visas?" Nadira looked up at him, suspense caging a swarm of butterflies in her stomach.

"Why would I abandon a business I've spent years building and go overseas where I'd probably end up pumping gas? What kind of life would that be for us and the children?" Sohail said.

How could he acknowledge the gravity of the situation in one breath and refuse to consider leaving in the next? Her heartbeat quickened and body quivered as the scattershot of her anger focused on one target. Clutching her dupatta to still her hands, she stood up.

"And life here is so good? In addition to all the usual shortages and daily inconveniences our politicians have bequeathed to us, we're held hostage by terrorists and criminals. The children's school is shut down at least once a term because of bomb threats, and we no longer feel safe traveling in certain areas of the city." As she talked, the sense of foreboding she'd been experiencing lately grew stronger, constricting her chest. "And it's only going to get worse."

"Nadira please, I don't have time for this now." Sohail waved her away.

"Does that mean you'll discuss it later?"

"Unless there's a dramatic change in circumstances, I don't see any reason for another go round."

Nadira looked at Sohail's face, which on close inspection carried the weight of more than just the passage of years and regretted losing her temper. She moved next to him and rested her hand on his arm and in a soft voice asked him to at least think about what she'd said.

"Enough," Sohail said, shaking free of her touch. Do something useful. The new cook is totally unreliable. Go see if he's started breakfast."

Nadira, startled by his brusque treatment, stared at his stiff back as he turned and went back into their bedroom, closing the door behind him. She felt like a servant, dismissed when her presence was no longer required. Anger and sadness battled for precedence as she thought about his uncharacteristic behavior. In the past, he soothed away her fears or joked about their situation, until he coaxed a smile from her. Lately, things were different. His once limitless patience and optimism were gone, and dealing with the changes in his mood was as difficult as finding her way through the unfamiliar streets of a foreign city. Thinking back over the last few months, Nadira felt Sohail had pulled away from her, and didn't know why it had happened, or how she could help him return to his old self. She was lonely in their crowded house and couldn't think of anything she wanted more than to recapture their former closeness. Well, Sohail was right about one thing; she should at least make sure the household ran smoothly, not just for him – since at the moment she had difficulty caring about his needs - but for all of them. She'd go check on breakfast. Her prayers would have to wait.

As Nadira entered the kitchen, she interrupted an argument between the cook and the driver. Although their angry words had ceased the minute she came into the room, they still stood facing each other like two scrapping dogs pulled apart and restrained by invisible leashes. The short, stocky, middle-aged driver, now red faced with bared teeth showing beneath his mustache, looked like a mastiff growling a warning. A half smile played over the face of the young cook as he took a couple of steps back, his loose limbed movements reminiscent of a playful puppy dancing out of harm's way.

"What's going on here?" Nadira looked first at the driver and then at the cook.

"Begum Sahib, I was just telling this boy he should make my breakfast right away so that I'll be ready to take

Sahib to the office," the driver said. "And, he's giving me back talk."

Nadira studied them like a politician trying to determine which constituency will offer the most influential backing in the future. She considered the driver who had been with them for almost three years - a long time these days - and had excellent driving skills, a qualification difficult to find. Many so-called drivers had only recently acquired licenses in some questionable manner. This would be revealed when you were seated in the car on a test drive, jerked about to the tune of grinding gears and avoiding collisions by such a small margin, Allah's name sprang to your lips. The cook at nineteen was barely out of adolescence. He had turned up on her doorstep one day looking for work. A distant cousin of a former gardener, he had left his small village in Kashmir to supplement his family's meager income. He was a good boy, if not overly bright, with a penchant for daydreaming. He had minimal skills when he arrived, and she'd been giving him cooking lessons for the last few months. His cooking had improved, but he had trouble showing up on time and disappeared during the day when it was least convenient, her time wasted as she searched for him. Unfortunately, experienced cooks demanded salaries beyond what their budget would bear, so she was stuck with less desirable candidates. She was certain given enough time she could train him to be an adequate cook. But she also knew once he was competent, someone would entice him away with a larger salary, and she would have to start all over again with another young boy or girl. It was clear she should try and placate the driver, but her sense of fairness overrode her practicality, and she sided with the cook.

"You know you're supposed to have breakfast at home before coming here. I'll make an exception today, but if we're feeding you more than just the midday meal, there will be an adjustment to your salary."

"But, Begum Sahib, the other drivers on this street get two meals a day, and they're getting paid more than me." He looked at her without the slightest sign of embarrassment over this subtle form of blackmail.

It annoyed Nadira that the driver gave no consideration to the fact they had paid for a doctor's visit and medication when he was ill a few weeks ago and had given him a modest raise the previous year. She crossed her arms over her chest and pressed her lips together to stifle a hasty retort.

"That's not our arrangement. You should discuss any changes you want with my husband," she told him, unhappy because having to deal with the driver would not improve Sohail's mood. Although she had most of the supervisory responsibility for the servants, adjustments to terms of employment, hiring and firing came within Sohail's purview. It was a recurring area of disagreement between them, for if she didn't have the final say regarding the servants, then she lost most of her control over them.

Having temporarily dispensed with the problem, Nadira instructed the cook to get the tea and toast ready, including some for the driver, and reminded him about Samir's cereal and Arif's boiled egg.

"I'll be back in twenty minutes, and I expect to find the table laid and breakfast ready." She gave him a last stern look.

"Yes, Begum Sahib." The cook dropped his head and stared at the floor.

Nadira sighed as she went back down the hall to the bedrooms. The morning's events had tired her out, and she wished she could crawl back into bed and start her day over again.

Wouldn't it be nice if life with servants could be like the old English TV series "Upstairs, Downstairs" where the staff was unquestionably loyal, and a magisterial butler relayed all the orders from the mistress, supervised all the work, and took care of disputes out of the sight and hearing of the family? But not even the British had that anymore. The old attitudes and way of doing things had crumbled along with the Raj, and the British had left a legacy of disagreements on the Indian subcontinent much more serious than mere servant squabbles.

On her way to her bedroom, she looked in on Samir. She found her younger son sitting on his bed, fully dressed with his head stuck in a book.

"As salaam aleikum, Samir."

"Wa aleikum salaam, Amma." He looked up with a smile.

"Is that school work you're reading?" Nadira tilted her head to the side, trying to make out the book's title.

"No Amma, it is a new book on reptiles my friend lent me." Samir's eyes had already returned to his page.

"Have you done your homework?"

"I finished it last night. You must be mistaking me for Arif." He looked up to punish her with a scowl.

"Sorry, I asked without thinking." Nadira kissed the top of his head in apology. "Why don't you get your school things together while I give your brother a push."

The differences between her two sons always amazed her. Arif was relaxed, outgoing, and preferred sports over more sedentary activities, very much like his father - a fact neither of them wanted to admit. Samir was in many ways his opposite, serious, a reader, worried about everything, and soft-hearted. He seemed less worldly than Arif had been at his age, and she wondered if she'd been too overprotective. She had often questioned who Samir took after, thinking of their extended families and not finding an answer. Although, he did have a trait that reminded her of someone; the identity of the person always just out of her mind's reach. He seemed to know without being told when she needed comforting, giving her an unasked for hug, or surprising her with a chocolate bar he'd bought with his pocket money.

Later when they were all sitting at the breakfast table, Nadira remembered an invitation from her friend Sharnaz. She wondered if she should tell Sohail about it now or wait until the evening in the hope that their morning disagreement would be forgotten. She decided she might as well get it out of the way. Who knew if his mood would be any better after a day dealing with business problems.

"Sharnaz and her husband have invited us to lunch

at their house on Sunday. Should I accept?" Her husband glanced up at her, his face unreadable.

"I have a client meeting, but why don't you go," Sohail said, as he busied himself buttering a second slice of toast.

Nadira was puzzled as to why he had scheduled a business meeting on a Sunday when he had never allowed business to interfere with their weekends before. She wanted to question him about it but was afraid she'd precipitate an argument in front of the boys.

"I'll give her our regrets. It's no fun going without you." She waited for an apology from her husband for disappointing her.

"It's up to you." With almost no pause, he went back to eating his breakfast.

His answer made Nadira more unsettled, and she retreated into her dark thoughts. The rest of breakfast passed in relative silence as the four of them finished eating. Immediately afterward, Sohail left for the office and Nadira shepherded the boys out to the car for the drive to school, only to be delayed as Arif dashed back into the house to get a book he'd forgotten. At least one person's behavior was still predictable, she thought.

There was a time when she'd enjoyed driving, but now she dreaded it. The traffic in Lahore got worse every month. Bumper to bumper, side mirrors almost touching across lanes, you inched forward, your leg muscles aching from the repetitive use of the clutch. Impatient drivers ignored traffic signals and policemen, taking advantage of any opening. The worst ones played chicken with oncoming cars in order to pass a slow moving vehicle or get through an intersection. Every move was accompanied by the insistent blowing of horns, ranging in tempo and tone from staccato beeping to long noted wails, sounding like the brass section of an orchestra playing a dissonant, new age composition.

A block from the boys' school, they were halted by a line-up of cars, waiting to drop children off at the barriers.

"Amma, why don't you let us off here and we'll walk the rest of the way?" Arif said.

"Just stay in the car, please; it won't take much longer." She took her eyes off the vehicle in front of her and looked in the rear view mirror to check on her sons.

"Amma, you have nothing to worry about. If a kidnapper comes along, I'll give him a good bash with my cricket bat." Arif raised his bat up in the close confines of the back seat and almost hit Samir.

"Not much good against a pistol, Arif." Samir aimed an extended finger at Arif and imitated the sound of a fired shot.

"Samir, you're ruining our chances of getting out of the car." Arif cuffed Samir on the arm.

The boys' talk of kidnapping put Nadira on edge; still suffering the lingering effects of her dream, she found their boyish bravado disturbing.

"Enough! You'll both remain in the car until I say you can get out." She could hear a sharp edge in her voice and suffered instant regret.

Ten minutes later, having seen both boys pass through

the guards at the school gate, Nadira started on the return journey. As she crawled along in traffic, her mind returned to her morning exchange with Sohail. It astounded her that he'd cut off any discussion of possibly getting overseas visas as if it was solely his decision. But why was she so surprised? Hadn't men always been in control of her world? She remembered how as a child, she had wished for her brothers' privileges while never considering things could be different. And had she ever looked beyond her parents' marriage when forming her own expectations of her role as wife and mother? As a young woman, her thoughts on marriage, like those of her peers, had centered more on the looks, personality and prospects of her future husband. She admitted to herself that her marriage had more mutuality than she'd thought possible, but it was Sohail who governed the parameters of their equality.

When they became engaged, Nadira had just graduated from college, and Sohail was struggling with a nascent business. She remembered telling him how much she admired his ambition and courage, it being such a rarity for someone his age to take on the running of a company. He said it was more the hand of fate than a well-considered decision. Near the end of his MBA course, he had been struggling to decide where to apply for a job when his uncle came to him with an offer he thought would be advantageous to both of them. When Sohail's cousin flunked out of college, his uncle had put him in charge of a factory which made clothing for export, having acquired the failing business as payment for a debt. But, Sohail's cousin couldn't make the business a going concern due to a lack of knowledge, interest and energy. Exasperated, his uncle used his political connections and got his son a managerial job in the inflated bureaucracy of the state owned Pakistan International Airlines. This suited his cousin just fine. He had a job with an impressive title and a large salary for which he did nothing, leaving the real work to college graduates who were more qualified and earned far less than he did. Meanwhile, his uncle was left with a business he had no time for and suggested Sohail take it over while he remained a silent partner. His uncle would receive a percentage of the profits, paid on a monthly basis until he'd recovered his investment, at which time the company would revert to Sohail's sole ownership.

Once they were married, Sohail had asked Nadira to help him with the business by taking over the books, which he had been tackling with some difficulty. He explained that in addition to saving on cost, he would have more time to deal with clients and oversee the production side. Nadira had been thrilled by his confidence in her, and it made her feel she was contributing to their future. So she gave up looking for work, and instead joined Sohail in his new enterprise, increasing the amount of time they spent together, and giving them something in common beyond their social life. As they lived and worked together, they discovered where their personalities meshed and where they differed and learned to adjust to each other as they created a family. Their initial attraction and early friendship grew into something more, something that fit Nadira's vision of love.

After a year of marriage, Nadira thought Sohail had begun to overlook her gender, at least at the office, her femaleness masked by her work. Then she presented him with irrefutable proof of her womanhood, evidence that couldn't be hidden behind balance sheets and account ledgers, and his attitude shifted. When she became pregnant with Arif, he didn't like her coming into the office, which was situated at the factory, and suggested she work from home in case she needed to rest during the day. At the time, Nadira appreciated his solicitousness. He became even more protective once Arif was born. Then one night when she was pacing their small apartment with Arif in her arms, cranky with a cold, she was unexpectedly thrust back into a more traditional role. Without preamble, Sohail informed her he thought it was time she retired. She remembered thinking it was one of his jokes, waiting for a punchline and a laugh that never came.

"Why? Have I done something wrong?" She had paced their small lounge, and jounced a wailing Arif as she waited for his reply.

"No, not at all. But, handling Arif and our move to the new house is keeping you very busy, and having you work from home isn't the ideal situation. There are times when I need someone on site and now that the business is doing well, I can hire an accountant."

"But I enjoy doing the books and participating in the business." As much as she would miss watching the changes in Arif, which seemed to occur almost daily, his needs at this stage of his life were elemental, and she desired more, an activity that exercised her brain and was hers alone. And, she already missed the more collaborative aspects of her relationship with Sohail. "Can't we hire a nanny who'll watch Arif when I'm working?"

Sohail must have been surprised at her reaction since he had already taken steps to replace her, and Nadira had been very upset with his unilateral decision on such an important matter. But after being up with Arif for several nights, she was too exhausted to argue.

She wondered; if she had lived her dream for just one or two years longer, until it was well rooted, as much a part of her as the nervous habit of twisting the end of a lock of hair around her finger, would she have let it go when the first real obstacle appeared? Or had she been fated to become lost among the tangled undergrowth of society's traditional directives?

She remembered reconsidering what Sohail had said after she'd calmed down. Was Sohail right or should she persuade him to change his mind and continue on with their original arrangement? Her eyes had fallen on Arif who was finally sleeping, his face peaceful and enchanting. She had reached out and smoothed the hair off his forehead, thinking maybe Sohail's reasoning was correct and she did have other, more important things taking up her time.

Now years later, she realized the impact of ignoring her nani's advice. In a weak moment, she had given up the future she had planned and prepared for and had accepted the role played by so many generations of women before her. Just as they had, she occupied a place in the background, taken for granted like an object in a room that you see day after day until it recedes from view. And, her brief discussion with Sohail this morning made it apparent she no longer had a part in making the big decisions that affected all of them. The question was: what was she going to do about it?

And then there was the Sunday business meeting. Why would he make a business appointment on a Sunday? Was it just a fabrication so he could get out of the house? And if so, why? Her head began to throb, with the beginning of a headache.

Once she reached home, she dismissed her thoughts and concentrated on the morning's tasks. Entering the house, she went to the kitchen, but the cook wasn't there, gone again contrary to her instructions. Nadira stood there for a moment, frustrated and annoyed. She felt like screaming. After searching the house, she finally found him outside leaning against the back wall. She could tell he was chewing betel nut by the red stain around his mouth and the lump he tucked into his cheek when he saw her coming. Nadira found the practice of chewing betel nut, which acted as a mild stimulant, disgusting but it was very common, particularly among villagers, and she only forbade it inside the house.

"Get rid of what you're chewing and come into the kitchen. There's cooking to be done for lunch and dinner." Nadira waited for him to do as she asked, afraid if she went inside ahead of him, he might disappear again.

She had taught the cook that spitting was unsanitary.

So, as he rose to his feet, with an irritating slowness, she watched him pull out a small, dirty square of cloth from under the wristband of his kurta, deposit the repulsive, masticated lump, fold up the piece of material and then palm it. Nadira shuddered. She'd have to ensure that he threw out the cloth in the kitchen bucket and washed his hands before he started cooking. At times like this, when she became impatient with him, when he irritated her with his obtuseness and his village habits, she reminded herself that he was someone's son. Somewhere he had a mother who thought about him, prayed for him, and missed him. At the very least, she could give him a few more chances because she knew with certainty, one more chance would not be enough.

Once inside, she opened her purse and looked for her house keys but couldn't find them. Not for the first time, she wished her shalwar had pockets like the blue jeans she wore when she was younger. Then she might not put her keys down and forget where they were. She told the cook she would return in a minute and with hurried steps went into her bedroom. Sure enough, her bunch of keys hung from the lock of her clothes cupboard. She turned the key, tugging on the door to make sure the cupboard was locked before removing it. Returning to the kitchen, she unlocked the refrigerator and the pantry cupboard, taking out the meat, vegetables and dry goods necessary for each lunch and dinner dish. After getting the cook started, she said her prayers and took a quick shower before the sweeper arrived.

When Nadira returned to the front of the house, the

cook had already let the sweeper in, and she was at work in the drawing room. She stood in the doorway and watched her perform a task that had been done in much the same way for centuries. Squatting on bare feet as hard and cracked as old shoe leather, she tucked her kameez between her legs and crab walked across the terrazzo floor, using a bundle of twigs tied together at one end to corral the dust into small piles. Her arm swung rhythmically back and forth, banded by thin bangle bracelets that clinked with each motion, keeping time like a metronome. Once she had swept a section of the room, she dampened a rag in her water bucket and wiped up the dust piles. The repetitive motions were hypnotizing after a poor night's sleep. Rousing herself, Nadira crossed the room.

After exchanging salaams, she reminded the woman about changing the water before it became too dirty. Even though the sweeper had done the same tasks every day for years, she could not be left on her own, and Nadira would check on her now and then until she finished. The last time she hadn't supervised her, she'd damaged the computer keyboard by cleaning it with a wet cloth, an instance of good intentions gone awry, so she hadn't scolded her. Now the entire computer was covered with an old towel like some exotic caged bird, and the sweeper wasn't allowed near it.

The morning's events conspired to scatter her thoughts in different directions, and she found it hard to enter into her normal routine. She paused to look out the window and saw a feral cat seated on top of the wall licking itself clean. These cats were such a nuisance. They dug in her flower beds and defaced the clean, green surface of their lawn with clumps of feathers, bones and beaks; all that remained of their prey. She decided to run the intruder off, but stopped when the cat stood, revealing a tight, swollen belly. It embarrassed her that her first unselfish act of kindness for the day was directed at a cat instead of her husband. She turned away from the window, her brief detour over. There were still the boys' rooms to check to see if anything needed doing before the sweeper got to them.

Samir's room was first – fine as usual. His desktop was cleared off, his cupboards closed and locked, and even his books marched in neat rows across the shelves. On an impulse, she walked over and pulled out one of the later "Harry Potter" books, sat on the bed and leafed through it. She was only familiar with the first book in the series having read it to Samir when he was younger. She missed the days when she read to the boys before bedtime. Now there was no time for reading. Her daily chores were like the prayers of cloistered Buddhist monks, the same round repeated day after day after day. She put the book back on the shelf and crossed the hall to Arif's room where chaos reigned. His clothes from the previous day were bunched up in a pile on the floor, and his cupboard doors were wide open. A couple of shirts, clean she thought, had fallen off their hangers onto the shelf underneath, a football was on his bed, and books and papers lay in piles on his desk and chair. She set about putting his room to rights.

Over the next few hours, she got the maid started

on the laundry and ironing, worked with the cook in the kitchen and every so often checked on the sweeper. She often wondered why supervising these tasks took up almost as much of her time as doing them. It was almost 1:30 when she let the sweeper out and left to pick up the boys at school. She drove with only half her attention on the road, part of her mind taken up with what she had to do during the course of a busy afternoon, catering to the needs of both her sons. At least there was one novel event to lift her day out of its usual routine. She was dropping Arif off at his new friend Jameel's house, her first opportunity to meet this boy who, for the last several months, had taken up so much of her son's free time.

When the three of them returned, the aroma of spicy masalas from the large pots on the stove welcomed them. The enticing smells sharpened Nadira's hunger after a morning so harried she hadn't had time for her usual second cup of tea, and they also prompted pleasant associations. She had always looked forward to family meals, both as a child and now in her own home. Meals were a time for sharing news and ideas, a time to connect with one another. When they were first married and his business was in its infancy, Sohail came home for lunch, but now he was only home for breakfast and dinner. Nadira was not as strict about table manners, having inherited her father's preference for open discussion over the formal etiquette her mother had tried to instill in her, and when her husband was absent the boys were a little rowdier. Today was no exception.

"Amma, I want to lodge a complaint," Samir said.

"Who talks like that?" Arif looked up from his plate at Samir and shook his head. "Lodge a complaint? Samir, you're strange."

Clearly, Arif's comment was the opening salvo to an argument, but she kept eating and remained quiet, wanting them to learn how to resolve their differences without her always being pulled in as a referee.

"Amma, he's making fun of me," Samir said, the faint beginnings of a whine in his voice.

"Is that your complaint?" Arif pointed at Samir with his fork before bending back over his plate and resuming his meal.

"No it's not. Stop interrupting me when I have the floor." Samir leaned across the table and swatted at Arif who in one quick movement leaned back in his chair out of range of his brother's hand.

"You have the floor? Since when do we go by Robert's Rules of Order? This isn't the debating club, Samir."

"Amma, he's doing it again." Samir turned away from Arif, and looked at her.

"Samir, when will you learn to ignore Arif?" Nadira leaned over and placed another spoonful of his favorite spinach dish on his plate, hoping to distract him. "If you ignored him, he wouldn't keep teasing you."

"Wrong." Arif shook his head. "I will always tease him whether or not he ignores me."

Nadira had hoped the boys would be close instead of fractious like she had been with her siblings. How old was she when her brothers stopped being adversaries and became friends as well as family? The boys got along better when Sohail was around, which had Nadira wondering if his more frequent absences were affecting them too. Their bickering was becoming annoying, and she finally gave up on them working out their problems by themselves, convinced the argument would go on indefinitely, and too tired to put up with their quarrelsome behavior.

"That's enough. I don't care what either one of you did or didn't do to the other one."

Her sons ignored her and continued their protests, each talking over the other, their sentences diced into small, incomprehensible bits by their overlapping voices. Nadira slammed her hand down on the tabletop, sloshing water over the side of her glass and rattling the spoon on her plate. The silence that ensued seemed more profound after the previous commotion. She could hear the ticking of the clock on the buffet, and the cook banging pots in the kitchen. Her sons looked at her wide eyed and then glanced at each other, telegraphing some silent, coded message with raised eyebrows and shoulder shrugs.

"You heard me; not another word. I don't have time for this. Samir, I hope you haven't forgotten that you have your Qur'an instruction in an hour. Your nana is coming over to stay with you while I drop Arif off at Jameel's house. Now let's finish lunch, or we'll be late."

It was amazing how universal disapproval could unite her sons when they were otherwise so divided. Nadira thought it was a good sign, an indication that in times of trouble, they would forget their differences and support each other. And these days when solidarity and peace appeared to be lacking outside their walls, she felt it was even more important to have it at home.

Chapter 2

Hameeda's favorite time of the day was early morning after the children left for school. With her mother-in-law sleeping in, she and Zubair had this time all to themselves. Often, it was the only chance they had to talk without interruption. This morning, like every weekday morning, they sat next to each other at the table, relaxing and having a second cup of tea before Zubair left to check on his patients at the hospital.

"Isn't Jameel's new friend coming over this afternoon?" Zubair asked, as he took the milk jug from Hameeda and poured some in his tea.

"Yes, the timing couldn't be better," Hameeda said. Whenever Jameel has his class fellows over, the noise is a little too much for your mother, and this afternoon she'll be out visiting a friend."

She smiled as she watched Zubair stir his tea, his spoon circumnavigating his cup exactly two times. In all the years she'd known him, she had never caught him stirring one turn more or less. Once, a few years ago, she'd asked him why he always stirred his tea twice, thinking it might be an unconscious habit, but he had an answer ready. He told her, one time did not sufficiently combine the tea and the milk, and any more than two times was wasted motion. During the course of their marriage, she'd found that he approached most things in a methodical way, and maybe it was his systematic nature that had made him such an excellent surgeon, the one his colleagues turned to when a family member needed a procedure.

"I'll be interested to hear what you think of Jameel's friend. It's hard to imagine anyone could be the paragon he describes," Zubair said as he handed the milk jug back to her.

"I'm also looking forward to satisfying my curiosity," Hameeda said. "Jameel has been talking about this friend for months. It's Arif says this and Arif does that. The girls have gotten so tired of hearing his name they put their hands over their ears every time the subject comes up."

Zubair laughed. "Well, soon the suspense will be over."

A little while later, he took his suit jacket off the back of his chair and put it on, pulling his shirt sleeves down, before buttoning the top button. She accompanied him to the front door for their goodbyes, and then stood there and watched the car exit the courtyard, prolonging her early morning pleasure for a few more minutes before going back to her bedroom.

As she entered the room, she heard her mother-in-law's aggrieved voice through the connecting door, calling her name.

"Hameeda, Hameeda, where are you? Come here at once."

Was it just a coincidence, or did she wait for the very

second Zubair exited the house to begin her daily demands and complaints. Never easy to deal with, after the death of her husband, she had become even more vexatious. Hameeda had thought life would be easier once her children were out of infancy, but now it was her mother-in-law's cries she was running to answer.

She walked over to the door which offered slim protection from her mother-in-law's intrusiveness. But then, it hadn't been installed for the old woman's convenience. It had been put in when she was pregnant with their first child, Daliya, the adjoining room set up as a nursery. When the children were very young, it had proved to be a great renovation, the door left ajar at night so she and Zubair could hear the smallest whimper or call for attention. But when her father-in-law died, her mother-in-law had insisted on moving from her much larger room at the other end of the house to the adjoining room. Daliya, then age four, and Jameel, age two, had been sharing the bedroom, while three month old Rabia was in a crib in Hameeda and Zubair's room. To accommodate her demand to relocate, Daliya and Jameel were moved to bedrooms across the hall, and for several years afterward, Hameeda never slept well, always worried the children's cries were going unheard. It had also created a problem with Rabia whose asthma and fear of the dark kept her in their room until she was almost nine years old, probably why she was their last child.

"Hameeda, are you there?"

She took a deep breath before entering the room. She saw her mother-in-law still in her night clothes, sitting on the edge of her bed. When Hameeda had first met her, she was only a little overweight, but years of inactivity and devotion to food had drastically altered the landscape of her body. Now, even the tent of her kameez couldn't hide the terraced folds of fat that rolled down the cliff of her chest and abdomen. Despite her age, she retained her vanity and insisted on dying her gray tresses with henna; this chore ceded to Hameeda when the old woman could no longer manage it. This morning her uncombed, orangey-red hair bloomed on white stalks of untended roots, adding another task to Hameeda's weekly list.

"Hameeda, that donkey of a boy has not brought my tea yet."

Her shrill tone plucked at Hameeda's nerves.

"Ammie, we only have the one cook, and he's busy in the kitchen," Hameeda said. "I'll get it for you."

"Well, where's his wife? Let her bring me my tea. I need your help to get dressed."

Her mother-in-law was getting more forgetful lately, not like Hameeda's father, just the normal forgetfulness of old age. For her mother-in-law, the past was no longer stored away like outdated clothes in a trunk, but readily accessible and occupying a space in her mind so close to the present that the two sometimes got confused. Hameeda hesitated before answering, trying to find the most tactful way to inform her of her mistake.

"Ammie, there's just the cook who comes in daily to help with the meals," Hameeda said. "You might be thinking of the couple we had in the house a few years ago." She bent down and retrieved the comforter that had slipped off the bed onto the floor.

"I know that couple left. Do you think I'm senile? There's nothing wrong with my mind." And she tapped her temple with her forefinger as if the solidity of her skull was proof an unaffected brain lay within. "If as you say there's nobody else, get my tea and then help me get dressed."

A damning thought began to form in Hameeda's brain, and she weeded it out before it could take hold. She reminded herself of her duty to be respectful and forgiving, and pushed her unspoken grievances into a far corner of her mind. She still felt guilty, as if her internal dialogue was something observable and subject to judgment. Not for the first time, she worried that her thoughts defined her as much as her deeds.

"Do you want me to help you into the shower before I fetch your tea?"

"And what if I should slip and fall while you're gone? Sometimes I wonder what those two years of college did for you. I'll wait until you get back."

She tried not to take her mother-in-law's comments to heart. But the old woman seemed to find just the right words to penetrate Hameeda's defenses, leaving her feeling battered.

When Hameeda reached the kitchen, she decided to make the tea herself, rather than have the cook do it. She wanted to be sure it was just the way her mother-in-law liked it. Once the tea had steeped the required amount of time, she placed the teapot, a cup, sugar and warm milk on a tray, and started back.

She'd hoped the morning would pass without incident, and give her plenty of time to prepare for the arrival of Jameel's friend and his mother. She knew it was important to Jameel for her to make a good impression. Normally, providing tea for a guest would be routine, but her son had proffered the invitation without consulting Hameeda, and had forgotten to tell her about it until the previous day. It didn't help that he kept asking her about the preparations, his desire for perfection making her anxious. She just prayed her mother-in-law would still go to her friend's house in the afternoon as she had planned and eliminate one worry.

What would her life have been like if she and Zubair had lived in a separate residence? She knew women her age who for one reason or another were not able to move in with their in-laws, starting their marriages in apartments of their own. It was evident from the beginning she and Zubair would move into his parents' large home since Zubair was an only child, born when his parents had resigned themselves to childlessness.

Her old friend Nadira came to mind, sneaking into her thoughts in the same way she had snuck up behind her during her childhood, making her jump when she placed her hands over Hameeda's eyes and whispered, "Guess who?" It was strange she still thought about her and wondered where she was and what she was doing, questions certain to trigger recollections that overpowered her with a bittersweet feeling. Hameeda smiled as she pictured Nadira in her situation. It was doubtful she could have kept quiet, and she envisioned an ensuing civil war that would have had her husband retreating to his own residence within the first year.

Had she known in advance what Zubair's mother was like, would she still have married him? Now, it was impossible to imagine any other life. During their engagement, her mother-in-law had seemed pleased with her, often complimenting her on her beauty, her cooking, and her knowledge of the Qur'an. Not for the first time, she wondered what she'd done early in their marriage to set his mother against her.

Sometimes, she studied the old woman for some word or gesture that would indicate any connection between her and Zubair, but for the most part, she found it incomprehensible that his mother had given birth to him. When Hameeda asked her husband what his mother had been like when he was a child, he drew a picture of a woman very different from the person Hameeda knew.

Even if she had been the person Zubair described, she thought he took after his father, a quiet, gentle man who spent a large part of his time in the library reading. He delighted in finding books he thought Hameeda would enjoy, and once she finished reading his selection, they would sit in the library together after lunch and discuss it. She was very sad when this wonderful man, who had made her feel so welcome, had died so soon after the marriage.

Hameeda was jerked out of her reverie by the sound of

her mother-in-law calling her name, and she picked up her speed, walking as fast as the heavy tray would allow.

"Hameeda, why did it take you so long to bring my tea from the kitchen? I've been waiting here forever."

"I'm sorry to have kept you waiting," Hameeda said as she placed the tea on the trolley near the bed and moved it in front of her. As her mother-in-law dawdled over her tea, she sat in the corner, not saying a word, like a naughty little girl being punished. After helping the old woman bathe and dress, Hameeda had to offer her arm for the walk to the dining room since her mother-in-law refused to use the cane her husband had gotten her. They made slow progress, the old woman's feet shuffling across the floor like polishing cloths, forcing Hameeda to move at a snail's pace. The walk seemed endless. Once Hameeda seated her at the table, she stuck her head into the kitchen and asked the cook to bring in her mother-in-law's breakfast.

When the plate was placed in front of her, she crooked her finger at Hameeda.

"Come here and look at this."

Hameeda looked down at the plate of food. The pale yellow omelet was set but still sheened with moisture, its surface patterned with flecks of minced onion, tomato, cilantro and green chili, and next to it was a chapatti still hot from the tava, its flat surface bubbled and brown, everything still warm and done to her mother-in-law's strict standards.

"It looks fine to me, is there a problem?"

"This is not what I asked for." Glaring at the cook,

the old woman told the servant to take the plate away and bring her two soft boiled eggs, toast and jam.

Hameeda was positive her mother-in-law had not requested anything other than her usual breakfast. She excused herself and went after the cook to apologize for the mix up. If Zubair were here, he would be annoyed. He kept telling her that dealing with last minute changes was part of a servant's job and not to worry about it, but she pictured herself in the servant's place and remained regretful.

The cook shifted from one foot to the other and avoided looking at her while she spoke to him. As she left, she caught him staring at her, an expression of pity imprinted on his face. She could imagine his thoughts, the words as clear as if they had issued from his mouth. You're just as much a servant as I am, not in charge of the household, merely here to dance attendance on the old woman. As she headed back into the dining room, her inadequacies gnawed at her.

She was startled when her mother-in-law asked her to keep her company while she waited for her breakfast. Usually she preferred her own company at this time of day because she said Hameeda's chatter was annoying so early in the morning. Hameeda took a seat opposite her and called to the cook for a cup of tea.

Her mother-in-law granted her one of her rare smiles. It should have pleased Hameeda, but it only made her wary.

"I'm looking forward to spending time with Farah today since we don't often get together. All my other friends are gone and only Farah, my oldest and dearest friend, remains. Did you know our husbands were college class-mates and introduced us when we were both new brides, still young and inexperienced?" her mother-in-law asked. "We've been a comfort to each other ever since."

Hameeda was bewildered by her disclosure since she usually didn't talk about anything of a personal nature. What had prompted her to share this bit of nostalgia?

"It must be wonderful having a close friend for so long," Hameeda said, feeling sad as she remembered when she too had a friendship she thought would last a lifetime.

"Not so wonderful when you're moving to a foreign country and she's staying behind," her mother-in-law said, referring to their upcoming move to Canada, her voice cold and hard.

Hameeda suspected she'd allowed herself to be lured into a trap. This feeling was confirmed when her mother-in-law began to harangue her about their ill-advised decision to leave Pakistan, and accused Hameeda of pushing Zubair into it. If mere assent made her culpable, then Hameeda had no grounds to protest her claim. When Zubair had received the offer of a job as a staff physician at a Canadian hospital, she had agreed with his decision to accept the position despite her misgivings, as she felt a good wife should support her husband.

Really, her mother-in-law should be castigating her son. Despite the unfairness of the attack, it was difficult not to sympathize with her. Hameeda also wanted to stay in Lahore. She had struggled to convince herself that it was a good opportunity for the entire family, career advancement for Zubair, a chance of a better future for their children, and a healthier environment for asthmatic Rabia. But as hard as she strove to maintain a positive attitude, she still felt disheartened every time she faced the details of their exodus. Throughout the visa process, she kept hoping unforeseen bureaucratic red tape would keep them from leaving. After all, so few people obtained visas for entrance into Canada, and she could see no difference between them and family and friends that had been turned down. As Pakistanis they were undesirables, citizens of a nation on the West's list of suspect countries, so why would Canada accept them?

When the five of them went for their visas, they stood outside the Canadian consulate inching forward in a long line for four hours. They watched people enter the building, stacks of documents clutched to their breasts like precious infants, only to come out later, their arms dangling by their sides, looking like they'd aged ten years. As each dejected person exited, Hameeda's mood lightened. But once inside, their interview had only taken about fifteen minutes. A woman had looked over their completed forms, asked a couple of questions and then picked up a stamp and banged it down on each page with a loud thump.

"Your visas are approved, good luck," she'd said with a broad smile.

Suddenly, she realized her mother-in-law had gone silent, and was waiting for a response from her. She tried to remember the last thing she'd heard.

"I don't appreciate being ignored," her mother-in-law

said. "Go do your chores, and tell the cook to hurry up with my breakfast."

As she walked away, she thought about her mother-in-law's attachment to her friend Farah, and how great a loss it would be for her when they moved. It brought Nadira back to mind. There had been no contact between them for the last eighteen years, and when she left the country, she'd lose any chance of ever making amends, her regrets and uncon-fessed repentance carried with her to their new home.

Despite their long estrangement, her memories of her old friend were sharp and clear; their school days and the outside activities they'd shared, even the more important conversations they'd had and the myriad feelings evoked by their friendship. She wished things had been different, that she'd been stronger and had contrived a way to reach out to Nadira before letting their friendship die.

Everything had altered the instant the rock made contact with her dada's head, and she remembered entering a period of confusion when she had sorely needed guidance and her friend. But, Nadira had no longer been approach-able, and she hadn't known who to turn to for advice. Her dada was gone, and her dadi stayed at her prayers longer and longer every day until she was spending most of her time in her room. Her mother was almost always occupied with the needs of her father, trying to act as a buffer between his anger and the rest of the world. When her mother was available, she was harried and distracted. Even her brothers offered her no solace. Avoiding the unremitting gloom at home, they stayed out for most of the day, only appearing for the evening meal. Hameeda had tried to take up as little space as possible, being good, staying silent, afraid if she said the wrong thing, it might be the spark that caused her father to explode. She had never felt so melancholy. It took over a year for some semblance of normalcy to return. And through it all, she suffered the pain of knowing she had deserted Nadira.

Sadness and guilt had haunted her ever since, sometimes muted or even dispelled by life's preoccupations and joys but reasserting themselves now and then in the days' empty spaces – the minutes before sleep came, or right after prayers. If only her life could be rewound like a tape recording; a new track laid over the old one so she could reclaim what she'd once had.

Hameeda wasn't sure how her mind had gravitated to this well-worn path, but she would have to turn it to something else. She wanted today to be enjoyable for all of them, and in an attempt to sweep the past aside, she tackled her chores, focusing on mundane details to forestall any more thoughts of Nadira. Her daily household duties had multiplied as servants became more expensive and unreliable. Now it seemed like all but the very wealthy were trading supervisory roles for tasks for which they'd never received any training. After instructing the cook, she went into the laundry area and pulled the wash out of the machine and into a basket. She took the basket out onto the sunny part of the veranda where she dropped a skin of wet clothes over the skeletons of her drying racks. The rest of her responsibilities were attended to with one ear cocked for her mother-in-law's voice. But all was quiet right up to the time her mother-in-law was picked up by her friend's driver. She helped her into the car, and sighed with relief as it pulled out of the gate.

As she made her way back through the house, she looked around her to see the public rooms through a visitor's eyes. All the furnishings had been here when she arrived; the heavy, fringed curtains, the dark, old fashioned wooden side tables, and the overstuffed couches and chairs covered in outdated, stained fabrics were all her mother-in-law's choices. And when she entertained Arif's mother, the tea would be poured from her mother-in-law's teapot and the food served on her china. The few household items she'd brought with her as part of her dowry and their few wedding gifts languished in a storage closet. Nowhere was there any evidence of her personality or taste. Observing her surroundings, she realized this place she'd lived in for so many years was not her home, and would never be her home as long as Zubair's mother was alive.

Hameeda glanced at the clock, almost 1:30! Where had the morning gone? She must send the driver to collect the children from school, and see how lunch was coming along. When she reached the door of the kitchen, she found the cook washing dishes at the sink.

"Is all the day's cooking done?" she asked.

"Begum Sahib, the gas has gone off," the cook reported.

"Oh no, not again! How far along are you with lunch?" Hameeda said, dismayed it had happened on a day that was so important to Jameel.

"The lunch is done, but I haven't started on the kebabs and samosas for the tea or done any of the cooking for dinner."

Hameeda couldn't believe her bad luck. Load shedding was difficult enough, but at least when there was no electricity they could eat by candlelight. When the gas went, the most she could manage was cold salads and meat paste sandwiches for meals. And now she'd have to rethink what she'd serve with the tea.

"I'll just have to make do with what I have," Hameeda said as she opened the freezer and moved items around until she found a date cake and some pakoras which she handed to the cook.

"You can microwave these for our tea, and maybe the gas will come back on in time for you to make dinner."

"Begum Sahib, when the driver picks up the children, can he get some sugar? The last of it was finished at breakfast."

Sugar had been in short supply for weeks, and having made a futile trip to three stores the previous day, Hameeda knew the shortage would continue for the foreseeable future. But, she couldn't possibly serve tea without sugar. She immediately called her mother to see if she could spare some. When her mother said she had some extra, she left at once, hoping to get back before the children arrived for lunch.

Going home had always been a comfort to Hameeda, the house the same reassuring place it had been in her childhood, and weekly visits inured her to the small, incremental changes in her aging parents. Even the beginning of her father's dementia was so benign it became a family joke, his inability to find his glasses or remember a name a cause for teasing. It was Zubair who had suggested he see a neurologist, and accompanied him to the appointment.

"Did you know your father was beaten up by two of his class fellows in primary school?" Zubair had asked her. "Apparently, he fell and suffered a concussion, and the doctor thinks this brain trauma as a child predisposed him to dementia."

Hameeda had never heard anything about it. Her abu never talked about his years in Karachi, or shared any other stories of his childhood. But, she knew you could never leave the past behind; at any moment it could stretch into the present and grab you.

These days, she was never quite sure if the man she visited would be the father she remembered or a distant relative of the person she'd known. Today when her mother ushered her into the lounge, he was sitting in a chair by the window, his eyes closed, his head tipped up toward a beam of sunshine. Lately, he had developed an affinity for the sun's warmth. He sought it out like the lizards that crept out of hiding early in the morning, the exposure turning his skin dark and wrinkled so he looked much older than his real age. It was almost as if he was making a conscious effort to synchronize his outward appearance with his decline in brain function.

"He's having a so-so day," her mother whispered in her ear.

Her father opened his eyes and smiled.

"You … come…" her father frowned, shook his head, and pounded his fist on the arm of the chair in frustration when his brain wouldn't yield the words he wanted.

"Yes, isn't it nice that Hameeda came for an unexpected visit," her mother said.

"Come …" he said pointing to the chair next to him.

"Sorry, I think he wants you to sit next to him," her mother said, and her father nodded his head in agreement.

Hameeda sat down, and reached out to take his hand. She explained she was there to borrow some sugar and couldn't stay long because she was expecting company. She saw tears well up in his eyes, his dementia pulling emotions up to the surface that used to remain hidden. She stroked the back of his hand and assured him she would return the next day for an extended visit.

In the car, she had to sit for a moment to regain her composure. It still shocked her to see her father this way. Once back home, she gave the sugar to the cook, checked on the children and then went to change her clothes. She worried that in the rush to get ready she had forgotten something. Were her instructions to the cook detailed enough? Had she remembered to have the maid dust the drawing room this morning? It was too late to do anything but hope for the best. She passed her hand over her face as if the gesture would erase the worry lines and turn up the corners of her mouth so she could present a cheerful countenance when she met Jameel's friend and his mother.

Chapter 3

Nadira sat in her back garden staring straight ahead; her eyes sought out a tree branch in the same instinctive way the fingers of a rock climber searched for a solid handhold to keep from falling. She needed something concrete to steady her as she re-examined what had transpired at Arif's friend's house.

Over and over again, she saw the door open and Hameeda standing there; a slightly different version of Hameeda with a rounder face framed by a hijab and a fuller figure, but without a doubt, Hameeda. In the months after their friendship ended, Nadira had daydreamed about bumping into her on the street, or in a shop, or at the cinema, scripting a speech that would be polite but dismissive, forcing Hameeda to beg her forgiveness. But her sudden appearance so many years later left Nadira flustered and mute. How long had the two of them stood there without saying a word? As she waited for Hameeda's reaction, it felt like each second was expanding beyond its normal borders, and she was caught, suspended in time's web. She stared at Hameeda, hoping for a smile, an outstretched hand, the smallest sign of delight, anything that would loosen her stiff limbs and reluctant heart. Finally, Hameeda had said "Nadira?" in a voice bordering on a whisper as she crossed the threshold and moved toward her. A residue of anger had clung to Nadira like the dregs of tea in the bottom of a cup, and she could feel the heat of the scarlet stain that spread across her cheeks.

All those years ago, she had admired Hameeda's goodness, a characteristic that appeared too pure and effortless to be anything but innate, something Nadira couldn't replicate no matter how hard she tried. Because of this trait, she'd judged Hameeda to be incapable of betrayal, and entrusted her with her heart, confident it was in the safest hands. But what had Hameeda done when her family had allied Nadira with the insane mob that caused her grandfather's death? There was no evidence Hameeda had protested, only arguments for her acquiescence - a refusal to speak with her and years of silence. And when the vortex of Ashura had pulled her under, her dreams filled with visions of black cloaked men chasing her through streets slippery with blood, the one person she felt would understand had left her friendless and alone.

Now, the once unknown distance between them had shrunk to an uncomfortable dimension. As Hameeda had advanced, Nadira had stepped back and watched as she visibly stiffened and stopped; her voice tentative, she invited her to come in. But Nadira couldn't imagine doing something as normal as sitting across from Hameeda, sharing tea, acting as if common courtesy could expunge their past. The impulse to flee overcame her, and without the slightest feeling of guilt, she excused herself, inventing a gathering where she was expected.

Now, Nadira struggled with the fact that Arif had been pulled into her troubled past by his friendship with Jameel. She felt as if she had run away from danger only to find herself at the edge of a precipice, trapped, cut off from all safe avenues of retreat. Looking back at their encounter, she realized her reaction had been impulsive and immature. After such a long time, shouldn't she be able to be more dispassionate? But, the collision of her past with the present had created a whirlwind of emotions that stripped her of everything subsequent years had taught her. If there was a way to resolve the impasse between her and Hameeda, she didn't have the will to find it.

When it came time to pick Arif up, she sent the driver. Now she waited for his return, dreading her son's reaction to her abrupt exit, preparing her lines like a child waiting for a scolding. She knew Arif would question her. Unlike his younger brother, he was not a boy who held back. He often showed a lack of awareness of his position in the family, behaving in a manner that sometimes bordered on disrespect. His youthful charm and wit had saved him on many occasions - her fault for allowing herself the luxury of falling prey to it. Admittedly, he deserved an explanation for her rude behavior and the obvious lie. She would have to tell him the truth, or at least some variant of the truth, since she wasn't sure she knew what constituted the truth. She and Hameeda each held their own truth. Would she ever be ready to hear Hameeda's version of it, and would it change anything? Without the answers to these questions, there was nothing she could say to Arif that would satisfy him.

She heard the door open and close, and a few moments later Arif stood in front of her. She looked at him to gauge his feelings. He didn't seem angry, just puzzled, his head cocked to the side, and the skin between his eyebrows pulled into pleats.

"Why?"

That's all he said. Her son, who could fit more words in one breath than anyone she knew, had only one word for her. Whatever she said wouldn't be enough.

"I'm sorry I lied about being expected elsewhere and left so abruptly. Hameeda and I were once friends and had a falling out a long time ago. It's a long, very complicated story and not something I can readily explain to you. You'll just have to trust me."

It was a parental answer she never would have accepted as a child.

"Can I still see Jameel?"

It was painful to hear this question. For once, she was absolutely certain she knew how he felt.

"This has nothing to do with you and Jameel. You can continue on as you have been. If you want to go to his house, I'll arrange to have the driver take you."

"Amma …"

"Arif please, I'm really very tired and would like to be alone."

Arif looked hurt, and uncharacteristically didn't try and argue with her.

Nadira felt the tug of regret as she watched him turn and walk into the house. But her remorse only extended to involving Arif in her private anguish. It didn't change the effect of Hameeda's reappearance which had awakened feelings she thought she'd dispensed with long ago. She searched her heart for forgiveness but it eluded her. Instead, she rediscovered a deep hurt that had never been assuaged.

*   *   *

After Nadira left, Hameeda forced herself to be cheerful with the boys, ignoring what had happened as if it was a normal occurence. She stood talking with them much longer than usual so she could study Arif, hoping to get a glimpse of his mother in him. Physically, he looked nothing like her, but he had an energy that charged the air around him like static electricity, and when he talked, his hands were in constant motion, underlining his words. These Nadira-like qualities made her feel an immediate attachment to him, and she longed to question him about his mother. She knew without asking that her name had never been mentioned in Nadira's house just as Nadira's name had never passed her lips. She was sure the one thing they still had in common was this secret part of their lives kept hidden within them. It would be wrong to ask Arif questions that were Nadira's to answer, so she left them on their own.

Alone in her room, Hameeda thought about all she had lost since her friendship with Nadira dissolved. Though the same age, Nadira had not only been her closest friend but a surrogate older sister, protecting her, teaching her, showing her how to color outside the lines, drawing her into a larger, more vibrant world.

What would she say when Nadira came to pick up Arif? When they were first separated, she had many internal conversations with her, picking words and then discarding them as too weak to express the strength of her emotions. When she finally found the words she wanted, she had practiced them over and over like an assigned poem she had to memorize for class, so even now they were committed to memory. But after so many years, the words she'd chosen had lost their power. Once her father had been the only impediment to their getting back together, now a thicket of obstacles appeared to be in the way, too tangled and thorny to attack with a young girl's vocabulary. The expression on Nadira's face was proof of that – her features collapsing in pain until they were rearranged by anger. If only Nadira had stayed and given her an opportunity to explain, and ask for forgiveness. If she had, Hameeda was convinced, at this very moment, they would be repairing their relationship.

As she struggled to come up with a plan, she remembered an incident that had happened the year before their separation. One day as she was leaving the school building, one of her classmates had hissed an insult at her and bumped into her hard enough to cause her to stumble and drop her books. Nadira had been a few yards behind her and saw what happened. Furious, she'd forced the girl to apologize and stood over her as she picked up Hameeda's things and handed them back. The vehemence of her reaction had not only intimidated the girl but scared Hameeda. She'd felt guilty about failing to defend herself, compelling Nadira to act as her proxy. Afterward, she had hoped her friend's hostility was momentary and would disappear by the next day. But Nadira turned icy, never speaking to the girl again and making disparaging remarks if the girl's name came up in conversation.

Today, that same emotion had been imprinted on Nadira's face, and it had been frightening to be its recipient. Now, she was afraid her old friend's implacability would destroy any chance of regaining their friendship. Was the ability to reconcile already lost? Maybe it was the unexpectedness of their encounter, which had been a shock for both of them, that had caused her reaction. It could be Nadira only needed time to absorb what had happened, and she was worrying needlessly. She imagined Nadira also watching the hands of a clock move with agonizing slowness as she marked time until they would meet again.

Hameeda saw to the boys' tea and then found odd tasks to keep her busy in the vicinity of the foyer, waiting for Nadira to return to pick up Arif and hoping to forestall her from leaving right away. When the driver arrived instead, she was chagrined. Had she been too optimistic in expecting reconciliation, or was she only rushing something that would take more time? She refused to lose hope. It had to be that it was too soon for a conversation. She would wait before contacting Nadira; not too long, just a few days, and then she would call and ask to see her. By then, she would find the healing words she needed.

The Qur'an said that before birth, Allah breathed some of his spirit into each and every soul, where it waited to be manifested. Therefore, forgiveness wasn't just the province of Allah and the prophets, but also within reach of every human being. With all they had meant to each other, surely Nadira's heart would soften, and she would pardon her.

Chapter 4

Salima opened her eyes to the darkened geography of her room, and turned her head to check the time. The luminous, green hands on the face of the ancient wind-up clock indicated it was 1:45 a.m. The late hour blanketed the house in silence, and the only sound that reached her was the occasional shrill tweet of the neighborhood guard's whistle, warning away intruders as he made his rounds up and down the street. A dream had pulled her out of her slumber, a strange fantasy of dark images that fled as soon as her eyes opened, leaving her with no desire to tempt them from their hiding place by returning to sleep. When she had been more mobile, she'd been in the habit of getting up and making herself a cup of hot milk if she was having trouble sleeping – her mother's remedy. But now her shaky sense of balance and her body's weight anchored her to the mattress, and without any other distractions, her unoccupied, restless mind wandered in her past.

She found herself walking through Lahore, heading for the place where she grew up. Red sandstone row houses faced each other across a narrow street; each house had a tiny garden in front with a spindly tree and stunted plants pointing their leaves toward whatever meager sunlight fell between the tightly packed buildings. She stopped and stood before the carved wooden door that would lead her back into her childhood.

Her large family - grandparents, parents, brothers and sisters - had filled the three story house, all the space in every room occupied with no place left for privacy. Viewed from decades later, she could see her fate had been determined in part by the accident of her birth order - born two years after an older brother with three brothers and two sisters following soon after her - and in part by her appearance. Her father was a distant figure having little time for any of his children, and what time he had was spent with his sons. Younger siblings kept her mother busy, and when they no longer needed her constant care, her mother was out of the habit of focusing on her.

A pain shot up her right leg, and she shifted her position to ease its sharpness. She could no longer remember a time when she moved around with not even the slightest ache. She wished she had enjoyed her early years more and paid attention to the pleasures of a young body instead of taking them for granted.

Trying to take her mind off her discomfort, she sank back into a pleasant memory, the sole time she could recall capturing her mother's undivided attention. She must have been about three years old and was howling after a fall scraped the skin off her knee. Two strong arms lifted her up and held her while a hand patted her back. Her mother's cheek touched her cheek, and the breath from her mouth tickled her ear as she soothed her with whispered words until her crying ceased. Salima kept that one memory safe inside her like a precious picture stored in a locket, and gazed at it with her mind's eye whenever she needed comforting.

The annual family portraits showed that from infancy; she had been unattractive with muddy skin, squinty eyes, a receding chin and a nose too large for her face, the ugly duckling in a family of swans. Her only redeeming feature was her hair, falling as straight as a plumb line down the length of her back, as thick and shiny as a panther's coat. Her extended family either ignored her or commiserated with her on the misfortune of her looks. Aunts and uncles would gaze at her and shake their heads, assuming this wouldn't communicate their opinion. Cousins and siblings teased her, calling her names that through conscious effort she'd forgotten. At school things were no different, and she formed friendships based on the shared fate of being cast out of the group. In the crowded house of her childhood and the territory she navigated outside of it, she felt very much alone. Her one consolation was her books; engrossed in their stories she could discard her life for a short while and inhabit the life of someone else.

Thinking back, she realized her childhood had ended when she was thirteen. One evening, her mother had sat her down and told her that after school she would start to take lessons from the old man who did their cooking. She would also help her mother supervise the cleaning, laundry and other household chores.

"Being accomplished at cooking and running a house

will give you an advantage when it comes time for marriage. With the dowry we can afford and your household skills, maybe there will be a suitor who will overlook your homeliness," her mother had told her. Whenever she remembered that conversation, the words still stung.

At age fourteen, she was forced to leave school because her father believed it was more than enough education for a girl. About the same time, her parents let it be known they were looking for a match for her which initiated a parade of suitors through the house. None of them returned for a second visit. Finally, after almost four years, she'd met Daud. Before the first meeting, her youngest sister came to Salima with gossip about him.

"Even though he comes from a good family and is an engineer with an enviable position, he has been rejected by a number of girls," her sister told her. "There must be something terribly wrong with him."

She was sure after so many years of being unclaimed, people were saying the exact same thing about her, and she had resolved not to be too harsh when it came time to judge him.

When Daud walked through the door, she saw a prematurely bald man who was rather nice looking but so thin he appeared to have some kind of wasting disease. He was also so shy he had to be encouraged to speak, and even then he failed to look anyone in the eye. His parents had done most of the talking, and when he spoke, she couldn't make out what he was saying because he mumbled. Then right before they left, his mother asked Salima what she did in her spare time. She told her she liked to read novels and poetry. At once, Daud's head came up.

"What are your favorites?" he asked.

She didn't remember the books she'd listed, but he had also read and enjoyed them. The next visit, while his parents were busy sampling her cooking, she and Daud talked about books. A few days later a marriage proposal was brought to her father, and Salima needed no encouragement to give her acceptance. But her mother still felt it was necessary to tell her how lucky she was such a fine young man wanted to marry her. She had no misgivings about the marriage, and was not the least bit anxious about moving into her in-laws' home. She thought nothing could be as bad as sharing a room with her two sisters and residing in a house where she was ignored most of time, unaware there were worse things that could happen to you.

Surrounded by the formless evening shadows, she considered her life-long struggle to rid herself of the influence of her beginnings and become her own creation. When she left home, she'd thought she could come out from behind the defective lense of her family's opinions, turn herself inside out, and show the world the person that existed behind the façade built by their treatment. Now she realized, even at her advanced age, she still hadn't escaped the childhood that formed her. She was like a burn covered with skin grafts, the new skin never looking natural, a constant reminder of the damage underneath.

From the beginning, her mother-in-law had been very demanding and critical. She kept Salima at her beck and call from early morning until her husband came home. Her time with him was like being served a banquet after months on a bread and water diet. After the evening meal, they would retire to their bedroom. She loved lying next to him as he described his day. Often, they would read to each other from books of poetry and fiction. Day by day, they had fallen in love. After five months, her mother-in-law began berating them about the fact she was not yet pregnant. Salima was just as disappointed as her mother-in-law about her failure to conceive. Almost a year passed before she got pregnant the first time. She lost the baby at four months. She started saying additional prayers for a successful pregnancy, but it still took another year before she got pregnant again. The second time she only carried the baby for three months. Two years later she lost her third child, also at three months. Each time, she and her husband had been devastated.

Her mother-in-law blamed Salima and screamed insults at her, cursing the day she'd agreed to the match. After the third miscarriage, her mother-in-law tried to convince her husband to divorce her, but in his only show of strength during their entire marriage, he refused. From then on she was hounded by Daud's mother. Nothing she said or did was good enough. When she displeased her mother-in-law, she would get a hard slap or a pinch. If her mother-in-law was in a particularly bad mood, she would beat Salima with a ladle, a mop handle, or whatever instrument was closest to hand. These beatings often left her with swollen, red welts or painful bruises. And as much as her husband loved her, he was too weak to stand up to his mother. Year after year, Salima did her duty to Daud's family, behaved in a righteous manner and like Abraham's wife Sarah, prayed for a child. It was her belief that Allah finally took pity on her. At age thirty-nine, a year after her mother-in-law's death, she gave birth to Zubair.

Salima heard the tchak, tchak, tchak of a gecko climbing the plastered concrete wall above her head. It reminded her of today's visit with her friend Farah. They had been sitting outside in her garden when a lizard had scampered up the leg of her chair and stared at her with an impertinent expression before she shooed it away with her hand. She had so enjoyed her friend's company today. She imagined her daughter-in-law thought she spent her visit with her friend complaining about her. Neither she nor her friend wasted their precious time grumbling, although they agreed that the life of a widow was harder than they could have imagined. Instead they talked over old times and read the Qur'an together. However, today her friend had complained about her grandson's behavior after he passed through the lounge where they were sitting, wires snaking from his ears to some device he had in his hand. The boy had actually waved at them instead of coming over and greeting them in a proper manner. Her friend was so embarrassed and Salima had comforted her, telling her manners were no longer taught the way they had been when they were children. It was a small lie, one she didn't regret telling if it made Farah feel better. However, she had always been very strict about manners with her son, and spent much more time with him than most mothers of her generation. She remembered how it was.

She and her husband doted on Zubair. When he was an infant, Daud would come home from work early so he could play with him before they put him down for the night. Salima hadn't used a nanny and did everything for him, including changing his nappies. Whenever they went out, her son went with them, and when he started school, she insisted on sitting in the back of the classroom for the first two weeks. Zubair was a well behaved, thoughtful child who had rarely caused them any worry. As she took care of daily chores, he often followed her around the house, watching what she did and asking a question when something puzzled him. His company always lightened the drudgery of her day. The three of them had been a very close, happy family. But as her son got older, he started turning to Daud more and more. Part of it, she'd always reasoned, was just a boy's affinity with his father, and part of it was their common interest in math and science. Also, as he got older, her lack of a formal education beyond age fourteen seemed to have discouraged conversation between them. By the time he was getting ready for University; he spent most of his time with his friends or his father and had little time for her.

One day, a day she would never forget, Salima heard shouting from the library. Concerned, she'd hurried in, and found Zubair holding up an envelope as he and his father danced around in excitement.

When she asked what the commotion was about,

Daud explained that their brilliant son had gotten a scholarship to Oxford.

"Oxford? Is that a new school; I've never heard of it."

Both of them laughed making her burn with embarrassment.

"Oxford is a very famous university in England," her son said.

"England? I thought you were living at home and going to Government College here in Lahore." How could she allow her only child, her heart's blood, to go so far away? It was unthinkable.

Her son explained that at first he had planned to go to college in Lahore, but when the opportunity arose to put in an application for an Oxford scholarship, his father thought it was worth a try.

"Why wasn't I told about this?" She felt the old sense of exclusion, the pain of it heightened by the unexpectedness of its origin.

Her husband told her they didn't know what his chances were and didn't want her to worry unnecessarily. If he got in, it would be a nice surprise for her. Remembering her husband's excited, smiling face, she wondered if he had ever known her, or she him.

She argued it would be much better if Zubair stayed home and went to Government College. Everyone told her it was a first rate college, and England was too far away. If something should happen to him, if he suddenly needed them, they would be unable to reach him.

Her son's face fell, and he turned and looked at his father.

Daud hadn't hesitated. "It was Zubair's decision. If he wanted to accept the scholarship, they should let him go." Then he'd asked their son what he wanted to do, and she'd held her breath, waiting for her life to continue or end.

And without knowing the devastating effect of his determination on her, Zubair had chosen to leave home and go to Oxford.

"Then it's settled," her husband said without even glancing at Salima.

Although she hadn't said anything, she never forgave her husband for allowing their son to leave. But, once Zubair was gone, Daud suffered the pain of his absence just as she had, and she relinquished her hold on her resentment. Yoked together by memories and habit, she and her husband clung to each other, rediscovering the closeness they'd felt when they were first married.

Once at Oxford, her son only returned home during summer vacations, and then he was busy at one job or another he got with his father's assistance. He continued with medical school in England during which time he had only come home twice, and when he was doing his training, he hadn't come home at all. When he finally returned to stay, he was no longer the boy she knew but a quiet, confident man with no need for her.

Salima remembered how certain she had been that she could ensure the future happiness of her son and herself by finding him the perfect wife. His wife would be like her own daughter, the second child she'd never had and a bridge between her and Zubair. She would give the girl advice on how to please her son, and they would commiserate over the common foibles of their husbands. The last year of his medical training, she thought about the personal qualities that would satisfy both their needs, and started investigating marriageable girls. Even now she remembered how naïve she had been, so sure of her ability to make the correct choice, as if she could discern the fabric of a girl as easily as that of a garment. But in the beginning, her ignorance kept her happy.

She had been very patient, waiting a month for Zubair to settle in before she broached the subject of marriage.

"Beta, now that you have a steady income, you must find a wife and start providing me with grandchildren."

"Amma, I'm just starting my career; I think we should wait until I get established," her son said, turning to his father for support.

"No, your Amma is right. You shouldn't wait until you're too old."

"All right, you can start looking, but I don't want someone who is only interested in clothes and parties. She must enjoy staying at home and have similar interests."

She and her husband had smiled at each other. Unlike his choice of college, this time they had been in agreement. Salima made sure of that.

"We understand beta. We'll find someone you'll like," Salima told him.

Zubair was introduced to several girls, but before he could decide if he liked any of them, she had wielded her veto power because they did not meet her exacting standards. Finally, her husband suggested the niece of one of his friends and from what he related to Salima, she sounded very promising.

The first time she met Hameeda, she was sure she was the right person for her son. She had fair skin and was very pretty. She also had a modest way about her and was not forward like some of the girls they had met. In addition, she had some cooking skill, something rare in those days. Her husband had also liked Hameeda, and after a few visits they asked Zubair if he would accept the match, and without hesitating, he said yes.

Once they were married, Hameeda moved in with them. Salima had spent a great deal of time doing over Zubair's bedroom. She had the walls repainted and bought a floral patterned bedspread and curtains in pale shades of green and pink. Her daughter-in-law had brought some bedroom furnishings as part of her dowry and what was lacking she purchased for her. Pleased with what she'd done, her husband said he hoped it would help Hameeda feel welcome.

But when Hameeda first arrived, Salima perceived a weakness in her that she hadn't noticed before. Her new daughter-in-law always seemed at the edge of tears, and her once warm smile had become half-hearted. Salima also thought she visited her mother far too often. It was true Zubair had worked long hours, and most of Hameeda's friends were still busy with college, so it was rare for her to have visitors, but was that so terrible? Salima hadn't remembered being so afflicted when she was first married and thought her daughter-in-law was putting on an act to get attention. And, it worked. Her husband made a special effort to keep Hameeda entertained, taking her for walks and having her join him in the library after lunch, so he could share selected poems with her. Her son also tried to keep her spirits up, and whenever he was home, they would go out to a restaurant for dinner, visit friends or closet themselves in their room. When she passed their door, she heard pieces of conversation or sometimes laughter, and felt left out.

Hameeda took over Zubair's life and made Salima feel like the outsider. After all those years of his being away, years counting the days until he would return, she'd lost him again. She also resented the time her husband spent with her daughter-in-law, and found it difficult to respond to him in the same loving way. Her husband acted puzzled and hurt by her new attitude, but feeling pushed aside and ignored, as she had been as a child, gave her reason enough for her behavior. She waited for Daud to recognize the unfairness of what he was doing and turn away from Hameeda and back to her. After her husband was gone, she was mired in regret over their lost intimacy and the hours with him she'd missed during their last few years together. Hameeda was to blame for all of this.

At least she couldn't fault her daughter-in-law for not providing her with grandchildren. Her granddaughter, Daliya, was born ten months after the wedding, soon followed by her grandson and younger granddaughter. Daud had loved his grandchildren and would somehow bend his arthritic joints, and play with them as he had once done with Zubair. Salima, who had been impatient as she awaited their births, found she was not as enthusiastic once they arrived. In her seventies, she couldn't bear the noise and running around, and she no longer had the patience for playing and talking with them like her husband. By the time they were old enough for her to take an interest in them, the children viewed her as an old woman requiring respect and deserving politeness, but with whom they had only a genetic connection. She blamed her daughter-in-law for this as well, believing Hameeda had turned the children against her.

And when Salima decided life could not be any worse, Daud died and left her to manage on her own. After decades of marriage, she had been set adrift without anyone to anchor her days.

Tears wet her cheeks, drawing her out of remembrance and back into the solidity of her darkened bedroom. Bereft, she tallied up what was left to sustain her in her last years. She had one remaining friend whose memory stretched back as far as hers and who saw the world the way she saw it. When it came to family, Zubair, Hameeda and the children were a planet unto themselves, and she a distant satellite orbiting around them. In her loneliness and despair, she cried out to Allah and asked what she'd done to receive such a small measure of happiness and then have it taken away.

Chapter 5

The spill of light from her bedside lamp pushed away the gloom in her room, and she wished it could dispatch her brooding just as easily. Was it only two days ago she'd had her unexpected meeting with Hameeda? Nadira felt as if her control over events had been compromised for much longer. When she was unoccupied, like now, she was aware of the hectic pumping of her blood and thoughts racing through her mind too fast for her to hold on to any one of them. The last couple of nights Hameeda had appeared to her in strange dreams and stayed with her after she woke up. She tried to distract herself by focusing on the page in front of her, but the printed words would not stay still, and her old friend's face appeared before her like an apparition.

Years ago, she had banished Hameeda from her world, convinced that because she was absent from her life, she had also left Lahore and relocated not just to another school but to a distant city or even a foreign country. Of course in retrospect, this had been a self-protective mechanism that made no sense. Confronted with reality, she could no longer deceive herself with a childish fantasy. Hameeda was still in Lahore, so close by it was amazing their paths had never crossed before.

At least she hadn't tried to contact her – Nadira had expected it, and started every time the phone rang, but there was no call. The girl she remembered would have called, but her old friend must have changed, just as she had, the passage of time refashioning both of them. She should be relieved but for some reason wasn't. She frowned, annoyed at herself for letting Hameeda remain in her thoughts. She tried to remember what formula had worked to drive Hameeda's spirit away the last time. Focus on something else, she told herself. If you allow her to take root in your mind now, she will plague you for another night. What did the advice columns tell you to do to relax? Think pleasant, happy thoughts, and turn your mouth up in a smile to call up a corresponding emotion. Unfortunately, her mind found nothing pleasing to latch onto, and the corners of her mouth would not cooperate.

These days, nothing seemed to be going right. Sohail was still not his old self, and Arif, who had always come to her with his goings on, thoughts and complaints, had stopped talking to her. She missed their old comradery but knew Arif's current reticence was her fault.

Now, she was waiting for Sohail. Hours ago, he had telephoned saying he wouldn't arrive home until quite late, giving her no further explanation. She accepted that owning a business often meant irregular hours, but the occasional late night had now become a weekly event. She assumed the factory had finished a large order on a tight deadline and he was double checking the shipment before it went out, and would stop somewhere for dinner on the way home. Waiting for his return, Nadira felt empty, as if her heart had slipped from the cage of her ribs and drifted away, leaving a cavity behind. Once again, she tried to immerse herself in her book while she waited, but her inner turmoil interfered with her concentration.

She remembered a dream she'd had a few weeks ago. She was at one end of a long corridor, and Sohail was at the opposite end. She ran forward, reaching out for him, but no matter how fast she pumped her legs, she never got any closer. When he turned and started walking away, she yelled, "Sohail, come back." She threw the words out like a fisherman casting his net to capture an elusive fish. He didn't stop or even turn his head, traveling farther and farther away. The only thing that came back to her was the echo of her own voice.

She closed the book lying open on her lap and moved over to her dressing table. Picking up her brush, she began running it through her hair in preparation for going to bed. A minute later, she heard footsteps coming down the hall, and Sohail called her name in a soft voice. She waited for him, not moving, her arm stretched out on the dressing table, her fingers still locked around the brush. Soon, his reflection joined hers in the mirror. He reached out his hand and stroked the hair on the back of her head. When he came to the end where her tresses brushed her collar bone, his hand continued down her back as if stroking the ghost of the length that had once been there.

Bending down he whispered in her ear, "How is my choti billi?"

Nadira smiled, and happiness flooded in, drowning all her dark thoughts. He hadn't called her little cat for a long time. Early in their marriage, he'd told her she reminded him of a tabby he'd had as a child - both soft and fiercely independent. It warmed her heart to have him use this language from their earliest days together.

"Your choti billi missed you," she said in almost a whisper as she turned to him.

"That's reassuring," He pulled her up into an embrace which she settled into, wanting to stay nestled up against his chest as long as possible.

"I'll just get ready for bed; be right back," he said as he eased out of her arms.

She contemplated how a few well-chosen words and an embrace could dispel the sense of unease that had dogged her the last few weeks.

A short time later, he returned, slid into bed beside her, and pulled her close. "You never told me about meeting Arif's friend Jameel," he said, nuzzling her neck. "Is he as amazing as Arif claims?"

Nadira had never spoken to him about Hameeda. She had walled off that part of her past, deciding it was useless to talk about something unsettling and long over. And, she'd avoided mentioning what had happened when she'd dropped Arif off at Jameel's house. She didn't know where to begin the recitation of her history with her old friend, or how to explain her reaction on seeing her. Would her husband think she'd been unreasonable? He wasn't the sort of person to hold a grudge, and she didn't want to tell him something that would result in a lecture, or change his view of her. No matter how understanding he generally was, only someone who had lived those years with her could comprehend how she felt.

"He seemed like a very nice young man," she said, and then changed the subject. "What kept you so long at the office?"

"Just a little busier than usual."

"Why, what's going on?"

"Nadira, when I come home I want to relax, not discuss the business. I'm tired; let's go to sleep." His voice sounded tense as he reached up and turned off the lamp next to the bed.

"Sohail, is something wrong?"

"Everything is fine. Now, can we go to sleep?" And he rolled onto his side away from her.

His denial didn't change her certainty that something was amiss, and she was hurt that he didn't feel he could discuss it with her. And, her question had ended their brief moment of intimacy. She wished she could take it back. Settling down proved to be difficult; her thoughts did gymnastics in her head, and her limbs wandered restlessly back and forth between the sheets long after her husband's even breathing indicated he'd fallen asleep. It seemed like hours before she finally dozed off.

Nadira woke up just as tired as when she went to bed. As they both got ready for their day, Sohail's cheerfulness held a false note. It had been this way for the past few months; he sometimes seemed to be playacting or was so preoccupied he was present, yet absent. When they spoke to each other, their conversations were limited to the minutiae of everyday life or the children. We could both be politicians, she thought. We say so much without really saying anything at all. This distance in their conversations made her feel as if she was living a singular existence.

Later that morning, Nadira was already engrossed in her daily routine, studiously avoiding troubling thoughts about her husband and her friend. Her body weighed her down, and she felt as if she was moving in slow motion. It didn't help that the sweeper hadn't shown up for the second day in a row. She guessed she'd gone home to her village because of some sudden family problem. There was no way to find out the reason for her absence or when she would return since she had no phone. Without the sweeper's presence, the house showed evidence of Lahore's dry, dusty climate in an instant. An army of dust motes parachuted down from above, invisible until they drifted across a searchlight of sunshine. Regiments of them collected on tabletops and congregated in large parade formations on the floor. She sat with a cloth in her hand and watched the invasion as if the specks were some new micro species she was classifying for further study. The gate buzzer pulled her out of her pensiveness, and she hurried to answer the intercom.

"Who is it?"

It was the driver shared by her father's two older sisters.

"Just a minute, I'll have someone open the gate."

In one swift movement she slipped the dust cloth into

a drawer. Once outside, she asked the part-time gardener to open the gate and then stood at the bottom of the front steps to wait for her aunts. After the car was parked, the driver helped the old women out. A stranger would never guess they were sisters. Although they were both short, Saabira had a slim, angular body and a narrow face with a long nose, the same almond shaped eyes Nadira had inherited, and full lips bracketed by the deep parentheses of age. She wore her grey hair cut in a short bob. If Saabira could be described as a number one, then Afrah was a number eight. She had large breasts that strained at the fabric of her kameez, a narrow waist and large hips. Her face was a generous oval with the same long nose, deep set eyes hooded by heavy lids and a down-turned mouth. She had kept her still youthful, black hair long and pulled it back in a bun at the nape of her neck. Nadira walked over and greeted them.

"As salaam aleikum, Afrah Auntie, Saabira Auntie, what a nice surprise," She leaned over and hugged them both.

"Nadira, I hope we're not disturbing you, "Saabira said.

"No, it's wonderful seeing you," she replied, wondering if the lie had rearranged her features in a noticeable way. She led them into the drawing room. "Please sit down while I go make us some tea. I'll just be a minute."

"Don't go to any trouble for us," they said in unison.

"It's no trouble at all; I'll be right back."

As she prepared the tea, she cursed the cultural habit of showing up uninvited at the doorstep of family and friends, creating all sorts of problems. It wasn't that she didn't love her aunts, she did, but sometimes their timing was unfortunate. Widowed and in their late 70's, with all their children having immigrated overseas, they did little with their time besides making the rounds. It was just bad luck they'd chosen her house as their destination today.

Once she'd served the tea and passed the plate of snacks, Nadira reclined in her chair, and decided since there was nothing she could do about it; she might as well enjoy the unexpected interruption in her day.

"We were just talking about the sad state of help these days," Afrah said as she filled a plate with biscuits and two heaping spoonfuls of fruit chaat.

"Were we?" Saabira asked, raising her eyebrows. "I don't remember that subject coming up."

Nadira suppressed a sigh. It was obvious her aunt had noticed the condition of her house, and she was sure to add it to her list of stories when she visited other family members, including her mother. At least she could try and minimize the damage. She proceeded to agree with her aunt's statement and complained that her sweeper hadn't shown up for the last two days, in the hope this information would account for the state of things.

Afrah recalled how loyal and reliable servants had been when they were children; hired in their teens and growing old in their family's service. She lamented the fact that it was now difficult to keep servants for more than a couple of years.

"It must be you, Afrah," Saabira said, putting down

her cup and looking at her sister. "My servants have been with me for many years."

"Why would they leave? You treat them like they're your family," Afrah said, waving the hand holding her half consumed biscuit in a dismissive motion and scattering crumbs across her chest. "You know Nadira, the other day I stopped by Saabira's, and she was serving the sweeper tea!"

Saabira reached over and brushed crumbs off the front of her sister's kameez. "Afrah, you have no compassion. The woman has been with me for fifteen years and is nearly as old as I am. She had already done most of the work and just needed a bit of a sit down before she finished."

"See what I mean."

"What do you hear from my cousins?" Nadira asked, in an attempt to divert the conversation to a safer subject.

"They're all doing well and are very busy. I was hoping they would visit soon, but it doesn't seem likely," Afrah sighed deeply. "Life is very difficult and very lonely when you're by yourself. If it wasn't for your brother Asim, I wouldn't have anyone I could turn to for help. He's such a good boy. And thank goodness Saabira lives next door. I've often thought we should save on expenses and move in together, but she thinks it's a bad idea."

"It's a terrible idea Afrah; think of my mental health," Saabira said, the corners of her mouth twitching.

"What on earth are you talking about, Saabira? Sometimes you say the oddest things."

Saabira raised her eyebrows at Nadira, and she had trouble suppressing a laugh. Despite their arguments, she knew they were very attached to each other. Maybe it was the contentiousness of their relationship that kept them so lively.

"But Afrah is right about one thing," Saabira pulled one end of her dupatta, which had slipped off her shoulder, back into place. "With all the young people emigrating, there are a lot of elderly people like us, living on our own without any help in an emergency."

"Yes, and it seems young people will go anywhere just to get out of the country," Afrah said, nodding. "My friend's son moved to Sweden. Can you imagine? He didn't even take ice in his coke because he said it was too cold, and now he's living in the frozen North. But who can blame them. Load shedding, shortages of our most basic needs and terrorists have made our lives so difficult. It's all due to interference by CIA operatives of the United States."

Nadira sighed. "Whether or not that's true, we should find ways to solve our own problems."

"But what can we do?" Afrah said, shrugging her shoulders. "Either our ineffective, corrupt politicians are thrown out by military coups, or at the next opportunity we elect more of the same."

Nadira wasn't sure if her aunt's question was rhetorical or not, but she chose to ignore it. Political discussions went on all the time, no matter where you were or who you were with. Conspiracy theories attributing their woes to outside elements circulated daily. People talked and talked and talked, creating edifices out of words. Some people had complex ideas that were like elaborate, elegant buildings while others built crude structures from many uninformed and unconsidered opinions. All the babble created a continuous background noise, changing nothing. Their economy was as legless as a double amputee being both a victim of the lack of overseas investment and a bloated defense budget. Years of political wrangling and corrupt politicians lining their pockets had held up infrastructure projects like dams, so they were living with water shortages and a lack of adequate electricity and gas. These fragile threads that kept them tethered to the modern world were stretched more and more every year, closer to their breaking point. In addition, there was continual conflict between local factions, an increase in terrorist attacks, a justice system that ran on bribes and influence, and the constant threat of war with India. All this made life uncomfortable and precarious. Sometimes she parsed all that she saw, heard, and read but still couldn't come up with any possible solutions to their problems. It was like being lost in a labyrinth. Each corner turned, each path chosen led you deeper and deeper into the maze and farther and farther from finding the way out. She would finish these sessions with an aching head and a depression that lingered for hours.

What if she and Sohail stayed in Pakistan and their children decided their only option was to leave? It was difficult to even imagine them out of the house never mind thousands of miles away. So much of her life revolved around her sons, her feeling for them unique and unyielding. A voice on the phone would never satisfy her need to have them physically present. Her heart ached with loss just thinking about a separation.

Nadira brought her attention back to the conversation and realized her aunts had moved on to another subject. She abandoned her mental meandering and listened to them with her full attention. For the next hour, Afrah gossiped about family, friends, acquaintances and strangers, her only criteria being that the story had to be colorful or scandalous. Saabira confined herself to mocking Afrah or commenting on current news reports. When they had appeared at her door, she had been dismayed at the inconvenience, but in the end her aunts brought her a welcome distraction.

Right before they left, Afrah went to the toilet, and she was alone with Saabira.

"Remember our lunches at the Gymkhana Club when you were a little girl?" Saabira asked.

"Yes, they were a special treat. I felt so grown-up giving my order and being served by the waiters in their white turbans and black sherwanis. My mouth is watering just thinking about their fancy cakes."

"Well, you look like you could use an afternoon out," Saabira said peering at her. "I'm still a member; why don't we have lunch together next week."

"That sounds lovely; thanks for the invitation," she said and gave her aunt a hug.

Saabira looked like she was about to ask her something else when Afrah walked into the room.

"Thank you for the tea, Nadira," Afrah said. "It was such a nice visit."

"It was wonderful seeing both of you."

She walked them to the car and waved as they drove away. As she went back into the house, she couldn't prevent her worries about Sohail and the problem of Hameeda from resurfacing and trapping her like an animal caught in a snare.

Chapter 6

Hameeda had come into the library for a book when exhaustion folded her into a chair and thoughts of the previous week held her there. The beginning of the week had been uneventful, and the only thing that stood out in her mind was how upset she'd been with Jameel over an ink stain on his brand new shirt. Now, she couldn't imagine her concern over something so trivial. If she'd known what would happen next, she would have gathered in the quiet of those ordinary days to serve as a cushion, and steeled herself for what was to come. But not knowing, she was unprepared for the landslide of events, one tumbling into another.

It began three nights ago when her mother-in-law's screams had pierced the connecting door to their bedroom. Hameeda was jerked awake. Confused, she blinked to adjust her eyes to the lamp-lit room. She noticed the empty space in the bed where Zubair should have laid, and heard his mother exclaiming over and over again, "My legs, my legs, I can't move my legs." The words became tangled with a nightmare she'd been having, and she had trouble making sense of them. Maybe the old woman had also had a disturbing dream, and once her husband got her calmed down, they could all go back to sleep. But when she entered the room, she saw Zubair was by his mother's side, his medical bag opened on the bed. She watched still half-asleep and muddled, as he did a quick examination, questioning her, shining a pen light in her eyes, prodding her feet with a pointed instrument and testing her reflexes with a rubber mallet. When she heard him tell his mother he'd make arrangements to have her admitted to the hospital, Hameeda had wondered if this was an attempt to placate her.

The seriousness of the situation had only hit her when she saw the two ambulance attendants enter the room with a stretcher. She knew Zubair would never frivolously tie up resources that might be needed elsewhere.

It's odd what the mind holds on to and what it discards. The events of that night appeared to her like an out-of-focus picture except for her recollection of the men who had transported her mother-in-law. That memory was strangely clear and detailed. Maybe it was because they'd been such an odd couple, one young, tall and scrawny, and the other appearing to be middle-aged with grey hair, and as square as a box except for a large, protruding paunch. They'd looked incapable of lifting his mother's considerable weight but had somehow managed it. She wondered what type of person would spend their life suspended between boredom and adrenalin pumping, life and death moments. What did they do between calls? Were they also pulled out of sleep, rubbing their eyes and fumbling for keys as they ran for their vehicle, or had they waited up night after night, carrying on aimless conversations while downing multiple cups of tea, and smoking cigarette after cigarette until their butts overflowed an ashtray?

A line of sunlight slipped through the narrow space between the closed curtains and the window casing and landed on her hand, rousing her from her musing. In the dimness of the library and submerged in a dark mood, she had forgotten the day was sunny and pleasant. Maybe she should open the curtains and let some light in, but she couldn't find the energy. Held in place by her despondency, she yearned to be somewhere else, to be home. She remembered how it felt to be cosseted by her mother and longed to inhabit her old room, sleeping and waking in a space devoid of another person's presence. How wonderful it would be to spend a day without thought or motion, held within a calming stillness like the dreamless quiescence when sleep first overtakes you. A moment later, the light-bleached band of skin decorating her hand disappeared and the room's gloominess deepened. Maybe it was a cloud passing across the sun, a portent of further evil. She shivered, remembering.

Hameeda had always dreaded Zubair's rare absences from home. No matter that her mother-in-law, the children and the servants were there, the house always felt empty when he was gone. When his mother was hospitalized, he had stayed with her, reviewing tests that provided no clues to her paralysis and sleeping on a cot in her room. Despite missing him, she had been glad he felt it more important that she stay home with the children. She was sure Zubair's loving attention was more beneficial than her dutiful presence. What could she do for a woman with whom she had the most tenuous relationship?

By the second day of her mother-in-law's hospital stay, Hameeda had felt obliged to visit. Her mother volunteered to pick up the children after school and suggested they stay for dinner, removing any excuse she might have had to stay away. She told her husband she would come to see his mother in the afternoon.

She recalled meeting Zubair in the lobby, a memory attached to an astringent, antiseptic smell that would forever trigger in her mind what came after. His phone had rung and after he'd held it to his ear for a moment, she saw the color leach from his face. Everything that followed was a tangle of recollections tripping over each other. Zubair had pushed through the crowd surrounding the reception desk, ignoring the protests of those in his way and asked the woman to page two nurses. The woman had consulted a list and told him both of them were absent, one on leave and the other out sick. He had grimaced and shaken his head before turning and grabbing her by the arm. As he pulled her along a corridor, he said something about an attack on a shrine, and told her they could use her help with the patients' families. When they entered the emergency room, fear had gripped her as images of the Ashura riot passed through her mind in rapid bursts like sunlight bouncing off a distant mirror. Was it then she'd pulled back? But, it was too late. An instant later, she heard the blaring of ambulance sirens. Watching through the glass doors, she saw them squeal to a halt. Behind the ambulances, a number of cars fanned out. Victims were handed down from the emergency vehicles while the doors of the cars were flung open, disgorging men carrying wounded in their arms like oversized packages. A stream of stretchers entered, and the room was flooded with people. Bellowed instructions competed with shrieks and moans, the clamor making it difficult to differentiate the screams of the injured from the cries of panicked relatives. A nurse winnowed the crowd, separating out the uninjured like chaff from wheat, then sent them in Hameeda's direction. Nothing seemed real, and she moved toward these unknown people as if in a dream. Hameeda was not sure it mattered what she said, and spoke in what she hoped was a calm voice as she went from one person to the next. She found once she got them seated, either incomprehension held them in place, or they were so agitated, they wandered about like lost dementia patients she had to retrieve again and again. Victims kept coming, overwhelming the capacity of the emergency room. Some of the less serious cases were moved into one part of the lounge area. Despite a queasy stomach, Hameeda found it impossible to look away. Colors took on new meaning; the bloody crimson which painted the doctors' coats in abstract designs, the striated pink of muscle and the white of protruding bone. Later, disconnected scenes from the day would flash through her mind like a poorly spliced film; a sobbing mother pried from her son so the doctors could check his injuries; a woman who kept looking for her husband despite being told repeatedly he had died; and a man clutching a cold cup of tea like a talisman, while waiting for news about his wife and daughter. Soon she could read expressions with a fluency founded on repetition: the blank shocked stare, the grimace of pain and the relaxed smoothness of relief. Faces of strangers became as familiar to her as her own family, and their grief became her grief.

It was early evening before Hameeda was conscious of the imposition of some sort of order. Zubair never reappeared but sent a nurse who told her their driver was picking her up, and she should go home. It was only then she remembered her own children and called her mother. Fortunately, they were just finishing up dinner and had not thought anything was amiss. Hameeda heard conversation in the background and recognized Jameel's voice. She told her mother she'd been delayed at the hospital, without giving any explanation that might elicit questions she couldn't answer yet. Thinking of them sitting around the dinner table, talking and laughing, untouched by this latest attack, was a welcome bit of normalcy she desperately needed. She asked her mother if she would wait and drop the children off after she reached home. Her mother told her she'd leave as soon as she got her call.

Last night, on the way back from the hospital, she'd been astounded to find the familiar streets of Lahore were unchanged by the bombing. The shops and restaurants were open for business, and people carried on as if nothing had happened. But she was not the same. The experiences of the last few hours had left her feeling different in a way she couldn't define. It was as if her life had become an earthquake zone, the ground beneath her no longer solid but instead shifting and keeping her off balance. She'd thought about her unresolved issues with Nadira and again promised herself she would call her in the next couple of days. The thought of something happening to her before she was able to explain and apologize had been unbearable.

Sunk in her chair, she heard footsteps coming down the hall accompanied by the sound of Rabia's coughing. Even sunshine couldn't dispel the smog that curtained the sky in a brown haze, worsening her attacks. Hameeda looked up as her daughter walked into the room, a hand shielding her mouth, as each cough bent her slim frame forward like a sapling in a heavy wind. It hurt to watch her struggle for each breath. If only Rabia's asthma was an external burden like her school backpack, one she could lift off and place on her own shoulders.

"Amma, I've been looking all over for you. Do you know when Abu will be home? He promised to help me with my science project."

Hameeda tucked her daughter into the curve of her arm, reached up to push the sweat dampened hair off her forehead, and kissed her on the cheek. Thinking of all the children lost in the attack, she didn't want to release her from her protective custody, but Rabia grew impatient and squirmed in her embrace.

She told her daughter her father would be home for a short while that afternoon, and after reminding her to use her inhaler, she reluctantly let her go. The interruption motivated her to get up and look for a book to take with her to the hospital the next day. Once again, she was resolved to visit her mother-in-law, but she felt it necessary to arm herself with an aid to interaction; a book to read to her.

She switched on the lamp on her father-in-law's old desk. She still thought of this room as his library. If he could somehow return, he would find his sanctuary unchanged since his death. She stepped over to one of the bookcases and opened its doors; the volumes gave off a musty smell, and she thought she could still detect the faint odor of his cigarettes. It was as if he had left a bit of himself behind to keep her company. And for an instant, she was positive she saw the reflection of his gentle face in the glass pane of the door. Nadira had called these manifestations of what Hameeda considered a sixth sense, her overactive imagination, and lectured her on reason and the laws of physics. But, she knew there were things in the world beyond human understanding, as incomprehensible as Allah, blessed be his name, and as invisible as the angels sent to watch over them.

Hameeda studied the titles on the book spines, and selected a volume of Wordsworth's poems. She was sure the old woman would be pleased she had remembered her affinity for this poet. As she held the book, her imagination created a scene of her visit. A companionable conversation played out in her mind, along with a vivid picture of the transformation in her mother-in-law as she responded to her thoughtfulness. She knew this was the hope of an optimist, but she couldn't seem to help herself. As far back as she could remember, her mind had the habit of constructing cheerful scenarios whether or not previous experience warranted them. Aware the trait often led to disappointment, she still couldn't seem to adopt a more realistic outlook.

As she passed by the foyer, Zubair was entering the house, his jacket slung over his shoulder and a newspaper in his hand. He was disheveled and when he came up to her, she saw he hadn't shaved and his eyes were bloodshot.

"You look like you could use some rest," she said as she put her arms around him, and felt the roughness of his beard abrade her cheek.

"I'll feel much better after I clean up and have something to eat more palatable then cafeteria food," he said smiling at her and taking her hand. Walk with me to the bedroom, and tell me what I've missed here at home."

Hameeda filled her husband in on household matters, remembering to mention Rabia's need for a consultation on her science project. What an ordinary exchange it was, she thought, even while the horror of the attack still lingered; life went on as if this monstrous event was a mere wrinkle in the fabric of their lives.

When her husband went to shower, she picked up the newspaper he'd dropped on the bed and took it into the lounge. There was a large headline on the front page, "Suicide Bombers Attack Sufi Shrine." Who would have thought something like this could happen in Lahore? She remembered her dada calling Lahore the cultural capital of the country, without the group conflicts of Karachi. He had taken them on tours of the ancient architectural sights, and the family took full advantage of the museums, public gardens and parks in a city where dissension seemed absent. He always said moving here was one of the best decisions he'd made. Did he have time to regret his choice during the Ashura riot which cost him his life? And if he were alive now, what would he say? She continued reading the article which reported that two suicide bombers had blown themselves up at a time when special prayers were being offered, and the shrine was most crowded. The current toll was estimated at 42 killed and 175 injured, including many women and children. It was ironic the bombers chose a shrine to Data Ganj Bakhsh, one of the earliest Sufi saints, who like the Prophet Jesus and the Prophet Muhammad, peace be upon them, promoted love and the spirit of brotherhood. Why was it such voices were so often drowned out by the strident cries of hatred? These days there were always many questions without answers. She sat there, her mind filled with the image of white garbed, tall hatted Sufis whirling to their external and internal music in cosmic synchronicity.

Before Zubair left to return to the hospital, he joined the family in the lounge. She watched as he talked and joked with the children. Hameeda considered what he dealt with every day. How did he come home appearing undisturbed, the same person who left in the morning? After the previous day's catastrophe, her respect for him had increased immeasurably. She felt very lucky to be his wife.

As she walked him to the door, she said, "Tell Ammie I'll come tomorrow afternoon."

"Are you sure it's not too soon?"

She really wasn't sure. Even before the attack, she had been uncomfortable visiting family and friends when they were hospitalized. Her three hospital confinements for the birth of her children had not erased the dark associations acquired during her days spent by her dada's bedside as he lay dying. Now with the scenes of carnage fresh in her memory, it would be even more difficult to step through the hospital's doors. But it was her duty to go, and she told him she would manage. Thinking of what she had accomplished the previous day gave her some confidence she could cope with the visit.

The next afternoon, she went to the hospital. There was no evidence of the previous day's terrible events, only the usual visitors with their bags of food or bouquets of flowers. Zubair was busy, so she went up to her mother-in-law's second floor room by herself. When she entered, she saw the old woman lying like a leviathan under an ocean of blue blanket and white sheet. Her head was turned away from Hameeda toward the window until the sound of her footsteps swung her face around. When her mother-in-law saw who it was her countenance remained unchanged as if the paralysis had moved from her legs up to her facial muscles. Hameeda crossed over to the chair placed beside the bed.

"As salaam aleikum Ammie. I hope you're feeling better."

"I am as I was two days ago. Now leave a dying woman in peace." She turned her head away from her again.

It was not so much the words that shocked her, but the tone of her mother-in-law's voice. Normally, the old woman was agitated and her words leapt from her mouth, rising and falling both in volume and tempo as if they were landing on a trampoline. Today, her voice was low, flat, lacking in emotion, as if straitjacketed by an unfamiliar mood.

She reached out and touched the old woman's hand. "I can imagine how difficult it must be lying here unable to move your legs and thinking the worse, but I'm sure you're not dying."

Her mother-in-law looked at her with an annoyed expression, irritation creeping into her voice. "And how do you know this? Neither my son nor all the doctors at this fine hospital can discover what's wrong. But I know it's Allah's way of telling me I should prepare myself for death."

Hameeda couldn't think of a reply. She certainly wasn't able to foretell the future. In this respect, Zubair's mother was correct; only Allah knew the fate awaiting each of them.

"Ammie, think of Allah's compassion toward us, his children, and it will give you hope you'll be cured."

There was no response; she just turned her head to stare out the window again.

Being used to the thrust and parry of their usual conversations, she was unprepared for her mother-in-law's retreat into silence. Denied conversation, she pulled out the volume of Wordsworth and began to read. For an hour she read poems whose verses inspired thoughts of the world's beauty. Her voice served the words like fine food at a feast the old woman refused to share. Her head remained turned away, her body so still Hameeda almost checked her breathing in case she had died as predicted. But before she leaned close to her mouth, she saw her hands plucking at the sheet, drawing it up closer to her chin. At the end of an hour, discouraged with her failure to comfort her mother-in-law, she got up.

"I'll be back tomorrow afternoon. Is there anything I can bring you from home?"

Her mother-in-law finally focused on her again. "You may be attending my funeral tomorrow."

She shook her head. "Oh Ammie, please don't say that. I'll say a special prayer for you tonight."

"Save your prayers for someone else."

She decided further argument was useless and gathered up her purse and the book. "Allah be with you, Ammie."

The lack of a response followed her out the door.

That night, her husband again stayed at the hospital with his mother. When she talked to him on the phone, she questioned him about the old woman's health, and told him his mother was convinced she was dying. He said he'd assured his mother, a number of times, she was in no danger of dying, and explained that although they hadn't found the cause of her paralysis, she was otherwise in good health for her age. All the tests had been negative. The only remaining possibility was some sort of auto-immune response which would resolve itself over time.

Hameeda wondered how you could be positive, one way or the other, about the imminence of death. She remembered when she had the flu. The preceding day there had been no symptoms, just a sensation something was different, an indescribable, internal shift and a vague tiredness which could have been attributed to lack of sleep. Couldn't death be like that, already stalking you but not close enough to be detected? And how near would its shadow have to come for you to be aware of it – a month away, a week, a day? Would you sense its approach before renegade cells were identified under a microscope, or a bomb exploded? Or was there never any warning, leaving you to live with the assumption death was always one step behind you.

"We'll both be coming home tomorrow," her husband told her. I've arranged for a physical therapist to come in and exercise her legs. I'm afraid it will mean a lot more work for you."

"Don't worry about it; I'm sure I'll manage. What will we do about the move now Ammie is ill?" Although she'd been thinking about the effect of her mother-in-law's paralysis on their move to Canada, it was the first time she had mentioned it to her husband. She was surprised with everything else on his mind, he too had thought about it.

"We still have a few months. We'll wait and see what happens. I'll make a determination once the situation becomes clearer. I still hope Ammie's paralysis will resolve itself."

"I'll keep praying for her recovery," she said, her

thoughts already on arrangements, schedules, and having her husband back home.

"Over the years I've witnessed miraculous cures with no scientific explanation," her husband said. "I've exhausted all the medical solutions for Ammie. Now it's in Allah's hands."

Chapter 7

Yesterday, almost two weeks after their cataclysmic meeting, Hameeda had called her, but fortunately she hadn't been at home. Nadira had held the slip of paper, now their only connection, and read the maid's message several times as if it was written in code and its hidden meaning could be deciphered if she pored over it long enough. But it was simply her old friend's name, a phone number and a request to call. And afterward, she ignored it. Even before the call, she had made up her mind, and then Hameeda's delay in contacting her just confirmed her decision. That's the end of it, she'd thought, and without examining why, she tucked the note in the back of one of her cupboard drawers.

This morning, she was determined not to think about anything that might spoil her day. The weather outside was beautiful and Sohail was in a rare mood, humming an off-key tune as he got dressed. Picking up their discarded night clothes off a chair and, encouraged by his apparent equanimity, she told him she'd need an additional 10,000 rupees that week.

"Why do you need such a large sum?" He stopped in the midst of pulling on a sock and looked over at her.

"Arif and Samir need new outfits for your niece's upcoming wedding."

"They can wear what they have," he said, sticking his other foot into the remaining sock.

She hadn't expected him to disagree and was annoyed he was questioning her judgment, since as a rule she was not extravagant. She sighed, all at once tired of the necessity for discussion and compromise. Wouldn't it be nice to be a despot like the ancient Mughal emperors, whose every request was instantly granted by a retinue of obsequious ministers and retainers? She tried to picture Sohail saying, "Your wish is my command." A laugh rose halfway up her throat before she smothered it. Her need was not enough unless she could cloak it in a reason he would find acceptable – something clear cut and unassailable.

"It's not a matter of making do; they've outgrown every suitable outfit," she said, the memory of the trouble she'd had getting the boys to try on their existing wedding clothing still fresh in her mind.

There was no response from Sohail as he busied himself buttoning his shirt, and she felt ignored. Nadira wondered if he was doing it on purpose to discourage her from continuing, but it didn't deter her.

"Sohail, are you listening to me?"

"I heard you Nadira. If they're growing so fast, you should find outfits which aren't as expensive. I'm sure 5,000 rupees will be sufficient. And I hope you're planning on wearing something you already have. I can never understand why women have to have a new outfit for every occasion."

She knew if Sohail had looked over at her, he would have seen the danger signs – her hands on her hips, chin thrust forward, lips compressed into a thin line. But he didn't even favor her with a glance; he was busy observing himself in the mirror as he looped his tie around his neck.

"Obviously, you haven't been shopping for clothes in a long time. I can't get two suitable outfits for that amount, and I haven't asked for anything for myself. If you took the time to notice, you'd know I usually wear outfits I already have or remake old ones so they fit the current style," While speaking, she heard her voice increase in volume beyond a civil, conversational level.

She watched Sohail's reflected image change as his clenched jaw dug shallow trenches across his cheeks. Just minutes ago he was in a good mood, and now, she knew, she would be blamed for spoiling it.

"Raising your voice isn't necessary, Nadira. I can hear you perfectly well."

She felt herself tense and knew her morning, which had started so well, was rapidly disintegrating. For a brief moment, she considered backing off, and might have if another way out of her dilemma had occurred to her. But she had already examined her problem from every possible angle and had found no other solution. Besides, she was tired of being told what to do.

"I'm not a child Sohail." Nadira said. Despite her protestation, for an instant she felt juvenile and longed to express her frustration by stamping her foot and beating his chest with her fists. She moved between him and the mirror so he would have to look her in the eye.

"I resent the fact you don't trust me with household decisions."

Sohail's voice went up a few decibels as he proclaimed her current behavior proof of her immaturity. She snapped back that his need to be in control all the time was a sign of an insecure personality. The argument deteriorated from there, falling into sink holes of discontent. They sullied the air, both of them saying regrettable things that would leave behind hard feelings.

Finally, as she pressed her lips together, Sohail also went silent. Maybe he was as shocked as she was at the heat of their fight. She couldn't think of anything to say that was strong enough to sweep away the acrimony that seemed to hover over them.

"Since I'm the one responsible for supporting this family and keeping our finances in order; I have the final say on how money will be spent, something that gives me no pleasure," he said as he yanked the knot of his tie up under his collar. "Find a way to work with the amount I'm giving you."

She knew he meant these words to end the conversation, but she was beginning to feel remorse and wanted to try and repair some of the damage. A few seconds passed while she gathered the right words.

"You don't have to do it alone. I'm perfectly willing to share financial responsibility. Just tell me the current state of our finances. Has something changed? Is there something we need to discuss?"

He hesitated, and his body relaxed its stiff pose. For a moment it looked as if he would respond to her questions, but then he turned his back on her and started to leave the room.

"Wait, Sohail; we haven't finished."

"We have as far as I'm concerned," he said as he walked out the door and left her upset, her day already in ruins.

A little while later, Nadira was halfway home after dropping the boys off at school and still agitated from the morning's argument. She didn't understand why a normal conversation on mundane matters had turned into such a fierce disagreement? Where had things gone wrong? She couldn't rid her mind of his dismissive exit from their room, and it made her furious all over again. If she didn't talk to someone about it, she would explode. Ordinarily, she would have called her friend Sharnaz, who'd known Sohail long before they'd been introduced. Unfortunately, she was away at a conference in Islamabad.

Her friend had continued her college activism, and was involved in various women's rights and political organizations. Whenever they got together, Nadira enjoyed hearing about her activities, and they always had spirited discussions. But a few years ago when Sharnaz had asked her to join a group and become more involved, she had begged off claiming a lack of time.

"What's happened to you, Nadira? I remember when

you thought social action was important. Have you forgotten the protests you organized?"

"I hardly think demonstrations against the terrible food in the cafeteria or the censorship of student articles in the school newspaper qualifies me to address weightier matters," she had said. "Really, I can't shoehorn one more thing into my schedule right now. Maybe when the boys are older."

"There's never enough time, Nadira. You should reassess your priorities," Sharnaz had said, waving her pamphlets in front of her. "Believe me; housework will always be waiting for you."

If she had listened to Sharnaz, and created an outside life separate from her role as wife and mother, would she be in the same position she was in today? Would Sohail take her more seriously and be more confiding? She shook her head and wondered why she was wasting time mulling over a past miscalculation?

With Sharnaz absent, she decided to talk to her father. Maybe he could provide some insight into her husband's behavior, and suggest a different way to deal with the problem. She might also talk to him about Hameeda, a subject she'd thought was closed, but it still tugged at her and demanded her attention like a persistent toddler. Her usual rational thought process didn't work when she dealt with the problem of her old friend. Whenever she approached this subject, her normally orderly mind fell apart and emotion took control. Part of her desired the catharsis of a final confrontation, but she was determined not to do anything which might have unintended consequences for her son. His friendship with Jameel put her in a quandary. Probably the best course was to continue to ignore Hameeda's overtures and regain the silence they had settled into for so many years. In a way it was an elegant solution, her response identical to her friend's all those years ago, resulting in a perfect balancing of accounts.

When a car horn blared at her, she was startled to find she had started to drift into the next lane. She looked at her surroundings, and found she'd traveled a significant distance without being conscious of it. She felt her worries were becoming too much of a distraction, and she wanted it to end. Not being far from her parents' house, she didn't bother to call and drove directly there. It was her mother who opened the door.

"Nadira, what a nice surprise."

"Amma, I hope I haven't come at a bad time?"

"No, I was just watching the news on TV. Food and gasoline prices are up again. All too disturbing, I'm happy for the interruption. Come in, come in."

Her mother led the way into the lounge and shut off the TV before sitting down next to her on the sofa, angling her body so they were facing each other. She studied her for a moment.

"I guess you came to see your father? I'm afraid he's out visiting a friend."

"Why do you think I want to see Abu?" She was surprised her mother had guessed the reason for her visit.

"You're chewing on your lower lip which you only

do when you're upset about something, and when you're upset, you always want to talk to your father."

For some reason, it bothered Nadira that her mother knew her so well. She wasn't sure why her relationship with her mother was so tenuous and combative. Was it because her mother had favored her older brother and been the parent who almost always disciplined her, or because the natural affinity she felt with her father was absent with her mother? As often happened, she found herself contradicting her mother's statement.

"That's not true, Amma, sometimes I talk to you."

"Yes, you do, but it's on subjects like fashion advice or when you need a recipe for a dinner party. We never talk about anything important. Maybe now's the time to start. What's going on with you? Saabira visited me yesterday and mentioned you seemed distracted and troubled when she saw you last week." Her mother reached out and laid her hand on Nadira's forearm.

She was annoyed her aunt had talked to her mother rather than approaching her directly. She escaped from her mother's hand, crossed her arms over her chest and leaned back.

"Why must everyone in the family always stick their noses in other people's business?"

Her mother frowned and straightened up. "She's concerned about you. You should be grateful you have people who care about what happens to you."

The admonishment reminded her of everything her favorite aunt had done for her in the past. Realizing her interference must have been motivated by the desire to help, she felt contrite.

"I'm sorry, I shouldn't have said that, but I had a huge fight with Sohail this morning, and I'm in a bad mood."

"Nadira, I know you think I couldn't possibly understand your situation, but I've been married a long time, and I might be of some help," her mother said, looking at her over steepled hands.

She was tempted to talk to her mother and tried to remember the last time she'd told her anything personal, but nothing came to mind. Not knowing where to begin, she sat there in silence, twisting her wedding band around her finger.

"What was the argument about?"

"I'm not sure. He disagreed with me about a household expenditure, wedding clothes for Arif and Samir. But what made me angry was he didn't trust my judgment, and he no longer takes me into his confidence. When we were first married, it was different. This last year, he's treated me more like an offspring than a wife."

"It sounds like this is about a larger issue than this morning's argument."

Nadira was becoming uncomfortable with their exchange. She paused before she continued and searched for a way to redirect the conversation.

"I'm sure I'm overreacting. By tonight, it will be forgotten. Maybe I expect too much. My life just isn't what I envisioned when I was younger." She was surprised at her statement of discontent. It was as if the words had come from someone else, but the moment she heard them; she knew they were true.

Her mother sighed. "What happened to my fearless daughter, the one who fought so hard for everything she wanted? Don't give up on your high expectations."

Nadira couldn't believe what she was hearing. All during her childhood she'd argued with her mother every time she'd pushed a traditional boundary. It didn't seem fair for her mother to change direction now.

"If that's how you feel, why did you always discourage me when I was young?"

"As a child you scared me. I remember a trip to the beach. You were so small and the waves so big. When we stood at the edge of the surf, I held onto your shoulders to keep you from getting knocked over. But you escaped my grip and ran forward, laughing with delight when a wave sat you down on the sand and covered you up to your nose. And as you got older, you continued to do things that put you at risk. What choice did I have but to try and protect you from youthful mistakes?

Nadira couldn't remember any close calls, at least not ones she had engineered. But, she did remember feeling constrained by very narrow boundaries governing what she could and could not do. She lifted her head, and met her mother's gaze.

"So what made you change your mind?" she asked.

Her mother stared at some distant point off to the side. "Nothing is the same as it was … nothing," A shadow of sadness darkened her face. "These last few years, I've realized what it must have been like for you, to want one thing and have to accept something else because you couldn't control your own destiny."

Nadira didn't think her mother was just describing her. Their world had been twisted and mangled until it was unrecognizable. And in this new variant of their life, nobody's dreams could be safeguarded. She knew this fact could change you in unintended ways. She had become superstitious. Now before she left the house, she stopped to touch the Qur'an, as if her fate could be changed by that one act. And when a family member departed, even on the briefest errand, she interrupted what she was doing, stood in the doorway and held onto them with her eyes to memorize them like an understudy learning the lines of a play she might have to recite at a moment's notice.

"There are times when I wonder how much my life has been determined by where I am instead of who I am – maybe if I lived somewhere else …"

"Every place comes with its own set of difficulties. Do you think if you changed your location, your life would all of a sudden be better?" Her mother shook her head. "Even if you could find a country where you wouldn't be treated like an unwelcome guest, you can't leave problems behind like superfluous furniture. They follow you wherever you go, and having to deal with new issues makes it harder to address old ones."

"Well, it doesn't matter. Sohail would never leave Lahore."

"Is that what this is about? You want to leave Pakistan and Sohail doesn't? Maybe he has good reasons for his decision, Nadira. You'll never know unless you talk to him about it."

"But that's just it; he won't talk to me."

"Maybe he's just not ready. Give him a little time." A hint of a smile crossed her mother's face. "It wouldn't hurt you to practice some patience."

Nadira grimaced. "Patience is not one of my strong points."

Her mother laughed. "Yes, I know. You'll have to work on improving that trait by yourself, but I may be able to help you with a wedding outfit for Arif," she said, switching to a more neutral subject as if she didn't want to test their new rapport any further. "Your father has an outfit he wore once or twice before it got too tight, and I'm sure it can be taken in for Arif. Do you think he'll mind wearing a hand-me-down?"

"Arif hasn't reached the point where he's too concerned about clothes, except for his cricket outfits. If it can be tailored to fit him, it will help a lot. I hadn't thought about it, but I can have a look in Arif's closet and see if there's anything I can have altered for Samir. Thank you, Amma; I think you've solved my immediate problem." Nadira reached over and gave her mother's hand a squeeze.

While going through the clothes in her father's closet, they retreated into the ease of their usual superficial chit chat. Her mother finally found the outfit she was thinking of for her grandson. After handing it over to Nadira, she opened up a drawer in her own closet and lifted out a large flat box. Opening the box, her mother removed a layer of tissue paper and held up an outfit she had never seen before. It was a silk shalwar kameez in the palest shade of blue. The unadorned shalwar complimented the elaborate kameez, whose mandarin collar, cuffs and hem were embroidered in a dense ivory, pale pink and silver floral design. In addition, the sleeves and body of the kameez had tiny, ivory Jasmine blooms stitched at random as if scattered by a passing breeze. A matching dupatta completed the outfit.

"I think this will fit you if you'd like to wear it to the wedding," her mother said, smoothing out the creases on the front of the kameez.

"Amma, it's exquisite. Can I really borrow it?"

"It was part of my dowry. Your nani and I worked on the embroidery together," her mother said as she fingered the stitches. "It no longer fits me; why don't you keep it."

"Are you sure?"

"Yes, I'd love you to have it."

Nadira could picture the two women sitting side by side with sewing needles in their hands, embellishing the garment her mother now placed on top of the box. Tears blurred her vision as she felt anew the loss of her nani, and was touched by her mother's gift of something which must still be precious to her. She had to wait a few seconds before she could answer. "Thank you so much," she said, wrapping her arms around her mother in a long embrace.

Her mother gave her a hug and wiped away a tear with her fingers before turning to fold and repack the outfit.

She had just finished wrapping up the clothes for

Nadira when they heard footsteps coming down the hall, and her father appeared in the doorway.

"Isn't this wonderful; the two most beautiful women in all Pakistan here to greet me on my return from the war," her father said with a broad smile.

"What war is that?" her mother asked, returning his smile.

"The war of words I was having with my friend over the latest political contretemps. He's an apologist, while I expressed my indignation, leading to the construction of battlements and the marshaling of opposing forces." His cheerful expression conveyed the sense of a very amiable war.

"And who won?" her mother asked.

He laughed. "Oh, we both had to declare a truce so we could enjoy our tea."

"Nadeem, I hope you haven't spoiled your appetite for lunch," her mother said with a shake of her head.

He looked down and patted his belly.

"Unfortunately, my appetite is unaffected as my waistline bears witness. Will you stay for lunch, Nadira? You can tell me all about what you've been doing since I last saw you and help me devise arguments for my next engagement."

She looked at her watch and was alarmed at how late it was. "I'm afraid not Abu; I'm already behind schedule, but I'll come again soon."

"Yes you must. We haven't seen enough of you lately," he said as he kissed her on the forehead.

"Come Nadira, I'll walk you to the door. Nadeem, will

you please take a look at the hot water heater for the guest bath? It isn't heating properly."

"You see; how can I solve the country's problems when my time and services are in constant demand at home?" he said with a shrug.

"Oh, please spare me," her mother said and waved him away.

When they reached the front door, her mother kissed her goodbye. "I'm glad we talked."

"Me too, Amma," Nadira said, realizing, with surprise, she meant it.

As she stepped outside, her mother's quiet voice followed her down the steps.

"You know Nadira, I would be very sad if you left Lahore," and then not waiting for a response she closed the door.

It didn't occur to her until she reached home that she hadn't broached the subject of Hameeda and was once again left with the burden of it.

Chapter 8

When Zubair's mother returned home, Hameeda had to adapt to a new schedule and take charge of two additional people. There was a full-time aide, a young village girl who often seemed to need mothering, and a physical therapist who came for an hour, four days a week, and whose presence at the gate always surprised her even though she was expected.

As hard as she tried, Hameeda had trouble adjusting to her new circumstances, the transition taking longer than she thought it should. Her handling of the situation reminded her of learning to operate a clutch on an automobile, her progress a series of stutters and stalls. Twice, the children had to wait when she was late picking them up at school, and the house was beginning to look orphaned with mail piling up on tabletops, clean laundry still not put away and misplaced necessities requiring an almost daily search of her rooms.

Hameeda's mood was also affected. As soon as her eyes opened in the morning, she felt out of sorts. She would lie in bed and review all the new tasks she had to tackle and then linger a few more moments, her body a weight that took a conscious effort to lever into an upright position.

Her day took an inordinate level of concentration, not unlike the tests she'd taken in school. Realizing how settled she'd been and how much she'd relied on familiar routines, she longed for the reflexive nature of her recent past.

Despite the new demands, she made it a priority to call Nadira, allowing enough time to have a lengthy talk. But she was disappointed when a maid informed her of Nadira's absence. She left a message with all the necessary information and a specific request for a return call. One day, then two passed with no response. She began to wonder if her message had been received but was afraid to call again. She was encouraged by the fact that Nadira still allowed their sons to spend time together. The previous weekend Jameel had met Arif at the cinema for an afternoon movie. It reminded her of all the times she and Nadira had gone to the cinema together, and the thought brought back pleasant memories. She became impatient to resolve their impasse so she could enjoy her old friend's company again, and considered mailing a note, but in the end lacked the courage to do it. She tried, unsuccessfully, to put the silence between them out of her mind.

Once days became weeks, she was crushed and her chest felt sore, as if a forgotten accident had left a bruise. She didn't consider being angry because she felt she had no right to it. Her pain was like a star, burning with the glittering, white heat born of an explosion she had ignited long ago, waiting all these years later to reveal itself. She embraced her discomfort as long deferred punishment and found it lessened her guilty feelings. But even if she'd wanted to wallow in her emotions, she was distracted by her mother-in-law who continued to devour most of her energy, time and attention.

Taking care of the old woman's physical needs was not easy but dealing with the change in her personality was far more difficult. Her mother-in-law had lost her appetite, and it was a struggle getting her to eat. In the four weeks since she'd been taken ill, she looked noticeably thinner. She lay in her bed fingering her prayer beads as hour after hour her lips formed the words of Quranic verses. What had once passed as conversation between them had ceased. When Hameeda was in the room, the air was so thick with silence, it suffocated any of her attempts to talk. The absent words pressed against her with more force than the ones which had once assaulted her. It was not that the old woman had gone mute because she would still talk to Zubair when he sat with her at the end of the day. One night, before they dropped off to sleep, Hameeda asked him what they talked about.

"I do most of the talking, but once in a while she gives me instructions on the upkeep of the house and what to do with her possessions when she dies."

Hameeda didn't find this information very helpful when it came to finding an avenue of conversation for herself and pressed him to give her a more detailed account of what he said to his mother.

"I tell her what happened at the hospital during the day or read the newspaper to her. You should carry on as usual, discussing the same things you did before she became ill."

"I suppose I could do that."

Long after Zubair had fallen asleep, she lay awake puzzling over what she and the old woman had said to each other over the years. She remembered being lectured or chastised but not much in the way of mutual exchange. After a couple of sleepless hours, she realized during her eighteen years of marriage, they had never had a meaningful conversation. When she was first married, Zubair's mother took on the role of a teacher. She instructed her on how everything was done in the house and showed her how to make her husband's favorite dishes, so she in turn could instruct the cook. She had been careful to behave in a respectful manner, which consisted of making affirmative responses to all her mother-in-law's requests or statements. When she looked back, it was as if they had been actors in a movie, each of them reciting pieces of dialogue already written for them by previous generations. When they were all together, her father-in-law or her husband initiated and took control of the conversations, which were general in nature.

When it came to forming a relationship with her mother-in-law, she had taken the path of least resistance. From the beginning, she had not been comfortable with her. She was so different from her own mother and aunts who had always been loving and affectionate. Zubair's mother seemed intent on keeping her at a distance, and whenever they were together, her eyes were always on her, watching and judging her. It made her self-conscious, and she found it much easier to focus on Zubair and the children. With great difficulty, she admitted to herself that after her father-in-law's death, their lack of a relationship left her mother-in-law alone in the house most of the time. She wished she could go back to the beginning and start again. She longed to retrieve the person she'd been before she married, a time when her mind's narrative and her actions were congruent. For how could her acts be defined as kind if she had to suppress contradictory sentiments to perform them? Examining her dilemma from every angle, she reached a helpful realization. Even if going back in time was impossible, it wasn't too late to make amends and thereby regain her self-respect and Allah's good graces. She decided to embark on repairing their relationship first thing in the morning. And with the hope of winning her mother-in-law over and the pleasant sound of amicable conversations playing out in her mind, she fell asleep.

All week, Hameeda took extra care with her mother-in-law and spent as much time with her as she could. She told her about her day, how Zubair and the children were doing, and gave her any news of the extended family. She was very disappointed when days passed without the old woman's behavior altering in the least, and no indication she even noticed Hameeda's serious attempt to connect with her. But she refused to be discouraged and remained confident she'd find a way to get through to her.

Over the next few weeks she continued her efforts. But all her striving was fruitless, and each day she prayed for the strength to keep working at it. One day, she found she didn't have much in the way of family news, and she was getting tired of talking about her day, so her sole audience must also have lost any interest she might have had. What could she talk about? Then she remembered her father-in-law's stories. When she was first married, he shared stories with Hameeda of the early days of his own marriage. She thought it was his way of illustrating that all newly married couples have to overcome difficulties and make adjustments. One story in particular was very funny and just thinking about it made her smile. In fact, it was so heartwarming, how could the old woman fail to respond to this memento of her past?

Still, she had never been very good at anticipating her mother-in-law's reactions and was apprehensive. As she began, she looked down at her hands.

"You know Ammie, when Zubair and I were first married I was having trouble adapting to the way he did things, and was shy about talking to him about it. Abu was always so observant, and I think he noticed I was upset when Zubair corrected me. So, he told me a story about the two of you.

As she began the story, she tried to remember her father-in-law's voice and mannerisms when he had recounted it, in the hope it would draw his affable spirit into the room.

"One hot day, Abu came home from work with his clothes as wrinkled as the skin of an elephant and complained about the unkempt appearance of his clothing. 'How am I to gain the respect of my colleagues when I look so rumpled?' Hameeda said as she grasped the edges of an imaginary jacket and examined it with a frown, trying to replicate her father-in-law's pantomime. "Then he offered the opinion, more starch would solve the problem. The way Abu remembered it, you took it upon yourself to supervise the maid the next time she did his laundry to ensure it was done properly."

Coming to the main point in the story, she remembered her father-in-law's dramatic pause and his chuckle when he described the results.

"Two days later, everything including his underwear was starched as stiff as a board." Hameeda did not have the courage to waddle stiff-legged across the floor as her father-in-law had. "When he looked at you, the expression on your face told him how pleased and proud you were of your accomplishment, and he didn't have the heart to say anything. A few days of chafing had him limping in discomfort; he had no choice but to beg you to starch just his shirt and jacket."

She decided she didn't have her father-in-law's talent for storytelling because when she glanced over at her mother-in-law, there was not even a hint of a smile. Was another mistake about to be added to her already long record? Maybe her mother-in-law was just waiting for her to conclude her recitation before reacting. She was looking at her, but her expression offered no clues to her present state of mind. Now very nervous, she spun the tale out to its conclusion.

"Abu thought you would be upset with him for complaining since it was his fault for not being more specific. But instead, you laughed. Once you started laughing, he started laughing too. From then on, whenever anyone mentioned starch, you had to avoid looking at each other or risk laughing uncontrollably."

As she finished speaking, she looked over at the old woman, who turned her head away from her. Maybe she had gone too far by revealing she knew something her mother-in-law would have preferred her husband had kept between the two of them. She began to be afraid she had made matters worse.

Hameeda noticed a pillow had fallen off the bed, and she went over and retrieved it. As she put her arm under her mother-in-law's shoulders and repositioned the pillow behind her back, she saw there were tears in her eyes. She didn't know what to say, so after replacing the pillow, she cradled her mother-in-law against her chest, and with one hand rubbed her back, up and down, up and down.

In a voice close to a whisper, her mother-in-law said, "Thank you, beti."

Hameeda was startled and very touched. It was the first time the old woman had called her daughter.

She lowered her back onto the pillow. "You're welcome, Ammie."

*　　*　　*

Salima lay in her bed staring at a ceiling she had mapped in detail since she arrived back home. Every crack and stain was now as familiar to her as the wrinkles on her face and the age spots on her hands. All bore testimony to the passing of many years. She and the house were both very old and reaching the end of their usefulness. A few years ago, Zubair had suggested they sell it and buy a smaller, more modern place closer to the hospital. But she couldn't bear to leave, not even for her son's sake. Every room in this ancient place held an imprint of her married life. She was afraid without the physical cues to pull her memories back up to the surface, everything would be forgotten, and she would be left without anything to comfort her.

A spider forded one of the muddy tracks flowing across the white plaster. It climbed part way down the wall and began weaving a silken bridge across the corner. A fly buzzed as it banged against the window glass. Her clock ticked away the seconds on her bedside table. Every small sound in the room was amplified against a quiet background. She wished she could still her mind so it remained as motionless as her legs. Instead, thoughts rushed around like traffic in a busy city. A strand of recent memory teased up a memory from long ago, and the two became knitted together. She felt Hameeda's arm encircling her and her hand stroking her back. It awoke in her one of the strongest memories of love she still carried with her. For an instant, the wheel of time halted and tracked backward. She was no longer old and infirm but a toddler receiving comfort in her mother's arms.

*   *   *

In the days that followed, a little at a time, her mother-in-law resumed talking to Hameeda. It wasn't anything special, just requests or a simple thank you when she did something for her. Even when Zubair's mother complained, a habit which also resumed, it wasn't directed at her but was about some unmet need or annoyance.

She expected Zubair and the children to comment on the old woman's miraculous transformation and was astonished when nobody said a word. The difference in her mother-in-law was so obvious to her; why didn't anyone else notice? Then the answer came to her; it wasn't Zubair's mother but she who had changed.

Chapter 9

For days after she returned from her mother's, Nadira rehearsed conversations with Sohail in her head. She practiced what she would say, anticipated what he would answer and then formulated responses to his replies. She went over her lines like an actress before opening night, but the curtain never went up. Sohail worked such long hours by the time he came home she had fallen asleep. In the morning, he would rush off after grabbing a couple slices of toast. One morning, Nadira managed to corner him before breakfast.

"Sohail, can you go into the office a little later today so I can talk to you?" She came up behind him, slipped her arms around his waist and leaned against him, hoping the warmth of her body would soften his resolve and hold him there for just a few minutes longer.

"Not possible," he said, wriggling out of her embrace.

"It's important, what about tonight?" she asked, her hand catching his sleeve to detain him long enough to get an answer. "I'll wait up for you."

"I'll be home very late. I have mountains of work to finish if I'm going to take the four days off for my niece's wedding." He escaped her grasp with ease and headed for the door.

It was clear to Nadira, even if she managed to stay awake until Sohail came home, he would not be in the mood to talk. Frustrated, she spent the day on her own preparations for the wedding in Attock. She brought her husband's wedding clothes to the dry cleaners and picked up Arif and Samir's altered outfits from the tailor. The majority of her time was spent shopping for some decorative items her sister-in-law had requested for the wedding ceremonies: the distinctive Lahori designs unavailable in their small city or in the capital city of Islamabad, an hour west of it.

Nadira could never comprehend why Sohail's brother, Latif, had given up the excitement and advantages of Lahore to live in a rural area. His own father, despite being an only son, had been quick to leave Attock behind for college and a professional career. At eighteen, Latif had surprised the family by deciding to study agriculture, part of his long-term plan to take over the management of their land from the local man employed to oversee the property after his grandfather's death. Latif still seemed satisfied with the life he'd chosen, and for that she envied him.

When it came time for Sohail's brother to marry, he had his parents investigate the local marriage pool for a wife rather than arranging a marriage with someone from their circle in Lahore. He ended up marrying an Attock girl, the granddaughter of his grandfather's close friend. Although his wife, Ameera, hadn't had the advantages of a formal education beyond high school, she had an intelligence that went beyond book learning and a personality that kept you smiling. Nadira enjoyed her company and was looking forward to seeing her.

Despite all of her planning, on the morning of their departure, she was still rushed and irritated by the usual delays. She intervened in a disagreement between the boys and had her own argument with Arif who couldn't understand why she wouldn't let him bring his cricket bat. While she was dealing with all of this, Sohail was off talking on the phone. Every time she went into their room for his assistance, he waved her off and continued with his conversation in a low voice. It aroused Nadira's suspicions again. What was going on?

They were over an hour late by the time they climbed into the car. She decided to let Arif sit up front with his father. Separating him from Samir was the only way she would avoid the boys' squabbling during the five hours it would take them to reach Attock.

The rushed feeling she had made it difficult for her to settle down. In an effort to distract herself, she stared out the window and took in her surroundings as they navigated the streets of Lahore. In the tangle of traffic, their car was just a few inches away from a donkey pulling a tonga. There were two men in the small, two-wheeled, wooden cart. One man held the reins and a long whip, which he flicked against the donkey's flank when it slowed down. The second man steadied a roll of carpet that hung a good two feet off the back of the tonga and extended forward over the shoulders of the donkey. She could see the donkey's eyes rolling back and forth, not surprising given the noise that must be assaulting its sensitive ears and the proximity of its unprotected body to the cars. Ribs showed through the donkey's rough coat, and there were sores on its side. She couldn't bear looking at the poor creature and turned her head away. Many people in Pakistan ignored the underfed and sometimes mistreated domestic animals. Although the evidence of mistreatment bothered Nadira, she understood how difficult it was generating concern for animals when there were people scavenging in the same piles of garbage as the stray dogs and cats.

Once the traffic cleared a little, their car pulled away from the donkey straining against its load. As they passed through the outskirts of the city, she closed her window to keep out the smoke from charcoal fires burning outside the small tin roofed huts which housed the businesses lining the road. Once on the motorway there was not much to see. The open, empty plain stretched for miles on either side. Sometimes a skirt of wind brushed its hem along the dry earth, raising a cloud of dust that it dragged across the landscape. An hour later, they drove between columns of eucalyptus trees that divided the motorway from rice fields and citrus groves. The tree crowns of dense, elongated leaves cast shade in irregular patterns across the motorway. At times she glimpsed the low, rectangular shapes of village houses off in the distance. It reminded her how the villages still lived in a past the cities had shrugged off years ago.

Trapped in the car, she had no way to distract herself

from thoughts of Sohail, and even the scenery that rushed by only served to push her back into the shared history of their past. Well before she'd seen Attock, she'd heard Sohail's stories of the wonderful summers he spent with his brothers at his grandparents' house, hunting, fishing and enjoying the novel sleeping arrangements necessitated by the season's heat. Sohail would recount how in the hottest weather, old fashioned charpoys, their wooden bed frames strung with taut rope, and fans were moved up to the roof where it was cooler. There the family slept under the dome of the night sky, watching orbs of starlight wink at them until they were lulled to sleep by the whirring of fan blades. He made it sound so appealing, Nadira wished the advent of water coolers and air conditioning hadn't made this practice unnecessary.

She had her own memories of the Attock District. Sohail had introduced her to this agricultural area early in their marriage. Nadira sometimes accompanied him and his father when they visited their tenant farmers in one of the villages. Traveling to a village was like journeying back in time. Their car bucked along rutted dirt roads that hadn't been designed for modern transport but were serviceable for the horse drawn tongas, camels or bicycles used by the locals. The families they visited lived in one story mud brick houses, often consisting of as few as two or three tiny rooms. The village had no electricity or running water. The women drew water from a community well, carrying the filled vessels balanced on one shoulder with a grace born of years of practice. Wooden yoked water buffalos pulled ancient plows to till the fields, their dried dung serving as fuel for the village fires. Once out of the car, she was assailed by sights, sounds and smells that were foreign to her city sensibilities. Standing at the edge of the village, sight lines continued uninterrupted until the flat land met the foothills of the distant Salt Range. The occasional voices of the people working the crops carried across the open space of the valley and were punctuated by the shrill chirring of crickets, the lilting notes of bird-song and the creak of wooden wheels against hard packed earth. The smell of dust, animals, cooking fires and drying chilies perfumed the air of the village. Nadira realized how easy it was to romanticize this place as long as you avoided looking into the lined, weary faces of the people and failed to notice that only the very old and the youngest children inhabited the village during the day. Men, women and children worked long hours so they could survive, with no respite except for religious holidays and weddings.

Nadira wondered if the villagers ever saw their surroundings as she did, and if the natural beauty offered any compensation. Did they marvel at the startling emerald green of irrigated fields that appeared like a mirage in an arid landscape barren of vegetation except for the occasional stunted acacia tree? Had they ever paused late in the after-noon to watch as the sun sank low in the sky and stroked a wash of lavender over the distant hills? At night when the darkness was so profound the moon and stars glowed with a white hot brilliance, did they stand outside and stare in awe while listening to the sounds of nocturnal creatures?

Or was appreciation of the pastoral landscape reserved for a visitor who wasn't fighting it for his livelihood day after day? Her mind continued sifting through past memories of Attock until a noise startled her out of her reverie.

Nadira looked over at Samir. His book had slipped to the floor as sleep tucked his chin to his chest. She picked it up and placed it on the seat between them. Sohail and Arif were discussing the details of a recent cricket match. Sohail glanced over his shoulder and gave her a smile which warmed her, so she returned it with one of her own.

Maybe there was no problem between them but the press of work, and while away they would recapture their old ease with each other. That was her last thought before she joined Samir in sleep. When she woke up, they had left the flat land behind them and were at the Kallar Kahar rest stop in the foothills of the Salt Range. Sohail had stopped so they could refuel and eat something before tackling the steep twisting road over the craggy hills.

"All right everyone, we shouldn't waste too much time eating. We're way behind schedule, and we need to arrive in time for the Mehndi preparations," Nadira said as she stood by the open car door and attempted to get a still sleepy Samir to move a little faster.

"Amma, we've just gotten out of the car, and you're already trying to get us back in it," Arif said as he stretched his arms over his head. "Anyway, they'll never start on time."

"They're having the Mehndi at the house, and I promised Ameera we'd be there early so I could help her with some of the decorations." Nadira started to walk toward the building in the hope it would encourage the rest of them to make a move. "Let's go, let's go," she called over her shoulder.

"I'm sure we'll all do our best to make this a short stop, right, boys?" she heard Sohail say.

Nadira looked back and smiled at Sohail, mouthing a silent thank you for his support. For weeks, doubts and regrets had been her companions, and it felt good to have a reason to let go of them, if only for the moment.

Once back on the road, they were forced to reduce their speed in order to navigate the switchbacks up to the plateau of the Salt Range and then descend in the same manner to the long pillared bridge across the Jhelum River. By late afternoon, they neared Rawalpindi where they got off the motorway and turned west toward their destination. It wasn't long before they were passing through Attock City, almost there. Latif's house was in Cantonment, a somewhat new area adjacent to the city limits. It was situated at the end of a long street, sandwiched between another house and a vacant, weedy lot where someone had staked three goats on long lines so they could graze. As their car passed them, the goats lifted their heads and their belled collars chimed out a greeting which Sohail answered with a beep of his horn. Approaching the house, they saw the gate in the high, boundary wall swing open, and Latif and Ameera walked out to welcome them.

"Are we the last to arrive?" Nadira asked her sister-in-law.

"Yes, the rest of the family is inside having something to eat before getting ready for the Mehndi." Emotion was evident in Ameera's voice. "For a year, I've been so involved with all my preparations, I forgot once they were complete, it would mean the wedding was just hours away. I'm having difficulty accepting that my daughter will soon be Usman's responsibility and will no longer be with us."

Nadira gave her an encouraging hug. "It's not as bad as it could be. Remember, she's marrying your nephew and will be living thirty minutes away."

She couldn't imagine marrying a first cousin, probably because she'd spent her childhood in a constant state of war with male cousins who seemed intent on finding ever more creative ways to infuriate her. But, marriage between first cousins had been a common practice and sometimes still occurred. If anything, going outside the tight circle of family and close friends for a marriage partner was some-what new, happening often only in the last two generations. Her own parents' families had been very close friends. Even when the bride or groom was from outside those circles, he or she was almost always found through a network of long-time friends and relatives. She remembered how shocking it was for her parents when they received a proposal, indirectly, from their future son-in-law. She felt a rush of emotion when she contemplated how passionate Sohail must have been to have taken such an unusual step. When the proposal came, Nadira couldn't remember feeling any hesitation about accepting. Everything seemed so clear to her then. Now returning to how she'd felt during the early years of their marriage was as difficult as swimming against a strong current.

She drew her attention back to her sister-in-law who had continued talking while her mind was elsewhere.

"Having Ruksana close by is a blessing, but the house will seem empty without her. You're lucky Arif and Samir will be bringing brides home, not going away," Ameera said reaching out and ruffling Samir's hair as he stood by the back of the car and waited for his father to hand him a suitcase.

"That's assuming they end up in Lahore and don't want a place of their own. Look what happened with Latif," she said, a sweep of her arm taking in the neighborhood.

"It's true. Only Allah, blessed be his name, knows what the future holds for us."

While she talked with Ameera, Sohail and the boys unloaded their things from the car and brought them into the house. As soon as Nadira joined them, she was surrounded by family members. After she exchanged greetings, she listened to the chattering of excited females and thought about the couple soon to be married. Her sister-in-law's nephew, Usman, was twenty-four and already embarked on an engineering career. Although Sohail had been just two years older when they married, to her mind, the groom seemed very young. Her niece was even younger, nineteen, and Nadira worried about her marrying at an age when her ideas on what she wanted from life were still incomplete and susceptible to change. Marriage was difficult enough when you were older.

Nadira knew when arranging the marriage, their parents had considered them well suited for each other, and having grown up together, they knew each other well. But, nothing in life was certain and while a decision might be right when taken, people and circumstances were never static. Or maybe, she was just projecting her own situation onto the couple. She promised herself she wouldn't think about her problems during the wedding and would concentrate on enjoying the occasion.

Nadira walked into the dining room and got a cup of tea. She passed Arif and Samir as they headed back into the lounge, juggling cokes and plates of food. In the middle of each of their plates, they had a pyramid of rice topped with generous portions of dal and chicken curry. This precarious mountain was fenced off from the plate's edge by pakoras, a samosa or two, and spoonfuls of mango chutney.

"Are you sure you've taken enough?" Nadira asked. "After the starvation diet we've had you on, I'm surprised that's all you're going to eat."

"Don't worry Amma; we can always go back for seconds," Arif replied with a smile.

She cuffed the back of his head as he went by, and after pouring her tea, found a seat next to her sister-in-laws. Although their family did not adhere to the rules of purdah, it was inevitable for the men to gravitate to one side of the room and the women to the other. Nadira had grown up in a household where men and women mixed at social occasions. She often chafed at the formal or informal segregation that discouraged her from joining the men's conversation when the women's talk concerned mundane topics she found uninteresting. At least for the present, she was happy discussing the lighter subject of the wedding while on the other side of the room the men talked about crops and politics.

Ameera came over to her. "Nadira, come see the arrangements for the Mehndi, and tell me where you think we should hang the decorations you've brought."

The two of them walked out to the back lawn. The once empty expanse of grass had been transformed. Lengths of heavy, turquoise fabric with a gold and white paisley design hung on a structure of poles that formed a high, flat roofed, rectangular tent. To one side of the tent, a long buffet table was set up under a green and white striped canopy. Inside the enclosure, the support poles had been wrapped with alternating diagonal strips of gold and paisley fabric. Swags of tiny fairy lights hung in rows across the ceiling and twinkled like strings of diamonds caught in sunlight. The ground was covered with a tarp, overlaid with beige Bokhara carpets, and a line of chairs, three deep, formed a perimeter around a large open space for the singers and dancers.

Nadira complimented her sister-in-law on the design of the tent, and told her nothing else was needed. Instead, she suggested they use the decorations for the front of the house.

"That's a terrific idea," Ameera said. "With a little help, I'm sure we can get it done in plenty of time."

For the next hour, she worked to finish the decorating,

happy to be kept busy, and then while Ameera answered a phone call, she went to her niece's bedroom to see how she was getting along.

Her niece was seated in a chair, a noisy crowd of female cousins and friends clustered at her feet like acolytes. There was a tray table drawn up in front of the bride, and one of her friends sat opposite, applying henna in beautiful, intricate designs to her palms and fingers. The designs on her feet had already been completed, and the thick, mahogany colored henna paste looked dry. When her niece noticed her in the doorway, the smile on her face widened.

"Nadira Auntie, I didn't realize you'd arrived. I'm sorry I wasn't there to greet you, but as you can see I can't move at the moment." Her niece nodded her head in the direction of her hands.

"I'll reserve my hugs for later. I don't want your Mehndi ruined. The designs are beautiful. You're lucky to have such a skilled, artistic friend."

Nadira walked up to the table to get a closer look at the workmanship.

"Yes, isn't Fauzia doing an absolutely smashing job," Ruksana said. "She does the best designs."

"We've all made Fauzia promise that she'll do our Mehndi as well," one of her niece's friends said. "The question is, who will do Fauzia's when it's her turn?"

"She'll train one of us to do it," one of the other girls suggested.

"If she has her way, I don't think there will be enough time for that," someone else chimed in. The whole group dissolved into laughter at some private joke, their loose limbed bodies collapsing on the floor in positions Nadira would find impossible to attain without severe discomfort.

Had she ever been this silly and carefree? Probably, but those days seemed distant, and her memories of them hazy.

"Well, I just came to say hello. Enjoy the rest of the afternoon."

"Oh no, you must stay for a while," her niece said.

Nadira smiled. Her niece was such a sweet girl, and she appreciated the invitation. But the company of girls her own age was what Ruksana needed now, and she would just dampen their fun.

"Don't worry; we'll visit later on."

It might have been her closeness with Ruksana or the timing of the wedding which brought forth so many memories of her own marriage. She remembered her excitement in the months leading up to the ceremony. Every day involved some type of preparation for the event. She had gone on many shopping trips with her mother and her nani, buying household items, new shoes and fabric for new clothes. Her nani's arthritis prevented her from helping with the stitching, but she was involved in designing each outfit, giving detailed instructions to their tailor and attending every one of her fittings. Nadira also helped her mother select the wedding gifts for Sohail and his family based on the limited information she'd garnered during the two or three chaperoned visits she'd had with him. Although their meetings had been curtailed, they'd spent hours talking on the phone. It seemed like there was never enough time for all the things they wanted to say to each other. During those months, she'd felt like she was the center of a more beautiful, ever expanding universe. Now her world seemed to be shrinking, offering fewer and fewer possibilities.

When she reentered the lounge, she looked around to find her husband and the boys. She saw Sohail across the room, talking with his brother and Samir in a corner with some of his cousins, but Arif was nowhere in sight. She went over to her husband.

"Where's Arif?"

"He's in my son's bedroom with the door locked. When I knocked, they told me no one was allowed in," her brother-in-law said. "There was music playing, and they're definitely up to something."

"I should have known. Those two are always getting into mischief," Nadira said. "Should I try and find out what's going on?"

"I'm sure we'll find out soon enough, Nadira," Latif said with a smile.

"That's what worries me," she laughed.

"They don't have access to weapons or incendiary devices, so I think we're pretty safe," her brother-in-law said.

Nadira knew she didn't have a fraction of the imagination Arif had when it came to thinking up schemes that often got him into trouble. If Latif thought two fourteen year old boys conspiring together were no threat, he had a very short memory. She looked at her brother-in-law and just shook her head.

"I think I'll go see if Ameera needs help with anything."

Ameera told her everything was done, and if she was still running around, it was because she needed to keep occupied or she would fall apart. She left her sister-in-law to her tasks, and went back and visited with the rest of the family until it was time to get dressed for the Mehndi.

That evening, after the groom's family had been greeted and led to the tented lawn, Nadira found a seat next to a cousin and chatted while she waited for the groom's entrance. After a few minutes delay, he arrived under a colorful fabric canopy raised on four corner poles by young, female relatives. As she watched, he was seated in a high backed chair on the men's side of the tent, and for a moment he looked like a king overseeing his subjects as he awaited the arrival of his queen. Then, he glanced around, adjusted a sleeve, and crossed and uncrossed his legs as if searching for a way to get comfortable, and the illusion was destroyed, no longer a royal personage, just an untried young man. She thought about going up to him and saying something reassuring, but a line of well-wishers had already begun to form in front of him.

On one side of the groom was a decorative tray with a platter of sweets and a small brass bowl of oil. Women and girls went over to him and taking some oil from the bowl, rubbed it on his head and then fed him a sweet. This was supposed to bring him good luck and longevity in his married life. The girls teased him without mercy, and despite his protests, used more oil than necessary and stuffed his mouth with sweets until his cheeks bulged. At that point, a couple of his friends came to his rescue and dismissed the girls.

How different it was for Ruksana. Although the manner of her entrance was the same, she was hidden from sight by a sheer veil, her head bent as if in prayer. Hampered by a hazy view, she had to be guided to a seat across the enclosure from the groom.

Nadira remembered how difficult it had been to keep her head bowed in a proper display of modesty. She had wanted to look around and see who was there and what they were wearing. When she peeked through her veil, everything was suffused with the color of the saffron yellow fabric, her surroundings out of focus, as if she was wearing someone else's prescription eyeglasses.

Once Ruksana was seated, she was also fed sweets. As each person went up, a friend lifted the bottom of her veil just enough for a bite size piece to be placed between her lips. It reminded Nadira of a helpless, baby bird waiting for its mother to drop a worm into its mouth.

While this was happening, the young people set up for the singing and dancing, taking seats on the carpet in front of either the bride or groom. She saw Samir and Arif sitting next to her nephew on the far side of Ruksana's group. Someone had placed a portable CD player on the carpet between the two sides.

When Nadira had gotten married, accompaniment had sometimes been provided by musicians playing the harmonium and a flute called the shahnai while beating out the rhythms on the traditional dholki. But now, most people had abandoned instruments in favor of instrumental CDs, and the dholki was added if you were lucky enough to have a friend or relative who had mastered the small drum. She reflected on the list of "remember when" stories she was acquiring at an alarming rate, and recognized her sentimentality about those days as a sure sign she was out-of-date.

At some unseen signal, someone pushed a button on the CD player and the competition began with singing on the bride's side. The young people raised their voices as loud as possible, their hands clapping to the beat. It was evident from the level of performance both sides had met for practice sessions. In between wedding songs, the girls got up for their dances, their bodies swaying as they went through the intricate steps and graceful arm movements dictated by tradition. The groom's side had just completed a dance, and everyone was waiting for the next performance from the girls on Ruksana's side. A CD was slipped into the machine, and six girls rose to their feet. Before they could take the floor, her nephew and Arif ran into the center of the open area. Dupattas, probably commandeered from Ameera's closet, hung from their shoulders. They stood there with their lips pursed, one hip cocked to the side and their arms stretched out in front of them. Once the music started they took mincing steps, swiveled their bodies and moved their arms in a clumsy imitation of the girls' routine. Ruksana's side reacted with cheers while catcalls came from the groom's side. Laughing, Nadira looked across and found Sohail clapping for his son and nephew. Their eyes met and Sohail pointed a finger at her, as if to say "That's *your* son." Nadira returned the gesture, and they both smiled. Competitive to the last, the other young men from both sides got up. Forming a circle around her nephew and son, they stomped out their own dance. It was as if some sort of spell had been broken. Now the remaining young people crowded the floor, each trying to outdo the other. When the song finished, they all stood there for a few seconds, caught up in the moment, before returning to their respective seats. After that, the once choreographed evening developed an untamed quality as the energy in the room increased. Two hours later, a break for dinner was announced. It was a relief to leave the now overheated tent and go outside to fill a plate with kebabs and curries. Nadira waited near the buffet table for Sohail. When he came out of the tent, she went over to him.

"So what do you think of our son?" she asked.

He smiled, a real smile, a smile she hadn't seen in a long time.

"I think he should stick with cricket since it appears he has no aptitude for dancing."

"Oh, I don't know. With a little practice he might be very good."

"If he follows his usual pattern, having done it once, he'll be bored with the idea of doing it again," Sohail said. "Come on, let's get something to eat." His hand rested on her shoulder for a moment before they were pulled apart by the noisy gathering of people lining up for food.

After eating, the singing and dancing continued. The

joyous sounds bringing with them an excitement that pushed fatigue aside. It was after midnight when, despite the protests of the young people, the adults called a halt to the proceedings. Tomorrow would be another long day.

The Mehndi was just the beginning of the wedding activities, each event steeped in tradition, one following another in recognizable fashion, no different from any other wedding Nadira had attended. Many months later, certain recollections, like Arif's dance, would be included in a pastiche of scenes unrelated in their magnitude, held in memory by the ordinary pleasure they had brought. And, they would acquire an out-of-proportion importance, artifacts, to be unearthed and preserved like ancient bones from an archeological dig.

*   *   *

Breakfast the next morning was a piecemeal affair. The cook was kept busy ferrying eggs, toast and tea to everyone in shifts as they arrived in the dining room dressed and ready for the day. Yesterday's atmosphere of fun had been replaced by a serious air. Ruksana did not appear, choosing to have breakfast alone in her room. Nadira wondered if her niece was as nervous as she had been the morning of her Nikah.

After months of being excited and enjoying the idea of getting married, upon waking the day of the wedding ceremony, Nadira had come down with a case of the jitters. She'd known, in a few hours, her life would undergo a significant change and there would be no turning back. As she'd looked around her bedroom, she had been struck by its perfection; everything in it a personal choice, the quilt in her favorite colors, the coordinated rug and wall decorations, and the shelved books, their covers worn from frequent handling. It had been her private domain; everywhere something referenced her past and nowhere was there any evidence of a compromise. She had questioned whether there would be enough space for her in her marriage. Would being part of a couple require her to become someone else? She hadn't yet understood that learning new behaviors was not always a negative, and in the best of marriages, you could both become better versions of yourselves.

Midday, Nadira watched as the immediate families of the bride and groom exchanged gifts to solidify their new familial ties. She thought about how a marriage's expansion of close connections brought about an inevitable change in a couple. Adjusting to a new family could magnify the best or worst in you, and either way if you were aware, teach you more about yourself. Based on her experience, there were always missteps in the beginning, and it was sometimes difficult to loosen the bonds of first impressions. One of Sohail's aunts still thought of her as shy simply because at their first meeting she'd had a splitting headache and had been so focused on keeping a pleasant expression on her face, she'd been almost silent. At their next meeting when she was more herself, the aunt claimed credit for "bringing her out," and to this day felt she'd been instrumental in helping Nadira overcome her reticence in company.

Once the servant ushered the imam into the drawing room, Nadira left with the other women and girls and went into her niece's bedroom. Her niece was seated on the edge of her bed; hands folded in her lap, her duputta clad head once again at a modest angle. When they walked in, she looked up and gave them a quick smile before looking back down. If she was nervous, she wasn't showing it. Ameera sat next to her daughter, and the rest of them took seats on the chairs placed against the walls. They heard the imam's voice through the partially opened door as he read the sermon for the marriage and recited verses of the Qur'an. Soon the door opened and Usman's grandfather, father and Latif, acting as witnesses, brought the marriage contract over to her niece and read it to her. When asked if she would accept the proposal of marriage, she replied, "I accept," and signed the marriage contract. Latif put his hand on top of his daughter's head for a brief moment before leaving with the other two men to repeat the procedure with the groom.

As Nadira observed the formalities, vivid memories of her wedding came back to her. When she'd been asked for her acceptance, a sense of panic had gripped her and she'd started to tremble. Her mother was standing behind her chair and at that moment placed her hands on Nadira's shoulders and gave her an encouraging squeeze. It reminded her she was not alone but following generations of women who had taken this step knowing far less than she did about their futures. They had placed their trust in their parents and their faith in Allah, and now she would have to do the same. She had taken a deep breath, spoken her acceptance and signed the contract with a steady hand.

She heard Usman asked if he would accept the marriage contract and his clear, strong voice as he accepted. Then the imam completed the Nikah ceremony by reciting a prayer from the Qur'an and various blessings upon the Prophet. Ameera held her daughter in a long embrace, and the rest of them came forward to congratulate her. Leaving the bride, the women went into the drawing room and congratulated Usman before serving dishes of dates and sweets to him and his family. Then Ameera and Latif escorted their daughter in and seated her next to the groom. Wisely, Nadira thought, her niece had chosen not to wear the veil and go through the "showing of the face" ceremony. At one time, it would have been the groom's first glimpse of his bride's face, but both the groom and the bride decided it was old fashioned and silly in their circumstances.

Nadira watched the couple as they accepted congratulations, their happiness evident in the way they kept turning toward each other. A need to see Sohail took hold of her, and she searched for his face in the crowd. She found him across the room, leaning against the wall in his old relaxed fashion conversing with a family friend who was laughing at whatever he was saying. Sohail always had a talent for entertaining people and making them feel at ease. It was one of the traits she'd admired when she first met him. It didn't take long for other people to gather around him. Watching him, she forgot her grievances for the moment and thought about all she loved about him, his intelligence, sense of fun and easy going, kind nature. Surrounded by his admirers, he appeared unchanged. What was going on that had so altered him when he was with her? She observed him as he charmed his audience, and felt a sharp pang of envy. All at once, she was a young girl again, awash in a mix of contradictory emotions. Desire, confusion, anger and sadness overtook her in rapid succession. The sadness lingered through lunch, and immunized her against the joy that infected the gathering. She was glad nobody appeared to notice the change in her mood.

Later that evening Nadira got ready for the Shaadi. Just out of a hot shower, her skin was moist, her cheeks flushed, and her face framed by the silky, black curtain of her hair which shone in the lamplight. Taking care, she lifted her mother's cleaned and pressed shalwar kameez off the hanger and slipped it on over her still slim body, then turned to look at herself in the mirror. The outfit was a perfect fit, and the contrast of the pale blue material emphasized her golden skin and dark eyes under the long, thick fringe of her eyelashes.

She heard the intake of a breath behind her. Swinging around, she saw Sohail in the doorway, looking very handsome in his white shalwar and black achkan.

"You look beautiful, Nadira. I'm afraid you'll outshine the bride tonight."

She blushed with pleasure. "I don't think there's any danger of that. Youth has its advantages."

"Then you don't see yourself as I do. You're even more beautiful than the day we met."

The unexpected compliment left her searching for something to say. "Thank you, Sohail. You're looking very handsome tonight as well. Maybe we should get dressed up more often."

Her reply sounded facile to her ears. It didn't reflect what she was feeling. The wedding had pulled her memories of their earliest days up to the surface and reawakened feelings for him she'd lost over the last few months. She wanted to ask him what had changed and come between them. How could they return to the couple they had been not so long ago? But it was not the time for a talk. They would be late for the bride's reception, and everyone would be wondering what was keeping them. Maybe tonight when they were alone, she would brave her uncertainties and discuss the questions that disturbed her days.

When they joined the family welcoming party, they were lined up in two rows in the courtyard by the gate armed with rose petals to anoint the groom and his family as they passed between them. The basso of a large drum announced the groom's arrival. Walking in between his parents, Usman looked handsome in his cream colored sherwani and elaborate turban, a garland of red and white roses decorating his chest and his feet clad in embroidered khussa shoes whose long toes curled over in front like a pug dog's tail. He held the hand of his cousin's six year old son, who was dressed in an identical outfit and would sit next to him for company throughout the evening. The groom and his companion were led down a center aisle bordered by round tables to a long sofa on a raised platform at the front of the room. Then there was a pause, and the guests turned away from the groom and watched for the bride's appearance.

Nadira was near the front of the room. All at once, she noticed Usman rising from his seat, his eyes wide, fixed on someone behind her. At the same time a murmur rose from the other guests. She turned and saw her brother-in-law and sister-in-law escorting the bride into the tent and understood the groom's reaction. Ruksana with her dramatic wedding make-up and attire was transformed from an attractive teenager into a stunning young woman. Her youthful beauty was accentuated by her glamorous outfit. She was dressed in a traditional gharara whose voluminous, floor length underskirt done in pale gold silk, flared out at the bottom and trailed behind her as she walked, showcasing the navy and burgundy embroidery. It was topped by a mid-thigh length, long-sleeved, over-shirt and a matching dupatta that fell from her head down to her ankles, both done in burgundy silk with gold and navy embroidery and the addition of tiny crystal beads that sparkled in the light. Her long hair had been parted down the middle, its length curled and pulled back and up, the elegant hairdo, just visible under her dupatta.

Wedding outfits seemed to get more and more elaborate every year, Nadira thought. Her sister-in-law had gone to a designer in Islamabad, but new, unique designs were now also available in boutique stores or could be copied by your tailor. In recent years, fashion had become an obsession with a segment of society and she wondered if it was an infection transmitted by their exposure to the West, or an extreme form of a native tendency. The expense of a traditional wedding, always high, was reaching ridiculous proportions, and she wondered where it would end. As she examined her niece's magnificent outfit, she pondered the cost. How many silkworms had lived and died to produce the yards of fabric? How many women had worked late into the night on the intricate, floral patterns placed with exacting regularity across the yards of silk, and compressed into a dense, four inch wide motif on the hem and cuffs of the over-shirt and the edge of the dupatta? How many hours had been spent picking up paper thin sequins, beads the size of sesame seeds, and making the thousands of motions required for the satin stitches and French knots. And what of the jewelry? A dowry's worth adorned her body: an ornate gold and ruby forehead medallion was pinned to the center part in her hair by a length of seed pearls; gold bangles encircled her forearms; rings studded with precious and semi-precious stones banded fingers on both hands; gold filigree earrings dangled beside each cheek; her neck was encircled by a six strand pearl choker; a gold filigree oval dotted with small gems hung from a necklace of heavy gold links, and a diamond stud pierced her nostril. How much of their parents' future ease was sacrificed to pay for them all?

It occurred to her that in addition to the ultimate cost to the purchaser, there was also a payment made by the creators of her niece's garments, in eyes, tendon and bone, with small compensation. She tried to envision a different, more modest tradition, where the religious requirements were met and the ceremonies dictated by long held local custom were simplified. What would she discard, and what would she keep? And if the families of her sons' brides held on to the old way of doing things, how was a change to be managed without hurt feelings? Would the next generation force their parents along a different path, revolting against the way things had always been done? Nadira thought about how her nani had been ahead of her time, persuading her to prepare for a career which failed to materialize for her but was now available for the young women of her niece's generation. Maybe it was up to her to find some way to weave a new vision of the future into a narrative for her sons and teach them to look at traditions from a new perspective.

Nadira looked back at her niece. With help, Ruksana had arranged herself on the sofa next to Usman, her smile still natural in the spotlight of the guests' attentive stares. She knew, by the end of the evening her niece would be battling fatigue to keep the smile on her face, and her muscles would ache from the effort of staying upright under the weight of yards of heavy fabric. This was one part of her youth she was glad to have behind her.

As she made her way toward a gathering of family members at a center table, she noticed many young girls were wearing saris, now back in fashion, and they carried them with a grace she hadn't had at that age. These days, the blouse covered all of the upper body and arms, the pleats were stitched down and snaps in convenient places held everything together. She had worn a sari for the first time at a family wedding when she was in college. Her mother had warned her she would be more comfortable in a shalwar kameez, but Nadira insisted on a sari. In those days, a sari was only a long length of fabric expertly wound beneath and over an abbreviated, short sleeved blouse that left a strip of bare midriff. She had been at a loss as to how to arrange it, and her mother had done it for her. Standing behind her, her mother had tucked one end of the sari cloth into the waistband of Nadira's petticoat, wrapped the cloth around her lower body once and then with her arms thrust under Nadira's arms, her nimble fingers gathered the cloth into even pleats just below her navel. The pleats were then tucked into the waistband. Her mother finished with one more half turn around the waist and the loose end was draped over Nadira's shoulder where her mother placed a safety pin, to ease her daughter's concerns about coming unraveled. Nadira remembered being impatient while her mother dressed her. Her recent détente with her mother made her think of that time with a fondness that she hadn't felt before. Had she thanked her mother for her help that night? How many times had her mother made an effort for her despite the fact that Nadira hadn't noticed or appreciated it? At that moment, her long formed opinions about the people in her life were as precarious as an unpinned sari.

After hours of picture taking, eating and small talk, the Shaadi ended with the Rukhsati. Sohail joined her as everyone followed Ameera and Latif, who escorted their daughter to her husband's car, ending her childhood. Ameera had her hand cupped under her daughter's elbow while Latif held a Holy Qur'an over her head. Nadira joined those crowding around the car for a last glimpse of the couple. As they shouted their goodbyes, she could see her niece inside the car, crying on her husband's shoulder. Ameera, and yes, even Latif, were also wiping away tears. Tonight would be the bride and groom's first night together. Tomorrow evening, they'd see Ruksana again at the Walima, the reception hosted by the groom's parents to welcome the bride into their family, which would take place at a marriage hall in Attock City.

As they returned to their room, Sohail looked thoughtful.

"Do you remember our first night together?"

"How could I forget that disaster? Your friends followed us to your house and stood outside the window to our bedroom singing and calling out to us until your parents drove them off at around 3:00 a.m. We were so exhausted, it took all our energy to change into our night clothes before falling asleep. The next day, I felt like everyone was staring at us, looking for a visible change when nothing had happened."

"Well, we made up for it after the Walima."

Nadira felt the heat of a blush on her face as if she were still an innocent girl. When they climbed into bed that night they were as silent as mutes, letting their bodies communicate their need for each other. Afterward, afraid of breaking the spell that had fallen over them, Nadira didn't bring up her concerns. Later, she would regret the lost opportunities she'd had during the wedding festivities to express her renewed feelings for Sohail and to somehow bridge the distance between them. The words she had left unspoken would be a burden she would carry for the rest of her life.

Chapter 10

It was Nadira's last day in Attock. The night before, the Walima had gone on for hours, and they hadn't returned from the wedding hall in Attock City until early morning. Everyone in the house had slept in, and once they were up, they had all moved in slow motion. A short while ago, they had finished afternoon tea, bid goodbye to departing relatives, and now had the dubious honor of being the last remaining guests. As she sat in the lounge with their hosts, replete and lazy, she knew it was past the time they had planned for their departure, and Sohail didn't seem in any great rush either. At this rate, though, it would be very late at night by the time they arrived home. Maybe she would let the boys skip school tomorrow. She sat on, as relaxed and satisfied as a well fed cat in a pool of sunlight, lulled into a state of somnolence by the whir of the fans and the murmur of amiable conversation. Still, she knew she should start the leave-taking process by having Sohail put their bags in the car, but she was just too comfortable to move. Everyone else seemed of a similar mind as they slumped exhausted on the sofa and chairs in the lounge and enjoyed what remained of their time together.

When Nadira heard a distant sharp, grating noise and

then several loud thuds like heavy objects hitting the stone floor in the back of the house, she saw that Ameera and Latif also noticed. Just as her brother-in-law rose to go investigate, footsteps sounded in the hallway. She expected to see servants enter the room, but instead, three strange men walked in showing no signs of discomfort, acting as if they were there by invitation. Smears of dirt covered the front of their shalwar kurtas, and automatic weapons were cradled in their arms. Two of the men also had coils of rope draped over their shoulders. Shocked into silence, the only sound was the slap of the men's leather sandals against the floor as they surrounded the family, their guns pointing at them like giant accusing fingers. Panicked, Nadira's eyes sought out Arif and Samir, and found them, their faces as bleached as cave dwellers, sitting cross-legged on floor cushions on the opposite side of the room. Arif had risen to a half crouch as if considering flight, while Samir's arms crossed his chest in a posture of self-protection.

A man with a dark beard, bushy black eyebrows and a wide, prominent nose stepped forward with a bowlegged gait, his kurta stretched tight over a protruding belly.

"Don't be frightened; if you do as we say, nobody will get hurt."

"Take what you want; just leave us alone," Latif told him.

The man smirked and told her brother-in-law he needn't worry about them helping themselves. Once he determined Latif was the house's owner; he forced him to stand by his side. Then, this bearded man, whom Nadira identified as the gang leader, instructed everyone near the windows to move to the seats on the far wall.

She was able to make room for her youngest son next to her but had to be content to face her husband and older son across a space, which though small, put them out of reach. Nadira thought if only all of her family was shoulder to shoulder, the situation would be easier to bear. It was similar to the way she felt about flying, always insisting they get four seats together. The boys complained because it meant they had to sit in the center section, never allowed the window seat they wanted. But, no matter how irrational her thought process might be, she was convinced if the plane ever had a problem, being together would somehow make a difference. And Nadira couldn't shake the feeling that disaster was imminent.

A fourth man entered the room with the two servants. The maid was crying, and the cook had a red mark on his cheek and a cut on his upper lip. The man shoved both servants to the floor. The gang leader, whom Nadira dubbed Black Beard, yelled at the maid to be quiet before turning his attention back to the rest of them.

"Now you'll give us all the jewelry on your persons, if you please. My friend here will collect it," he said.

When one of the men stood in front of her with an open cloth sack, she saw he was not a man at all but a smooth cheeked boy, maybe only a year or two older than Arif. Her bangles went into the bag without regret, but when she handed over her sapphire and diamond wedding band, she almost cried out in protest.

The collection process finished, Black Beard nodded his head in some prearranged signal to the men carrying the ropes. The men, with practiced motions, duct taped their mouths and tied their hands and feet together. Then a length of rope was looped between their bound hands and feet and all the knots tested. In Nadira's case, the looped rope was a little too short for her to sit upright, and she was forced to bend forward in a position of supplication. The man trussing her noticed her predicament and loosened the rope so she could sit up straight. Her tether adjusted, he reached over and as instinct pulled Nadira back away from his hand, he lifted her dupatta off her shoulders and placed it over her head.

"Begum Sahib, I know you don't want your head uncovered in front of unrelated men," he said in a soft, polite voice.

In other circumstances, the two acts would have been ones of kindness, but they made Nadira shudder.

"We're sorry for any discomfort, but you wouldn't believe the foolish things people do," Black Beard said. Then, making sure Latif had his house keys on him, he escorted him out of the room to unlock all the cupboards.

Nadira watched the young man who had collected the jewelry squat on his heels and light up a cigarette. She had exacted a promise from her sons that they would not pick up the habit of smoking and wondered if his mother knew he smoked. It was true; his age made her think of him in a different way. When she'd noticed his youth, her first thought was he'd been coerced into criminal activity, a naïve conclusion she was sure. Did she think only middle-age men committed these acts? Past media reports told a different story; neither age nor gender was an impediment to immoral, violent behavior. Still, when she had looked into his young face, it had been hard for her to accept he had chosen to be here.

It was difficult not to stare at the man guarding them. What was it about guns that drew your attention and repelled you at the same time? Nadira saw how his finger twitched close to the trigger, and it sent an icy stream through her veins. When he redirected his gaze at her, she ducked her head. She didn't want him seeing the naked emotions she was sure were on her face.

Samir leaned his body against hers. She strained her bonds to their limit so she could grip his hands with her fingers. She glanced across at Sohail and Arif. Sweat adhered Arif's hair to his forehead, and his eyes were downcast so she couldn't get his attention. When her eyes met Sohail's, he raised his eyebrows in an attempt, she thought, to encourage her. If it had been possible, she would have offered a smile in return, but the tape over her mouth wouldn't allow it. Instead, she nodded her head.

Black Beard returned to the room with Latif, who was bound like the rest of them. Retrieving a chair from the dining room, he positioned it so its back faced the group. He sat down and made himself comfortable, balancing the barrel of his gun on top of the chair back. Then, he sent one man outside to keep watch and motioned the other two men out of the room.

"We'll try and get out of your way as fast as we can," Black Beard said as if he were an accommodating trades-person. His eyes darted from one person to the next. "Why so scared? I'm sorry if we've given you the wrong impression. We're just making a living. We have nothing against you and have no intention of hurting anyone. You know the famous outlaw, Robin Hood? I saw a movie about him when I was a young boy. The Pakistan People's Party candidate treated all the people in our village to a film show before the elections. It was a great movie and got him lots of votes. Think of me as Robin Hood. I rob you of things you can do without and give them to the poor – me and my men. You can count your lost valuables as part of your zakat for the year."

Far from comforting Nadira, if that was the story's intent, the man's mocking tone angered and disturbed her. And upon further observation, Nadira felt there was something familiar about him – the eyebrow deformed by a scar, the nose, and the scowl when his men didn't respond to an order fast enough. She studied his face, searching for the connection. Her stomach lurched when she realized where she had seen him before. Age had etched the lines of a disagreeable nature on his face; his mustache had become a beard and he had put on at least 20 kilos, but she was sure she wasn't mistaken. He was same man who had once guarded their neighborhood for a few short months when she was a child - the man who had been involved in the drug and gun trade. This realization sent shivers through her body.

From where she sat, she could see into the foyer and watch the robbers haul everything out the front door and load it into a truck. During the next three hours, the house was emptied of anything of value: cash, jewelry, electronic devices, small appliances, silver serving dishes and flatware, hand knotted Bokhara and Kilim rugs, decorative brass objects, and even the excess embroidered silk fabric left over from wedding outfits. As Nadira sat through each second, minute and hour, every smell, sight and sound left an indelible imprint on her brain. After a while, her body and mind went numb.

She shifted her stiff body as much as possible, but there was very little space between them on the sofa, and Samir continued to lean on her for comfort. When she looked at Arif, his eyes seemed to appeal to her for help. If only she had insisted on leaving at the appointed time, this wouldn't be happening. Even as this thought passed through her mind, she dismissed it. If she'd been born with hindsight, how different her life would be. She'd made so many mistakes. She was reminded of the Ashura riot. She and Hameeda had been a few months older than Arif was now, still children. In a contest of wills with her father, what chance did Hameeda have to succeed? She was ashamed she hadn't given Hameeda an opportunity to explain and at her stubbornness in withholding her forgiveness. She implored Allah, to give her an opportunity to make things right with Sohail and Hameeda.

The sun had long departed by the time the robbers were satisfied they had found everything worth taking.

324

With the exception of the outside lookout, the entire gang assembled again in front of them.

"Sahib, we're disappointed you haven't been more extravagant in your spending. The jewelry was nice, but there wasn't as much as we expected, and such an old TV and only two computers," Black Beard said. "Really, it's a very small return for so much planning and work. It pains me, but we shall have to make up the difference somehow."

He glanced around the room and then pointed his gun at Sohail. Nadira had never known such fear before; it clenched her stomach, closed her throat and made her heart jump in her chest.

"Ah, Mr. Factory Owner, I'll have to ask you to come with me."

How did they know Sohail owned a factory? Who had given them the information and pointed him out? Nadira glanced over at the servants and saw the cook bow his head. As if from a distance, she heard someone moan.

"Begum Sahib, please don't be distressed. I promise we won't harm him. He'll just spend a few days as our guest, how long will depend on how fast you get us our money. It will just be a slight inconvenience."

Sohail's feet were untied, and he was pulled upright. Arif made an angry noise and tried getting to his feet but quieted when Sohail shook his head and a gun was trained on him.

"Now, we must go. It was a pleasure meeting all of you. I hope we have behaved as gentlemen. The gate will be left open, the front door unlocked, and the outside light turned on so some curious neighbor or passerby will find and release you. Don't report this to the police. They're really a useless lot, and if they find us, we'll have to pay them a share, forcing us to increase the ransom. We'll be in touch soon and let you know how much we want for Mr. Factory Owner's return and where to deliver the money." Then, with a gun at her husband's back and a man on either side of him, they left.

Nadira was horrified at how the man had spoken of Sohail, treating him like a commodity, no different than a pair of diamond earrings or the latest Nintendo, just an item on their balance sheet. If they didn't recognize his humanity, didn't see him with a family like their own, what chance was there he would be returned once they got what they wanted?

As soon as Nadira heard the noise of their truck disappearing down the street, she tried reaching up to pull the tape off her mouth, but the rope attached to her feet prevented her from getting her hands up high enough. Her nephew, seeing her struggle, shimmied off his chair onto the floor. Then he pulled his knees up to his chest and tried reaching his mouth, but there was still not enough slack. After watching him, Arif, also got down on the floor and positioned himself next to his cousin. He tried to untie his cousin's hands but failed, probably because the hours of being bound had made his fingers stiff and clumsy. He did manage to yank the tape off his cousin's mouth. Her nephew yelped in pain as it tore away, leaving his face branded with a rectangle of dark red, hairless skin.

A minute later, she was grateful for this small accomplishment when there was knock on the door, and her nephew yelled for help. She saw the front door open a crack and a neighbor's voice rang out.

"Latif, Ameera, are you here?"

"Uncle, we're in the lounge. We've been tied up and robbed."

The neighbor rushed into the room. "Allah be merciful; what has happened here!" Starting with Latif, he peeled the tape off their mouths and untied their bonds.

As she waited her turn, a mantra kept repeating itself in Nadira's head - please hurry, please hurry, please hurry. Every passing moment meant the robbers were traveling farther and farther away with Sohail. Once freed, she tried to voice her concerns, but with her throat and mouth as dry as the Thar Desert, it took her a few moments before she could make an intelligible sound.

"Please, you must call the police at once so they can go after the robbers and free my husband."

"I don't think it's a good idea," the neighbor said. "The police can't be relied on, and it will only anger the kidnappers. I know a man in the business of getting kidnapped people released who has all the necessary contacts. He can take charge of the negotiations and the exchange of money for your husband. His fee is reasonable. With your permission, I'll call him for you at once."

"I don't know," she said, feeling paralyzed by indecision.

"Nadira, what my friend says is true. You know I wouldn't risk my brother's life," Latif said. "Hiring an expert is the best approach. You and the boys can stay here until Sohail is released."

How did Latif and his neighbor know so much about these things? Was kidnapping becoming so commonplace this information was available to everyone? Scared and uncertain, Nadira agreed to leave the police out of it, but she wasn't willing to accede to everything.

"I don't want Arif and Samir to stay. I want them out of harm's way. I'll call my parents to come get them."

"I won't leave," Arif said.

Samir clung to her arm. "I'm staying too."

"You'll do as you're told," she said, fear sharpening her voice. Watching Samir's face collapse in response to her tone, she put her hand on his shoulder to soften her rebuke.

The neighbor emphasized the importance of secrecy and suggested she let her sons stay, telling her they were in no danger, and with Allah's help, she would be leaving with her husband in a few days.

"What if the robbers come back?" Nadira asked.

"Believe me, I've never heard of an instance when they've done that. What would they come back for?" the neighbor said.

Nadira agreed to follow their suggestions but only if she were included in any conversations with the man who would negotiate Sohail's release. After a short argument, Latif agreed to let her participate. It felt wrong to argue with her brother-in-law at a time when unity was important, but she wasn't willing to step aside and put her family's fate wholly in the hands of others.

It was arranged for Latif's friend to call the negotiator. Nadira knew there was nothing else they could do until they heard from the kidnappers. She hoped they would call soon; she didn't think she could endure a long wait.

While her brother-in-law walked his neighbor out, the cook shuffled over to Nadira, his posture bent and his eyes averted. "Please forgive me, Begum Sahib. I swear, even after they hit me, I didn't give them any information. But when they said they'd harm my wife and children, I had to give in."

She remembered her fear for her own family, and her anger at the cook slid away.

"I don't blame you. You only did what you had to do."

"Thank you, Begum Sahib. You're most generous. May Allah bless you and your family, and may your husband be returned safely."

A pair of arms enfolded her and she smelled Ameera's perfume as their cheeks touched.

"Nadira, I keep thinking it was our neglect that put all of us in danger. I'll never stop blaming myself for this. I can't imagine what you're feeling, but you must have faith Allah will protect Sohail and bring him back to us unharmed."

Ameera's words made her realize, no matter how happy the ending, this trauma would never be over, its influence felt in some measure for the rest of their lives. As difficult as it was for her to speak, she managed to tell Ameera she was in no way responsible, in the hope it would at least lighten her burden.

"I think we should all try and eat something," her sister-in-law said as she motioned to her husband and son to follow her. "I'll come back to collect you when it's ready."

The air was thick as it entered Nadira's lungs making her ache with each breath. She could still detect the rank odor of dried sweat left behind by the robbers. She prayed she was caught in a nightmare that was more vivid than usual and any moment she would wake up. But when she glanced down, she saw the tattooed bracelets of abraded skin on her wrists, and her face burned where the tape had been peeled away. A tormented cry lay trapped in the back of her throat, and she was afraid she couldn't hold it in, but seeing her sons huddled next to her, she clamped her teeth together to imprison it before it escaped her lips.

Nadira put an arm around each of her sons. Samir started to cry, and Arif's face twisted in an attempt to still his own tears, but in the end, the little boy in him overcame his almost grown-up resolve. Her own tears had sunk so deep into a well of despair, she couldn't access them.

"Everything will be all right. You'll see; everything will be all right." Nadira said, in an effort to convince herself as much as her sons. They waited in silence, the only sound a few remaining snuffles from Samir. When she looked at her sons' faces, they appeared as dazed as she felt. It was only a short while before Ameera returned to tell them dinner was ready. Later, she would wonder how she had managed to sit at the table and encourage the boys to eat when she felt so close to collapse. She'd known she should also eat something, but difficulty swallowing and a rebellious stomach precluded all but a few sips of tea. Waiting for the meal to be over, she moved her food around the plate with her fork, exhaustion sparing her by emptying her mind.

It was almost midnight when they went to bed. Nadira hoped the unconsciousness of sleep would separate her sons from their fears for a brief period. Arif had gone back to her nephew's room to seek comfort in a familiar routine, she presumed, while Samir insisted on sharing her bed. She lay there stroking his back until he slept. She spent the rest of the night staring into the darkened room, trying to rid her mind of worst case scenarios always ending with Sohail's body in a funeral shroud.

When daylight worked its way through the gap between the window frame and the drapes, she slipped out from under the arm Samir had flung over her and went to shower and dress. Under the fall of water, Nadira's naked body showed the evidence of her ordeal. Her wrists and ankles were discolored and swollen. In addition, the muscles of her arms and legs were stiff and sore, and her back ached. She moved like an arthritic grandmother, she thought, as she rubbed her skin dry and dressed. She covered her head with her dupatta and wrapped it around her shoulders, to tame her shivers. Then she eased the door open and left Samir to sleep as long as possible.

Entering the lounge, she saw Latif sitting on the edge of a chair, deep in conversation with a stranger.

"Asalaam aleikum," Nadira said in a voice softened by uncertainty.

Startled, the men looked over at her.

"Nadira, you're up early. Let me introduce you to Mr. Siddiqi who will be negotiating Sohail's release. Mr. Siddiqi, this is my sister-in-law Nadira Malik. It's her husband who's been kidnapped."

The negotiator stood up and gave her a slight bow. "Asalaam Aleikum Mrs. Malik, I'm so sorry for your trouble."

Nadira didn't know what she had expected, but without a doubt, not this. Everything about the man was average, his height, his build and his facial characteristics. He wore his thick grey hair short and had a neat, trim beard. He was dressed in an expensive looking western suit, had bejeweled rings on his left ring finger and right pinky finger, and his feet were clad in black shoes polished until the light bounced off them.

"Thank you, Mr. Siddiqi," she said as she took a seat next to her brother-in-law.

No call had been received from the kidnappers, but the negotiator told her he expected them to call at any moment. Nadira questioned him about his experience. For the last three years, he had been dealing with the release of kidnapping victims, almost all from the Islamabad area but once as far away as Karachi. She asked how he'd gotten into this line of work, all the while thinking how bizarre it was to make such routine inquiries, as if she were looking for a driver or cook.

"I'm a retired army intelligence officer and have many contacts in the military and, shall we say, with the shadier segments of the population," he told her. "The first kidnapping victim whose release I secured was my cousin. Word of my success reached other people in similar circumstances, who asked me for my help." He leaned forward and his jacket sleeves rode up revealing snowy shirt cuffs. "After securing the release of a couple more people, I realized I had found a calling where, with Allah's help, I could return kidnapping victims to their families."

"And have you been one hundred percent successful?"

"When all the kidnappers' demands are met, yes, I have."

Nadira didn't ask the next logical question. There was no reason to. She would pay anything to get Sohail back.

She was assured by Mr. Siddiqi he would not leave until the kidnappers called, no matter how long it took. And, he would speak to them on her behalf.

It was done. With just a neighbor's recommendation and with no expertise in the matter, they had hired a nego-tiator, a stranger who held her husband's life and her fami-ly's future in his hands.

"Not to worry, Mrs. Malik, I'll handle everything."

But, how could she not worry? Did he think her concerns were something she could transfer to him and then forget? Her irritation at a comment she knew was meant to sooth her was evidence of her agitation and made her realize his dispassion was one of his assets.

Mr. Siddiqi went on to explain how the robbers had gained entry to the house. In his search of the grounds, he had found where they had climbed over the boundary wall from the empty lot next door. He suggested it must have happened while they were away at the Walima. The bars from the rear laundry room window had been cut out, puttied back into place and the cut marks coated with soot so nobody would notice. All they'd had to do the previous day was remove the bars and get in through the window.

Nadira shivered at how easy it had been.

"This is the wedding season. These robbers watch out for houses where weddings are taking place. It's not hard when they're advertised with wedding tents lit up with bright lights and the noise of music. Then they strike before the women have returned their expensive jewelry to their bank vaults," he said. "Although people hear about these things happening, nobody ever thinks it's going to happen to them. And, until very recently, it has been occurring mostly in large cities where strangers aren't as visible."

There seemed to be nothing else to say, and fixed in her seat, trying to make polite conversation only played on Nadira's nerves. She asked Latif to have someone come get her when the call came in and excused herself to go say her prayers and be available to her sons. At least it might reduce her feeling of uselessness.

She entered the bedroom, taking care to be as quiet as possible, leaving the door open a crack so she could hear the phone ringing. Samir was still asleep, his body crosswise on the bed wrapped in a tangle of sheets and blankets. She did her ablution, tented herself in her dupatta and began her prayers. But thoughts kept interrupting her recitation. Sohail was a good man; why would Allah let this happen to him? If he didn't come home unharmed, what would become of them? Again and again she pushed her anxieties away so she could continue. She was only able to focus her full attention after she'd finished the standard morning prayers and began special prayers for Sohail and the children. She chose each word with care, as if the form of her entreaties would determine whether or not Allah answered her requests. A long time ago, Hameeda had told her she could sense Allah's presence when she prayed. But only darkness enclosed Nadira, as if the ground had opened up beneath her and pitched her into a deep pit.

A soft knock on the door made her jump. "Yes, who is it?"

"Amma, it's me, Arif."

"Come in, beta."

When Arif looked at the bed, she saw his face light up for an instant before he realized the sleeping form was Samir.

"I can't believe Abu is really gone."

"He'll be back with us soon, beta."

"Do you really think so?"

"Yes I do. I've met the man helping us, and he's confident Abu will be released." Nadira wondered if she would be punished for lying but couldn't imagine any punishment worse than what she was enduring.

"What's happening?" a sleepy voice asked.

"Nothing Samir; Arif and I are just talking."

"You know, Arif, after this is over and we're back at home, we'll have to have Jameel and his family over for dinner so your Abu can meet them. What do you think?" Nadira asked.

Arif gave her a weak smile.

A phone rang in the distance. She directed Arif to stay with Samir and hurried out of the room. When she reached the lounge, the negotiator was on the phone. It was clear he was talking to the kidnappers. Latif held a finger to his lips and then led Nadira to the opposite side of the room.

Mr. Siddiqi's side of the conversation constituted only three words during the entire call – yes, or I understand. Would this be the extent of his contribution to Sohail's release? Either she or Latif could have done the same. She waited, impatient for the call to end. Since their lives had been invaded by Black Beard and his cohorts, she was always counting increments of time, seconds, minutes and hours which extended out farther than they had in the past. And, she no longer recognized herself. Once logical and organized, her brain had become a repository for discon-nected thoughts. When the negotiator hung up the phone, she felt sick to her stomach.

"The kidnappers have made their demand. They want $300,000," he said, his face expressionless. "It must be delivered to them within six days. Once we have the money, they'll give us further instructions."

Nadira gasped, and Latif put his head in his hands.

"But we don't have that kind of money!" Calculating how much Sohail kept in the factory's account in a normal month, Nadira said, "I could take most of it out of the account Sohail kept for his business operating expenses, but I would need time to raise the rest. When will the kidnappers expect an answer?"

"They said they would call back tomorrow."

"My sister-in-law and I will talk it over. I'll call you this afternoon when I know more," Latif told him.

"You have my number; call me anytime."

Her brother-in-law was pale and sweating when he came back from walking the negotiator out. "Nadira, there's something I have to tell you."

"You're frightening me, Latif. What is it?"

Nadira listened dumbfounded as her brother-in-law explained how over the past year the business had been going downhill. There was only about $35,000 in the bank account and except for a few small receivables, the business was on the verge of bankruptcy.

"How can that be? Just a few months ago Sohail was talking about new customers and increased sales."

"It must have been more than a few months ago." Her brother-in-law began to pace. "Last year Sohail spent a lot of money purchasing and running generators because of the unreliability of electric power. Then when the terrorist attacks increased, he started losing accounts." He paused and glanced at her. "In recent months, his biggest overseas customers wouldn't renew their contracts, and his oldest customer withdrew just a month ago. They were uncomfortable coming here for the necessary onsite meetings and were afraid the instability would lead to delayed or incomplete orders." He shrugged. "Nothing Sohail could say or do would persuade them to give him a chance."

"Why didn't he tell me?"

"He didn't want to burden you with the same worries. At first he thought he could save the business by switching to production for the domestic market, but it's already overcrowded with established firms. When he realized it was hopeless, he decided to sell the factory equipment, building and the remaining inventory. He has two potential buyers he's been talking to." Latif stopped pacing and looked at her. "He'd planned on telling you everything when he had some better news."

Nadira felt a slow build-up of anger and became furious with Sohail. How could he confide in his brother instead of her? How had she gone from a marriage partner to someone who needed protection? But her fury was soon replaced by despair. "Can we tell the kidnappers they haven't given us enough time to raise such a large sum of money?"

"They won't believe us." Latif shook his head. "They think all factory owners are enormously rich fat cats with ready access to cash. They'll assume we're just trying to cheat them out of their money. I'll speak to the interested buyers and try and push a sale along by reducing the asking price, and talk to family members and see how much they can contribute."

Nadira knew Sohail would be humiliated to have his failure common knowledge, but she couldn't think of any other solution.

"Do you think we can raise the $300,000?"

Latif hesitated. "In all honesty, Nadira, we might do it if we had a few months but …"

"If only they would give us more time. When they call tomorrow, Mr. Siddiqi must see if he can get them to extend the deadline." Nadira did a mental inventory of her remaining jewelry, which didn't amount to much, and their other possessions. "I can also put one of our cars and the house up for sale. I'll call my brother Asim and ask him to try and find buyers."

"I'll discuss the situation with Mr. Siddiqi, and then you can get in touch with Asim. I'll probably need his assistance with the factory sale as well."

"Yes, please call him right away." Nadira could hear the note of hysteria in her voice and calmed herself down. Now was the time for her to muster her strength. She could give in to her emotions when it was over and Sohail was returned unharmed. She let Latif make the call without her. He had more information about their situation, and Nadira didn't know if she could sit through a repetition of his shocking disclosures and still keep her composure.

The rest of the day was spent on the phone and closeted with her brother-in-law. Each person they took into their confidence was told Sohail's life depended on them not revealing the kidnapping to anyone whose involvement was not necessary. After discussing it with Latif, it was agreed Nadira could tell her parents so they could approach the rest of her family for any financial help they could offer, and put the newer car and the house up for sale. When they heard the news, her parents wanted to leave at once for Attock, but she told them they would be more helpful if they stayed in Lahore for the time being.

There were many times when Nadira thought she would collapse under the weight of her fears. She was thinking that nothing in her short life had prepared her to cope with her present circumstances when she remembered the ballet class she had taken as a young girl.

She must have been about eight years old. A friend had been attending classes taught by an English lady. Nadira hadn't been the least bit interested in ballet until she saw her friend's beautiful pink, satin toe shoes with matching ankle ribbons and a white bunny fur piece to pad her toes. She asked her mother if she could join the class, and her mother, pleased at her interest in such a feminine activity, signed her up. She could still picture her teacher, her brown hair pulled back in a tight bun, her chin up and back as straight as a soldier at attention. Her first day, Nadira was dismayed to discover, as a beginner, she would start with ballet slippers, not the toe shoes she coveted. Her ballet slippers were black and held in place by an elastic band which pinched the top of her foot. And, there was no standing on her toes in an elegant stance, only flat footed exercises with her arms held at unfamiliar angles. Fear of what her mother would say held her in the class for only a couple of months before she quit. But some lessons stuck with her. Her ability to stand in the five basic positions still remained, and she also recalled a posture exercise their teacher had given them while at the ballet barre. She summoned up her teacher's commanding voice with its upper class, British accent instructing the class.

"Young ladies, you must not slump like wet noodles.

Always strive for a still, lifted body. Imagine you have a string running from the base of your spine through the top of your head, and use the string to pull yourself up straight."

In the company of family, the only thing keeping Nadira upright was an invisible string and the vision of her sons' faces before her. At night alone in her bedroom, her body sagged into a comma, and her tears flowed across her pillow.

After five days, they were still short $53,000, leaving the factory sale as their best chance. They continued to talk to interested buyers, but the parties were taking their time examining the books and the property and would not be rushed. Their house was also up for sale, but that had never been a realistic solution. Meanwhile, the kidnappers would not extend the deadline and were calling once a day, asking when they would have their money. They wouldn't put Sohail on the phone, but e-mailed pictures of him holding a newspaper with the date displayed, proving he was still alive. Each picture increased Nadira's panic. At the end of the six days, when there was no further progress with fund raising, Mr. Siddiqi decided they should try and work out an agreement for Sohail's return with the money they had. Her parents had arrived unannounced the day before, bringing the funds they'd collected with them. She convinced them to take the boys and her nephew out for the day, so they wouldn't be around when they received the call.

It was hours before the phone rang. Nadira wondered

if the kidnappers were prolonging the wait on purpose as a way to torture them. During the call, she sat across the room, and it wasn't until later she found she'd been clenching her hands, leaving behind red quarter moons from her fingernails digging into her palms. Latif stood beside Mr. Siddiqi like a disciple waiting to do his master's bidding, so close, their bodies were almost touching.

As Nadira listened to the negotiator's side of the conversation, her fears intensified.

"Yes, we have the money for you, but we weren't able to raise the entire amount."

"No, we don't think you're fools. These people are of more modest means then you've been told."

"What does the servant know? To him a few thousand rupees is a fortune.

"The factory stands empty. Send someone to me, and I will take him there so he can see for himself."

"No, we haven't talked to the police, and this isn't a trap. His wife and children cry for him every day. May Allah strike me down if I lie; this is the best they can do."

After more back and forth, Mr. Siddiqi cited verses from the Qur'an and quoted the hadith like an imam sermonizing at Friday prayers. Finally his voice ceased its striving, and he just listened. From time to time, he wrote something down on a small pad he had taken out of his pocket. The phone call ended in the most ordinary way as if he was taking leave of an acquaintance.

"Will they release him?" Latif asked, his forehead furrowed with worry.

"Yes, they'll take what you've raised and return him to his family. They gave me instructions on where to go for the exchange of the money for Mr. Malik."

"When?" Nadira asked, finally finding her voice.

"Tomorrow morning."

Mr. Siddiqi's response elicited an enormous smile from Latif. But, when Nadira looked at the negotiator, she saw his shoulders roll forward and one hand cupped the back of his head like a man expecting a blow.

"You'll be in my prayers, Mr. Siddiqi," she said.

"Thank you, Mrs. Malik. We'll need all the assistance Allah can spare us. I'll go now. There's much to do before tomorrow morning."

When they were alone, Nadira told Latif she had no idea what to tell the rest of the family and expressed a lack of optimism. She asked him if he would talk to them for her. Latif counseled caution, suggesting they tell them about the meeting without mentioning the return of Sohail. Hoping he would refute the uncertainty she'd sensed in Mr. Siddiqi, she asked him if he thought something would go wrong.

He came over and put his hand on her shoulder. She noticed how untidy his clothes had become, how his once brisk step was slow and halting, how the creases in his forehead had deepened into trenches and lines had formed in the corners of his mouth.

"This has been a horrible time, particularly for you, but we must have faith."

It was not the answer she'd been hoping for. Nadira

wished she could respond in a way which would help her brother-in-law, who was taking such good care of them during this crisis. But whatever faith she had was gone. Faith was a luxury from a different time when the chaos and horror were kept at a manageable distance by the belief these things only happened to other people. Now, events which formerly had been just newsprint on a page, rushed to drown her like the turning sea at high tide.

Later, she had no memory of how she spent the rest of the day. But, somehow she got through both it and the night that followed. Before dawn, Nadira was in the room when Latif and Mr. Siddiqi made final preparations. The money collected with such difficulty during the week was packed into a new leather case. All the old rupee notes, which had worn their history in soiled creases and tattered edges, had been exchanged for crisp new bills and banded in small piles. Nadira knew everything which could be done had been done, but would it be enough?

She joined the family for breakfast despite a lack of appetite, adhering to a normal routine as a means of retaining her sanity. Very little was consumed by anyone, but they stayed rooted in their chairs and toyed with their food. Her father made a few awkward, unsuccessful attempts at conversation. Everyone appeared to be preoccupied with their own thoughts. Afterward, her nephew and Arif went outside and kicked a football around, Samir retreated to a quiet corner with a book, and Latif went into the library to go over accounts. Both Ameera and her parents asked her if she would like some company, but she told them she hadn't slept well and thought she would go lie down for a while.

Nights of interrupted sleep had left her feeling exhausted to the edge of tears. When she lay down, her head spun, making her dizzy and nauseous. So, she got up and mapped the room with her feet. Four strides down the side of the bed, four strides to the chair, two strides to the door, ten strides to the opposite wall and then back to the start. She paced until her legs gave out, and she collapsed on the bed. At some point she must have fallen asleep. She woke to loud knocking on the door, which jerked her upright. As she swung her legs over the side of the bed, Ameera's head appeared in the doorway.

"Nadira, Latif is in his office on the phone with Mr. Siddiqi."

Nadira ran out of the room to the office. Her parents stood outside, corralling the boys with their arms while her nephew stood nearby. Ameera stepped aside, letting her enter the office alone. She closed the door behind her just as Latif was saying goodbye. She saw no elation on his face. His eyebrows had drawn together over lightless eyes, and his cheeks were flushed.

"What's happened?"

"Mr. Siddiqi turned the money over, but Sohail had been moved to a remote location, and it will be another day before they bring him back. They've given him instructions on where he can pick up Sohail tomorrow."

Nadira shook her head. "No! They said he would be released today. It must be today, not tomorrow, today!"

"Nadira, it will be all right. It's just a few more hours."

"I can't do this anymore, Latif."

"Yes you can," he said in a gentle voice.

Nadira covered her eyes with her hands, forcing back tears. "All right, will you tell everyone? I don't think I can."

"Yes. Come, they'll be wondering what's happening."

Latif updated the group huddling outside the room, making this development sound like something they had expected. But Nadira could see they didn't believe it any more than she did.

"I've heard they avoid detection by moving kidnapping victims around," her father volunteered.

"Yes, that's what Mr. Siddiqi indicated," Latif replied, grasping the lifeline her father had thrown him.

"So, tomorrow then," her father said.

Nadira spent the rest of the day making sure she and the boys were distracted with activities. She stayed busy with tasks reflecting a forced optimism. She supervised the servant in the washing of the family's dirty clothes so she would have one less chore when they reached home. She repacked their suitcases and helped Ameera and her mother prepare breaded goat chops and a sweet rice dish Sohail was fond of, as a special treat for the next day's tea. While they cooked, her mother talked about happier times or asked about events from the wedding, anything to take their minds off the current situation.

After days of tension, Nadira felt lifeless and claustrophobic, and asked Samir if he would go outside with her for a walk. It was the first time she'd been outside the house in a week. She and Samir walked side by side, sinking into the sandy soil the wind had piled up on the edge of the road, imprinting it with evidence of their existence. A while later, turning around and walking back to the house, she noticed a breezy broom had already swept away her footprints, as if to demonstrate her insignificance.

When they returned, she asked Ameera for a book and then found herself reading the same page three times without one word registering. She avoided company whenever possible; the effort to stay positive and not break down was becoming an almost impossible task. Once in bed, having spent the day focused on finding ways to push the hands of the clock forward, she wished time would reverse itself so she wouldn't have to face the uncertainty of Sohail's release.

In the morning nobody even made a pretense of eating breakfast. They all sat in the lounge waiting for the phone call, as motionless and silent as when they had been bound and gagged.

Nadira didn't know what time it was when Latif's mobile phone rang. It could have been minutes or hours since they had started their vigil. Latif stepped away from everyone and cupped the phone to his ear. Nadira studied his expression as he listened. When she saw his face crumple, taking on the appearance of an old man, any hope she had kept alive disappeared. He turned away for a second, and Nadira heard him thank Mr. Siddiqi in a strangled voice before he hung up the phone. When he faced them, there were tears streaming down his cheeks.

Nadira couldn't ask the question. It was her father who said, "What's happened?"

Latif raised his hands, palms up in a pleading gesture before he spoke. "When Mr. Siddiqi arrived at the designated place, the police were already there. They had received an anonymous phone call a short time before, directing them to the meeting site where they found Sohail's body."

The anguished scream, which had taken up residence at the back of Nadira's throat the day they took Sohail, escaped its flimsy prison before she collapsed to the floor.

Chapter 11

"Please Amma; can I stay home from school?" Rabia, pleaded. I don't feel well."

"Beti, your father just examined you and found nothing wrong."

"My stomach hurts."

"Once you're at school you'll feel better." Hameeda stroked her daughter's back. "Be a good girl and get dressed. Your father will be leaving in a few minutes. If you don't hurry, you'll be late."

Rabia sniffled, and her eyes leaked as she pulled on her school uniform. Hameeda felt powerless to help her daughter, certain fear was the cause of her pain. It had become a common malady, with no available cure.

Two days before, there had been a bombing at a girls' school in Peshawar. Twenty-eight children were buried in the rubble. Although it was quite a distance from Lahore, the attack hit Hameeda almost as hard as if it had been her children's school. When she'd watched the TV footage, she expected to see familiar faces among the mothers, and in a way they were all known to her, because but for Allah's grace, she could easily have been any one of them. It was horrifying to think Rabia might be identifying just as much with the dead and injured girls and pictured herself buried under a pile of concrete debris.

Hameeda tried remembering life before terrorist acts. Once a rarity and related to local sectarian disputes, they had proliferated after the Afghan War. Now, almost every week there was some type of violent incident. She and Zubair had tried to reassure the children, told them their school was well protected, and classes would be cancelled if there was the slightest chance of danger. After repeated attacks, Jameel and Daliya appeared to have armed themselves with a protective shell, but Rabia was more upset after each bombing. Hameeda understood her daughter's increasing apprehension since her own fears had been heightened after witnessing the aftermath of the bombing at the Sufi shrine. Intermittent nightmares still troubled her. If she had a choice, she would keep all three children home from school, but Zubair insisted they live as normal a life as possible.

After Rabia finished dressing, Hameeda took her into the bathroom and bathed her face, wishing she could wash away her fears as easily as the tear tracks on her cheeks. Although eleven-year-old Rabia had been braiding her own hair for a while now, it soothed Hameeda to go back to a chore she associated with her daughter's younger, innocent years. As she plaited, she wove in a length of pink ribbon in the hope this special touch might cheer up her daughter, who was still so miserable; Hameeda felt heart sore.

"Look how pretty you are, beti." She stroked her cheek, still as soft as an infant's, and gave her a quick hug, then walked with her to the lounge where Zubair was waiting.

"Beti, are you feeling better?" Zubair asked as they came through the door.

Her daughter glanced up at him. "Yes, Abu."

"Good." You can sit up front with me this morning. Would you like that?"

The front seat next to Zubair was a coveted spot and not so long ago Rabia would have been overjoyed, but this morning she just nodded her head. Her husband reached out and grasped her hand, as if to keep her from changing her mind and retreating back to her room. "All right, it's getting late; let's go."

After they'd left, Hameeda tried to find comfort in her familiar, daily routine. Once she had savored her early morning solitude, time to do nothing more than sit and enjoy the garden, her body still, her thoughts tucked away. But now she craved motion and interaction to crowd out the press of her worries which sometimes crept into the unoccupied moments of her day. Her mother-in-law's needs had become a surprising blessing. Now, by the time she finished with the old woman's breakfast, helped the maid get her bathed, dressed and settled into her wheelchair, the morning was gone; then lunch, the usual tyranny of afternoon chores and the children's after-school activities held her captive.

A few hours later, she opened the storage cupboard in the laundry to return the iron the maid had forgotten to put away and noticed several lengths of unfamiliar black cloth hanging on a hook in the far corner. When she pulled them out, she discovered it was a burqa a former servant must have left behind. It seemed wasteful for it to go unused, and she decided to wash it and give it to someone who would wear it. As she held it in her hand, she wondered what it was like to dress in one. From adolescence she had adopted modest dress in accordance with the prescriptions of the Qur'an as she understood them. In recent years she had switched to a hijab instead of covering her head with her dupatta, and even when fashion dictated a form fitting shalwar kameez, she had kept to the traditional style of baggy shalwar and loose, long kameez despite the protests of her tailor who complained she dressed like a tasteless, old woman. These days, burqa clad women, once a rarity, were becoming a more common sight in the streets of Lahore.

Carrying the burqa over her arm, she closed herself in her room. The coat-like abaya slipped on easily over her clothes and the burqa's head covering, similar to her hijab, felt comfortable. But, when it came time to attach the niqab and draw it across the lower part of her face, she had a moment of hesitation and almost retreated back to her familiar clothes. But curiosity drew her onward.

Cloaked in the burqa, it was as if she inhabited someone else's body. The former servant's life was revealed in the cheap cloth, as coarse and rough as a burlap rice sack, its fibers pricking her skin, and in the garment's odor, an amalgamation of dust, smoke, rancid cooking oil, stale spices and sweat. She walked over to the mirror and was startled by the stranger looking back at her. She was shapeless from shoulder to hem; even the shelf of her breasts was obscured by the folds of the overlapping head covering. The black fabric bleached out her skin, and with just a narrow strip of forehead and her eyes visible, her face was a blank mask. Only when she frowned, furrowing her forehead and the space between her eyebrows, did any expression or emotion register. Feeling strange and uneasy, she pulled the burqa off, straightened her clothing and went back to the laundry. Filling the old tin wash tub with water, she added detergent and scrubbed the burqa. As her hands kneaded the garment in the soapy water, she contemplated the small, but increasing minority who wore them, and the confidence they had to step outside the bounds of established societal norms. She admired them for their indifference to what other people might think, and the way they limited their concern to the rigorousness of their religious observance. But she couldn't quite identify with them since wearing a burqa was foreign to her upbringing. She told herself she had no need for it and would give it away, but once dry, it found its way into her clothes cupboard.

At lunch time, Hameeda went into the kitchen and retrieved the tray the cook had prepared for her mother-in-law and herself. She was now in the habit of having an early lunch with the old woman before the children came home. Hameeda found the dramatic change in their relationship miraculous. Her husband had dismissed this depiction, stating it was more likely appreciation for all the care and attention Hameeda was giving her. She wondered if the difference in her behavior over the last few weeks had worn away her mother-in-law's sharpness like the constant action of water against stone.

Her conversations with her mother-in-law had graduated from the mundane to the personal, and more and more she looked forward to their time together. In the beginning, Hameeda asked her about her childhood in an effort to see her as a whole person, rather than just an elderly woman. She told Hameeda she'd had a mother, father and the usual complement of brothers and sisters and would say no more on the subject. Instead, she recounted stories from her marriage and Zubair's childhood and encouraged Hameeda to share her own experiences when she was younger. Most often they read and discussed passages of the Qur'an. She loved listening to her mother-in-law's low voice reciting the holy words Allah spoke to the Prophet Muhammad, and it was a large part of what drew them closer together.

Today when she entered her mother-in-law's room, the maid was sitting on the floor next to the bed, her eyes glued to the TV screen where a Pakistani soap opera played out. The maid had been hired to help her mother-in-law who, for one reason or another, needed constant attention during the day, which Hameeda wasn't always available to provide. She was also supposed to help out with housework when she had free time. But since the maid was closeted in her mother-in-law's room, it was difficult keeping track of what she was doing. Hameeda asked the maid for an account of her morning activities, and when she was satisfied, sent her to the kitchen to have her lunch.

"Before we start eating, shut off the TV. That ignorant girl has become addicted to these ridiculous dramas. I'm afraid she believes they're not made up, but are as real as her own life. You'd think her harsh upbringing would make her sensible, but instead she seems drawn to fantasy." Her mother-in-law grimaced and shook her head.

"I'm sorry Ammie; shall I tell her she can't watch the TV?" Hameeda searched for the remote and located it on the floor near the bottom of the bed.

"My poor hearing has become a surprise blessing. Just tell her to keep the volume low. I'd tell her myself, but I seem to have lost my authority along with my ability to stand upright."

Hameeda promised her mother-in-law she would take care of it. She remembered when the old woman had been in charge of the household and everyone in it. In those days, ignoring her would have been unthinkable. How long ago had her power and control started to erode? She thought about how difficult it must have been to turn over her home to a younger woman and be side lined, little more than a guest. She wondered why it hadn't occurred to her before.

"Thank you, beti. Now tell me, what was Rabia crying about this morning?"

"She wanted to stay home from school. The bombings have made her afraid to go out of the house."

"Again, we're tortured by extremists." Her mother-in-law sighed. "You'd think the epidemic of heinous murders during Partition would have satisfied the appetite for violence in our country. Beti, I've lived too long. I wish I had died with Daud, not survived to see my own country become a foreign land. When I was young and not so young, everyone always got along. Our friends were Sunni, Shia, Christians; it made no difference. We lived together in the spirit of the Qur'an. Here, take the tray for a moment so I can read something to you."

Hameeda slid the tray out of the way, and her mother-in-law lifted the Qur'an from her bedside table and after combing through the pages, found the passage she wanted.

"It says here in Qur'an 49:13, '*Behold, we have created you all from a single male and female, and have made you into nations and tribes so that you might come to deeply know one another (not to hate and despise each other).*' In my youth, I believed in an Islamic State where everyone would come to recognize the wisdom of Allah, blessed be his name, and follow his commandments. I thought as the years advanced, people would evolve and surpass their ancestors. Instead they have flung themselves backward, embracing their primitive instincts, no less susceptible to disobedience then Adam and Eve were when they ate forbidden fruit. Now, just as Cain slew Abel, Muslims kill their own brothers in a slaughter of innocents."

"I don't understand why people don't follow the teachings of Allah, blessed be his name," Hameeda said. "The Qur'an tells us, on the Day of Judgment, those who reject its teachings will face the torment of hell, while if we heed them, we are promised heaven's bliss."

"People twist and distort the words of the Qur'an to

serve their own purposes in this life, refashioning sin into holy action. If you haven't learned that already, you will soon enough."

Hameeda thought about the vast numbers of good people in the country and couldn't let her mother-in-law's words go unchallenged. "But, it's only a tiny minority."

"When people remain silent, it's the few, loud voices that are heard." Her mother-in-law sighed and passed a hand over her eyes. "This subject distresses me; let's speak of something else."

Hameeda was happy to comply since she also found the turn the conversation had taken upsetting. And so they talked of the weather outside, about the cousin with a new grandchild, how tall Jameel was getting, and what food the cook should prepare for the coming week. When the maid returned, Hameeda cleared away the dishes in preparation for the arrival of the physical therapist. Once the therapist arrived and was tending to her mother-in-law, she left to pick up the rest of her responsibilities.

Back in the kitchen, she oversaw the cook's preparation of their afternoon tea, and sent the driver to pick up the children. She tackled all the repetitive, familiar chores that made up her day, and was happy to do it, because in doing them, she felt normal when nothing else was as usual any more. And who or what was to blame for that? She thought about her earlier conversation with her mother-in-law. She wasn't sure she fully understood the old woman's point about the terrorists. Did she blame their fellow citizens for the violence? Her mother-in-law didn't grasp that outside interference was the root of their problems. How could it be otherwise? How could a Muslim act against the tenets of Islam and their own people? It was incomprehensible. She accepted that some Pakistanis had been involved in attacks, but they must have been brain washed or seduced by huge sums of money. She wished she hadn't started thinking about it again. It was the last thing she wanted on her mind. It was fortunate the children appeared in the doorway, giving her an excuse to turn her attention elsewhere.

The next day, Hameeda gathered up some clothes for the tailor and picked up her shopping list in preparation for going to the marketplace. When she opened her cupboard to retrieve her purse, she saw the burqa hanging there. How would it feel to wear it in public? After a moment's hesitation, she took it off the hanger and put it on. This time, the ghost of the previous owner had decamped, and the burqa was as familiar as a seasonal outfit worn for the first time in months. It smelled of the same detergent which perfumed her regular clothes, and the washing had softened the feel of it a bit. She picked up her purse and went outside where the driver was sitting near the car waiting for her.

"Is it you, Begum Sahib?"

Though the driver's question was understandable, it irritated her for no apparent reason. "Yes, now open the gate and let's go."

It might have been her imagination, but the clerks in the shops seemed more respectful when they waited on her, and as she moved about, she was less nervous than usual.

Donning the burqa, she felt hidden from the eyes of men, giving her a feeling of greater safety. The garment became a shield, a symbol of Allah's protection. As she walked through the crowded streets, she had the impression people gave her more space, as if she had gained in stature. The entire time she was shopping, most people didn't even glance at her. The only exception was two teenage girls in blue jeans and kurtas, who stared, whispered to each other and then laughed. When she passed by another woman in similar attire, she nodded her head at her as if they weren't strangers but in some way acquainted.

After this first experience, Hameeda wore the burqa when she went out, but only if she was alone. When she took it off, she stored it in the back of her cupboard where it wouldn't be noticed. The next couple of days, Hameeda found excuses to make trips to parts of the city she hadn't gone to since the bombings started. She shopped for fabric in Fortress Stadium and even went to Anarkali Bazaar, although she wandered around without perusing any of the shops since she had no particular reason for being there. After the first day, her driver accepted her new garb without question. She wasn't worried about news of her behavior getting back to Zubair. The servants might gossip among themselves, but it was not a subject they would discuss with their employer. She considered telling him herself, but she didn't feel comfortable with the change. It felt like a temporary exploration of what life would have been like if she'd been born someone else. She was concerned about following the true word of Allah, as given to the Prophet

Muhammad. But if she thought her current manner of applying the modesty requirement was incorrect, didn't it bring into question other areas of her observance? Wouldn't it also be an indirect criticism of the teachings of her imam, and her parents and grandparents? For days, Hameeda stayed longer and longer at her prayers as a means of working through her confusion. Each time she prayed, the words, spoken since childhood, came unbidden. She forced herself to focus on each one as if she were voicing it for the first time, while in the same moment imagining her body as a vessel, filling with Allah's presence. Once finished, she remained still for a moment, gathering the energy to emerge from the chrysalis her prayers had spun around her so she could return to the everyday world of solid objects and commitments. But although her prayers soothed her, they failed to provide her with any answers.

A few days later, a conversation with Jameel pushed her own quandary aside.

"Amma, Arif went to a family wedding last week and was only supposed to be gone a couple of days, but he still hasn't returned to school. He's already missed an important cricket match, and I know he would never be absent unless something was wrong. I've called the house, but the servant won't tell me anything."

"Beta, I'm sure there is a simple explanation. I've been meaning to call Nadira Auntie. I'll call her today and find out why Arif isn't in school."

Hameeda was glad Jameel had come to her with his concern. It gave her a perfect excuse to call Nadira, a pretext to start a conversation with her. Wasting no time, she called her old friend's home number. Her call was answered by the servant who told her the family had not returned from Attock. She asked for her mobile number and then tried calling her again. It appeared Nadira's phone was not on, so she left a message explaining Jameel's worries. She waited the rest of the day and the next day to hear back, but her call wasn't returned. Nadira might not want to talk to her, but she was certain she would have let Arif call Jameel. Hameeda decided to try calling her parents. Again a servant answered the phone and told her they weren't at home. Was their absence a coincidence? It was very worrying. She hoped nothing serious had happened.

Chapter 12

Hameeda finished her morning prayers but couldn't capture her usual post-prayer serenity. One phone call had changed everything.

The mystery of Arif's absence had been solved when Nadira's mother contacted her upon their return from Attock. How could it be? Nadira's husband kidnapped, killed by a single shot to the head and dumped in a back street in Attock City? After the call, she wondered if she'd dreamt it, and only the solidity of the phone in her hand and the uneven rhythm of her breathing convinced her it was true. She had called Zubair at once, and he had left the hospital early so they could tell Jameel together.

The news bruised her son's face as if he'd been punched. His previous experience with death had been confined to the aged or ill, and even then, the sole person who'd been close was his dada. She tried to remember how old he'd been when Zubair's father died; four or five, she thought. For a short while, he'd asked where his dada had gone, but otherwise there had been no indication he was upset, or was that what she'd chosen to believe? What was it like for a child who knew nothing of death for a loved one to disappear without warning, never to return? She imagined it being similar to the days when people believed the earth was flat, and sailors who failed to come back from a voyage were thought to have lost their way and fallen off the edge into a black void. She couldn't remember if or how she had explained it to him, and though she knew she couldn't change the past, it bothered her.

When her dada died, she had been old enough to understand, and despite the comfort of knowing his soul must surely reside in Paradise, she did not escape the emptiness of loss. Now, the worst of all possible fates had touched Jameel's close friend and, she imagined, made life seem frightening and unpredictable. She could never quite reconcile how random fate seemed to be, good people dying while evil people flourished. She had to believe that Allah had a purpose for everything that happened, but it didn't make accepting it less heartbreaking.

She wondered what advice to give Jameel if he asked her how to console his best friend. What do you say when death is delivered by another person's hand? She had no trouble remembering how destructive a violent end could be to surviving family. When her dada was killed, his death had spawned a fierce anger in her father, which had sharpened and distorted his grief and prevented healing and acceptance. He had changed in such a dramatic way, she'd felt as if he too had died and someone else had taken his place. And the words people had offered as a balm to his suffering, only made him angrier. She would tell Jameel what she had learned; words were inadequate, and the best he could do was to stay by his friend's side and refuse to be driven away by discomfort.

After the children had gone to bed, Hameeda had stayed up late talking with Zubair. She unraveled her complicated history with Nadira as if she were summarizing the plot of a novel she'd read, equal parts love, adventure and tragedy. She wished she could have provided a different, happier ending, but it still concluded with sorrow and guilt. She finished her story and waited for her husband's reaction, afraid of what he might say. She was relieved, but felt no less guilty, as he insisted it couldn't have ended any other way. She didn't mention her dream of renewing their friendship and putting all the wasted years behind them. It seemed too tenuous, and she was worried close scrutiny would destroy the hope it was built on. Even before Nadira's personal tragedy, she hadn't known if her old friend would accept her back, and now this possibility seemed even more remote. How could she approach Nadira when she was so fragile? She didn't want to be the person who caused her to break.

The next day, Zubair and Jameel attended Sohail's funeral while Hameeda and the girls said prayers for Nadira and her family at home. On her husband's return, he reported on the large turnout, including many of Sohail's friends, some who came from quite a distance, a tribute to how well liked he had been. Placing his arm around her, he told her he had something for her. Arif had mentioned to his mother they were planning on attending the funeral, and Nadira had entrusted her son with a note for Hameeda. As Zubair handed it to her, she burst into tears. He stroked her back and told her not to worry; the note had been handed over with an encouraging smile.

Alone in her room, she opened the envelope and took out a single sheet of plain paper. She recognized the handwriting, still so familiar. An extension of Nadira's personality, it was extravagant with large, forward slanting letters sprawling across the page. Looking at it made her smile. When they were in the primary grades, she remembered how Nadira had struggled to restrain her letters and stay within the lines of the ruled sheets of paper. She took a deep breath and began to read.

Hameeda, my old friend,

Since our surprise meeting, I have been thinking a great deal about us. And upon honest reflection, I found you inhabited my happiest childhood memories, which says a lot.

You were very special to me, and when we were first separated, I missed you terribly. Even after I denied you in anger, I lived with the feeling of having an unsatisfied need, which I suppose was another way of missing you.

Life is too short to let false pride or self-righteousness govern decisions.

I'm ashamed of the way I treated you when we met at your house. Please accept my apology. I hope you will forgive me, and we can become friends again.

Nadira

Hameeda wiped away her tears, careful to keep them off the page. She was astounded Nadira was asking for her forgiveness. What had she done to deserve such a friend?

Even if she couldn't oppose her father when she was a child living in his house, why hadn't she searched for her after she married? Why had she assumed it was too late? A thought frightened her; had she subconsciously blamed Nadira for the actions of a few Sunni extremists? No, she refused to believe it. But it was true when she'd had the chance, she'd let time pass without doing anything.

The day after the funeral Hameeda and the rest of the family paid a condolence call on Nadira and the boys, who had moved into her parents' house upon their return from Attock. Entering the house which had been the backdrop for so many activities during her younger years, Hameeda saw reminders of her time there. She noticed the dent in the wood skirting in the foyer, caused by a cricket bat Nadira's brother had flung down during an argument. As they passed the lounge where she had spent most of her time, she peeked in and saw everything remained the same, except for the old sofa which had been refreshed with new fabric. It was almost as if they had known how disappointed she would have been to find her childhood memories altered. Being ushered into the drawing room, a place reserved for guests or special occasions, seemed peculiar and made her realize how much a part of the family she had been.

She put her arms around Nadira, who felt as insubstantial as a hollow boned bird yet still weighed Hameeda down as she sank into her embrace. When Hameeda disengaged herself, she saw a face with red, swollen eyes, sallow skin, and a torn lower lip where her teeth had worried it. She found it difficult to look at her. Although she could only imagine what it was like to lose a husband, she could well understand the pain of losing someone for whom there was no substitute. She often thought of her grandparents and her unique personal history and relationship with them. Deprived of their company, feelings and thoughts, she had only felt comfortable sharing with them accumulated and were forever left in her keeping.

Unable to think of anything to say, she offered traditional words of comfort. "By the will of Allah, you'll be united with Sohail on the Day of Judgment, after which there is no parting."

Tears gathered at the corners of Nadira's eyes, and she squeezed her hand.

"Thank you for coming, Hameeda," she whispered.

Hameeda drew Nadira to her again. "I have never stopped being your friend. I'm the one who owes you an apology for cutting you out of my life without any explanation. I hope someday soon we can talk about it, insha Allah."

"Yes, insha Allah," Nadira replied.

When Nadira's parents welcomed her, she felt the same warmth she had experienced as a child, and it was as if she had never been away. Although it wasn't the time to have an intimate conversation with her friend, she had hoped for some interaction. But, after their brief exchange, Nadira became subdued and almost non-responsive, letting her parents keep up the conversation. At least Arif seemed to benefit from Jameel's company. Talk of school and sports appeared to dispel his air of melancholy and disorientation.

*　　*　　*

Having received the note, Hameeda felt the next move was up to her. She waited a little over a week, and then called to see how her friend was doing and if she might have time for a visit. Nadira's mother gave her discouraging news. After she had fulfilled her obligation to receive visitors during the three days of mourning, she had closeted herself in her room and refused to see anyone. Although Hameeda understood she was not the only one banished, it made her uneasy, and she took to rereading her friend's note whenever she needed reassurance.

Nadira and her family weren't the only ones affected by Sohail's death and the manner in which he died. Overnight, Jameel had become quieter, and when he was in the house, he kept to himself. Daliya eschewed her usual hectic social schedule to spend more time at home, and sometimes late at night when Hameeda lay awake, she would hear her daughter's low voice calling outside her younger brother's room, a creak of a door opening and then silence. Hameeda was glad her son was talking to his sister since he refused to talk to her.

Rabia, her obedient child, became uncharacteristically rebellious in her firm resolve to stay out of school. Two days in a row she refused to leave her bedroom when it came time to go. Hameeda had thought it was reasonable for her to fear attending class when you could no longer count on the safety of your own home. She hadn't known what to say or do, and instead, Zubair had gone to her, first trying to cajole and reason with their daughter, and then insisting she get up. Both days, Rabia had remained adamant and became so hysterical that she had triggered an asthma attack, the second one so severe, it left Zubair white-faced and on the verge of taking her to the hospital. That night, he told Hameeda how shocked he'd been by Rabia's behavior, and was surprised when Hameeda told him their daughter's fears had been building up for quite a while. Without further discussion, he hired a tutor for her and the very next day began to return from work earlier. Maybe, like Hameeda, he no longer took for granted the time they had together. Now when the family congregated, Hameeda listened to every word they said, savored the smiles and laughter, and found excuses to touch them, wiping away a stray piece of food at the corner of a mouth, straightening an article of clothing, or smoothing down a cowlick.

Days passed and still nothing felt normal. Even the weather pattern was unusual. Summer's heat had already arrived even though it was only April. Now, despite the early morning hour, Hameeda could feel beads of sweat forming under her arms and breasts. She gave in to inertia, and continued kneeling on her prayer rug, her legs stiffening against the unyielding floor. It was becoming more and more difficult to remember how she had once sailed out into the yet unexplored hours of her day. The terrorist attack at the girls' school and Sohail's murder had crushed her, and feeling as if she had been present at both tragedies, she stumbled around like the relatives she had observed in the emergency room after the bombing.

As she eased off her knees and stood up, the cook dropped something in the kitchen, and it hit the floor with a clang. Her body quivered as the sound played on her nerves. She had become as fearful as a young child at bedtime, but it was not the dark, or jinn, or her dreams of drowning that frightened her. It was not her imaginings but reality that petrified her. The nature of people was changing. More and more of them had tunnel vision, focused on their own resentments, needs and personal view of the rules that should govern behavior. They presumed to know what was best, not just for them, but for everyone, failing to acknowledge that it was Allah's judgment that ruled all mankind. And once Allah was forsaken, there would be no safe haven.

If it were just the outside world that was unsettled, she could have managed better. But the previous night, Zubair had again brought up the topic of their move to Canada. With everything else going on, Hameeda had pushed this subject to the farthest recesses of her mind where it laid almost forgotten. Zubair had called the hospital in Canada and discussed their situation with a member of the hiring committee. After consulting with his colleagues, his start date had been extended so he would have more time to see if his mother's condition would resolve itself. She could tell he was relieved by their decision. But it made her tense, another unwelcome change she might have to come to terms with in the future. Even though life at home had become difficult and sometimes nightmarish, it was a life she owned. She had adapted to each new discomfort with her own strategies or those borrowed from others. It was remarkable how soon any other existence was difficult to recall. However, if she were honest, her memories of the years before the engine of progress had reversed itself, made their current reality feel like a world from one of the dystopian novels her son liked to read.

And her religious dilemma was also distracting her. The violence perpetrated by terrorists and criminals had proven death was never far away, and she was determined to correct any laxity in observance before it was too late. Over the next couple of days, every time she opened her closet, the burqa tucked into the back taunted her with still unanswered questions.

With Zubair at home amusing the children with a board game one Sunday, Hameeda took the opportunity to visit her mother, arriving at her parents' house just as they were finishing their lunch. With the death of her grandparents and her father's worsening health, they had shifted downstairs and given over the upstairs to her oldest brother and his family.

Her father sat in a chair, his eyes fixed and unresponsive. Hameeda stroked his hand and talked to him, hoping for a reaction that didn't come. After sitting for a while, her mother called the maid in to stay with her father and suggested she and Hameeda relocate to her sitting room. As they walked together, Hameeda found she had to shorten her stride so as not to outpace her mother. She had never thought of her mother as old, but she realized age was catching up with her, and caring for her father must also be taking its toll. And here she was, still running home for comfort and advice. Returning home seemed to be an established pattern for her. Too soon, she would be caring for her mother; what would she do then?

Once they were settled, her mother turned to her, an interested expression on her face. She asked after Zubair and the children and then inquired about how Nadira was doing. Hameeda had to tell her Nadira didn't seem to be doing very well.

"Well, it's not surprising under the circumstances," her mother said. What a fierce, resilient child she was. I'm sure she'll get through this in time, insha Allah."

"Insha Allah. Sometimes I wonder how well I would do in such a devastating situation. I've never been as strong as Nadira."

Her mother smiled and took her hand. Hameeda was surprised and puzzled when she told her she had something else that would serve her even better.

"You have an enduring faith in Allah which will guide and support you no matter what you encounter in life."

Her mother had presented her with the perfect opening. "My faith is really the reason I'm here. I've been having doubts about how conscientious I am in my observance of Allah's commandments."

"I can't imagine anyone more conscientious. Since you were a very young child, you have been exacting in your fulfillment of all Allah requires of you. Is this about Hajj? You and Zubair should consider going on your pilgrimage to Mecca now that the children are older."

Hameeda explained her confusion over the dress requirement. Her mother responded with the same instruction she had received as a child, citing the Qur'an's requirement to cover the entire body, except for hands and face, with clothing thick and loose enough to hide her form.

"But don't the hadith tell us we must veil our faces?" Hameeda asked.

"It's true that different Islamic scholars have adopted varying interpretations of the original texts. Our imam does not interpret the hadith that way. Remember, the veiling of women was a custom in Arabia before the Prophet's time," her mother said as her eyes examined her. "But I know you're sincere, and if you truly feel the shalwar kameez you're wearing isn't modest enough, and wearing an abaya over your clothing makes you more comfortable, then make a change. I don't think it's necessary to wear a niqab since based on our teachings, your face doesn't need to be covered."

Hameeda was disappointed because her mother had placed her almost back where she started. And instead of feeling as if she'd found her answer, it left her with the same sense of uncertainty. "There seems to be so much confusion over religious interpretation these days," Hameeda said. "It's just something I was thinking about."

"On the Day of Judgment, the strictness with which you interpret the modesty requirement will not matter as much as your collective observance of all Allah asks of you." Her mother looked at her with her head tilted to one side, as if she were trying to see her from another angle which might explain her sudden inquiry.

She knew in her heart what her mother said was true. But, if one had the capacity for strict observance in all things, there seemed to be no excuse not to obey. She would have liked to discuss the subject further, but her sister-in-law came in looking for her mother. Hameeda had never quite gotten over the strangeness of her brother's wife living in the house in her stead, and this feeling was most pronounced when her sister-in-law welcomed her almost like a guest. Was it jealousy she felt? No, her love for her was real, and she couldn't picture herself in the house as anything other than a child – a position, she was sure, she now only occupied in her mother's eyes.

The next day still feeling conflicted, Hameeda remembered a weekly Qur'an study group the mother of one of Daliya's friends had told her about. She hadn't gone to a study group since college but remembered how much she had gained from those sessions. She called the woman who taught the group and was invited to join them. The timings of their meetings worked with Hameeda's schedule and she began attending.

The woman who led the group grew up in Karachi but had lived in Saudi Arabia for many years and while there had attended classes in Arabic and the Qur'an. Given her background, Hameeda trusted her interpretation of the Qur'an and the hadith. As she studied with these women, all of them in search of a stronger connection to Allah, she felt both calmer and energized by her new insights and experiences. It reminded her of her lessons with her dada, and his voice which had faded over the years came back to her as sharp and clear as it had once been.

Hameeda was aware of her difficulty with embracing change. At every stage of her life some person or event had dragged her onward when she would have been content to have things remain the same. While her friends looked forward to birthdays, anticipating the new privileges and possibilities that came with an added year, she worried about what she would lose by getting older. When she turned eight, she was afraid she might be considered too old to sit on her mother's lap or be put to bed at night. And when she attained an age which brought with it new responsibilities, it always took a while for her to become confident enough to handle them alone.

Without the support and assurance her study-group classmates had given her, she knew she wouldn't have had the courage to adjust her beliefs. Once her mind was made up, she should have been relieved, but her choice did not affect just her, and she wasn't sure how her family would react when she explained it to them. She would talk to Zubair first because if he objected, that would be the end of it. She felt it would be selfish to endanger their relationship and disturb family harmony. Maybe in that respect, her mother was right. There was more to observance than obeying an individual commandment. Unlike her dada, she could not and would not make decisions for the rest of the family. Observance was a personal struggle, and this decision would be hers alone. Besides, she thought, setting an example was the best way to promote a change.

It took her two days to bring up the subject with Zubair, but as it turned out, the discussion wasn't as difficult as she anticipated. He listened to her explain the changes she wanted to make, the wearing of the burqa being the most dramatic, and the education process she had gone through before making her decision.

He disagreed with her basis for wearing the niqab, setting forth his own reasons. But when she remained unconvinced, he said the decision was up to her. When she discussed her adoption of altered religious practices with the children, Zubair sat with her but made no comment. The three of them were very accepting, and Daliya even mentioned the mother of one of her friends who had started to wear a burqa in the last year.

When Hameeda thought of the emotional upheaval of the last few months, she imagined her new interpretation of Allah's commandments must have seemed inconsequential to her family. But it felt momentous to her in a way she found difficult to describe. She thought she would feel guilt or regret over disagreeing with her husband but instead she was, what - satisfied, elated? She was certain she felt different and tried to find a way to define the change. It occurred to her that, at last, she was beginning to form ideas and opinions without reference to someone else, and follow her own inclinations. She realized this had raised her self-confidence to a level she hadn't known before.

Chapter 13

Nadira found slumber, once sweet and soothing, was now a bitter pill she swallowed as soon as she lost consciousness. Nightmarish visions, like slides dropping in front of a projector lens, flashed on an interior screen. As much as his death, it was the image of Sohail's last moments that haunted her. She couldn't bear the thought of him alone with the belief his family had not cared enough to ransom him. Had the kidnappers informed him of the negotiations? Had he been confident enough in their love to know they wouldn't desert him? And what of his last moment when the hard, cold steel of the gun barrel was pressed against the soft skin of his temple? She couldn't stop thinking about the terror he must have felt in that last instant. And so, during her waking hours while she kept sleep at bay, Nadira fabricated a story and practiced it over and over until it was no longer a product of her imagination but a truth stronger than any reality.

To keep Sohail tractable, the kidnappers drug him every day into a state somewhere between awareness and insensibility. In this condition, Sohail dreams of the reunion with her and the boys, a counterfeit experience so vivid, when he visualizes pulling Nadira and the boys into his arms, he can feel the softness of their bodies and the pressure of their returned embrace. And it's while he's in this induced deep sleep, unaware of his surroundings, happy in the belief he's back with his family, his captors administer the fatal shot.

In the morning, still exhausted from battling her nightmares, she would hear the boys enter the room to say their salaams before they went off to school. Sorrow and regret mired her in a quicksand of fatigue that made lifting her head off the pillow or speaking a Herculean task. After the door had closed behind them, she was not certain whether or not the response she had formed in her mind had left her lips. She yearned for quiet, but voices attacked her like bothersome gnats, imploring her to eat or wash or get up when all she wanted was to sink deeper into her stupor. Then one night, she escaped the bonds of her nightmares and fell into a dream.

Nadira was back in her grandmother's sewing room, leaning against her nani's comforting bulk, as she stitched together a kameez. Her nani's warmth unlocked the cold that stiffened her body, and she felt her limbs loosen and sensation return, starting in her fingertips and moving down to her toes. She had thought of her nani so many times, and now she told her how often she'd missed her and how she still remembered the times they'd spent together.

Her nani looked at Nadira over the top of her glasses and said with a frown, "If you hold me in such high regard, why have you forgotten the most significant lesson I taught you?"

When Nadira protested that it wasn't true, her nani

asked her what she'd learned. Because her nani had instructed her in so many things, it took her a minute to realize what she was waiting to hear.

"You told me to always remember, family is more important than anything else in life."

"Then why are you more concerned with yourself than your family? You lie there nursing your pain as if you're the only one suffering. What about your responsibility to your children? What about the worry you're causing your parents?"

Nadira looked over at her nani who stroked the wheel of her sewing machine like a fortune teller passing her hand over a crystal ball and was certain she possessed the power to see her future. Apologizing for her actions, she promised she would make amends and asked what else she could do to find her way out of her confusion and despair.

"I always made sure your clothes had generous seam allowances, so they could be altered as you grew and changed shape. Sometimes life, like clothing, has to be re-stitched to fit changing circumstances. Stop trying to squeeze yourself into something you've outgrown. It's time you started on alterations."

Nadira didn't understand and asked her for an explanation, but her nani did not oblige.

"You were always a smart child. Think hard and you'll find the answer. Now, I'm late for an important tea party, so I must go."

She begged her to stay but, murmuring "no time, no time," her nani slipped through a door which vanished as soon as her ample figure crossed the threshold and left Nadira unable to follow.

Slumber's coils loosened their hold, and she woke to the sound of the muezzin's call to prayer. Bits and pieces of the dream remained, and she tried to grab on to them before they disappeared, but they escaped, leaving behind clarity of mind she hadn't had in days. As she sat up, her body felt so tender, she searched her skin for bruises but found not one mark. Swinging her legs over the side of the bed and onto the floor, she pushed herself up. Her head spun and her legs shook, forcing her to lean against the wall until the room stood still and she was able to stand without support. A nose-wrinkling odor enveloped her and she realized it emanated from her own body. Disgusted, she immediately made her way to the shower.

The simple pleasure of clean, fragrant skin and hair felt wonderful. But soon sorrow crept back in again and threatened to suffocate her. She forced herself to get dressed, with the hope that if she kept moving, she could somehow stay ahead of her emotions. When she opened her closet, all her clothes hung there, clean and pressed just like when she was a girl. She ran her eyes over her wardrobe, amazed her outlook had ever been cheerful enough to choose fabric in such bright colors. After going through all her clothes, she pulled out something in a subdued beige print. Once dressed, her outfit hung so loose on her frame, she had to pin the waist of her shalwar to keep it from falling off. Her mirror image showed a much thinner person with prominent collar bones, hollowed out cheeks and somber, lifeless eyes. She stood staring at her reflection while she decided what this new version of her would do next.

Being as quiet as she could, she opened her door and walked across the hall to the room Arif and Samir shared. They were both sleeping. Arif was on his back with one arm tucked under his head and the other flung out to the side; the thick, unruly hair he had inherited from his father stood up in spikes on his head. In the other bed, Samir was curled up with a pillow clutched in his arms. Nadira sat in the chair and stared at their faces smoothed by sleep into expressions of peaceful innocence. It was like glimpsing a scene from the past, and she was afraid waking would alter them. She didn't know how long she sat there before Arif rolled over and opened his eyes.

"Amma, is it really you?" Arif leapt from his bed and threw his arms around her. "You're up, you're up," he exclaimed, waking his brother.

A moment later, a second pair of arms cinched her waist as Samir pushed his way in next to Arif.

"If you two have finished smothering me, I need to talk to you."

Arif and Samir pulled back and sat down next to her feet. Samir kept one of her hands hostage while Arif rested his arm on her leg just above her knee. Did they think she would float away if she wasn't anchored in some way?

She apologized for leaving them to cope on their own when she should have been there to help and promised it wouldn't happen again, assuring them, with time, things would get better. Whatever the future held, she told them, they would face it together as a family. She wasn't surprised when Arif challenged her.

"How can we be a family without Abu? Nothing will ever be right again," Arif said with an anger Nadira understood all too well.

How could she convince her sons when she also felt buried in the debris from their shattered lives? "Abu will always be a part of this family," she said. "What he taught us and our memories of him will be with us forever."

"That's not the same as having him here, Amma," Arif protested, his face beginning to flush.

His words tore into her. She knew the terrible ache of wanting to hear her husband's voice and feel the warmth of his body. She had to push her feelings aside and talk to Arif about the necessity of learning to live without him, of going on because they had no other choice. Her words did nothing to dispel the anger in her son's face, and her own anger at the unfairness of it all resurfaced. She didn't know why this had happened to Sohail and to them. She needed there to be an explanation and there was none.

During her conversation with Arif, her younger son had remained silent. Now he cried out. "Stop it, Arif; you're upsetting Amma."

"It's all right, Samir. Both of you should feel you can talk to me if something is bothering you."

"Please, don't be sad anymore, Amma," Samir said.

Her son's concern was her punishment, driving home how hard her withdrawal had been on them. "Sometimes sadness is unavoidable, Samir. But just having you and Arif around is a big help. When I'm sad or you're sad, that's when being together will be important."

Nadira wanted to end the conversation for the time being and get the boys into their routine for the day. Was it a weekday? She realized she had lost track of time and was forced to ask her sons the date. Thursday already? Somehow three days had passed without her knowing it. She saw her sons' worried expressions and made a joke about it. Then, she told them to get ready for school. When they asked to stay home with her for the day, she refused them, and her usual parental reaction seemed to ease their concerns. At least they had the routine of school to provide some stability. Sohail had been her polestar, and his loss left her feeling dizzy and free floating. She took a deep breath to steady herself before taking the next step, talking to her parents.

Once outside her parents' bedroom door, she paused. How many times during her childhood had she stood in this very spot to give herself time to frame a request, concoct an excuse or rehearse an apology? In those days, the words scripted themselves without any effort as she drew on her intimate knowledge of individual personalities and viewpoints, and the family dynamics she learned over the years. But this time, she had no idea how either she or they would react. She was on an unfamiliar road traveling to an unknown destination. Despite having the solid landmarks from her past around her, she felt uneasy. Her knock on the door was soft and hesitant, and if her father hadn't answered so fast, she might have lost her courage and turned away.

"Yes, who is it?" her father's voice called out.

"It's Nadira, Abu."

She heard a thud as his feet hit the floor, and an instant later he flung open the door and enfolded her in his arms.

"Beti, it's so good to see you up. You feel cold. Come into bed with us and get warm." Her father closed the door and led her inside where her mother pulled her down next to her and covered her with the blanket. It was years since she'd climbed into bed with her parents. It was both strange and comforting.

"How are you feeling, beti?" her mother asked.

Nadira paused to think so she could choose an ordinary response from all the new emotions whirling around inside her. She told them she was a little hungry. This answer galvanized her father into action. He pushed the covers aside, and declared he would run out to her favorite shop for halwa puri, her breakfast of choice on special occasions like her birthday. Her mother saved her, telling him a big, heavy breakfast would make her sick and the best thing for Nadira was tea and toast.

"I'll go tell the cook to start preparing it at once," her father said. "Now where have my slippers gone to?"

As her father looked around, Nadira reached over and grabbed his arm. "Before you go Abu, there are some things I need to talk to both of you about."

Her mother propped herself up on an elbow. "Certainly beti, what is it?"

She asked how her sons had been doing the past few days and told them she thought she remembered the boys coming into her room dressed for school but wasn't sure.

Her parents explained her sons had been attending classes with a great deal of reluctance. Their friends had been awkward with them, and even Samir was having trouble concentrating on his studies. Arif had been spending time with Hameeda's son Jameel in the afternoon and insisted Samir go with him. Both boys seemed to benefit from the time they spent there. Her mother also mentioned Hameeda had called about seeing her.

"You should call her today Nadira. She's been very worried about you."

Even dealing with her family required more energy than she thought she possessed. She couldn't imagine speaking with anyone else, and most of all not Hameeda since she was sure any conversation they had would be an emotional one. "Not today Amma, I'm not ready to talk to anyone quite yet."

"The family has also been asking after you. The aunts have stopped by a couple of times. I'm sure hearing you're doing better will cheer them up."

Nadira felt very self-conscious in her new role as a widow. She no longer understood where she fit into the family or how she was supposed to act. She resisted the urge to go back to bed and pull the covers over her head. She could see that retreating from life was an attractive trap she must avoid falling into again. She took a deep breath in preparation for asking the difficult questions before she lost her nerve.

"What's happened with Sohail's business and the

house?" Just speaking his name aloud caused a sharp pain in her chest.

Her father reported that the factory had been sold and the proceeds deposited in her account. They hadn't found a buyer for the house yet, but they were starting to receive some requests for viewings. Her mother suggested they go through the house and remove any household items which would help her and the boys feel more at home. They could even bring over their own bedroom furnishings. Nadira said she would discuss it with the boys to see what they wanted to do.

"One thing I do know, I'm taking the profits from the sale of the factory and the house and paying back the ransom money contributed by the family," Nadira said. Will it be enough?"

"Nobody expects that of you, Nadira," her mother said in a soft voice.

"Nevertheless, I'll pay back every rupee. That's what Sohail would have wanted and that's what I want."

Her father told her the proceeds from the factory and the house would likely be enough to repay everyone, but afterward, what remained would maybe cover the boys' education and not much else. "You have to think of your future," he told her.

"I'll find a job as soon as possible."

Her father suggested she wait awhile before making long-term decisions. He felt with all the adjustments she was already facing, to start a new job might be too much. He told her they were prepared to take care of her and the boys.

The story of her nani's aunt came back to her. She did not want to have her life co-opted by her parents, no matter how well meaning they were, and become some-one's child again.

"Abu, a job is just exactly what I need right now and my sons are my responsibility."

Her father looked concerned. "Nadira, I think…"

"That's enough discussion for now," her mother inter-rupted, "Nadira, why don't you check on the boys, and I'll see about breakfast. It will be nice sitting down together again."

The short conversation left Nadira feeling battered and exhausted. She composed herself before she knocked on the door to the boys' room, and called out to them, asking if they were dressed. Samir opened the door already in his school uniform. She reached over and straightened his tie. She noticed the sleeves of his blazer were now about an inch too short. When had that happened? Arif was still getting ready, and she told Samir he should wait for his brother and then meet her in the dining room.

A little while later, she joined her parents and her sons at the breakfast table. The chair next to her father which she had occupied as a girl, stood empty for her.

"Nadira, are you sure all you want is toast?" Her father asked, patting her hand where it rested in her lap. "I can have the cook make you an egg."

"Toast is fine, Abu. Stop fussing."

"That's good advice, Nadeem. You sound like a mother hen," her mother commented as she slid the toast rack in front of her.

Nadira took a slice and accepted a cup of tea from her mother. Sunshine slid across the room, as it had on countless mornings, settling like a warm shawl on her shoulders. She watched Samir spoon up his cereal while Arif started on his customary soft-boiled egg. Her father spread a thick layer of honey on his toast, and her mother scolded him, as always, for his excess. Nadira marveled at how life could carry on like it always had when her own situation had altered in such a fundamental way.

After a long silence, Samir asked her if she was driving them to school. Nadira didn't even know what had become of their remaining car, and even if the car was here, she couldn't picture managing this task. Not just unsteady on her feet, her emotional state made everything around her tilt and slide as if she were on the deck of a ship, and finding her equilibrium took a constant effort. She claimed fatigue and said she would wait a couple more weeks before chauffeuring them again. Her father volunteered to carry on with the driving duties until she felt up to it.

After her father and the boys left, Nadira sat with her mother and finished her breakfast at a slow pace. After days of not eating much, her stomach was sensitive and her appetite was sated after consuming a small amount of food. Her mother asked her if there was anything she wanted to do before the boys returned from school. Nadira's mind was a blank. In her parents' house, she had no regular responsibilities and felt as if someone had sent her on an unwanted vacation. She should offer to help her mother, but she couldn't bring herself to do it. She wished it was time to go to bed.

"I think I'll sit in the lounge for a while."

"Take things slowly until you get your strength back," her mother said. She reached over and tucked a length of hair that had fallen across Nadira's face behind her ear. "I just finished reading a book I think you'll like. I'll go get it for you. You can read while I get my housework done. Then we can talk about a special dinner for all of us tonight, and you can advise me on dishes you think might tempt the boys' appetites."

"All right," she said, not caring one way or the other.

Her mother brought her the latest novel by one of Nadira's favorite authors. She thought she might be too distracted to read, but she soon became involved with the characters and engrossed in the story. With relief, she fled reality and submerged herself in another place and time with people both different and familiar. After a while, her eyelids drooped, and she dozed.

In the distance, she heard her mother's voice. "Nadira, wake up."

She opened her eyes and found she was slumped against the arm of the sofa with her head bent at an awkward angle.

"I'm sorry to wake you, but I was afraid you'd get a stiff neck in such a contorted position. Why don't you go into your bedroom and lie down for a little while?" her mother suggested.

When Nadira realized where she was, not with Sohail as she'd been dreaming but alone, forever without him, tears formed in her eyes. Sleep had become a body snatcher, digging up Sohail's corpse again and again, teasing and tormenting her.

"What's the matter, beti?" her mother asked.

"I was dreaming about Sohail. It was so real."

"I'm so sorry, beti," her mother said gathering her into her arms. "I'm so very sorry."

She leaned her forehead against her mother's chest and waited until the dream's hold on her dissipated and the waves of sadness subsided. Her mother suggested she come into the kitchen and keep her company while she helped the cook get things started for dinner.

A while later her father joined them. "Hard at work already?" he asked Nadira.

"I'm only working in a supervisory capacity today," she said.

"Yes, Nadeem, she's temporarily taken over your job."

"Being a supervisor takes a special talent that I've obviously passed on to my daughter," her father said as he winked at her.

She studied her father's face. His sad eyes did not match his joking manner, and she realized she was not the only one putting on an act.

"If sitting and giving voice to your opinions is a talent, you have definitely perfected it," her mother said with a smile. "Since one supervisor is more than enough, you can help by getting out of our way. Why don't you go read the newspaper."

Her father left, and Nadira and her mother entered into a mundane conversation. There were few neutral subjects they didn't discuss: the weather, the traffic, Samir's growth spurt and the neighbor's new landscaping. They avoided any mention of her situation or Sohail. But Sohail was there. He stood in front of her, his spectral eyes burning a hole in her heart, occupying a portion of the room elephantine in comparison to the space he had taken up when he was alive. Nadira was uncertain which was more disturbing, talking about him or avoiding any mention of the subject.

When the boys returned from school, she sent them to do their homework and didn't see them again until they sat down to have dinner. How do you carry on a normal conversation when conditions are anything but normal? But she asked the standard questions about their day, and they obliged her with their standard unrevealing answers. Again, everyone skirted any mention of Sohail or their present circumstances, leaving large gaps in the conversation which her father filled with nonsensical monologues. Nadira knew talking to Arif and Samir about their father would be one of her most important motherly duties. As difficult as it was, they all needed to hear his name spoken aloud so his ghostly presence was fleshed out into something warm and human they could continue living with. At this instant, she was still too raw to give voice to the necessary words, but she must do it soon before silence became a habit.

Chapter 14

Salima lay in her bed unable to sleep, her internal clock turned upside down. Doing little but reading in her room all day, she found she often dozed, which left her preternaturally awake once night fell. It was then she perused the unexamined thoughts she had collected during the daylight hours.

Since her paralysis, her physical world was severely restricted. But with her mobility taken away, unexpected developments had expanded her life beyond the old, well-established boundaries. Instead of feeling more isolated, she felt more connected to her family. She now looked forward to the time Hameeda spent with her during the day. Well, she shouldn't be surprised. After all, she'd chosen Hameeda for Zubair, so it just confirmed her original good judgment. And then there was Rabia; what a strange child she was. Now that her granddaughter was being tutored, she was home all day. Whenever Hameeda had to leave, except for the servants, the two of them had the house to themselves. One day, Rabia must have been feeling lonely and wandered into Salima's room.

"Dadi, would it be alright if I read my books in here with you?" she asked.

Rabia's request surprised her. She had never been close with her grandchildren, and none of them had ever sought out her company. If that had ever caused her regret, it was forgotten long ago. She didn't know what to make of this sudden change but told her granddaughter she could take the chair opposite her. With Rabia immersed in a book, she'd studied her. She was at an awkward in-between stage where her various parts hadn't yet aligned themselves: her teeth too big for her face, her legs overly long and her middle still that of a pudgy child. She could tell, one day Rabia would be beautiful, very much like her mother, except for the remarkable hair she herself had bequeathed to her.

The first afternoon, Rabia worked on her homework without saying a word and left as soon as Hameeda returned. Afterward, her granddaughter got into the habit of coming into her room when her daughter-in-law was out. In the beginning, she kept to herself and read, but after a while the girl started asking her questions, and this led to a number of long, surprising conversations. When Salima spoke to her, she listened with great attention to everything she was told before answering; in that respect, she reminded her of Zubair. And, she also didn't hesitate to disagree with her, although she was always polite about it, which secretly pleased Salima. Maybe Rabia wasn't aware of her reputation for being sharp tongued; oh yes, she knew what the family and servants said about her; not even a whisper in the house escaped her notice. Or, maybe Rabia just had the unthinking honesty of youth. Either way, Salima looked forward to her visits.

One afternoon, her granddaughter was in Salima's room working on her lessons. She watched her as she turned the pages of her book and scribbled on her notepad.

"So, do you like being tutored at home?" she asked.

Rabia looked up at her, the pencil in her hand suspended in mid-air.

"It's all right. Sometimes I miss my friends."

"Then why not go back to school?"

Her granddaughter was silent for a moment. "There are people who bomb schools and kill schoolchildren."

"It's true some children have been killed in bombings, but it's not common and not a reason for staying at home."

"They killed Arif's father, too."

Salima hesitated over what she should say. Rabia was too young to have learned about the cruelty human beings inflicted on each other and the heartache of life. These were lessons which should wait until adulthood. Once they had protected their children from such things, but now it was no longer possible.

She motioned to her granddaughter to sit down next to her on the bed. Cupping her chin in her hand and looking into her eyes, she informed this most precious of her grandchildren that she would remain unharmed because Allah had other plans for her. When Rabia asked her how she knew, she said Allah had spoken to her.

"Allah spoke to you?" Rabia asked, her eyes opening wide.

"Not in the way you mean," Salima said. "You don't

hear Allah's voice with your ears but with your heart. It happens to me most often when I am deep in prayer."

"Why haven't I heard Allah?"

"Allah's voice is softer than the sound of a feather falling through the air. It takes many, many years of practice to interpret it properly."

Rabia sat there thinking, her brow furrowed as deep as a plowed field. Then she picked up her books and started for the door.

"Where are you going Rabia?"

"To say my prayers and start practicing."

Salima felt no guilt over what she had said to her granddaughter. She had a strong feeling nothing bad would happen to this child. When she looked at her, she had a clear vision of Rabia's future stretching out in a long unbroken line. Now, thinking of her granddaughter's statement as she left the room, Salima chuckled. At last, feeling tired, she settled her head into her pillow and pulled the blanket up to her neck in preparation for sleep. As the blanket moved over her legs, she concentrated on feeling even the smallest sensation but felt nothing. You couldn't have everything in this life. If paralysis was the trade-off for the improvements in her family ties, she was more than willing to endure the difficulties it brought with it. She was like a blind person with acute hearing, robbed of one faculty while blessed with an increase in another. It was amazing to find, at her age, life was not only about contraction but also about expansion. It made her curious to see what else Allah might have in store for her.

Chapter 15

Nadira opened her eyes and watched as the late morning sun painted her walls in shades of yellow and gold. After two weeks of nights offering little sleep, the only thing she recalled of the previous evening was slipping between her bed sheets, and for the first time since the kidnapping, she felt rested.

Another day with empty hours to fill stretched in front of her. Where once she had longed for the free time to do as she wished, now her freedom felt like a burden. At first, she had tried to take over some of her mother's chores, but her mother had her own routine and way of doing things, and the servants were accustomed to their employer's habits. After she caught her mother redoing something she'd already done, she gave up trying to be helpful. And once the boys were convinced she would no longer burrow back into her sorrow, they settled back into their usual routine and were busy most of the day.

There were times she tried to think about future plans, something concrete to carry her forward. One day she started a proper outline. She penned in Roman numeral headings labeled long-term and short-term goals. Underneath, she added letters to act as space holders for the steps to achieve these still unspecified intentions. But no matter how long she stared at the paper, she couldn't fill in the blanks. It seemed as if Sohail's death had formed a black hole in her universe, and she'd been sucked into it.

Tomorrow, they were expecting her aunts for afternoon tea, and though it should have been a welcome distraction, it felt more like a test. Widowhood often acted like a severe head injury which required her to relearn basic life skills, each day presenting a new set of challenges. She had forestalled seeing anyone up to now, but she couldn't keep postponing her re-entry into the larger world. Yesterday, when her mother had asked her if she would be joining them, Nadira could tell she was losing patience and knew it was unfair to once more request she offer excuses for her absence.

She remembered an old man, a hermit according to local gossip, who lived up in the back country outside of Murree, about a two hour hike from the town where they had vacationed. She would see him once a month on market day, buying rice, dal and cheap, end-of-the-day vegetables. He had looked much like any local man except for his dazed eyes, the way he startled at human noise and his spare, halting speech. He always arrived after the crowd had thinned and left as the sellers were packing up their wares, the tension in his face receding as he started out for home. In her present situation, she felt a bond with the old man and his seeming unease with the world beyond his front door.

Like most mornings, she left the solace of her bed with regret. Her energy level was still low, and getting ready for the day took her longer than usual. Her parents had finished their breakfast but sat down to keep her company while she ate. She saw them smile as she reached for an egg to add to her usual toast. She appreciated all they were doing for her and the boys but was uncomfortable being the center of attention and having their happiness depend on how much she ate or the nature of her mood. She now knew what was meant by living under a microscope. If things had turned out differently, they would have been home now, she thought, and in an instant regretted the direction her mind had taken.

She hadn't been to their home since they returned from Attock. Their first week back in Lahore, her parents had collected their clothing, toiletries and the boys' school books from the house. Later, they'd taken the boys over to go through their rooms for whatever personal items they wanted. But she couldn't face the most potent reminder of her old life with Sohail, and her lack of courage embarrassed her. She had become an example of what not to do, and she was determined to redeem herself.

And since she was in the process of making difficult plans, she should also get in touch with Hameeda. She owed her a phone call, and she wanted to thank her for all she had done for her sons. She frowned trying to picture the two of them together again. She'd thought having made the decision to reconcile, her worries would cease. But now, other concerns assailed her. What if they no longer remembered how to talk to each other? Could they recapture what they had before, or would they find the years had changed them so much they were no different than strangers meeting for the first time?

"You're very quiet this morning," her father said. "Care to share your thoughts?"

Nadira brought her attention back to the breakfast table. "I'm planning to go check on the house this morning," she said before lifting the last forkful of egg to her mouth.

Both of her parents offered to go with her, but she told them she would prefer to go on her own. Since they'd returned from Attock, her mother and father had been managing everything for her, including overseeing her residence and her car, now parked in their drive. They still had her keys and she felt like a teenager when she had to ask for them. After a moment's hesitation, her mother questioned her on her readiness to drive, and she assured her she would be fine. Why did her mother do that; call her competency into question instead of encouraging her? Did she appear so fragile? She hated how different she felt, as if pieces of her were breaking off, and she was becoming smaller and smaller. She was afraid she would keep disintegrating until she became as insubstantial and empty as a line drawing. Maybe handling something on her own today would make a difference, restore her solidity.

Her house keys hung off a large ring attached to a black and white plastic cat. The second year they were married, Sohail had seen the key ring while they were out shopping one day. He'd bought it for Nadira while her attention was elsewhere and surprised her with it at dinner.

"In light of your nickname, the little cat seemed appropriate," he'd told her. "Maybe now you'll be able to keep track of your keys."

A bittersweet feeling overcame her. No matter where she turned, in every corner of her life, Sohail had left part of himself, making her wonder if she was going to the house too soon and would be ambushed by memories too difficult to handle. But if she didn't go today, when would she go?

Nadira closed her hand over the keys and felt the ears of the cat press into her palm. She straightened up, elongated her spine and lifted her chin until she'd reached her full height. She no longer had the luxury of choosing the perfect moment; it was best not to postpone any further.

Later behind the wheel of her car, she was amazed at how good it felt to be out of the house, on her own, independent. The heavy traffic on the roads gave her more than enough to focus on and cleared her mind of troublesome thoughts. When she overtook a slow vehicle and cut back in front, the driver's shouts and hand gestures made her laugh. As far as he knew, she was just another aggressive driver who deserved no special consideration.

Turning into her street, she drove past the neighborhood guard. Dressed in his pseudo uniform of khaki shirt and trousers, a bandolier across his chest and a rifle slung over his shoulder, he strode along the roadway, head swiveling left and right as he surveyed his small domain. Once he had given her a sense of greater security, now he was a joke, no more effective than a cardboard cutout.

At the house, she rang the bell, and the servant, retained to keep watch over it, opened the gate. She was surprised at his appearance because she thought her father had mentioned hiring an older man. This tall, broad shouldered fellow looked to be about her age. As she passed through the gate, he raised his hand in a salute and smiled at her. By the time she stepped out of her car, the servant was busy on his phone, and she was happy not to have to engage in conversation with him until she was on her way out.

She had never seen the house look so unwelcoming. Not so long ago, it had been inhabited by the chorus of sounds accompanying their daily lives. Outside, the water from the gardener's hose had swished and pattered against the plant leaves, while the cook had provided the syncopated squeak, bang beat of the kitchen door as he went in and out. Through open windows, you heard the sounds of leather sandals drumming against terrazzo floors and multiple voices sliding up and down the scale to fashion an original melody. Today the house was mute and blank faced, and no interior lights beckoned her to approach. Drapes drawn over the windows turned the glass into mirrors that reflected a view of the boundary wall back at her. It seemed like years since she'd been here, and she took a deep breath before opening the door. As she stepped inside, hot, dead air pressed against her skin, and it took a moment for her eyes to adjust to an interior lit only by filtered sunlight. If she had turned on a lamp she could have seen better. But the dim light fit the atmosphere inside, as hushed and solemn as a mourner, and disguised familiar sights, soothing her in a strange way. Bodies were everywhere. Lifeless flies lay scattered across the floor like raisins, and she felt a crunch as the sole of her shoe came down on the corpse of a desiccated cricket.

She wandered through the public rooms where they had come together as a family and entertained friends. Without the trappings of everyday life, the house was robbed of the homely look it used to have. Only the lounge, where they had spent most of their time, still seemed to have some vitality. The comfortable furniture still held the imprint of their bodies, and the boys' art work on the walls and her nani's handmade pillow covers gave the room warmth the other rooms lacked. She picked up a lopsided ceramic ashtray Samir had made in grade three and ran her finger over its bumpy, glazed surface. This reminder of the past dispirited her, and she sank onto the jula her nani had given her a short time before she died. Pushing her toe against the floor, she started the jula swinging back and forth and gave in to the rhythmic motion as she'd done as a child. It felt like an eternity since the jhula had been the vehicle that fostered her romantic dreams of the future. Now, this idealized picture of her life was mutilated beyond recognition, an unknown hand scissoring Sohail out of it.

A sheet of light flowed from the direction of the foyer, across the opposite side of the room, and she realized someone had opened the front door. She must have forgotten to lock it behind her when she'd entered the house. Beads of perspiration broke out on her skin. How could she have been so careless! A large shadow stretched across the floor and up the wall as footsteps sounded, coming closer and closer. It had been foolish to come alone; what had she been thinking? Whoever had come in was blocking her way out. She looked around for something she could use as a weapon and picked up an onyx paperweight. This time she would fight back. Her heart raced as she moved as far back in the room as she could, her hand tight around the stone. A man stood in the entrance to the room, the light behind him making it difficult to see his face, and then he spoke.

"Begum Sahib, I came to see if you needed anything." He stepped closer and she saw a flash of white teeth.

Was he going to attack her? Why was he smiling?

"You don't remember me, do you?" he asked.

She was so confused she forgot to be on guard. "Have we met before?"

"It's Hasan; we used to play together as children."

Hasan? She moved over so the light wasn't in her eyes and studied the face of the servant who had opened the gate. And then it came to her, and she laughed with relief. "Little Hasan, my nani's driver's son; I can't believe it." She felt sheepish as she put the paperweight down and switched on a lamp.

Hasan told her he'd noticed the house was still dark and had come in to see if anything was wrong with the lights. He extended his condolences, and they talked for a few minutes before he left, leaving her to think about what might have happened. She waited for several minutes for the rapid beating of her heart to slow down and then thought to leave. But no, if she retreated now it would be another step backward, and she was determined to move on.

For some reason, she had expected her room to be the same as the day they had left, but all evidence of their hasty departure for the wedding had been cleared away. The bed was made, and the clothes flung over the chair and the shoes left scattered on the floor had been removed. She found the scrap of paper with Hameeda's phone number still tucked into the back corner of her dresser drawer and slipped it in her purse. Her cupboard was next. Her mother had moved everything out except for a kameez with a tear under the collar and an older outfit laundered so often, it was almost sheer. A small, carved wooden box sat on the otherwise empty shelf. She picked it up and took it with her to the chair. Opened, it revealed the odds and ends of her childhood. There was a packet of postcards from California tied with a piece of string, and a cheap metal ring with an enameled heart was jammed into a corner. It had been given to her by one of her classmates when she left Stanford to return home. She strained to bring up the image of the girl who had thought enough of her to give her this token of friendship. But she only had a vague memory of someone with curly hair and blue eyes. She lifted up the postcards and as the box shifted, four multi-colored glass bangles collided and chimed. Hameeda had given them to her for her birthday the year they met. She unfolded a sheet of paper and found a note from her nani on the occasion of her graduation from primary school. There was also a seashell, a tarnished English two pence coin an uncle had handed her when emptying out his pockets after a trip abroad, a brown, dried up sprig of pine needles from a family vacation in Murree, a length of satin ribbon, a pen jacketed in an iridescent green, and at the very bottom a stained envelope – the soldier's testimony she'd found in her nana's desk. Nadira felt a sudden kinship with this unknown man whose secret she'd kept. They had both been damaged and their lives upended by a single event. She closed the lid and placed the box next to her purse to take home with her.

Before unlocking Sohail's cupboard, she had to brace herself. Then, standing in front of the open doors, she sniffed the air like a dog hunting for the scent of a lost child. But the pungent odor of moth crystals overpowered anything that might have remained of him.

Sohail was a collector, and it resulted in a closet packed tight with hanging clothes and shelves that overflowed. He held on to his things even when they no longer had any utility. Pushing each hanger over to one side was like flipping through the pages of his personal history. Here were the jeans he had worn the first time they met, at least a size too small and yet, he kept them. His wedding outfit was here, a cricket shirt imprinted with the name of a recreational team he had captained, business suits and the shalwar kameezes he wore around the house on weekends. At the end of the rod were the clothes he had brought to Attock. The sight of them shocked her, as if someone had left his body dangling there for her to find. Wave after wave of pain slammed into her. She pushed her arms into the rack of his clothes and hugged an armful to her chest. She didn't know how long she stood in that position, tears soaking into the fabric that pressed against her face, craving the touch of something that had once been in contact with his body. After wiping her eyes with a sleeve of one of his suits, she relocked the cupboard and hurried out of the room.

Soon, she hoped, the house they worked so hard for would be sold. Whoever bought it would make changes that matched their own needs and aesthetic, and the house as they knew it would no longer exist. She and the boys would be where? Even her active imagination could not conjure up a picture of a future residence. She felt the empty house sucking all the air out of her and wished she had come with her parents who would have distracted her with questions and suggestions. Had she thought Sohail's spirit was here, and like a shy boy would only appear and communicate with her if she were alone? But the empty house just emphasized the finality of Sohail's absence. He was gone, and no amount of wishful thinking would produce some part of him to take away with her.

Outside, she squinted, the sunshine blinding her after the gloom of the house. Sunglasses in place, she pulled the car into the street, away from the guard's questioning eyes. Then she sat with her forehead pressed against the steering wheel and waited for the sick feeling in her stomach to subside. She was exhausted, and there was still the majority of the day and her aunts' visit to get through before she could let the mask of sociability slip off and tend to her grief-inflicted wounds.

*   *   *

Nadira stood in front of the mirror, brushing and arranging her hair in preparation for her aunts' arrival. She noticed the hollows in her cheeks were almost gone, but no amount of food could fill the hollowness she felt inside. At least looking closer to normal, she would garner fewer comments and less sympathy. She couldn't bear pitying looks or being treated as if she were a child to be lifted and carried. The assumption of helplessness reminded her of the widow in her nani's story. A woman she refused to become.

As usual, the aunts arrived well after their appointed time. When Nadira and her parents approached their car, they could hear the sounds of an argument. Her aunts saw them, became silent and smiles appeared on their faces as they stepped out into the courtyard. Salaams exchanged, Nadira received long hugs from both of them.

"Sorry we're so late, but Afrah couldn't find her eye glasses."

"At my age, a little absentmindedness is to be expected. You're just annoyed because I refused to take your advice and wear them on a chain around my neck – so unattractive."

"Afrah, there is nothing little about it. We go through this every time you step out of the house," Saabira said. "I was only offering a solution to save us time and frustration in the future."

Nadira waited, knowing Afrah would never let her sister have the last word. Sure enough, the bickering continued. Her father, accustomed to defusing their arguments, asked them if they were auditioning for a drama or a comedy; whichever one, he was sure they were providing the afternoon's entertainment for the servants. His comment halted the altercation, at least for a short while. Nadira wondered at what age her father had become the referee for his two older sisters. He was quite expert at redirecting their attention. She thought about her place in her own family. Her older brother Samir was the obedient, reliable one and her younger brother, Kareem, the lively, irreverent one with her father's sense of humor. And, how would she describe herself? Once she would have said she was adventurous but no longer.

They settled themselves in the drawing room, where tea and platters of chicken samosas, vegetable pakoras, tiny sandwiches and two kinds of cake waited for them.

"You shouldn't have gone to so much trouble. Just tea and biscuits would have been fine," Afrah said to her mother.

Her father glanced over at Nadira and gave her a knowing look. Afrah was notorious for her fondness for elaborate afternoon teas, and the entire family knew she would be disappointed in the extreme if she were served something simple. Nadira couldn't help but smile in return and relaxed just a little. But too soon, it seemed.

"You're looking so much better today, Nadira," Afrah said. Your appearance the last time I saw you was quite distressing."

"Thank you," Nadira said, unsure of how to respond to such a statement. She noticed Saabira frowning at Afrah.

"Please excuse Afrah. It seems she loses her tact as easily as her glasses." Saabira gave a sigh.

"Don't make excuses for me, Saabira," Afrah said, glaring at her. "I can excuse myself when it's warranted."

"You two have not changed since we were children," her father said, shaking his head. "You were always at war. Do you ever have a peaceful moment together?"

"Oh, it's just our way," Afrah said with a wave of her hand. "We're actually quite fond of each other. Aren't we, Saabira?"

"Yes, I'm quite fond of you when you're not driving me crazy," Saabira answered.

They all laughed.

How many times had she heard similar exchanges? There was an ease when you were in the company of people whose traits you knew well. Conversation wasn't a struggle, and you couldn't lose your way because no matter what the topic the responses were predictable. There were times when these very things made family gatherings uninteresting, but today she was grateful for it.

As the conversation swirled around her, she caught herself pushing her thumb against her ring finger. Her wedding band had always been a little loose and over the years she had developed the habit of shifting it back into place. Now a ghostly band of skin had been substituted for her stolen ring, but her thumb wouldn't stop searching for it. She half listened as Saabira talked about her plans to visit a college friend in Islamabad for a few weeks. Other people had plans, but as yet Nadira had none. So far, with the exception of this morning's trip back to her house, she had failed to do more than navigate the hours of the days without collapsing. There were short periods when her mind was sharp, and she felt ready to move forward, but then something would trigger a memory of Attock or Sohail, and she would find herself slipping back into melancholia.

"Do you have any plans for the summer?" Saabira asked.

Her father answered for all of them. "Well, we haven't discussed it with the rest of the family yet, but we thought we might take everyone to Murree for two months. It will get us out of the heat, and I'm sure the boys would enjoy seeing how Nadira spent her summer vacations when she was young."

Should she let her father's statement go unchallenged? It would be so easy to stay silent and postpone taking responsibility for a while longer. But, inaction was a trap that would hold her in place. If she stated a plan of action out loud, her aunts would, without a doubt, spread the word, and it would force her to follow through. She must do it now before she changed her mind.

"That's a very generous, tempting offer, Abu. But I'm going to start looking for a job over the next few months and will need to stay here. However, I'm sure Arif and Samir would love it."

For a few seconds, nobody said anything. It was Saabira who spoke first, asking what type of job she had in mind so she could ask around among her friends for contacts and possible openings. Her father gave her a long, questioning look, and then he said he would also help with the job search. Her mother put her arm around her shoulders and gave her a squeeze. And Afrah, after frowning and shaking her head as a prelude to disagreement, she thought, surprised her when she asked Nadira to let her know how she could be of assistance.

During good times, it was not always easy to appreciate family when their constant presence and advice felt more like interference. But when things went wrong, as her nani always said, they were there for you. At that moment, she glimpsed a way forward for herself and the boys, but she knew it was only the first small step, and she would have to be single minded in her resolve if she was to stay true to her vision of their future.

Chapter 16

The day before Nadira was scheduled to visit, Hameeda made the children clean their rooms and followed the maid around the house peering into corners for dust balls and running her finger over surfaces. As the cook was preparing the special dishes she had requested for their lunch, she kept checking on him, even though he was the expert and she the amateur when it came to preparing meals. It was rare for her to be so exacting, and she thought her behavior was an effort to relieve her anxiety by taking control of small matters. What she most wanted was to find a way to convince Nadira of the importance of their friendship and prove to her she'd never been discarded or forgotten. And, she remembered something that might help if she could manage to retrieve it from the box room.

Of course, the steamer trunk she was looking for was way in the back, untouched since she'd arrived after her marriage. By the time she'd cleared a path through piles of books, children's toys, an old bird cage, a small table with three legs and their suitcases, she was filthy and had a cut on her thumb. Maybe she should have asked someone to help her, but it was such a personal matter she could only imagine doing it by herself. It took her a few minutes to find a key that looked like it would fit, and she whispered a prayer as she inserted it into the keyhole. She was relieved as it slipped in and the mechanism turned, but the lid was stuck and she had to yank hard before it would open. Nestled on top was a pile of folded bed linens and tablecloths. Once as white as dandelion seed heads, the years had turned them the color of elephant tusks. At least the sealed container seemed to have prevented any insect damage. The linens were part of a larger collection of household goods she and her mother had taken pains to select for her marital home. The rest of her things were in some of the boxes stacked against the side wall, never used, waiting for the day when she became mistress of the house and could set her mother-in-law's things aside. Once she had been saddened by the waste and had resented the way the old woman had made her feel like an interloper, but she realized these feelings had disappeared. She knew if there was blame to be assigned for their difficult years together, they both deserved a share of it.

She wiped the inside of the trunk lid clean with the hem of her kameez and piled the linens on it. Underneath, between sheets of glassine, were the remnants of her distant past, items having little but sentimental value: an old scrapbook, an envelope filled with cinema ticket stubs, juvenile hair clips, school diplomas and a velvet pouch containing the child-size bracelet Nadira had brought her from the States. At the very bottom of the trunk, she found the object she was searching for – a small cardboard box. When she opened it, she was relieved to find a packet of blue aerograms tied together with a satin ribbon, looking the same as the day she'd placed them inside. She put the cardboard box and the bracelet to one side and repacked the rest of the items. If there was time, she wanted to read the letters once more before giving them to Nadira. She wished she could keep them, just in case they couldn't retrieve what they'd once had as children. They were her only concrete evidence of how entwined their lives had once been, and of the care they had taken to continue sharing all their experiences and thoughts even though a great distance had kept them apart.

The next morning, she was awake long before it was time to get up, and while she waited for the sun to rise, she daydreamed about what it would have been like if she and Nadira had never been separated. She relived her wedding and the births of her children with her friend present, and eavesdropped on missed conversations that shared fears, worries and secrets, and gave advice, support and comfort. How different her life might have been if Nadira had remained her friend. She couldn't expect things to be the same after so many years and made a promise she would be grateful with less as long as they could still have some sort of relationship.

The hours leading up to Nadira's arrival had Hameeda vacillating between excitement and nervousness, her emotions inscribing a rash on her arms. Once they faced each other across the threshold, Hameeda felt a force field of uncertainty between them. The easiest part of this first moment was when they entered each other's open arms. It was a familiar and unconstrained exchange, its etiquette making it no less meaningful. It made her wish words were unnecessary and they could communicate solely by touch, their bodies clothed in lines of braille whose hills and valleys would reveal truths and yearnings as the pads of their fingers traveled over them.

Before seating herself in the drawing room, Nadira handed her a gift wrapped package, telling her it was a very small thing in comparison to all she had done for her children.

"It was no trouble at all. We've enjoyed their company," Hameeda said as she looked at the package. "Should I open it now?"

Her friend told her to go ahead. As she unwrapped her gift, she took the time to fold the paper and roll up the ribbon from the bow. Nadira smiled and remarked that Hameeda still had this same habit of saving gift packaging, while she still used her old rip and crumple approach. Hameeda laughed and nodded her head, remembering past birthdays when her friend had sat amidst a pile of gift wrap reduced to rubbish.

Inside the box was a beautiful aqua dupatta hand painted with an abstract design. She thanked her friend and told her how much she loved it. Nadira told her to look closer; there was a second gift in the box. She lifted the tissue paper and saw a small, leather book with the word *Memories* embossed in gold on the front cover. Inside, tucked into plastic sleeves mounted on heavy ivory paper, were photos of the two of them. Hameeda couldn't help gasping with pleasure and tears started in her eyes.

"This is the best gift I've ever received!" she said. "Come closer so we can look at it together." They sat with their heads almost touching, rediscovering their friendship as they turned the pages. There they were at age six, both in school uniforms with long braids hanging over their shoulders. Posed portraits were interspersed with candid shots, some with just the two of them and others as part of a larger group, but none where one of them appeared without the other. Sometimes they both remembered when and where a picture had been taken without an effort and they reminisced together, while other photos set off a debate. She found the words she was so worried about came without a struggle, and Nadira also seemed relaxed. Then Hameeda came to a page, about two thirds of the way through the book, where there were only empty pockets. She couldn't help thinking about all the photos which might have filled the rest of the book, and took the blame for their absence. A lump formed in her throat, and she was afraid she would cry.

"What's the matter?" Nadira asked.

Hameeda took a deep breath. "I should have fought harder for us, or at least disobeyed my father and gotten in touch with you," she said, a tear rolling down her cheek. "I know you would have found a way to contact me if things had been reversed."

Nadira reached over and dried her cheek with a gentle sweep of her thumb. "I'm not so sure that's true. You never know how you will face difficulties until you encounter them. I always thought I could take the hardest blows life meted out and still remain upright. But I was wrong. And, I should have trusted what I knew about you, instead of assuming the worst."

Nadira told her they shouldn't waste any more time dwelling on a past they couldn't change. Hameeda thought of the formal apology she had practiced and felt a little guilty that her friend had made it so easy for her.

The cook entered the room to tell them lunch was ready. It wasn't until they sat down at the table that she saw her gift to Nadira on the sideboard.

"I almost forgot; I also have a gift for you," Hameeda said. "I'm sorry, but I didn't have time to wrap it."

Her friend opened the box, and after staring at the packet of aerograms, she blushed. "Oh, Hameeda, I can't believe you kept my letters all this time. I'm really touched."

"I thought you might like to have them as a reminder of your time in the States."

"It's a wonderful gift, thank you so much," she said as she crossed to the other side of the table and gave Hameeda a hug.

Lunch went well. Nadira exclaimed over the fact that Hameeda had remembered some of her favorite dishes, and there were no uncomfortable breaks in their conversation. They both talked about the intervening years and their families. As expected, she saw disappointment in Nadira's face when she mentioned dropping out of college, but her friend didn't say anything.

As they were saying goodbye, Nadira suggested getting together for lunch again sometime soon, maybe at one of the new cafes. Hameeda told her it was a wonderful idea, and she would look forward to it. One embrace and Nadira was gone, and an instant later she felt deprived. Afterward, their afternoon together seemed like a dream, a much better dream than she could have imagined.

*   *   *

Late that evening, alone in her room, Nadira thought about her time with Hameeda. She was amazed at how quickly she'd felt at ease, the old sense of a natural connection reasserting itself. She hoped Hameeda had felt the same. Their conversation had covered their years apart in broad strokes, and she knew they would continue to fill in the details as they spent time together in the future. Some of the retelling had been difficult for her, more difficult than she'd imagined it would be. As she told Hameeda about meeting Sohail and their marriage, her heart ached. Nadira had always loved Sohail's name; the soft sibilance of its components soothing to the ear. But now the sound of it hanging in the air was as sharp as an unsheathed knife with the same ability to wound. But in retelling their story, Sohail and their relationship came back into focus. Each event she described reminded her of his wonderful qualities. From the beginning, she told Hameeda, he had the ability to make her laugh. She asked her friend if she remembered how she could be stubborn and argumentative, and told her even at those times, he was slow to anger and forgiving. When she talked about the day each of her sons was born, she pictured her husband's expression of wonder and delight, as he held them for the first time, and thought what a good father he had been. She realized her feeling of being adrift was because his death had deprived her of the calm, loving center of her existence. She wanted to believe that Sohail's soul had ears to hear her praise, and it would act as the apology she'd never had the chance to give him.

And the special gift her friend gave her, more than anything else, told her Hameeda was the same person she remembered from so long ago. Just thinking about the letters brought a flood of emotion. She was eager to read a few of them and satisfy her curiosity about her younger self. Would the letters surprise her and reveal something she had forgotten or never known about herself? Undoing the satin ribbon, she picked up the aerogram on top and opened it. Frequent handling had broken the microscopic, wood pulp fibers, softening the paper's original slick stiffness until its surface felt like suede. Folds were held together in places by brittle, yellowed cellophane tape. As she flattened the sheet, some pieces of tape broke off and fell into her lap. The letter was dated the day after she arrived at Stanford. She remembered how comforting it had been to write to Hameeda, her tether to the familiar associations of home when the strangeness of her situation overwhelmed her. How young she sounded, excited about each novel experience and optimistic about the future. Refolding the aerogram, she leafed through the letters all arranged in chronological order; every one she'd sent, saved. She couldn't take her eyes off her missives, so obviously read, reread and guarded over the years. Hameeda had preserved the record of a part of her life that would otherwise have been left to memory's unreliability and had shown the constancy she couldn't claim. When they were children they had promised never to keep secrets from each other. But sometimes you had to hold back to guard a person's feelings. She would never tell her friend that a few months after they parted, in a fit of temper, she had ripped up and burned all her letters, regretting it almost as soon as they were reduced to ash. She hoped she'd changed since then and finally learned forgiveness benefited not just the person you forgave, but also yourself. She found it sad that even the photos she had given her had been culled from her parents' albums since her own photos had been discarded or lost. She realized she had been a lot more careless with Hameeda than her friend had been with her. Just as in the past, she'd have to run hard and fast to catch up to her.

Chapter 17

Nadira wondered if she was expecting too much. It had only been two months, but already she was sinking into despair. Every day she purchased the four newspapers with the largest circulation and went through the employment advertisements. For many accounting jobs she was under qualified, lacking a chartered accountant designation. The previous week, she'd answered a promising ad and wasted half a day waiting her turn in a roomful of applicants only to find out it was a combination of secretarial responsibilities and some bookkeeping with a salary she wasn't sure was worth the effort. She'd felt betrayed as if they'd intended to mislead her. Her confidence at a low point, she might have taken the job anyway, if only to pad her resume for the future, but they said she was over qualified. What had been the point of her carefully selected courses and her hours of studying to ensure nothing less than an "A"? And her truncated resume, the obvious sign of a working life cut short by motherhood, was a difficult disability to overcome. She couldn't believe how unknowing she'd been in her youth, missing opportunities and making poor choices, and how naive she'd been when she started looking. Only a marrow deep stubbornness and her responsibility for her sons kept her going. For the first time, she understood the full extent of the stress Sohail had been under.

In the end, she was saved by her aunt. That's how she thought of it later, as if she had been drowning and Saabira Auntie had thrown her a rope and pulled her on to solid ground.

Late one afternoon, her aunt rushed into the house calling her name. She was smiling and her eyes danced. "I've found you the perfect job!" she said. She had been to dinner at her neighbor's house and met a woman who was the headmistress at one of the better girls' schools. Her aunt had managed to work Nadira into the conversation, mentioning how she'd earned a first in math, and her interest in a teaching position.

"Not really a lie since I was sure if a job was available, you'd turn me into an honest woman," Saabira said, nodding her head as if agreeing with her assumption on Nadira's behalf. "You won't believe it; Allah must be watching over you. One of her advance math teachers has recently resigned with no notice."

Nadira frowned. She'd never considered teaching; it had always seemed like an ordinary choice, an old fashioned occupation for women from another age. More important, she had no teaching credentials or experience and didn't even know if she still remembered calculus and trigonometry well enough to explain it to someone else. But, as she thought about it, her skills in math were no rustier than those in accounting, and she didn't have the luxury of dismissing any potential job out of hand.

It was no longer about her wants and needs, only about necessity.

"They're having trouble finding someone, and are rather desperate. You'd start at the beginning of next term so you would have the entire summer to prepare. Promise me you'll call for an interview."

Nadira thought it unlikely the headmistress would be interested in her once she heard her particulars. She wondered if it was worth going through all the trouble and possible embarrassment when there was such a low probability of success. But how could she hand back the chance her aunt had given her as if it were a small, worthless thing.

"I'll call tomorrow morning," she said. "After all, I wouldn't want to ruin your reputation for truthfulness." And as she hugged her aunt, who was so dear to her, she considered the hurdles in front of her and tried not to give in to relief.

The next morning, she talked to the headmistress and agreed to come in for an interview the following day. She suffered a panic attack as soon as she hung up the phone and went in search of her father. She told him she had no idea how to interview for a job she had never considered. When asked why she wanted to teach, what should she say? Her father told her not to worry; she had more than enough time to prepare. He helped her write a resume geared toward teaching, including her stint as a math tutor for Hameeda, although she had never considered it tutoring in a formal sense. She also practiced answering the potential interview questions he posed. After she'd finished with her father, her mother helped her pick out something appropriate to wear.

By the time she appeared for her appointment, she had transitioned from panicked to nervous. When she entered the room, the headmistress rose and greeted her while remaining behind her desk. She motioned Nadira to the chair opposite her. It was the first time she'd been in a headmistress's office since childhood, and she was surprised at how intimidating it still was, even as an adult with no history of disciplinary problems. It helped that this headmistress in no way resembled the stout, grey haired woman of years ago. She appeared to be middle-aged and was wearing the latest style which had just begun to appear in the shops. Her hijab was held in place by an expensive looking pin, and her gold bangle bracelets clinked every time she moved her arms. On the wall facing Nadira were two rows of class pictures. Uniformed girls smiled down at her as if in encouragement while she tried to keep her hands still and a smile on her face.

Nadira offered up her resume and the headmistress glanced at it before putting it to one side. She congratulated her on earning a first in math before abandoning the subject of her qualifications. Nadira began to wonder which side of the interview she was on as the headmistress recounted her own experiences at Punjab University, including a physics course she had taken from Nadira's father.

"He was one of my favorite professors," she said, her voice syrupy and her fingers fluttering up and down like sparrow wings. I had avoided physics in high school, and he made it so interesting and easy to understand. I'm sure having the benefit of his example, you will do very well."

The faulty reasoning behind the headmistress's statement astounded Nadira and she felt forced to correct her, in the process ignoring her father's admonition to exhibit confidence in her teaching ability.

"I must tell you, I've never taught a class before."

"Well, you have tutored, and your record shows a mastery of the subject matter. In fact, I'm quite certain we've never had a math teacher with a first in the subject. I'm sure you'll make a rapid adjustment and be a welcome addition to our faculty."

Was it possible, it sounded like she was being offered the job? "Don't you have any more questions for me?" Nadira didn't know if she was asking because she wanted a chance to solidify her appeal as a candidate or was trying to sabotage her chances. Maybe this is how you felt after being home-bound for so long, all your enthusiasm and self-confidence gone.

"Normally, we don't hire teachers without either a teacher's certificate or teaching experience; however, your connections speak for themselves. I have a very high regard for your father, and my friend speaks well of your family," she said as she swiveled in her chair and picked up a pile of materials from the top of the bookshelf to her left. "The main reason I wanted you to come in was so we could discuss your salary, and I could give you the syllabus, the course textbooks, a copy of the class lists and school timings."

Nadira felt dizzy; events were moving too fast for her to assimilate them. The woman seemed to take it for granted she would accept the job. Was a response required at this point? She would have liked more time to think before she made her decision, but she worried that the headmistress might assume she wasn't interested and start considering other, more qualified candidates. She managed to thank her for the opportunity to teach at the school.

The headmistress slid the pile of materials across the desk to her. She named a salary figure that was more than Nadira had expected, and without querying further and with some relief, she agreed. Her new boss told her the first semester would be a probationary period, and if she did well, she would be kept on. Well, the woman was not being as precipitous as she first thought, and Nadira wondered if hiring her might just be a stop-gap measure until someone more qualified could be found. If that was the case, she would have to prove her worth as quick as possible.

The rest of the interview was spent in small talk which, to Nadira, seemed to have no purpose. Then, as the head-mistress ushered Nadira out, she told her she would see her in September and to call her if she had any questions.

Walking to her car, a sharp spasm stabbed her shoulders and her neck felt tight. She would only have a little over two and a half months to prepare for her courses. The idea of facing a classroom of girls made her uncertain about her decision to take the job. Later, it pained her to think of the questions she'd left unasked, proof of her inexperience. Going through the materials, she found she'd be teaching three classes of 18 to 20 girls, two in calculus and one in trigonometry, making the salary seem less generous. Maybe two months was not such a long time to search for a job. But it was too late to change her mind, and she would have a semester to find out if she would regret her haste.

Now the commitment was made, she wanted to put everything else aside and focus all her attention on preparing for the coming school year. Her father had gone ahead with his plans for a family vacation in Murree, and at first she insisted she would stay home by herself. But, her father argued she would find it easier to concentrate in the mountains than in the heat of Lahore. He also promised her uninterrupted time to work on her lessons. Remembering how she had suffered the previous summer with temperatures reaching 120° F, and load shedding shutting down their air conditioners for most of the day, she consented to go.

*   *   *

During the years preceding her marriage, summer vacation had been synonymous with Murree. Year after year, they had shared the same rental with her father's brother and his family, frequented the same shops and hired the same occasional labor. When she was in the marketplace and the locals called her by name, she felt special, singled out from the other visitors, and it pleased her in the same way being privy to a secret pleased her. All of these factors had made her feel as much at home in Murree as she did in Lahore.

As their car approached the mountain town, she looked out the window eager for her first glimpse and was disappointed to see how much it had changed during the years of her absence. Funny how she had expected it to be unaltered, as if her backward glance when she'd left had pinned it in place like a photo on a cork board. Among the new shops, restaurants and hotels that climbed up the hillsides and pushed the town out beyond its previous borders, she tried to find old landmarks to point out to the boys and was not very successful.

Their car was forced to slow down. Summer was high season, and the streets were crowded with visitors, the air thick with their noise. It was fortunate her father had rented a very small, but well-appointed guest house on the outskirts of town. Far from the center of activity, there was nothing to drown out bird song or the low soughing of the wind as it slipped through the tree branches. Once inside and before dropping her luggage in her room, she went over to the large window that dominated the lounge. Her spirits lifted as she took in a view of the same towering pines, magnificent mountains and azure sky she remembered.

She had a day to settle in before her father, as promised, put her to work. He became her teacher just as he had when she was waiting to begin school. Together, they went through the syllabus for the year and prepared lesson plans. They had some help from the teacher's guide that came with the textbooks and offered sample problems for homework and quizzes. But once school started, she suspected she would have to cull through the old A-level exams on file for additional homework and test problems. In the evenings, she worked on regaining her old facility with differential equations, theorems, vectors, trig functions, trig identities and other mathematical concepts. After spending a couple of weeks becoming familiar with the material, her father made her practice presenting her lessons while he played the role of a student. When Arif and Samir found out what they were doing, they insisted on joining the class. Arif looked everywhere but at her, asked the same question more than once, spoke out without raising his hand, and whispered to Samir while she was talking. Nadira hoped he was just playing the role of a difficult student and didn't present as many problems for his real teachers as he did for her.

"Arif, is this the way you behave in school?"

"I wouldn't think of it Amma. I just want you to be prepared for your most trying students."

"Somehow I doubt I'll come across a young girl with your qualities."

"I'll take that as a compliment," Arif said with an impish grin.

Nadira just shook her head.

"Don't let Arif distract you; let's go on with the lesson," her father said. "Arif, in my day, you would have already received a caning for your misbehavior, and I'm sure I could find a supple branch outside our door and give you a demonstration." Her father smiled negating the sternness of his voice. "Now, shall we continue?"

It took a day for Arif to become bored with his student role – too much like the real thing. But Samir became interested in the subject matter and was disappointed when he learned she wouldn't be practice teaching the entire course because of time constraints. To her delight, he began studying calculus on his own, coming to her for help when the book didn't offer enough of an explanation for him. Arif told Samir he was wasting his vacation, but Nadira did not find his fascination strange; rather, she saw in him a younger version of herself and hoped their shared interest would bring them closer together. She wished she could find a way to draw Arif back to the relationship they'd had when he was a young child. As a teenager, he needed her less and less, and she sensed there were conversations he would have had with Sohail on subjects he was uncomfortable talking to her about. While she was working, she often looked out the window and saw him sitting on the terrace, deep in conversation with her father, and felt better knowing he had a man to turn to.

As the practice sessions progressed, Nadira found she was enjoying her preparations, her love of math resurfacing. And, surprising her, she began to see teaching in a different, positive light.

After she had been in Murree for a while, she realized how wise her father had been when he insisted she go with them and balance her preparations for the school year with at least a couple of hours a day sharing family activities.

The way in which they filled their family time was the same as it had been when she was the boys' age. The horse wallah still arrived daily with mounts for riding, and she introduced her sons to the walking trails she'd trod so many years before. On rainy days they played board games or read the books left by past guests. The book selection was eclectic and both good and bad. Some of the books had handwritten notes in the margins, and she found it interesting to have access to another person's thoughts on what she was reading.

Right after early morning prayers when everyone else had gone back to bed, she and her father got into the habit of going for a short walk. It reminded her of their time at Stanford. As they walked the yet unpopulated paths, she was able to open up to him about her worries for the future. Although their conversations didn't solve her problems, it lightened her burden and she found she was more relaxed. And, when she returned to find her sons excited to start their day, and heard the sound of their laughter, she believed Murree had worked its magic on them as well. For the first time since Attock, she felt good, not just on the surface but through and through. There were still times when sadness overtook her, most often when she thought of how wonderful the vacation would have been if Sohail had been there to share it with them. But she managed to keep any sorrow in the background, no longer letting it take center stage.

One day, searching for a place to be alone, she found a flat rock on the hillside above the guest house. It was nearing dusk, and she stayed until the last of the sun's rays fanned out above the mountain tops, and the serpentine river splitting the valley below, so blue in the daylight, turned into a shining spill of liquid mercury. The land looked so empty and peaceful from her vantage point, it was as if she was seeing the world before Allah created mankind. It was amazing, she thought, how natural beauty could be a salve for life's heartaches. Maybe if all humans had access to moments like this, a clear illustration of the perfection of Allah's creation, they would take better care of this world and each other.

While they were in Murree she was able to keep her nervousness at a manageable level, but once back home and with only two weeks before the beginning of school, Nadira's thoughts never left her lessons and teaching techniques. At night she woke from dreams that made her heart pulsate like a struck drum skin. One night she dreamt that she was late for class. She kept running toward the school building, but instead of getting closer, it kept getting farther away. Another night she was in a classroom filled with expectant faces staring at her and waiting for the start of the lesson, but when she opened her mouth, nothing came out. She was in this state of mind when her first day of teaching arrived.

As she entered the room, the girls, all twenty of them, turned their attention to her. She arranged her books on her desk as a means of calming herself down, and then faced the class.

"Asalaam aleikum girls; my name is Mrs. Malik."

As she scanned the faces of the seventeen year olds, many of them looked more anxious than she felt. It occurred to her that these were the last few months before they took their A-levels, and now a novice teacher would be preparing them for the math exam. She still remembered how she felt going into her A-levels. All the grades she had earned over the years would mean nothing if she didn't do well on one set of exams, the results determining the universities who would consider her for admission, and influencing her future in other unknown ways. For these girls, she knew, a lot depended on her teaching ability. She made up her mind she would not fail them.

"All right, let's begin."

Chapter 18

All summer Hameeda had the feeling she was reliving an earlier part of her life. After their first meeting, she and Nadira couldn't coordinate their schedules and had to be satisfied with talking on the phone instead of meeting face to face. Once her friend left for Murree, they gave up speaking for the written word. It was just as it had been when they were twelve, except this time they didn't use aerograms – did they still exist? Instead they e-mailed, a skill Hameeda didn't possess, and she had to ask Daliya if she could show her how to do it. Her daughter sat with her at the computer half a dozen times until she mastered the process.

She missed her centuries old implements; the movement of pen across paper had always helped draw out her thoughts and feelings, as if her pen was a conduit linking her mind to her hand. Two-fingered typing on the computer was as alien to her as keying Morse code and amputated any connection between thought and written expression. She often found herself so focused on the individual letters, she forgot what she was going to say. However, she was enamored with one aspect of e-mail; she could save both the e-mails she sent and the ones she received from Nadira.

Years from now she would be able to revisit this second phase of their relationship even if her memory dimmed.

Memory was often on her mind these days, as every time she visited her father she was witness to how it could erode more and more until it disappeared altogether. Now, her father's good days were rare, and on a bad day he was word-less, his eyes empty, as if only his body occupied the chair. If she didn't know better, she would have concluded an angel had made a mistake and taken his soul before his life had ended. She avoided thinking about what it was like to have everything that defined you slipping away, until one day you woke up in an unfamiliar place not knowing who you were.

Hameeda stood before her open, bedroom window, let the refreshing, autumn breeze blow away her dark thoughts, and concentrated on getting ready to meet Nadira for lunch at the Pancake House. She was eager to learn how her friend's teaching was going. She never would have conquered math if it hadn't been for her friend's patient tutoring all those years ago. Nadira had never given up on her. If one way of explaining a concept failed, she kept coming at it from a different direction until she found one that worked. She was positive this talent would have transferred to the classroom.

Only one worry spoiled her anticipation of their lunch. Since they were meeting in a public place, she would be wearing her burqa, and she wasn't sure how Nadira would react. She knew she should care more about her principles and less about what her friend might think, but Nadira's opinion meant a great deal to her. She was tempted to leave the niqab off, but you couldn't pick and choose which of Allah's teachings you wanted to obey as if they were items on a menu. You either believed in the wisdom of Allah and the Prophet Muhammad, or you didn't. She sighed and took a final look in the mirror before drawing the niqab across the bottom of her face.

She selected a table at the back, facing the door so she could watch for her friend's arrival. Nadira appeared a few minutes later dressed in a red and black print kameez over narrow legged, black pants, a red dupatta draped around her neck. Since the last time she'd seen Nadira, her shoulder length hair had been cut in a chin skimming bob, and it was very becoming. Her friend looked around the room, her eyes not even hesitating as they passed over her. A feeling of dread filled Hameeda as she raised her hand to get her attention and saw Nadira take a long look at her before making her way to the table. Her small, tight lipped smile and abbreviated, one-armed hug made Hameeda's stomach churn, and she prayed Nadira wasn't going to lecture her. How well she remembered her friend's lack of reticence about saying what was on her mind.

Nadira settled herself in her chair, and their eyes met. Hameeda tried to divine her thoughts from the expression on her face, but only found her own fears projected there.

"Have you decided what you want to eat?" Nadira asked, her head now bent over the menu.

"Not yet." Hameeda waited for her to bring up the subject of her attire and when she didn't, she knew she should have been relieved, but it only made her more anxious. Forcing herself, she asked, "Do you want to talk about what I'm wearing?" Her friend looked up and was quiet long enough to sharpen her uneasiness.

"Let me ask you a question," Nadira said finally. "Does my uncovered head bother you?"

Her response caught Hameeda by surprise and made her smile. It was so like Nadira to answer her question with another, which if she thought about it, was also an answer. "No, of course not."

Nadira smiled, this time wide and toothy. "Good, I'm glad. Hurry up and decide what you want so we can order; I'm starving."

During lunch, there was no further mention of her transformation, but later she would wonder if there was some narrative she had not been privy to during Nadira's long pause. The rest of their conversation had a familiar feel to it, as if she had heard it before. Maybe, it was because she had once envisioned a long unbroken line of friendship where they shared their daily concerns at every age, including subjects like the idiosyncrasies of teenage boys. Of course, they were no longer children in the habit of letting words spill out before an internal censor could hold them back. But she hoped with time, a renewed trust would lessen their caution.

*   *   *

At dinner, when Nadira's parents asked her if she'd enjoyed her lunch with Hameeda, she didn't mention her shock at seeing her friend with her face covered, and later, she wondered why she hadn't told them. Maybe, she did believe it was unimportant and not worth discussing, or maybe she didn't want to appear narrow-minded. She wondered if it would have made a difference if she had seen her wearing a burqa before they'd spent time together. Would she have made erroneous assumptions about her and been more wary? She wanted to think not, but wasn't confident it would have been the same. If she had been honest with Hameeda, she would have told her she didn't like the fact she was wearing the niqab. Not only did she feel it was not required and was adopted from another time and culture, but by putting on the niqab, she felt as if her friend was hiding the person she'd known and presenting her with a stranger. At first she felt she was operating under a handicap, reduced to talking to someone she couldn't see well. Even her hearing had been affected, not because the piece of cloth muffled her friend's words, but because the sight of this black rectangle drew her attention away from what her friend was saying. Yet, by the end of their lunch she found herself adjusting, and she felt with time she wouldn't even notice the difference. After all, shouldn't the emphasis be on who Hameeda was, not how she looked? In the short time since their reunion, she'd had more than enough evidence of the enduring quality of Hameeda's character and personality.

The way the country was evolving, soon she, with her uncovered head, might belong to a dwindling minority. She harbored the slim hope that if and when it happened, tented women would remember how they had wanted to be treated when their numbers were small.

Chapter 19

A boy on the cusp of manhood paused at the entrance to the mosque and slipped off his shoes. Wearing a loose, bleached cotton shalwar kameez and a white knit topi over his close cropped hair, he blended in with the other men attending Friday prayers. Later, nobody would remember whether he was young or old, short or tall, bearded or clean shaven, fair or dark.

He crossed the floor without glancing left or right and found an empty spot in the center of the room where he spread out his prayer rug. When the man to his left greeted him, he returned his salaams in a low voice before turning his gaze toward Mecca, his ears attuned to the shuffling of feet as people formed rows behind him. The air thickened with the low hum of conversation until the imam appeared, and the talk thinned into silence. The boy marked time during the imam's khutbah, letting the sound of his voice move around him as if he were a stone in the middle of a stream. He remembered how his own imam's words had ignited an internal fire and then fed the flames until he was overcome by a feeling of rapture. Now, the fevered thoughts that had heated his body were replaced by a coldness that swept through him like the wintry winds in the mountain passes near his village. He felt a sense of detachment, as if his soul had already left him and was viewing, from a distance, the empty vessel that had once contained it.

If he was nervous at all, it was only about being discovered before he could complete his assigned task. But he remained calm and waited, his lips moving in unison with those around him. Midway into the prayers, as everyone prostrated themselves, their foreheads pressed against their prayer rugs, the boy ran his right hand over his shalwar, looking for the object taped to his skin just below the ridge of bunched fabric where a string gathered in his waistband. He found the button on its side, and whispered "Allahu Akbar," before pressing it with his thumb.

* * *

Months later, Nadira would look back at the event that separated her from her fears and propelled her forward, and puzzle over why this particular terrorist attack had affected her so much more than the others. It hadn't been noticeably different in execution or cost from preceding attacks. In the end, was it the horror of what they had learned to live with, or the accumulation of insults to her emotional balance that made it the tipping point?

The day it occurred, things had not been going badly; quite the opposite, she thought, recalling what should have been a celebratory day. During the lunch break, the headmistress called Nadira into her office to tell her that based on the many favorable comments from students and parents, along with her own positive observations, Nadira would be kept on for the rest of the school year. Thrilled, Nadira had looked forward to telling the family at dinner, but then remained silent that evening, her accomplishment forgotten in the wake of the latest violent act.

It's funny how ordinary things can stick in your memory if they're associated with something troubling. She even remembered the details of what she'd been doing and how she'd felt before this life-changing event. She was in the midst of grading papers when boredom struck; the pleasures of the classroom, both then and now, did not erase the tedium of this task. Daydreams pulled her away from her work until she was brought back to reality by the distant noise of the television and her father's raised voice. He was in the habit of directing tirades at the TV reporter in an attempt to rid himself of his frustrations, she supposed, and it grated on her nerves; one reason why she hadn't joined her parents in this pre-dinner ritual. In any event, spare time was at a premium her first year of teaching, and it was rare for her to watch TV or read a newspaper. In the beginning of the year, her lack of experience with the course material required additional hours to prepare for classes, and afterward she realized she didn't miss being well-informed since the news was invariably bad and only served to depress her. Lacking knowledge about something important was never a worry because her father acted as the household's newscaster of current events, complete with his own commentary. So when he brought up the latest atrocity as they were sitting down to eat, she hadn't been surprised.

"There was a suicide bombing at one of the Shia mosques today," her father said as he placed his napkin in his lap. "Something must be done about these extremists; right after dinner, I'm writing a letter to the editor of Dawn."

Nadira didn't respond. She stared at her plate and forced her thoughts on her father's disclosure to end with the period that finished his sentence. It was a necessary strategy because she'd lost the ability to distance herself from the heartache of strangers. The faces of victims and their families haunted her for days, awakening the sharpness of her grief, now settled into a dull throbbing like a decaying tooth.

"I don't think this is a proper subject for the dinner table, Nadeem," her mother said with a frown. "We'll all lose our appetites."

Her father cleared his throat, and Nadira waited for another comment. But then he glanced at her mother's face and must have seen something there that made him change his mind.

"You're right; I won't spoil this excellent meal with a discussion of the unspeakable contagion infecting our country."

"Nadeem, must you always put the tip of your toe across every line I draw in the sand?" Her mother wagged her finger at him.

For some reason, Nadira hadn't felt angry at first; maybe

she'd tamped it down or it had taken time to develop, creeping up on her over the next few days. Of course, in retrospect, there had been symptoms of her burgeoning outrage. That night, she woke up at odd hours, whatever pulled her out of sleep gone as soon as her eyes opened, leaving her perplexed over the cause of her restlessness. In the morning, she had felt sick with a queasy stomach, and a headache plagued her well into the afternoon. A day later while driving to school, a news report came on about the search for accomplices to the bombing and she'd switched the radio off so violently, the knob came off in her hand. And when she overheard one teacher telling another of her relief to learn the bomber's target was a Shia mosque because it meant it didn't affect anyone she knew, Nadira forced herself to turn away before saying something she'd regret. It wasn't until the metallic taste of blood filled her mouth that she noticed she'd bitten the inside of her cheek. Afterward, there was no hiding from her anger.

When she arrived home that afternoon, her father asked her to read his letter on the subject before he sent it to the editor of the newspaper. She saw he'd covered the same points other authors had eloquently argued in recent years, and Nadira found herself annoyed with him without quite knowing why. Even if she thought it would have no effect, at least he was doing something. What had she ever done?

She hated to think she'd become a coward, the type of weak person who would fail to act upon seeing someone else in danger. Look how strong her nani had been. Even her boys had dealt with their father's death better than she had. But then, as she handed the letter back to him, she remembered standing in their house, the puny paper-weight in her hand, ready to do battle, determined to fight and save herself, if only for her sons. As scared as she was that day, it had also felt good not to cower or run away. And in reliving that moment, she knew she'd become a hostage to fear. Furious, she felt compelled to do some-thing. But what?

It was possible she would have devised her own course of action, but instead, she thought, fate stepped in disguised as a luncheon invitation. What if she'd been busy and had postponed the date long enough for her anger to cool and her fears to reassert themselves? Would she still have taken advantage of the opportunity offered to her? She was glad she would never know.

*   *   *

Less than a week after the bombing, her friend Sharnaz called to see how she was doing at her job and to ask after the boys. As they talked, Nadira got the impression her friend had an ulterior motive for the call beyond a hello, how are you, since light chit-chat was not her usual style. So, when Sharnaz invited her to lunch on the following Sunday, she accepted, welcoming the chance to see her and curious to find out what was really on her mind.

Although, they had talked on the phone several times over the last few months, she hadn't seen Sharnaz since a few weeks after the funeral. They'd been close friends in college, and she regretted not making more time for her in recent years. After her marriage, she was so immersed in the life Sohail had brought with him, her old life had slipped away, and so gradually she hadn't noticed. When she'd realized what had happened, she thought it was a normal consequence of being married and having children. But, despite infrequent meetings, she and Sharnaz had remained very good friends.

It was interesting that her two closest friends were such opposites. Now, she realized Sharnaz and Hameeda had one thing in common; they both had traits she admired and wished she possessed.

Sunday afternoon, replete from a delicious lunch, Nadira eyed a canvas with random slashes of red, blue and yellow hanging on the sitting room wall, a new acquisition since the last time she'd been to Sharnaz's house. In her experience, her friend was drawn to objects that first startled you and then stirred your imagination.

Sharnaz's daughter had gone off to meet a friend, and her husband had retreated to the library. They were alone; maybe now her curiosity would be satisfied. Nadira turned her attention back to her cup of tea and studied her friend as she talked to her. Sharnaz had changed very little since their student days. She still wore her hair long with bangs cut straight across, brushing the top of thick, untweezed eyebrows. Her large, expressive eyes on either side of a Semitic nose, gazed at her, unmoved by any distraction, and whenever she paused in her rapid fire delivery of comments and questions, her generous mouth turned up in a smile. Nadira asked her about her latest causes, and listened as she described the various projects she was working on.

"Actually, one reason I wanted to see you was to get your help with an important event we've got in the planning stages," Sharnaz said, looking at her over her raised cup.

"I was wondering how much longer it would be before you told me why I'm here," Nadira said with a laugh.

Smiling, her friend protested. Then her smile disappeared, and Sharnaz began talking about the recent attack on the Shia mosque and other terrorist attacks. Nadira watched as her friend's passion lifted her out of her seat and set her pacing back and forth in front of her. She proclaimed how important it was for Pakistanis to show the politicians and the outside world they opposed terrorism, her hands stabbing the air like an exclamation point at the end of each sentence. Although there had been earlier, small demonstrations, she explained, as the attacks had increased the populace had begun to disengage and for anything to change, Sharnaz said, constant pressure needed to be applied to public officials. She went on to deride the government's pitiful response, not only to terrorist acts, but to the increase in criminal activity whose proceeds often funded terrorist organizations.

The possible criminal connection surprised Nadira, and her pain and anger returned as sharp as it had been in the days after Sohail was killed. She didn't know why the possible tie between crime and terrorism hadn't occurred to her before. The memory of her childhood encounter with

Black Beard, his evil aura, sensed even then, returned to choke her. Her eyes stung and she blinked a few times to clear her vision.

A conversation from long ago floated to the surface of her mind like a decaying fish set loose from the mud of a pond, the recollection of Black Beard bragging about the smuggling of drugs and guns between Afghanistan and Pakistan, now understood. She couldn't bear the thought that in addition to murdering Sohail, he had taken the ransom money and used it to fund more destruction and death. In that moment, there with her friend, she feared she might cry or be sick and wished she was home in her room. Concentrating on taking small, slow breaths, she waited until the beat of her pulse stopped pushing against the skin of her wrist, her stomach settled and her eyes cleared.

Grateful Sharnaz hadn't seemed to notice her distress, she listened as her friend continued talking about the coordinated women's anti-terrorism demonstrations being planned for Lahore, Karachi and Islamabad and that she was in charge of arrangements for Lahore. A political organization had promised to fund the events, she explained, but what she really needed was more people to help since it had to be scheduled quickly. To take advantage of the current outrage, the date set left only four months' time to complete arrangements.

Sharnaz sank back down on the sofa next to Nadira. "I need someone I can depend on to oversee the volunteers and coordinate activities," she said, her eyes searching Nadira's face. "Will you do it?"

The thought of taking on an unfamiliar role and the potential for failure, brought with it a grab of panic, like falling off a cliff in a dream and scrabbling to catch hold of the rock edge but finding nothing but air.

"Can you tell me how many hours a week it might be?" she asked, her mind first turning to everything she had to do for work and the boys.

Sharnaz shrugged. "I have no idea, let's just say all the hours you can spare."

Yes or no, what would it be? Doing something demonstrable against the extremists was still important to her. Hadn't she wished to do more than taking pen to paper as her father had? But she hadn't counted on a role that made her feel so intimidated and vulnerable. She dreaded disappointing Sharnaz and losing stature in her eyes, and there was something else. Just beginning to find her feet, and no longer suspended in a state of uncertainty about her ability to handle her responsibilities, she didn't want to surrender to anxiety. It would feel too much like a return to the days she'd been unable to get out of bed. Still, she couldn't get rid of her uneasiness. There was a ready supply of excuses she could use: her new job, and single parenthood, both understandable impediments. But it occurred to her that Allah had sent the answer to her earlier question of what could be done and left the choice of accepting it or not up to her.

"When do you want me to start?" she asked.

Chapter 20

Later, Nadira remembered her first foray into social activism as a period of discovery. She had felt like a child again, the world full of new experiences and revelations, her brain waking from the long sleep of established routines and opinions. Teaching started the process, she thought, but as she worked with Sharnaz and the other enlistees, her mind began to unfurl, opening up in the presence of individuals who, while working toward a common goal, differed in various ways. She discovered, for countless years, she'd been living among people characterized by a commonality of viewpoints on everything of importance. And although this might have made her interactions easier and more comfortable, she found it also left her with untested beliefs and narrowed her understanding of the real world.

In the beginning, Nadira and Sharnaz met several times, spending hours strategizing, developing a timeline for the various tasks and dividing up responsibilities. Nadira, reluctant to refuse any assignment given to her, was relieved when her friend took on the most difficult tasks and left the more manageable ones for her. Once they had developed a plan, they began working with their group of volunteers. She was able to relearn the complications of working as a member of a team and the satisfaction she derived from being involved in the preparations surprised her.

She met a number of interesting women, some from prominent families - the wife of a high court judge and the daughter of an industrialist, as well as women who had been directly impacted by extremism and still others responding to deeply held principles. Her fellow volunteers were smart, funny and creative. While serious about the work they were doing, they still found time to talk about the world at large, and to share personal stories and jokes, filling the room with conversation and laughter. Before, if she'd met any of her new acquaintances at a party or seen them on the street, she might have judged them in a different way. Her preconceived notions and expectations of people were being turned on end. She felt as if she'd been taken apart and put back together, resulting in a version of herself who could look people in the eye without embarrassment. And these vibrant women inspired her to take more risks, even if it might mean sacrifices on her part.

At first, she worried her role in such a high profile activity might threaten her employment. She could have chosen to keep quiet and hope word of her involvement didn't reach the school, but even in a city the size of Lahore, it was hard to keep a secret. It was better to inform the headmistress, she thought, rather than have her find out and think she was doing it behind her back. Whatever happened, she would deal with it.

Fortunately, the headmistress did not object to Nadira's participation but cautioned her not to involve the school, its staff or students in anyway. Then she surprised Nadira by asking her for information on the event. It was obvious she knew less about her boss than she thought she had. But she supposed everyone was an expert at concealment when they wanted or needed to be.

One day after a couple of hours spent working with Sharnaz, Nadira was finishing up early intending to spend some time with her sons. Since her involvement began, she'd made it a point to set aside at least an hour or two every day for them. As she picked up her notes and was on her way out, Sharnaz put her hand on her arm.

"One more thing, Nadira," Sharnaz said, bending over to pick up a sheet of paper that had fallen from Nadira's hand. "I think you should be one of the speakers."

"Me? I haven't spoken in front of a group since college."

"It's a skill you don't lose," Sharnaz said, smiling as she gave the page back to Nadira. "Besides, you're passionate about the subject, and the crowd will pick up on that," she gave her a pat on the back. "I realize this is a little sudden; just think about it."

A couple of weeks later, Nadira lay in bed staring at the ceiling. She thought she'd left sleepless nights behind her, but it seemed an unresolved question had the same effect as a crying infant. Whenever she had to make an important decision, it heightened her loneliness, and she missed Sohail even more. In the past, she would have gone to him for his advice, setting forth her pros and cons while he listened and waited until she fell silent to give his opinion or suggestions. Being the sole decision maker was not easy, and she wondered what Sohail would have said. Would he have supported her involvement in the protest? She used to be able to anticipate whether he would agree or disagree with what she wanted to do. But after months of unshared experiences and inhabiting a new set of circumstances, she could no longer predict what stance he would have taken, and it saddened her.

As time passed, she was losing bits and pieces of him. The sound of his voice was starting to fade, and she had somehow lost his laugh; no matter how hard she tried, she couldn't hear it anymore. And these were only the superficial aspects of him. How was it possible for her to know what his opinion would be? One thing was certain; he would want only the best for all of them, and now it was up to her to determine how to ensure a better life for their sons.

She plumped her pillow and rolled over on her side, her legs aching as if she were still having growing pains. She sighed, abandoned her efforts to sleep and gave in to her thoughts. What would she say if she decided to speak? Unbidden, sentences came to her. Maybe they had been developing for a while, waiting for the right moment to surface. But, she was surprised at how fully formed they were and afraid they would disappear if she didn't write them down. Turning on the light next to her bed, she found a notepad and pen in the drawer of her nightstand and began writing. At one point, she got up and pulled a biography of Jinnah out of her bookcase and consulted several pages. When she finished, early morning light was starting to outline her window shade. Rereading what she'd written, she was pleased. She'd call Sharnaz today and tell her to put her on the list of speakers. The thought of standing up before a crowd still made her nauseous, and it might help if she spoke first. She'd ask Sharnaz if that would be possible.

Since she'd started working with her friend, her family assumed her absences and long hours had to do with her job, and she didn't disabuse them of this notion. A convenient lie of omission, she knew, but she let it go anyway. It wasn't like her, she conceded, to keep something so important from her parents, but they had been so overprotective these last months, she didn't want to risk having to deal with their disapproval. If they opposed her involvement, she was aware of the difficulties that could ensue. Her father would turn her decision into the subject of debate, entangling her in elaborate arguments until she forgot the original reason for her position. Her mother was sure to withhold her approval, delivering her negative opinion with an absolute minimum of words, her frugality with language buttressed by what she and her brothers had designated "the stare." As far back as Nadira could remember, her mother could summon in her children the fear of dire consequences with just a facial expression. Her lips would compress into a thin line as her eyebrows rose to their maximum height, enlarging her eyes into owl-like, unblinking flint orbs. She could maintain this look in total silence for a long time; her younger brother timed it once at precisely one minute, eleven seconds; after all these years, it was still a frightening prospect.

The day before the e-mails were to be sent and the flyers mailed, she resolved to tell her parents what she'd been doing - before they heard about it from someone else. It would be a relief to abandon her secrecy. Since agreeing to work on the demonstration, she'd felt like a naughty child waiting to get caught. She decided to follow her father's pattern and inform the family at dinner, hoping her sons' presence would temper her mother's comments; Nadira was quite sure she would be very unhappy.

She waited until after her father and the boys had talked about their day and her mother had discussed an upcoming birthday party for her cousin. Finally, without preamble, she told them there was to be a demonstration and watched their faces as she explained what had been keeping her so busy for the past months. As she spoke, she felt the tension leave her body; she'd hated her deception. But, there was nothing in their solemn expressions to suggest encouragement, and her muscles began to stiffen again.

When she finished her monologue, her father wasted no time speaking up. He wanted to know if she was limiting her involvement to helping with logistics or was planning on attending. She told him she was going to attend. This incomplete answer, when she knew her father expected a full report, made her squirm inside, and she hoped her guilty conscience didn't show on her face.

"Do you think that's wise?" he said as he ran two fingers under the top button of his collar, a sure sign he was perturbed. "Even with the best planning, protests can get out of control, and you could find yourself in a dangerous situation."

Nadira remembered the information sheet Sharnaz had prepared for the demonstrators. The sheet listed rules for participants including not engaging in shouting matches with the police, military or any agitators in the crowd. It also suggested that participants park their cars a reasonable distance away from the site and walk in since Pakistani intelligence often took down license plate numbers to gather lists of the attendees. But she doubted the authorities would bother with a small women's demonstration. How many people attended these rallies anyway, her guess was a few hundred at the most. To the organizers, more than numbers, it was the media coverage of the event that would be important. And, as she was now too well aware, no place was totally safe anymore, so being in a crowd of women in public, surrounded by police and security didn't feel like taking an unreasonable risk.

"Driving is dangerous; should I give up my car?" she asked her father, leaning forward.

"That's quite different. Driving is essential for everyday life while attending demonstrations is not."

Nadira wanted to bring her father around to her way of thinking; his approval was still very important to her. She argued necessity was different depending on your perspective, and ensuring the safety of their daily life qualified as essential in her mind.

"Use your writing skills," her father told her, claiming

she could reach more people through the pages of a newspaper than from taking to the streets on one occasion. When she disagreed, he asked her to think of what was best for her sons.

"What if something should happen to you?" he said, looking over at the boys.

Why would he say something like that with the boys present? She half rose out of her chair, a feeling of heat flooding her cheeks.

"I am very familiar with the arrangements; steps have been taken to ensure everyone's safety," Nadira said, finding it difficult to keep the tone and volume of her voice at a respectful level. "And, I *am* thinking about what's best for my sons."

Their discussion had turned into an argument, and Nadira couldn't remember another time when she and her father had been on opposite sides of an issue. Their uncommon, open dispute disturbed her. She realized she was too old to be a child in her parents' house. Listening to her father, she was disappointed. He was no longer a man who remembered what it was like to be young, and for the first time, she could picture him white haired and arthritic, struggling with the changes delivered by each passing year. She wished she'd had the gift of foreknowledge at a young age to better appreciate the pleasures of their early relationship, one she had so often taken for granted. An unexpected longing captured her, and she wished for the old security of her father's lap. She was overcome with a yearning to sit there, as she once had, her back against his chest and her head on his shoulder. She felt tears start in her eyes.

Her father sat in silence for a moment, his gaze focused on his clasped hands. Then he raised his head and pinned her with a serious look.

"Nadira, trust me when I say you shouldn't do this," he said, in a quiet, deliberate voice.

His position shocked her. She had expected opposition from her mother but not from him. In particular, she remembered something from their time at Stanford.

One day, her father had taken the extraordinary step of keeping her and her brothers out of school so they could go with him to an activity on campus. Her mother hadn't approved and argued with him, but her father had been adamant and taken them anyway. As they walked toward the campus, her father told them they should pay very close attention so they would always remember what they were about to see.

At the Main Quad, there was a carnival atmosphere. Students waved colorful placards with sentiments like "Divest Now," and "Mandela Yes, Apartheid No." She remembered the excitement that jumped from one person to the next like a spark in a pile of tinder.

There was a platform set up at one end of the lawn, and two men and a woman sat facing the crowd. First, singers with guitars took center stage and soon had everyone clapping and singing along. Then the three speakers courted the crowd with moving and powerful words. Every speech brought cheers from the gathering. Afterward, the chanting mass of people marched toward the Administration Building.

As she watched them leave, Nadira had asked her father, "What is this?"

And she remembered him turning to her, his eyes gleaming, his mouth curved into a wide grin. "This is democracy," he had replied.

"Remember the student demonstration you took us to at Stanford?" she asked.

Her father's shoulders sagged and he put his head in his hands, and she knew she'd defeated him.

"Sabotaged by my youthful idealism," he said.

"What are you talking about, Nadeem?" her mother asked, looking first at her father and then at her.

He lifted his head. "Sometimes your children learn the lessons you teach too well."

"Stop talking in riddles," her mother said.

"I haven't dissuaded Nadira; she's going to this demonstration."

"Is that true, beti?"

"Yes," Nadira answered as she looked straight at her mother and waited for her objections.

"That's good because I'd hate to attend by myself," her mother said with a smile.

Nadira had never seen her father at a loss for words until that moment. He was struck dumb by her mother's response, and Nadira was astounded. A person couldn't change in an instant; she knew that. What had she missed all these years? Maybe her mother had always been awake to other possibilities, and a daughter's ingrained perceptions had kept her ignorant of her mother's true character.

At last her father collected himself. "Have you taken leave of your senses?"

"No, I think I've just come to my senses. It's not only your children you've taught too well. I think Saabira would also be interested in going, and maybe I can convince the rest of the aunts and some of my friends to go."

Emotions flooded Nadira - amazement, pride and love, and she couldn't find the words to express how happy she was to have her mother as her ally. She'd just received an amazing gift she hadn't known she wanted, and her joy caused her eyes to well up and a smile to spread across her face. She got up and hugged her.

Arif grinned and said, "I'll have to buy both of you a cape to go along with your Superwoman status." But Samir, ever her anxious child, sat with a frown on his face, his arms crossed over his chest, and his shoulders slumped as if he was bearing an invisible weight.

Nadira laughed at Arif and reached over to caress Samir's exposed neck, deciding to have a private chat with him later. She would try to explain to him why it was important not to let the extremists of this world or their own fears imprison them.

Arif, who had lately become less of a tease and more protective of his younger brother, also appeared to notice his distress. He turned to his nana and suggested the three of them go to the club on the day of the demonstration. They could go swimming and afterward, enjoy the barbeque lunch buffet. He put his arm around his brother's shoulder and said, "What do you say, Samir, you ready for a fun day?"

The remainder of the meal was taken up with a discussion of their plans for a "men's" day out. She was ecstatic to witness Arif's growing maturity and his concern for his younger brother. And she was delighted that despite her fears, her confession had ended well and brought with it some happy surprises.

Chapter 21

Salima looked forward to the hours between midnight and dawn, no longer wholly relinquished to the sweet oblivion of sleep, but often spent in solitary contemplation. She would reach into the furthest recesses of her mind and draw out her happiest memories; just like her favorite books, she never tired of revisiting them. Sometimes there were events of the day to mull over along with the thoughts and feelings they elicited.

In her mind, she perused a conversation she'd had with Hameeda that afternoon. She'd been gratified and touched when her daughter-in-law had come to her for advice as if she'd known her since birth and would intuitively have the right answer for her.

Hameeda was trying to decide whether or not to attend an anti-terrorism demonstration the following week and wanted to know if Salima thought it was wise to go.

Once, she would have said it was inappropriate for women to be out at such an event unaccompanied by their husbands, brothers or sons. For many years, she had equated the greater physical strength of men with bravery and looked to them for protection. But experience had taught her the foolishness of her belief. Had her father ever protected her from hardship and abuse? No, he had barely acknowledged her existence. When her mother-in-law was beating her and she turned to Daud for help, he had been afraid to stand up for her. Only when his malevolent mother was going to throw her out, did he refuse to allow it. Was it a brave act or had he been thinking more of his own loss than her plight, for she had no doubt he loved her. Still, she had forgiven him long ago. She knew people were often unaware of fault lines deep within themselves, weaknesses developed in childhood they found difficult or even impossible to overcome.

She had to admit she held strong opinions on most subjects, and the demonstration was no different. Yes, it was important to urge the government to take action against the evils in their society, especially killers masquerading as holy men. She was particularly incensed about the attacks on girls' schools, for they not only killed innocent children but were an attempt to prevent girls from getting an education. She remembered all too well the day when her father made her leave school at the age of fourteen, a tragedy for her, and much too young to give up the world of learning for mindless drudgery. Her lack of education had plagued her for the rest of her life and was one of her greatest regrets.

She was proud of these women who were willing to fight for themselves and their families, and if her legs functioned, she would join them. But she didn't tell her daughter-in-law what she thought; it would have been a disservice. She knew following someone else's advice, even if it took an act of daring, was not the same as making your own determination, since both the credit if you were correct and the blame if you were wrong would never belong solely to you. It was her decision and hers alone to make, she'd told Hameeda. Soon she would be gone, and her daughter-in-law had to learn to find her own way in the world.

She took a moment to say an extra prayer for her closest friend, who had died without warning in her sleep just two days ago. Salima's son, trying to console her, said it was a good way to leave this earth. But was it? Would she want death to take her unawares, or desire the time to say her goodbyes and impart last words? She puzzled over this question for a few minutes. She realized, for a while now, she'd been treating each day as her last, weighing with care what she said and did in light of Allah's judgment and, as far as her undemonstrative nature would allow, leaving nothing unsaid. She questioned whether or not anyone would even remember and value her words. Wisdom was often ignored or went unrecognized until individuals, either through maturity or experience, were wise themselves. You did what you could, she thought, and left the rest to Allah.

When she was younger, even during the most difficult times when life had lost its appeal, she had held on tightly to it, but now she could feel herself loosening her grip on her familiar existence in preparation for the new beginning to come.

* * *

While Zubair slept, Hameeda lay awake, kept company by her dilemma. How could he sleep so well every night and go about his days as if nothing had changed? Didn't he notice the downward slide they were on? Maybe he'd been inoculated against excessive worry and emotional upset from his days at the hospital. There, grievous injury and death had always been present, current events only changing the genesis and nature of his patients' wounds. An instant later, she felt terrible for having assumed Zubair was not just as affected. Men were more stoic then women. But even he had recognized an alteration in their children's personalities. How could he not? Not so long ago, the three of them had been heedless, barreling through life with a youthful belief in their immortality. Now, they seemed stiffer, more hesitant, as if waiting for the next blow to fall. These dangerous times, she feared, were robbing them of their childhood.

Earlier in the evening, Nadira had tried to persuade her to join a protest against the very people who were at the heart of one of their biggest problems. Listening to her friend talk about it, she could picture herself among a multitude of women standing shoulder to shoulder, insisting on being heard. Being moved by Nadira was an old familiar feeling. Since childhood, her friend's certainty had bolstered her courage and made her feel protected, and now, again, when she was in her company, there was no debate in her mind. But once alone, she suffered shivers of apprehension and couldn't picture herself anywhere but comfortably at home. Could she push away the terror that surfaced more and more often, sometimes paralyzing her?

There were days when she couldn't suppress the images of the victims in the hospital and the details of Sohail's kidnapping and murder. The burqa that had once made her so brave was now nothing more than flimsy material, and there were times when stepping outside made her breath come in short gasps as if she was asthmatic like Rabia. More and more often, she found herself sending the servant to do the shopping and avoiding all but the most necessary tasks outside the house. Images of the Ashura riot, undimmed by time, haunted her. How could she go to a demonstration, a certain magnet for conflict? Even if she went, what difference would it make? For once she felt Nadira was the naïve one. Life in Pakistan would go on in some fashion. They might be more restricted in their activities, but was that so important? Adjustments could be made.

She felt an overwhelming confusion about how they'd ended up in this situation. She tried to remember her vision of her destiny when she was young and recalled an afternoon when she was about nine years old. It had been an oppressive, hot summer day until an unexpected downpour released the heat, sending it upward in steamy columns. Her mother had gone outside to take in the laundry, the storm having left it soaked and trailing on the ground. As her mother crossed the yard, she'd left deep impressions in the saturated soil, and Hameeda had followed close behind, lengthening her stride to place her feet precisely in her mother's imprints. Remembering that, it seemed to her, she'd always wanted to duplicate her mother's life, an existence filled with family concerns, housed in a non-threatening environment. Instead, she lived in a hostile world, making one accommodation after another, her life once open and expansive, closing in on her. How had the parallel roads of expectation and reality diverged so radically in such a short period of time? Maybe, Nadira was right about taking action. Hameeda felt torn and still wasn't sure what she should and could do.

Earlier in the day, she had asked her mother-in-law for advice, but she'd had none to offer. What was she to do now? She was coming to realize that in the past, afraid of finding her own way in the world, she'd relinquished decisions on important matters to others, her parents, Nadira, her husband. Once she'd believed life would be easier and her happiness assured if she placed the needs and desires of those she cared for the most before her own. But by letting the opinions of others inform her decisions, her inner voice had grown softer and softer until it was a whisper. Who else could she turn to for help? She could feel her muscles knotting up and heard a thrumming in her ears, the same reaction she used to have when she was given a surprise quiz in school and felt unprepared.

And then something occurred to her, and she was amazed she hadn't thought of it before. There was one person she could go to for guidance in making her decision. Very soon, insha Allah, she believed, she would have her answer.

Chapter 22

The demonstration was set for 10:00 a. m., before the heat of the day became unbearable. Nadira planned to leave early to allow plenty of time for traffic jams, a possible long walk from their parking space, or any other unforeseeable event that might make her late. As she prepared to leave, she kept listening for the ring of her phone. She'd made one effort to convince Hameeda to attend and then left her to decide. Not having heard back, she had no idea whether or not her friend was coming, but she tried to remain optimistic.

When she'd set the time for their departure, she'd planned for the Pakistani habit of tardiness but entering the lounge she found her mother and the aunts ready and waiting for her. Saabira carried a furled umbrella, and Afrah held an old cardboard hand fan emblazoned with a Fanta advertisement. Judging from the size of her mother's purse, she too was well prepared for contingencies. With her father and the boys already out of the house, Nadira decided it was time to tell them about her speech. Remembering how her mother had surprised her with her decision to go to the demonstration, she had no idea what to expect and felt calmer than she otherwise might have.

Shifting from one foot to the other, she coughed and started in. "Before we leave, I have something to tell you," she said. "I…I'm one of today's speakers." She saw a hurt expression cross her mother's face and felt bad about having kept it from her.

"One of the speakers? Why didn't you tell us before?" her mother asked.

"I don't know," she said shrugging her shoulders. "There never seemed to be a good time." She had assumed that no matter what time she'd chosen, her parents would have been upset.

Her mother sighed and shook her head. "I suppose you were afraid we would try to talk you out of it."

"The possibility had occurred to me." Living with her decision to speak had not made her any more comfortable with it, she thought, and the smallest opposition might have persuaded her to withdraw. Perhaps that's why she waited to announce it when it was too late to back out.

"Well no matter, at least you told us before we found you on the speakers' platform," Saabira said, repositioning her dupatta and settling the strap of her purse on her shoulder. "Now we've been informed, all the more reason to be on our way." She flapped her hands at them as if they were a flock of chickens. "Let's go, let's go," she said shooing them toward the door.

Nadira remembered all the times her aunt had found a way to act as an intermediary between her and her parents and realized this was another instance of her trying to make a situation easier for her. As they walked out the door, she took her aunt's hand and gave it a squeeze and wasn't surprised when she winked at her like a co-conspirator.

Nadira's appetite had deserted her at breakfast and now she could hear her stomach rumbling in protest as she maneuvered the car through the usual heavy traffic. Her hands left a film of sweat where she gripped the steering wheel, and one at a time she wiped them on the side of the seat. Eyes on the road, she didn't try to join in the conversation.

Her mother and aunts were talking about their youth, remembering what it was like "before all this." Saabira Auntie reminded Afrah of a neighbor boy she'd had a crush on when they were teenagers.

"Remember how you spied on him all the time, peeking through the hole in the corner of the boundary wall?"

Afrah protested saying her sister must be thinking of someone else. Nadira's mother laughed and in a low voice began to sing a classic ghazal, a song of unrequited love with words by the poet, Ghalib. "It was not in my destiny to unite with my beloved," she sang. First Saabira joined in and then Afrah turned the duet into a trio, their voices somehow managing to navigate the swoops and trills of the vibrato. As a child, her parents had sometimes dragged her to concerts given by aging ghazal singers, their voices amazingly athletic despite bodies marked by the blight of elderliness, still able to soar over the tabla and harmonium accompaniment. Despite her early exposure, she didn't have a nostalgic attachment to these songs because, she

469

thought, they held no associations for her.

It seemed to her that memories and emotions were often tied to the music of your generation. Nadira had always considered ghazals old fashioned, the singers and tunes belonging to her grandparents and parents time. She and her friends had been caught in a wave of music from the West which had fit what they thought of as their more modern sensibilities. Still, the song's lyrics captured her and for a moment pushed aside her apprehensions. Somehow it was appropriate to be thinking of love at this moment, she thought, an emotion at the heart of everything most important to her and the impetus for her presence at this event.

When her mother and aunts finished the song, they giggled, sounding to Nadira like the giddy school girls they once had been. As they continued to reminisce, Nadira's thoughts turned once again to the demonstration. Her speech played over and over in her mind, practiced so often, she didn't lose one word. Still, it had been many years since she had spoken in public, and her one great fear was that stage fright might erase her lines. For the third time, she glanced at the outside pocket of her purse to check for the written copy – still there.

Participants were meeting at Faisal Square across from the Punjab Assembly Building, and she was relieved to find a parking space on a side street off Mall Road, a short walk away. It appeared they weren't the only ones arriving early. Other women, alone, in pairs and groups, were walking down the road in the same direction. As they neared

Faisal Square, she saw a familiar looking elderly woman proceeding at a slow pace with the aid of a walker.

"Amma, isn't that a friend of Nani's?" Nadira asked.

Her mother stared for a moment. "I can't believe it; it's Mrs. Ahmad."

"Really?" Afrah said, turning her head to take a look. "I thought she died long ago."

"She's either a shockingly energetic corpse or very much alive," Saabira said with a laugh.

The three of them walked over to say hello.

"How nice to see all of you after so many years," the old woman said, embracing each of them in turn. "Isn't this a wonderful turnout?" She smiled at her mother and then turned toward Nadira. "I expect your nani's spirit is hovering around here somewhere as well. This is just her kind of thing."

Her mother laughed. "Auntie, I believe you're right."

The Square already held more women than Nadira had expected, and it was still early. Armed police stood on the periphery of the crowd, although Nadira viewed them with a cynical eye, not sure how useful they would be if trouble arose. There were also suited men, scanning the area, mobile phones glued to their ears, fooling nobody, their affiliation with Pakistan's intelligence service clear to anyone with a good pair of eyes. She saw the raised speakers' platform in front with its row of chairs, a podium and a stand microphone attached by a long cord to a generator on the ground. Sharnaz was standing to one side talking to a man holding a walky-talky, most likely one of the private security guards they'd hired.

She watched her mother survey their surroundings before leading them to a spot close to the front on the far left of the crowd where they had a diagonal view of the podium.

"This is a good place; we'll be close enough so we can see without craning our necks and off to one side so we won't be hemmed in by other people," her mother said. "We'll stay right here, Nadira, so when you're speaking you can look out and find us." Her mother took her hand in both of hers. "I know your speech will be inspiring, insha Allah."

Nadira was starting to feel jumpy, and she imagined herself as a race horse in the starting gate, nervous but anxious to get going because, she thought, it was the waiting that gave her time to doubt she would succeed. "I'll be happy if I don't embarrass myself."

"You'll be fine," her mother said.

Once she reached the platform, Sharnaz introduced her to the other speakers and then was off to take care of some last minute detail. These women were strangers to Nadira, but not unknown; one woman was a local television personality, and she recognized the name of the main speaker as the well-known journalist, Safia Ashraf. Sharnaz had used her contacts well.

If she could have, Nadira would have withdrawn inside herself until she had to speak but, as always, people seemed uncomfortable with silence. She was seated between Safia and another woman who told her about her husband and three sons who had been killed in one of the mosque bombings, making her problems seem insignificant. Thinking of her own experience, she couldn't imagine surviving such a devastating, and to her mind, unmanageable loss. A desolate feeling overtook her, and eager for any distraction, she was happy when, from her other side, Safia turned to her.

The journalist asked her how she knew Sharnaz. Nadira explained how they'd met and then asked the same question of her.

"I'm a distant cousin," Safia said as she pulled her dupatta further forward on her head. "As a child, I stayed with Sharnaz and her family for a short time before we left for London."

"You lived in London? How long?"

"Fourteen years. I came back after college; the rest of my family is still there."

"Didn't you like London?" Nadira asked, even more curious.

"No matter how long I lived there, I could never stop being a foreigner, a Paki," Safia said, her nose wrinkling as if she'd smelled something bad. "It was my father's choice to leave Pakistan, and mine to return."

She remembered her own very different experience in California. Was it the time period and being in a college environment that had saved her from encountering a similar attitude in the United States?

"If you don't mind me asking, why did your father leave?"

Safia sighed. "Do you know about the Pakistani military's 1971 massacre of students and professors at Dhaka University?" The corners of her mouth turned down and her voice flattened. "It happened on the first day of the war between West and East Pakistan and was part of the army's Operation Searchlight, designed to hunt down and kill Hindus, journalists, academics, engineers and other professionals," she said, hugging her chest with her arms.

Nadira thought of the soldier's letter she'd found in her dada's desk, still in her possession, and remembered his account of the horrific events. And to think this was part of a wider plan; the barbarity of it was incomprehensible, and a shiver ran through her.

"Yes, I know about it."

The journalist looked surprised and told her very few people could say the same because Pakistan, like other countries, did not trumpet its shame but buried it as deeply as possible. She went on to explain that her father had been at the University, for reasons never made clear to her, and witnessed the slaughter before escaping. He'd left the country not long afterward and sent for their family a year later. He'd died when she was in college, and she'd found a graphic description of the event among his papers.

An incredulous thought struck Nadira. Could Safia's father be the same soldier who wrote the letter? His correspondence had revealed his wife's name, Gita; she only had to ask. She briefly considered it before rejecting the idea. It was not her place to reveal information Safia's father, if in fact he and the soldier were one in the same, had preferred to keep to himself. But she chose to imagine he was her father, surviving to return to his family and find some happiness in life.

She wondered if the information about this war-time event had influenced the other woman's career choice and asked her if she'd decided to become a reporter to find and disclose these sorts of truth.

Safia gave her a wry smile. "I decided to become a journalist because I thought reporting the truth would help people make better choices. But I was young and idealistic and now I am sometimes discouraged at how little impact my stories often have." Safia shifted in her chair and stared off in the distance for a moment before continuing. I am very serious about my responsibility to obtain complete, truthful and unbiased information from all possible sources. Yet, even after doing all that, my audience can still twist the facts, ignore them or search out biased articles to fit their perspective." She looked weary and shook her head, sighing.

"I see your point," Nadira said, nodding her head. She was about to ask another question when a woman Safia knew came up to talk to her.

Nadira turned back toward the crowd and became aware of the news cameras trained on the speakers' platform, making her very self-conscious. She realized her words might be included in the report of the day's events and began to regret her decision to speak. Would her sentiments touch a chord with others? What could she contribute to this august group? She began to think she should have stayed behind the scenes as an organizer.

She licked her dry lips and clenched the pieces of paper containing the speech she'd composed in such a rush. She looked out at a crowd that had grown until a solid, unyielding mass filled the Square. This was not the few hundred women she'd anticipated but a few thousand. She searched for the spot where her mother and aunts were standing, but they'd been swallowed up by new arrivals. She couldn't help but be astounded by the women in the crowd - college students, middle aged women and grand-mothers. Like a hive of bees, the air buzzed with their talk. She scanned the crowd a second time searching for anyone she knew and found her nani's friend, old Mrs. Ahmad, leaning on her walker and talking with the woman next to her. It had to be difficult for a woman Mrs. Ahmad's age to come and stand for such a long time in the heat, yet she was here. Nadira thought about what she had said about her nani's spirit being present and could almost feel her nani's hand on her head, reciting a blessing. This mental image created a feeling of protection, and she began to relax a little.

A few minutes later, Sharnaz left her seat and went to the podium. The crowd quieted as her friend began to speak. The words that came to Nadira were indistinct, as if she had cotton in her ears until the announcement of her name caught her attention and she saw Sharnaz motion to her. She walked up to the microphone in a daze. Feeling like something was caught in her throat and clearing it, she heard the sound amplified all over the Square. Not a good way to start. The hand holding her notes began to tremble. But then, she saw an arm rise up from the crowd and move from side to side. Even shrouded in her burqa, she was sure it was Hameeda, and Nadira was so grateful she had made it. Happiness bubbled up inside her, and she felt her stomach settle and her trembling cease as she stared right at her friend and began. After the first few sentences, she was able to steady her voice. Nearing the end of her speech, Nadira paused for an instant making sure she had the crowd's attention and then raised her voice a notch as she continued.

"I was asked to speak to you today as a victim of terrorism. But my personal narrative is only one among many. Everyone here and every person in Pakistan are victims of terrorism. It restricts our movements and preys on our emotional well-being on a daily basis. Yet, we allow a miniscule minority of our fellow citizens to steal our country from us, and let their acts distort the worlds' view of Islam, our country and each one of us, no matter how innocent we may be.

Those of us in attendance today are not here because we are fearless. We are here despite our fears. We are here not only to condemn past acts of terrorism but to protect our future and the future of our children and succeeding generations.

Mohammed Ali Jinnah, father of our nation, said in a policy speech given in August of 1947:

'If you change your past and work together in a spirit that every one of you, no matter to what community he

belongs, no matter what relations he had with you in the past, no matter what is his color, caste or creed, is first, second and last a citizen of this State with equal rights, privileges, and obligations, there will be no end to the progress you will make.'

Let us heed Jinnah's words and the principle of tolerance our religion teaches us. All of us who oppose the criminals who defame Islam and the precepts Pakistan was founded on, must break our silence and continue to raise our voices in protest. We must say by our words and our actions, we will not tolerate extremism and the violence that accompanies it. Pledge with me today to take up the task of fighting extremism, and rebuilding Jinnah's vision of Pakistan."

There was a burst of applause and then from somewhere in the crowd a shout rang out. "Pakistan zindabad; long live Pakistan." More and more women took up the cry while pumping their fists up into the air until the whole crowd was chanting. The roar of their shouting sent vibrations through Nadira's body, as if she were the sounding board on a string instrument. Then Sharnaz touched her elbow, and she somehow found her way back to her seat. The rest of the demonstration went by in a blur. It was as if her speech had primed an engine. The words of each of the following speakers were met with thunderous cheers and chanting.

When it was over, the crowd broke up so slowly that Nadira thought the women were trying to savor the moment as long as possible. Offering up congratulations, women encircled Nadira and the other speakers, capturing them in front of the platform, and when at last the crowd thinned out, she looked for Hameeda but didn't see her. She was disappointed to think she might have already gone.

Sharnaz was still talking to someone when Nadira left to find her mother and aunts. She caught sight of them at the edge of the square, their heads turning in one direction and then another as they scanned the departing women. And Hameeda was with them! Her mother caught sight of her first and hurried toward her, with Hameeda and her aunts close behind.

"Nadira, your speech was incredible," her mother exclaimed as her arms engulfed her.

"You've made us all very proud," Saabira said, giving her a hug.

"Yes, you certainly have," Afrah echoed, a wide smile spreading across her face.

"I wouldn't have missed this day for anything in the world," her mother said. "I wish your father could have been here. I can't believe how brave you were to speak in public before so many people."

Nadira smiled as Hameeda slipped in next to her. Above her niqab, she saw the corner of her eyes crinkle with happiness.

"Nani also deserves some credit for teaching us how to be strong and to stand up for ourselves," Nadira said. "If she were alive, she would praise all of us." She looked up and sent her thoughts skyward, imagining them penetrating the heavenly plane where, she had no doubt, her nani now resided. *See, I haven't forgotten.*

Nadira felt the rush of energy fueled by the event disappear, leaving her exhausted. As she linked arms with Hameeda, she stopped and looked back. Behind her, the square was empty, only the speakers' platform gave evidence that something out of the ordinary had occurred. Ahead of her, women pulled vehicles out of side streets and so fast, they disappeared into Lahore's busy traffic. Nadira recalled how enormous the crowd had appeared when she looked out from her place on the platform. But the actual number had been small when compared to all those who had not heard their message. How many people would be influenced by the women here today? She hoped it would be more than she could imagine.

As they walked, Nadira asked Hameeda what had decided her to come.

Hameeda told her she'd gone to the hadith and found the answer in the words of the Prophet Muhammad, peace be upon him. "Whosoever of you sees an evil action, he must change it with his hand. If he is not able to do so, then he must change it with his tongue," she recited.

Nadira thought, how like her old friend. It was not someplace she would have looked for a solution, but it didn't surprise her that Hameeda had sought help there; her reliance on their faith for guidance on life's questions was an integral part of who she was and what made her so special. Many people were scrupulous about adhering to the five pillars of Islam, but few lived every day in the spirit of the religion as Hameeda did.

"Remind me to use that passage if we ever organize an event like this again," Nadira said with a smile.

"I will," Hameeda said and gave Nadira's arm a squeeze.

A few minutes later, their small group stood by the car still talking about what had just transpired. Nadira felt reluctant to leave, as if the events of the morning would cease to exist once she left. Feeling a tap on her shoulder, she turned to see Sharnaz.

"I thought you would never manage to get away," Nadira said with a laugh.

"I was saved by a phone call; otherwise, I would still be standing where you left me," Sharnaz said, shaking her head.

As she looked at her friend, it occurred to Nadira that Sharnaz had changed very little in all the years she'd known her, still unafraid to engage in a fight if she thought it was for something vital. They needed more people like her. That was the way forward. She reached over and patted her on the back.

Her mother smiled and put her arm around Sharnaz. "Congratulations on a successful demonstration," she said.

"Whether or not we have been successful will be measured by the changes produced by our actions," Sharnaz replied. A voice called out a farewell; she waved her hand as she continued speaking. "But hopefully, this demonstration will make some people pay attention."

Nadira knew Sharnaz was right. If they wanted change,

they could only view this day as the first small step in a long journey.

Before Sharnaz left, her mother asked if she could get a picture of the three of them. Nadira slipped in between Sharnaz and Hameeda, and together they looked at the camera. As her mother focused the lens, a sudden breeze bathed Nadira's face and again she felt her nani's presence, bringing with it the certainty she, not fate, would control her destiny. Glancing over at Hameeda, she thought about the separate paths that had brought them together again to share in this day and interlaced her fingers with those of her friend.

"Nadira, face forward," her mother said.

Months later when Nadira looked at the photo; three very different women with the same goal stared back at her; women, she thought, who held the future in their hands.

EPILOGUE

A groaning sound came from somewhere close by and imagining her mother-in-law in pain, Hameeda jumped to her feet to go to her. In mid-step she halted, what was she thinking? It couldn't be, and she listened again with more concentration, identifying the noise as the vibrations made by water rushing through the ancient, narrowed pipes; the maid must have turned on a tap.

Once the vision of her mother-in-law had entered her head, she was foolish enough to let it draw her through the connecting door into the old woman's room, forcing her to once again confront the stripped down mattress on its wooden bed frame and the bare tabletops. Sitting down in the high-backed chair near the window, she waited for her mother-in-law's spirit to visit her, just as it had only hours after she died six months ago. She had never told anyone about the visitation because it hadn't been something she could prove, more of a feeling, the air heavier, and charged with energy, like the instant before a bolt of lightning splits the sky during a thunderstorm. And then, with a clap, her mother-in-law's Qur'an, unaided, had fallen open on the bedside table, and she'd been certain the old woman's spirit was in the room with her. But today, she remained alone, the hot, dry August air unchanged, her surroundings devoid of sound and motion.

Being in the unoccupied room only emphasized her mother-in-law's absence, and Hameeda felt herself being pulled down by an undertow of melancholy. She wished Rabia had moved into the room as she'd suggested, but her younger daughter had said it felt wrong, and she wanted to think of it as her dadi's room a little while longer. Hameeda thought her daughter shared her feeling that her mother-in-law was not entirely gone. She tried to steady herself with a deep breath and the faint smell of the bath powder the old woman had favored filled her nostrils. Tears coursed down her cheeks. A few years ago, she never would have imagined how much she would miss her companionship.

In a few days, she would have to face another major change in her life, and despite previous experience, she knew it would be difficult. Two years ago, Daliya started college in Lahore, and arguing for some independence, secured their permission to live in the student hostel instead of commuting from home. Now Jameel, along with Nadira's son Arif, was leaving for college much too far away in Toronto. When she had talked to Nadira about trying to dissuade them from enrolling in a college overseas, she'd said, "It's time to let them go," as if they were rescued baby birds fallen from a nest and tended for a few weeks, not the sons they had carried in their wombs and nurtured for eighteen years. Her friend's words made it sound easy when she was sure it would be the hardest thing she had ever done.

Already this year she had used up so much of her fortitude, she wondered if there was any left to deal with Jameel's absence. Maybe Allah was being kind, teaching her in steps how to spend more and more time without her children, until one day it would only be her and Zubair sitting across from each other at the table. The thought brought on another round of tears.

She hoped her committee work would offer some distraction. So long ago now, soon after the anti-terrorism demonstration, Nadira had convinced her to work with her on programs furthering women's rights and universal education. She smiled thinking about the vicarious pleasure her mother-in-law had seemed to derive from her activities. Still, even after all this time, she wasn't that comfortable with her involvement and always insisted on taking on tasks that maintained her anonymity.

And maybe she wouldn't be separated from her son for long, because for the last four months Zubair had again started looking for a position with a Canadian hospital. She'd made sure he focused on hospitals in the Toronto area. The remembrance of her mother-in-law also lessened her anxiety over the possibility of starting over in a foreign country. She'd learned from her that life was full of surprises, both negative and positive, and you had to have faith in Allah's wisdom to ensure everything would come right in the end.

For a while now, the country of her childhood had been lost to her. Since the day she was born, the dictionary of life in Pakistan had been rewritten and was now overcrowded with words and phrases like suicide bomber, drone, terrorism, sectarian violence, load shedding, shortage, pollution, disaster, assassination, economic failure and tragedy. But despite this, Pakistan defined home for her in a way nowhere else could. Even if she had to leave and live elsewhere, she knew her family and this place would pull her back over and over again.

*   *   *

The late afternoon sun filled the west facing room with light, illuminating a floor littered with suitcases and a staircase of open bureau drawers. Against the wall, cupboard doors hung ajar, revealing an interior, nude except for the same sculpture of tangled wire hangers that had greeted them the day Nadira and the boys moved into the apartment. She picked up the last one of Arif's shirts from the bed and folded it into a neat rectangle before placing it in an already overstuffed suitcase. Watching her step, she crossed the room and examined the inside of each drawer before pushing it closed, its emptiness producing a deep, echoey tone. The sound replicated the hollow feeling she had whenever she contemplated her oldest son's departure for college. When Arif was applying to universities overseas, she tried not to let her worries influence the process. She knew leaving Pakistan might alleviate some dangers while introducing others. She wanted him to have a good experience, untainted by negative perceptions of Pakistanis, but she had her doubts. What if his not uncommon name was the same as someone on a security watch list and caused him visa difficulties? Would other passengers or airport personnel be rude or antagonistic either on the plane or when he arrived? How welcoming would the other students be? Was she sending him into a hostile environment where some angry, ignorant fool might harm him because he imagined her son was a terrorist? That list of possible negative scenarios was long enough, and then there were the normal concerns of any parent. Would her son be homesick or hate the food? Would he be compatible with his roommate? How would he manage his money, his laundry, the new freedom from parental supervision? And, how could she possibly live without him for months at a time? But, when he was accepted at the University of Toronto and she had remembered herself at that age, wanting to be on her own in someplace new, she couldn't disappoint him. By the grace of God, Hameeda's son Jameel would be attending the same college, and knowing they would have each other to rely on, she felt a huge sense of relief.

If only Sohail was here to see the man Arif was becoming. It was hard to believe four years had passed since her husband's death. So much had changed since then. Arif had become more serious about his studies and done well, as if trying to please a father who was no longer there. Of course, she hoped her belated return to college, first getting her masters and now working on her PhD while working as an assistant professor of mathematics, had also set an example for him.

She knew Arif's absence would also be a loss for her younger son. Remaining the brilliant student he'd always been, Samir had thrived under his older brother's new attentiveness, and they had become close. In two more years, he also planned on going abroad for college. He was determined to qualify for a scholarship to MIT in the United States. She didn't know if Sohail's death had cut the ties tethering both her sons to Pakistan, or if they, like the flood of young people before them, saw no future in their own country.

As she thought of Arif's imminent departure and how much she'd miss him, her eyes welled up. She let the tears spill down her cheeks unchecked, hoping to cry herself out before he left. The last thing she wanted was to break down at the airport and embarrass him in front of family and friends. And afterward, somehow she would manage.

Completing the arduous work necessary to earn her PhD should help to keep her mind off how much she missed him. Whenever she thought of the possibilities the degree would open up for her at colleges in Pakistan or overseas, she felt optimistic and less claustrophobic. But completing it would take what little free time she had. One thing was certain; she wouldn't let anything interfere with her weekly lunch with Hameeda, all the more important now that her friend might be leaving the country.

Talking about what the future might hold, they had assured each other they would not allow physical separation to loosen the bonds of their friendship. Nadira knew this was not an empty promise, for they had spent the last few years building a shelter in each other's hearts, sturdy enough to withstand the forces of distance, time and circumstance.

Once Samir left, she would have to make her own plans. In the process of helping Arif decide on a college, it became clear to her that one day she might also leave her birthplace. She was aware either going or staying would take a great deal of courage, something she was acquiring a little bit at a time as she faced the country's difficulties head on month after month.

The previous evening, she and her sons had been up on the roof in an effort to escape the heat in the apartment and take maximum advantage of the little bit of breeze the evening hours had provided. Nadira had looked up at the stars dimmed by the city's lights and saw an invisible hand draw a white chalk line across the blackboard of sky. Was it simply the contrail of a jet or a celestial event? She'd thought of the shooting star that had appeared on the night of her birth. Maybe it *had* been a sign, not predicting a charmed or easy life, but a full life with both sad times and happy times, and the opportunity to discover and fulfill her dreams.

ACKNOWLEDGEMENTS

First and foremost, thank you to my husband, Zafar, who convinced me I could write this book and then gave me the time and space to do it while offering constant encouragement and support. And to the memory of my father, Phillip Harrison, whose special occasion poems and funny notes, inspired me to become a writer.

A special thank you goes to Jody Berman who saw the potential in my first draft and introduced me to my amazing editor, Laura Goodman.

Immense graditude to my editor, Laura Goodman who acted as my own personal MFA program, demanded the best from me, encouraged and nurtured me when I got discouraged, and cheered me on to the finish line.

The authenticity of my book would have suffered without the help of the following Pakistani friends and relatives who acted as expert readers or patiently answered my questions, provided information and recommended source material on Pakistan and Islam - Zafar Rashid, Nilofer Haider, Mehlaqa Samdani, Naveed Sobhan, Mobeen Afzal, Danyaal Afzal, Manezhe Afzal and Meher Aziz. Thank you to Ahmad Adeen whose photos and "writing challenge" inspired one of my favorite descriptions in the book.

Also, many thanks to grammar queen, Diana Hossain, for her editorial assistance, and to first readers Ellen Katz, Cheryl Hartell, Jay Harrison, Ellie Chaikind, Eileen Toomey, Diane Mack, Russ Murphy, Lyn Back, Mark Sacher and Carol Sanger.

NOTE

This is a work of fiction, and all the characters are imagined. Some historical figures, such as General Zia-ul-Haq, are real. Certain events, such as the massacre at Dhaka University are also real but the exact details of the event are imagined.

AUTHOR BIOGRAPHY

Susan Harrison Rashid practiced law for twenty-four years before retiring to begin her writing career.

Writing *Beneath a Shooting Star* was a long journey that began in 1980 when Susan married her husband in a ceremony in Lahore, Pakistan. Over the ensuing years, living as a member of a Pakistani family and annual visits to Lahore provided the background and the impetus for this book. *Beneath a Shooting Star* is her first novel.